TRUE STORM

L.E. STERLING

TRUE

True Born Trilogy

STORM

Entangled Publishing, LLC
2614 South Timberline Road
Suite 105, PMB 159
Fort Collins, CO 80525

Entangled Teen is an imprint of Entangled Publishing, LLC.

Visit our website at www.entangledpublishing.com.

Edited by Liz Pelletier and Stacy Abrams
Cover design by LJ Anderson, Mayhem Cover Creations
Cover art from iStock
Interior design by Toni Kerr

ISBN 978-1-64063-176-2
Ebook ISBN 978-1-64063-177-9

Manufactured in the United States of America
First Edition May 2018
10 9 8 7 6 5 4 3 2 1

an imprint of Entangled Publishing LLC

For C. W.
The perfect Agent Cooper
to my Diane

1

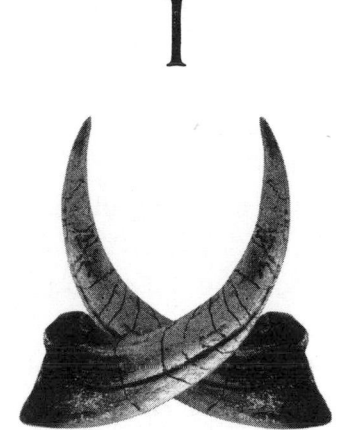

All our lives, the Harvest Moon Masque was but a fairy tale for my twin sister, Margot, and me. The Masque follows the last of the country harvest, attended by the elite and upper crust in Dominion's Outskirts. It had been my sister's dream to dance at this riotous ball in a matching gown and mask. So it's a bitter-tinged irony that I'm here instead, without her.

The rules of Dominion's Upper Circle society aren't followed out here. Here, at Senator Theodore Nash's sprawling plantation home in the Outskirts, surrounded by verdant fields I've never seen the like of, the country folk follow their own gods. The Plague may be gobbling up these people, same as in Dominion. But here the wealthy farmers, their mercs and field hands, seem less worried about the death and starvation that perch on each street corner of Nor-Am's capital city. Out here, under a stretch of endless gray sky, people may die, but they don't starve by the bucketful. Here, Lasters and Splicers aren't so different.

Lasters are those near certain to die from Plague—or the empty bellies and hard times that come hand and hand with it. Lasters don't last. Splicers survive. The wealthy Splicers attend Splicing Clinics, where new DNA is sewn in to take over from that spoiled by Plague.

In Dominion, there's no mixing of these social worlds. The Lasters are our servants. They are the mercs who guard, our cooks, our caregivers, while Splicers—those from the elite Upper Circle, like me—take up positions as politicians, socialites, doctors, and lawmakers. Splicers run our world. Splicers will inherit the earth. Or so it seemed, once upon a time.

I know better now.

If anyone is to survive this brutal Plague and its endless destruction, it's to be the one group that I've not seen in and around Nash's country estate.

Laster, Splicer…*True Born*.

To be True Born means you can't catch the Plague, though you're a pariah in so many other ways. They say True Born DNA has all but jumped back in time. A natural defense mechanism against the wasting sickness, they say. True Borns have special rogue DNA that has burrowed back into our ancestral past, turning some into what we all once were: not fully human. Some True Borns have the strength of cheetahs or the speed and grace of gazelles. Some have the hirsute bodies of our furry ancestors and some the scaly skins of our reptilian cousins. Near all I've met, I reckon, are extraordinary in some way. Hated and feared by all, too.

But here, in Nash's well-appointed ballroom, it's only rich and poor, Laster and Splicer, who dance side by side. As level as death itself.

Margot would love the romance of the Masque: the high and mighty of our elite world hobnobbing it with the sons of farmers. As for me? I love it a lot less, though likely because the romance of the evening is not coming alive in the arms of my current partner, Gordon Preston the Third.

"Y'know, you sure are the prettiest little gal," the Third slurs with a half note of surprise. He slips his mask up on his forehead and blinks at me owlishly. Drunk as sure as I'm a Fox. Gordon has not been withholding on a number of things this evening, booze being one of them. His identity being another—despite the nature of the event we are currently attending.

What he hasn't told me is anything useful. Though I play the role of flirt and ingénue, I'm here less to dance than to gather information for my guardian and leader of the True Borns, Nolan Storm. I've buttered up Preston the Third in a thousand delicate and flattering ways, all to have him answer a handful of questions: Have people in the Outskirts heard tales of a new, miracle cure for the Plague? Do the farmers trust the newly elected Senator Nash? Are the Outskirts at all worried about the reach of Dominion's rabble-rousing preacher men?

He's hummed and hee-hawed and grown so bold as to tell me not to worry, as he and his papa will protect me and the rest of the pretty gals of Dominion's Upper Circle. In other words, so far all I've really pulled from the Third is a lesson in lechery.

"Y'really not going to tell me? 'S just yer name." He jostles my arm as though I'm joking.

"No. It's a masque ball, Gordon. We don't reveal our identities until midnight. We've been through this."

My partner eyes me wolfishly. "You're gonna tell me your name. 'Ventually."

"Nah." I shake my head. "Spoil the fun." I'm ready to disappear, certain that even if Preston the Third has any information that would be useful to the True Borns, he's too glogged to give it to me. But farmers' sons, I'm coming to learn, are persistent.

"Where y'goin'?" he whines, halting me with a surprisingly strong grip on my arm. A shiver of apprehension rushes through me. Gordon's hair is a messy dark mop. It's bunched and pinched where his black mask rides up. His nose falls like a thin, sharp blade, but it's the curl of his bloodless, thin lips that I don't like, the sharp slant of his cheekbones. More than anything, I don't like the gleam in his black-black eyes.

I don't bother to smile from under my violet mask. He's too far gone to notice politeness anyhow, I remind myself. I had let Gordon lead me into a secluded alcove off the main dance floor, hoping the relative quiet would help him focus. Now I realize my mistake.

Gordon Preston the Third has begun to focus on only one thing: getting fresh with me.

I glance out from the alcove with its marble benches and exquisitely detailed walls and ceilings. In the ballroom proper, those ceilings rise a good twenty feet, high enough to have a band play on a little stage overlooking the dancers, who whirl as one under the bright crystal chandeliers. *It really is like a dream*, I think to myself. A lovely, old-fashioned dream. A dream where no one dies, shaking and sickened by the Plague. A dream where there are no poor, no desolate survivors.

And no Gordons, I think to myself wryly.

"Well, terrific to meet you, Gordon. Thanks for the dance," I chirrup brightly and take a step away. Any young man of breeding would recognize this as a clear signal that his presence is no longer requested by the lady in question.

Gordon, apparently, skipped this particular etiquette lesson.

"You ain't leavin'." Gordon lunges at me.

I recoil in shock, but it's too late. The thin strap of my dress snaps under his clumsy paws. I take another step back, holding the front of my dress. It's a fitted bodice, unlikely to fall. Still, I feel exposed, vulnerable to eyes and wagging tongues.

I glare daggers at my partner. "Oh, you didn't just do that. Who the hell do you think you are?"

Eyes glazed with as much excitement as drink, Gordon gives me a belching half sneer. "Oh, but I jus' did. Ev'y'one knows you Upper Circle girls are fast."

"You lecherous, arrogant ass!" I call Gordon out as he reaches for me again. My hand comes down automatically in a well-formed, defensive chop. I enjoy his surprised howl as I mentally scroll through all the ways I will murder him. Before I can make a second move, though, a shadow appears behind Gordon. It moves so fast, so silently, I almost miss it. Then one long finger reaches out and taps Gordon on the shoulder.

"May I cut in?" a voice rasps from behind a midnight-black mask. The candlelight from the wall sconces bounces off the tall figure, the pearly light absorbed by the black velvet of his suit. He's tall, lithe, and cuts the kind of dashing figure that makes girls feel dreamy.

Gordon frowns at the intruder. "I don't th-think," he sputters in protest.

But by then the masked man has inserted his more muscular frame between Gordon and myself and swept into a low bow before me. He wears his hair in the way common to the men here: slicked back and smoothed to one side. The mask covers most of his face, drawing shadows down over his lips. Even the color of his eyes is a secret, hidden by the dim lighting of the alcove.

"My lady, if you would care…?" the masked figure trails off and extends a hand to me.

I take the solid fingers, their flesh hot as coals against my own, and allow myself to be pulled into an alcove waltz. His steps are slow but sure, and when he turns me, I spy Gordon fuming at us from a distance.

"Is he still watching?" that voice purrs into my elaborately upswept hair.

"Yes."

"Good," rasps the voice.

Moments later the masked man's lips come down and sear me with a kiss I feel all the way to my toes. He pulls back a fraction of an inch while my breath hitches. His fingers stroke my waist. I sigh and lean my forehead against his tuxedoed chest, feeling the familiar shiver of comfort and crazy overtake me.

"I thought you'd never show," I murmur.

"And miss all this fun?" comes the man's sarcastic reply.

My partner turns me in time to watch Gordon storm off in a huff. A hand lightly skims the skin of my collarbone, causing a revolt of sensation to ripple through me.

"You okay? I thought I was going to have to decapitate him," my dance partner says, staring at me earnestly as he tucks the broken strap into the bodice of my dress.

"That would have spoiled my fun. I had it covered, you know. And anyway, Storm wouldn't have liked that."

"I don't care what Storm would like," he purrs with anger. "If that boy had laid so much as another finger on you, I was going to feed every single one of his digits back to him."

I sigh again and let my True Born partner twirl me around.

"Storm *really* wouldn't have liked that. I'm supposed to be gathering intelligence, not body counts."

Tense and ready for war, the True Born graces me with a terrifying smile. "You know what I think about Storm sending you off on recon."

I stop dancing and place my hands to the hard muscles of the True Born's chest. "We've been through this." I sigh. "Who better than me? All I'm doing is asking a few questions to people I would ordinarily be associating with. I can look after myself, you know. I'm not some helpless damsel in distress."

"Dammit, Princess. I know that, Lu. Doesn't stop me from wanting to do very bad things to anyone who so much as thinks about hurting you." My partner pulls his mask away from his face, revealing the cut and chiseled cheekbones and absurdly full lips of Jared Price. I try to calm the flutter of my pulse at the sight of him, but I'm about as successful as I was at pulling intel from Preston the Third: not at all. Instantly I'm lost in the green glow of his eyes, a sure sign he's about a whisker away from either ripping someone to shreds or dragging me into a shadow and kissing me senseless—that last would be my choice. But though I know Jared is one of the most dangerous creatures in this house—a close second only, I reckon, to my guardian, Nolan Storm—I'm not afraid this panther man will hurt me.

At least, not intentionally.

Mine. Not mine. My heart trips through the familiar ebb and flow.

I blink, forcing back the thought along with an unexpected welling of tears. Our situation is complicated. Jared is Storm's man. Though I don't think he'd give me up for Storm—should I ever be stupid enough to ask that of him—he'll be cautious about giving in to what some days feels like a Flux storm brewing between us. And then, everything is made more complicated by who I am. By *what* I am.

Whatever that may be.

"Don't look like that, Lu," Jared mutters as he curses under his breath.

"Like what?" I blink at his too-handsome face. The curved planes of his cheeks. The perfect softness of his lips, so strange in contrast to his killing nature, and the tiny scar that sits right beside them. But it's the eyes that hold me mesmerized. Jared isn't like most True Borns. When he's calm and human, his eyes are an indigo-blue sky filled with promises. When he's stirred, when his True Born nature is called, the monster that claws itself to the surface and screams like the hunting cat it is, his eyes turn a vivid emerald green. Like they are now. Those eyes momentarily blur before me as a tear gets tangled in my lashes. So soft and swift I almost don't notice it, Jared scoops up the tear and stares at it like it's a miracle. I watch, blushing and confused, as he kisses the damp drop from his finger.

We've stopped moving, though I hardly notice. I only know the hot strength of his hand on my back. Only the tug of my heartbeat, a steady drum gone haywire, and that peculiar scent of his, musk and cinnamon, that makes me feel at once calm and safe and utterly out of control. I don't even know if he's aware he's pulling me closer, tighter, his head tilting toward me as though he can't help but meet my lips with his own.

"What'd you get?" A bright voice pops up between us.

Not two hairs from us stands a gorgeous redhead in four-inch stilettos. Her low-cut sheath dress hides nothing from the imagination—save the pistol strapped to her inner thigh. Storm's assassin, Kira, cuts a pretty picture, but I'd as soon not cross her. I've seen what this True Born can do with a stiletto.

"Nothing, I'm afraid." I grimace and try to step away from Jared, but he holds me fast and glares at Kira.

"Our friend had a few too many," Jared drawls, looking pointedly at my dress strap, which has pulled loose once again from Jared's fix. "Do you have a pin, Kira?"

The gorgeous woman rummages through a tiny beaded handbag and pulls out a pin. "Ta-da!" She smiles and hands it over to Jared.

Jared's eyes cross as he concentrates on the tiny pin. "Hold still," he tells me. Despite his preternatural dexterity, I'm somehow not reassured.

"Do you know how to work these things?" I ask nervously.

A lock of slicked blond hair falls across his forehead as he stops to grin at me, a pure boyish grin that turns my guts to mush. "Relax, Princess," he tells me. "Can't be harder than surviving an arena fight. I got this." His fingers skim the skin beside my shoulder, leaving behind a tingling wake of sensation. Jared looks in my eyes and for a few long seconds I reckon the pin has been forgotten. Then with three quick twists, he wrangles it into the thin black strap of material. Though it's fixed well enough for now, he shrugs off his coat and drapes it over my shoulders anyway.

"What's this for?" I ask as my chilled flesh is suddenly enveloped by Jared's extraordinary heat, his scent tripping through my senses.

"In case the pin comes loose," he tells me with a dark look.

I can read murder written there, wrestling with something just as primitive: as though just by draping me in his jacket he claims me before all these country politicians and their reckless sons. But then the tall, lithe warrior laces his fingers through mine. And as he tugs me through the crowded dance floor into the heart of the darkest men of Dominion, my feet, like my heart, are light as air.

The True Born winds me through the buzzing, busy ballroom, up a marble staircase that rises into a curved balcony where the band plays something bone-jarring and sweet. He ducks me past them, into a black-and-white-tiled hallway. We flow beyond several pairs of armed men, none of whom seem to be concerned by us. They'll know which guests are which by now, I reckon. Jared's coat barely keeps me warm amid the arctic chill of the room I'm ushered into, flanked by two mercs in matching navy suits. They don't wear earpieces, these country mercs. Then again, I don't suppose they'd have to.

Criminals are sent here to the territories of Dominion, the Outskirts, to till and water the fields and harvest food, to be sold in the city. But once their sentences are up, many prefer to stay, putting to use their hard lives and harder bodies as the personal security to the Upper Circle elite. They say the mercs are reformed, more loyal and trustworthy than most. Still, when I pass the two mercs and one of them looks at me with the inklings of appreciation, I shiver with unease.

We pass through a heavy oak door and into a hallway lit only by candles shoved into wall sconces. The tiny flames make the hallway seem warm in contrast to the voices raised in anger coming from a room beyond. We follow the argument to the end of the hall and step into a brightly lit room fit for royalty.

Our host looks dapper for a dead man, I'll give him that.

"Ah, there. See? I told you she was fine," cries Theodore Nash. The new senator for the Outskirts lounges back in his chair with the smug satisfaction of a man who has everything.

He's got a cigar in one hand and a snifter of spirits in the other, while his bow tie has come undone and hangs down alongside his neck like a deflated balloon. The tux he wears is impeccable, and though he doesn't don a mask like the dancers in the ballroom, I'd swear his is the most deceptive of all.

Because just a few weeks ago, Theodore Nash sat before us sweating and patchy, clearly about to hurl into his end days: Plague-struck. Today, though, he's fine.

I can tell when they'll fall sick, when they'll die. It's one of my gifts. Or curse, more like. Sure as Sunday, Theodore Nash was halfway to death last time I saw him. Today, he sits calm and happy as you please, cheeks bright with health, eyes shiny and clear.

No one who Splices would look that good so close to death's door. So why does Nash seem so healthy?

Nolan Storm pulls himself from the desk to greet me. Though his voice was not among those I heard, I can tell my guardian is angry. A swirling, spectral rack of antlers rises into a crown over his head. Molten silver eyes, one of his most peculiar traits, roil like a storm-tossed sea. In his suit he looks like a prince of the Upper Circle. But as his foot impatiently stamps the floor, I see him for what he really is: the most powerful True Born in Dominion and beyond.

"Well," drawls Nash. "I think that pretty much concludes our business for today. Wouldn't you agree, Mr. Storm?"

Storm looks as though he'd prefer to rip Nash's head from his shoulders, something I'm certain he could do in ten seconds flat. Instead he dips his spectral crown in assent. It's a strange sight, and stranger still to think that I can see the weight he carries when others can't. His branching horns are visible to only a handful of people, I've been given to understand. Only

True Borns…and me.

His father was the First, we're told. The first of the True Borns, maker of Kings. Storm once showed Margot and me a stone etching, tablets from Babylon carved thousands of years ago. In the stone, trapped for an eternity, there were leopard men, and men who looked like Egyptian deities: half man, half beast. Though our genomics professors will tell us that our DNA devolved to allow some small part of humanity to survive the Plague, Storm tells us a different version of history.

True Borns are the old gods returning, Storm says. They come back when needed, the ancient DNA reasserting itself into family lines and allowing the children of gods to reign once more. And Nolan Storm, my guardian, would be king of them all.

If he can survive the two-faced wrath of Theodore Nash, that is.

"You were worried about me?" I ask, confused. "I was downstairs dancing with a boy named Gordon Preston. The Third," I add.

Nash snorts a laugh. "Ah, Preston. Such a fine boy. See? I told you everything was fine."

"You tell me that, Nash. But then you muck it up by sounding vaguely threatening."

Nash makes a show of feeling hurt. "I would never," he says unconvincingly.

"At any rate, our business is concluded. Wouldn't you say?"

"Yes, you're right. I've made my decision. The water project contract is canceled. Effective immediately."

Storm's voice is deceptively flat. "Jared, escort Lucy to the car, please."

Jared tugs my hand, but as I brush by Storm I whisper under my breath, "Please don't kill him." The subtle upturn of Storm's lips answers me. And then I'm swept from the room like a leaf, past the men with big machine guns and ill-fitting blue suits.

Jared escorts me nearly as far as the long, wide entrance that empties into the massive ballroom when I stop and squeeze his tuxedoed arm.

"One more dance, Jared. Please?" I plead.

And maybe it's the moonlight. Maybe it's the glitter on the mask. But for just about the first time since I've known him, Jared Price doesn't snark before doing as I've asked. Instead he sweeps me into his arms.

The band strikes up a stirring song, and the packed ballroom, filled with the very *crème de la crème* of high society in and outside of Dominion, executes the steps in unison. And while I've observed that the country folk of the Outskirts are not quite as fashionable as Dominion's Upper Circle, Nash's home could certainly give some of Dominion's senators a run for their money.

Gold braid plaster edges the exquisitely wallpapered walls of the ballroom. The rugs are the most sumptuous money can buy. Huge, ancient vases, the painted kind that used to store grain, run the length of the long entrance hall with its highly polished marble. And hovering over all that wealth are a half dozen three-tier crystal chandeliers. Still, I can't help the feeling that something is *off* about the whole place, right down to the polished servers wielding silver trays overloaded with food.

"Notice anything interesting about this place?" I ask my partner, who hasn't bothered to pull his mask back down over his beautiful indigo eyes that simmer with a hint of emerald as he looks back at me.

"Yes," Jared replies seriously. We stop moving. I try to mentally adjust to the sudden shift between us. He looks at me as though he's dying of thirst, and I wonder if my face betrays my confusion.

"I'm serious," I say, clearing my throat. We sway, our bodies just touching. I can feel the pull between us, a current as sure as electricity. And just as able to shock me.

"So am I," Jared rasps. For a moment I'm caught up in the sheen rolling over his eyes, a dead giveaway that he's caught up by some strong emotion. Sometimes I think that's what he feels for me. Other times, I remember that Jared Price will never lay claim to me. I'm a girl from the Upper Circle, intended to make a brilliant match—a political union. No hearts and roses for me. And Jared Price is my merc.

Once again I'm about to show just how different our backgrounds are, I muse with an inward sigh. I turn and run my gaze back down the hall, trying to scratch away at my instincts.

"What did you see in the gallery?"

Jared frowns down at me. "Lots of those urn things."

"They're not urns," I tell him.

"Well, cups, then. Cups for giants."

I hold back a smile. *"Vases,"* I correct. "What else?"

"Some paintings. Mostly these country scenes that look like they're from a thousand years ago."

"Exactly," I say as clarity washes over me. Jared continues to look mystified.

I ponder the scene before me. "Country scenes. Country vases. It's the perfect country seat, isn't it?"

Jared looks around him at the glowing opulence. "Well, yeah."

"You know what comes with country seats like this?"

The True Born shakes his head, amused. "I bet you're going to tell me."

I cock an eyebrow, giving him a haughty look. "It's a country *seat*, Jared. This is an ancestral home. It certainly looks like it's stood right here for generations. So where are they?"

"Who?" Jared's hands reflexively curl tighter around me.

"His ancestors. His family."

No portraits of long-dead patriarchs with their silvering hair and rounded country bellies line the halls. No idle housewives in finery stare down at the guests from the walls. The pictures are all expensive, yes, but not personal: There are only paintings of harvested wheat, ploughs, fields…

Nash was an upstart in the last election. He was an unknown, some third-rate senator who all but barreled over his competition. From nothing to king overnight.

What I still didn't know is, is that normal for the Outskirts?

I go up on my tiptoes and whisper in Jared's ear, "Where are all the dead relatives, do you reckon?" before giving his earlobe a not-too-gentle nip. I leave off the puzzle for now, knowing it will be easier for me to figure it out later. When I'm not so distracted by my proximity to Jared.

He doesn't pluck me away, but as I lean back, Jared's dimples appear as he bites back a smile. "Do that again and I'll—"

"You'll what?" I taunt. Grumbling under his breath, Jared closes his eyes and shakes his head. "You'll what?" I ask again, though this time I loose a silky voice on him as I run my fingers up his tuxedo-shirted chest, down his stomach. I slip two fingers between buttons. Along with the raised ridge of a long, puckered scar, the heat rising from his skin fascinates me. I close my eyes and feel as though I'm being washed out to sea as our bodies drift together across the floor.

Jared claps a hand down over mine, stopping my explorations, though our *détente* lasts a moment longer. His chest heaves a little more than usual, as though he's been running. But it's enough to shame me into stopping.

If we go any further I'll claim you. And then there will be no more choice for you, he'd said to me. We were in a cabin when he said those words, thick in the Russian woods. It would have been so easy to take advantage of me—to be with me, a willing and all-too-eager novice. And he didn't because he cares.

But there is no choice for me, I think a little bitterly. I am Lucinda Fox, daughter of Lukas Fox, the power behind Dominion's closed curtains. Daughter of Antonia Fox, social queen of the Upper Circle. My duty has always been clear: to make a good match that will help further my family's ambitions, to take care of my twin sister, Margot. It isn't fair for me to toy with Jared any more than it is for him to toy with me.

"I'm sorry," I tell him breathlessly.

Jared just shakes his head at me, lips pressed closed and flat, as he laces his fingers through mine and guides me off the dance floor toward the front door.

In the back seat of Storm's vehicle, Penny, whom I secretly call Mohawk on account of her intriguing hairstyles, sings off-key at the wheel while Jared and I avoid looking at each other. Or sitting near each other. Still, by the time Storm opens the door and bids me to move over, our fingertips have met on the seat between us, where Jared had been stroking the sensitive skin of my palm. Storm doesn't seem to notice our fingers recoiling, nor the blush that steals across my cheeks as we're pressed up against each other once again.

My guardian appears to have other things on his mind.

"Jared, when we get back, I want you to run another check on our good friend Senator Nash." Storm practically bites the name.

"Sure. Anything specific I should search for?"

"There's something not right here," Storm says, echoing my words as he rubs a hand over his cheek and chin in apparent frustration.

"Yeah, I get that," Jared replies, meeting my gaze.

Storm abruptly swings his attention my way. "Have you ever been wrong before?"

It's not an idle question. Not long ago, when I'd first met Theodore Nash, I'd called him a goner dead to rights. I always know with the Lasters—which ones will come down ill, though it's often just days before the Plague strikes with its vicious hammer. Sometimes I can even tell which Splices won't do the job of cleansing the body of the deadly rogue DNA.

"No," I answer truthfully. There hasn't been a single case of my knowing a person was going to fall full-on Plague-struck who has lived.

Not a single one.

Storm goes silent beside me. The vehicle pulls out from the pack of country cars, mostly open-topped jalopies and trucks with long beds for farming, and heads down the long paved drive to the gates. The moon is a wraith behind the white-gray veil of the sky. Out here, the night look darker, and every now and again I catch a pocket of thinner cloud cover where I see a glimmer of stars. For someone who's grown up with Dominion's constant cloud cover, this patch of midnight is a gift.

Storm breaks the silence. "People don't recover from the Plague; they survive it a little longer. See if you can trace Nash to Leo Resnikov or Lucy's father. I'm beginning to think we were too late."

Storm's words startle me out of my reverie. *Too late.*

Are we too late? Leo Aleksandrovich Resnikov was a business partner of our father's. Then he, or someone working for him, sliced open Margot and stole her eggs. Then he'd stolen my sister. Later, after we burned Leo Resnikov's factory to the ground, I had high hopes that we'd sent him to hell. But if Storm's instincts are right, not only could Resnikov be alive—some of his so-called "cure," harvested from my sister's body, could be circulating the Upper Circle and the even higher echelon, the Gilt...all the way through the ranks to the mysteriously risen Senator Theodore Nash.

I look over at the stern, unyielding profile of Nolan Storm. He shimmers with power and, I see now, carefully controlled anger. A shiver runs through me, cold as the grave. Could Resnikov be alive? And if we hadn't managed to destroy everything...what then?

The endless loop of questions is followed by one horrible thought. *How will I tell Margot?*

2

Pearly midmorning light breaks through the slatted blinds of the lab by the time I find Margot. Her long auburn hair is squashed in a ponytail, then squashed again by the elastic of the safety goggles she wears. Her arms are lost in the long white lab coat Doc Raines forces us to wear when running experiments.

She doesn't hear me approach, nor when I call her name. There's been a lot of that lately. Since we returned from Russia, Margot has become all but unreachable. For the hundredth time I find myself wondering what it was like—being held like a science experiment in Resnikov's factory.

While she was away I spent a lot of time worrying over this. The bond I have relied upon my whole life to tell me what Margot is thinking and feeling had stretched, thin and silent, until it was all but obliterated. It was the loneliest feeling in the world.

...

When we were born, my sister and I, we shared one skin—but that is only the beginning of our puzzle. Although we came into the world connected, stitched together at our big toes, we are not as similar as identical twins should be. Like the marks we bear on our toes, where they tore us apart—Margot's in the shape of a long, thin skeleton key and my own the perfect pear shape of a lock—we are mysteries of flesh and bone.

In Russia I'd met an old scientist who claimed he had helped bring us into the world. Test-tubers, he'd called us: babies born of laboratory cocktails and Molotov gene Splicing. But whatever they Spliced into us, Margot and I bear the traces of its magic. Whatever Margot experiences, I feel.

I've been left with other, even more dubious gifts: Like with Nash, I can tell who next will be gobbled by the diamond-toothed Plague. And sometimes my dreams walk into waking life.

Margot's talents have always been more useful. She'll charm birds out of the sky and men out of their mansions. She has but to walk into a room and it's lit with some indefinable incandescence. Our parents loved this about her. They've put her talents to use in the slippery wet world of Dominion politics. But then its tide carried her away.

Margot gives me broad strokes but won't really tell me what happened. All I know is that she is not the same. Sure as anything, she was betrayed: first by attendants of the Splicer Clinic, who stole the eggs from her body like foxes in the henhouse. Then by our parents, who sold her to the mysterious Russian count Leo Resnikov—sold us both. Margot was betrayed again by Resnikov, who transformed those stolen eggs into pale, lifeless bodies floating in long glass tubes, whose jobs were to pump the next generation of Margot's DNA into oily pills that could be fed to dupes by the millions.

He was making a cure of sorts. A cure for the ravages of the Plague. Bred from the blood and marrow of my sister's DNA. It was what we were born for — or so we are being led to believe. Though according to Resnikov himself, this cure would only last a little while.

"Margot," I say again, tugging on her loose ponytail. The elastic slips, and she turns to frown at me.

"Cut it out," she says crossly.

"Well, I reckon your attention was elsewhere now, wasn't it?"

Margot's frown lengthens. "What's wrong?"

"Why does anything have to be wrong for me to want to see you?"

Margot snorts. "Don't be daft. Have you forgotten who I am, little sister?"

Ouch. Born just seconds past Margot, I cross my arms at the "little sister" remark. It hurts. "One and a half minutes does not make you elderly," I retort. We've not had this childish fight for ages.

"No," Margot replies, lightning-quick. "Life has."

I reel back, struck again by the change in my sister, who I used to know better than myself. The smiling, carefree Margot, the Margot who used to be boy crazy, who'd skip school with her friends and laugh in the face of danger, is gone. Maybe for good. I miss that Margot: the girl who loved going to parties and being the center of attention, the Margot who lit a room when she walked in. A woman who will barely go outside has replaced that girl. This one is a silent stranger who has lived through more than I will ever know or understand.

But for that matter, I reckon I have, as well. Because I am the sister who followed her to hell and back.

My patience at an end, I frown down at my feet. "What is that about?"

"Don't try to change the subject."

"Mar, come on."

"Are you going to tell me?" she grumbles and takes hold of my arms. She's stronger than she looks. And I suppose she can't handle surprises that well any longer.

"Senator Nash," I blurt out, followed by a distinct, "Ow!" I rub at my flesh as she lets go.

"Okay, I'll bite." Margot stands defensively, fists on her hips. "What about Senator Nash?"

"Did Father or Resnikov ever talk about him that you remember?"

Margot bites her lip and retreats behind a shuttered expression. "Not that I can remember."

"It's important, Margot. Please try."

Margot stomps her foot. "I *said* I don't remember."

"Fine. Okay," I say as a silent moat opens between us. "Thanks anyway."

I turn to go, but Margot grabs at the sleeve of my tunic again. "Wait—you didn't tell me."

"Frankly, you haven't seemed that interested." I sniff.

"Lu. Don't. Please. Tell me about Nash. I'm sorry I lost my temper."

I relent in the face of Margot's solemn eyes. We have always been two sides of the same coin, my sister and I. In more ways than one. Blowing the hair from my eyes, I tell her, "He's better."

Margot shakes her head. "What do you mean? Better at what?"

"He's *healed*, Margot."

"Healed." My sister's face drains of color.

"As in, he was dying last week. This week he seems to be remarkably okay."

Margot spins and busies herself with gear on the lab bench. "Maybe he's just in that rebound phase." She shrugs. "They sometimes get spry just before the end, you know."

I did know. But that wasn't it. I pull at my sister's arm so she'll face me. "Not this time, Mar."

She stares at me. Her beautiful long eyelashes flutter over her blue-gray eyes. She tries to hide her reaction, but I can feel it, ricocheting through her body like a bullet. Margot turns her back abruptly. She sobs a deep breath, her entire body heaving with it while I sit inside her skin and battle wave after wave of nausea coming from her.

For a long while we just stand there. Then, as Margot grasps the counter like it will hold her up, I stroke her hair, as I've done her whole life long, and croon something wordless meant to soothe.

But no tune will soothe what this news implies.

Because what this means is that not all those babies hanging suspended in jars were destroyed in the fire at Resnikov's factory. Maybe something of that Plague Cure, fashioned from my sister's blood and bone, is still around, being bartered by the Upper Circle. Which further means that Margot and I are not safe.

Someone, eventually, will come looking for us.

A long moment later, Margot steps away and clears her throat. Back straight as an iron fence, she doesn't even look at me. "I need to return to work now."

"What are you working on?"

Margot shrugs. "Doc Raines said something about making DNA zippers. So I'm trying different recombinant sequencing."

My heart hammers in my chest. I stammer, "Y-You're splicing our DNA together?"

I don't know why I'm so horrified. It's the kind of thing I would do if I weren't so busy playing spy with Storm. Still, there is something terrible about Margot, my fun-loving, playful Margot, experimenting with our DNA.

"Why?" I ask as the silence between us lengthens.

A crease parts Margot's forehead. She turns her head, looking around, before telling me in one of our tiny mouse voices, "Because. There must be a reason. What if there's a cure? A real one?"

"You think Resnikov got it wrong."

"No." Margot shakes her head, a faraway look stealing into her eyes. "You don't understand."

"What don't I understand?"

"He wasn't looking for a cure, now, was he?"

This sinks in slowly, one sickening layer at a time.

They say the skies over Dominion were blue once. Once upon a time. Blue all the time, they say, fading to pink at dusk. Blue like a miracle. Now the sky is always white, a burial shroud thrown over the city to cover the mounds of dead. But I've seen it once. That miracle, a slice of blue sky. I turn away from the window stretching across one entire wall of Nolan Storm's office.

"Did you ever see a blue sky, Storm?"

The leader of the True Borns stands against his desk in one of his signature poses: black-trousered legs crossed, sweatered arms crossed. Over his head, humming, crackling lines of power intersect and merge and branch again.

"Yes," he says, but doesn't elaborate.

"What did it feel like?"

Storm snorts a short laugh. "It didn't hurt, if that's what you mean. It has no weight or substance," he tells me.

I shake my head. "I mean—did it make you feel...I don't know. Like there was hope in the world?"

Storm joins me at the window. I don't have to look. I feel him beside me like a live wire: electric, pulsing with power. "You know," he tells me now, surveying the world far below his tower-keep window, "it's only been a few months."

I hazard a glance at our self-titled guardian. If you can ignore the crown of thorns over his head, he looks the part of any Upper Circle businessman in his well-heeled suit. But there's wildness, sure as death, just under that veneer of civility and manners. I know better than to think that Nolan Storm is anything other than he is—a True Born god. A man destined to rule, and who'll do so with bloody hands or not.

"What did you make of Senator Nash's place?" he says now with an abrupt change of topic.

"I think it was... strange," I say carefully.

"That's an answer that a diplomat's daughter would give. Now give me your real impressions."

I picture again the black and white tile of the lofty mansion. The impersonal feel to its furnishings, as though someone had hastily moved in and claimed it as his own. The spoils of a political war.

"How long has that been the senator's home?"

Storm gives me a curious look. "Why do you ask?"

I shrug. "It seemed the home of a *nouveau arriver*, if you know what I mean."

Storm shakes his head. "Explain."

I sit on Storm's leather cream couch and relay the impressions I'd picked up with Jared. "How can any Splicer from the Upper Circle, even one from outside Dominion, live in such a stately home without even a hint of where all that wealth came from?" I outlay my impressions as carefully as I can. Even the richest senator's house in Dominion has some personal touches: portraits of their patriarchs, loving paintings of families, spouses, children and dogs. Nash's home, though, was free of all of these. There were no other family members in his receiving line, either. Not even a distant uncle or cousin. There's no such thing as a wealthy Splicer without connections.

Storm paces back to his desk, rubbing his jaw in a way that tells me he's thinking this through. He presses a button. Alma's voice crackles to life on the intercom. "Yes?"

"Alma, can you send in Jared, please?"

"Certainly, Storm."

Wintry eyes meet mine. "And what of young master Gordon?"

I stick out my tongue. "First-order letch."

Storm barks a laugh just as Jared gives a perfunctory knock and enters. He looks every bit the casual fly-by-night type in his brown-corded pants with the bottom hem unraveling. A faded lemon T-shirt with the outlines of OldenTimes bicycles strains across his muscular chest. But it's the flop of blond hair that falls across his forehead, the insouciant glint to his eye, that makes him seem so maddeningly casual.

Storm nods at his right-hand man. "I need further intelligence on Senator Nash. Particularly how he arrived at his country seat. When it was bought, who sold it to him. Everything you can find out."

Jared nods. "Already done. It was a Plague sale. Back channels, no real paper trail. Harrington was the original owner up until about a year or so ago. They perished within a month of each other. Last surviving member of the family tree was given very little choice in the sale, or so I understand," he finishes with a bland look.

Storm's face turns speculative. "Any family portraits hit the black market lately?"

Jared twists his wrist like it hurts and grins unpleasantly. I wince at his next words. "Black market won't take 'em anymore. They're like penny candy that only Upper Circlers would want."

The old bruise rubs between us. For Jared, the Upper Circle might as well be hell itself. And that is what I am, what Margot is: The epitome of Dominion's elite, we are its pampered, sheltered daughters. At least we *were*.

Feeling bleak, I turn toward the window and watch their spectral forms in the sparkling glass as Storm and Jared continue talking. "Good work. Still, I want you to keep an eye out in case any portraits turn up. And keep an ear to the ground with Nash. If any rumors of his involvement with our friends in Russia surface, I want to know about it immediately."

"Of course," Jared replies. I feel his eyes raking my back as he stands there a minute too long.

"Was there something else?" Storm asks.

"Nope. I'm good." A moment later I hear the door click behind him. And the weight in my chest grows heavier.

"Looks like you were right, Lucy. Nash isn't what he appears to be. Which makes me think that we need to be more careful about what and who he actually is."

Nolan Storm has sat himself on the corner of his desk, arms folded in his lap. He could be a suitor to swoon over, though I'd as soon say he's never given the matter much thought. Nolan Storm is concerned with one thing and one thing only: the welfare of the True Borns. *Then again*, I think as he launches into his next words, *perhaps I've been mistaken*. "I'd like your opinion on how Margot is faring."

"What do you mean?" In my confusion, the words tumble out like gravel. I clear my throat. "Is there something I should know?"

Storm tilts his head. His liquid metal eyes look through me, piercing my defenses. "I'm simply concerned. We both know that Margot hasn't quite readjusted to life in Dominion."

I hang my head. "I don't know what to do about it," I answer truthfully.

"Has she given you any indication as to her mental state?"

I shake my head. It's hard for me to admit that my other half, my *twin*, won't let me in. But at certain moments, I can feel it. The bleakness clawing at her. The overwhelming feeling of being alone. It's so awful I want to yell, *I'm right here, Margot*.

Storm is quiet for a moment, regarding me with his quicksilver eyes. "I'm worried about her. It might be time to start thinking about interventions." His words stab through my heart. Still, after a moment's agony, I realize he's right. I don't know how to reach her on my own.

"Like what?"

Storm's perfect shoulders give a quick shrug. "I'm not sure yet." He stands, towering over me like the True Born god he is. And some small part of me still trembles before him. He lifts my chin in his hand, cupping my flesh as gently as if I were made of fine china. "Perhaps you'd also benefit from a vacation from all this. You've the look of a scared rabbit in a foxhole."

But there's no safe place for the scared rabbits to go to ground—not in Dominion. Nothing is safe anymore. Certainly not for the Fox sisters. *Even when they're in their guardian's hidey-hole.* Silence hangs between us like a heavy fog. It's broken by a metallic *thunk* as the large, round clock over Storm's desk with its swordlike hands chops through another hour.

My smile is tight. "I'm fine." I say the words slowly and carefully.

"Sure you are," Storm drawls softly. He gathers himself from the desk and claps his hands on my shoulders. "You and I are going to have to come to an understanding, Lucy."

And once again, I'm met with the strange illusion, as though my eyes can't stick to Storm's form. "What do you mean?"

"I'll be blunt. As I think you are already abundantly aware, to obtain my objectives I need the help of the Fox sisters. Margot has said she will not help, even if she was in any sort of shape to."

For a moment I blank out the rest of his words. *She won't help?* Meaning: She and Storm have had a private discussion about this. And she's said nothing to me.

"So it falls to you," he continues. "You have been very helpful. It doesn't seem fair that so much would be asked of you. Still, I can't afford to coddle you both."

The conversation has dipped somehow below arctic waves of meaning. This is the kind of negotiation I understand all too well, having watched my father perform this dance for years. A pit of horror opens in my stomach.

I stare back at my so-called guardian with a carefully blank face.

"I see," I say. "Yes, of course, we must be able to contribute somehow. And since you already have a cleaning woman…" Storm frowns. I had meant it to come out more humorously. "Is there something more you'd have me do, then? More than helping you collect information, that is?" That last bit I toss in with a shake of my hair. I want him to know I count my services as valuable to him. I don't have to go asking questions of the likes of Gordon Preston the Third. And I don't have to share what I learn. I do it because I want to help.

And up until now, I thought we were a team.

Storm's hands feel like heavy weights upon my shoulders. His huge palms radiate heat. A moment later he tilts my head back with a finger and regards me carefully. A small smile tugs one corner of his lips, transforming the planes of his face into a sculpted work of art. "I'll let you know, Miss Fox," he says. Two of his fingers brush across my cheek, so softly I wonder if I have imagined it. In a blink he's at the door and calls out over his shoulder. "Get Kira to take you shopping again. We have some important outings coming up."

I sink down onto Storm's white leather couch. I reckon I've landed from one glass bowl to another.

Margot leans over the billiards table, her face a study in concentration. I can feel the hitch of her heart as she lines up her shot. Cracks the cue. Balls scatter expertly across the table. She smiles in triumph and the room lights with her beauty.

I'm not the only one who notices. Beside her, as Margot

tucks a strand of hair behind her ear, Derek, the boy who calls himself Torch, catches his breath and stares at her in frank admiration.

"Shark," I say as I breeze into the room.

"Canary," she replies, not even looking at me.

It's one of our oldest games, one of the thousand games that stretch between us like the skin we once shared. I stare at my beautiful sister. She holds herself like a regal stranger, the cue in her hands like a monarch's staff. *She's growing up*, it suddenly occurs to me.

I hadn't expected it to feel so lonely, as though I were being left behind.

A pair of eyes rakes at me from the far side of the room. It's just the True Born I was hoping to avoid. He holds a book in front of him but seems to be ignoring it in favor of glaring at me. I stick out my tongue at him. But as I turn away, I imagine I see the faintest ghost of a smile hover on his too-perfect lips.

I've just settled on a stool to watch the game when the door opens and Storm's woman, Alma, bustles in. Sometimes, like now, Alma is masked as a den mother in her severe bun and makeup-free face, her clothes functional and dull. Sometimes, though, like when she lets her hair down and it falls around her face like a curtain of rain, I see her as something more: a woman who was once a powerful beauty. A woman who hides out with the True Borns.

I have never yet seen evidence of her being one of them, though it's true you can't always tell. Once Margot and I were in a store and saw a woman with an elegant light-blue scarf wound around her neck. It wasn't until the woman adjusted the folds, looking uncomfortable, that we understood: Beneath the fabric of her scarf a set of gills ran up her neck like a line of tattoos.

Maybe they even could have been mistaken for those—if the gills hadn't started to shuffle in and out.

It's me Alma comes toward. She holds out an envelope, slightly creased in the middle. "Letter for you, Lucinda," she says, looking troubled.

"For me?" I echo hollowly. Beside me, Margot has stopped playing.

"Who's it from?" She frowns. "Our parents?"

I shake my head as I catch sight of the scrawling script. The rounded letters with the large, trailing ends are certainly not the work of someone who had finished Grayguard Academy, our very posh private school.

Alma stares at me awkwardly and nods at the letter in my hand. "That will be trouble, no doubt about it," she tells me before backing out of the room.

Margot nudges my arm. "Well, aren't you going to open it?" I stare at the letter as though it's an unwelcome houseguest. It hadn't occurred to me to open it right there. I was going to squirrel away to my room first.

And the reason for that gets up off the couch to tower over me, wearing a venomous expression. "Well, Lu? Aren't you going to answer your sister?"

"No." I turn heel and rush out the door. But I should know better by now. True Borns smell blood.

Jared's footsteps ring behind me, and a moment later he's before me, arm outraised to halt me. His voice is silk, but I can hear the iron underneath. "Who's it from, Lu? Open the letter."

"None of your business," I throw back.

"I'm your security. So it is my business. What if it's booby-trapped? In fact, that's a good reason for me to open it," he says, pulling the letter neatly from my grasp.

I gasp in outrage. "Don't you dare, Jared. That letter is addressed to me, and it's personal."

I don't really know this, in fact. But it stands to reason. I can count on one hand the number of letters I've received in my life. But I know that scrawl. From the look on Jared's face—eyes narrowing at the script even as his nose quivers, scenting the sender from the paper—so does he.

"So," he drawls. "Made yourself a pen pal for life, did you?"

"Yes, I did. And so did you," I argue, grabbing at Jared's arm. He holds the letter up high, away from me, like a schoolboy's prank. I lunge at him. I get no closer to the letter, but I end up just inches from his oh-so-handsome face. Close enough to be reminded that under all that beauty lies a feral animal. The bones in his cheeks carve out. He's not just angry. If Ali were to walk through the door right now, blood would be shed.

"You have no right," I seethe, though whether I'm talking about his anger or his actions, I'm not certain.

Jared's nostrils flare. I can tell he's atomizing my scent. He once told me it makes him feel calm. It's a reaction I can trace now, as rational thought creeps back into his eyes and he continues to stare at me with a haunted expression.

"I told you there would be problems, Lu." His words are oddly shaky as he hands me the letter. It hangs there, suspended between our fingers as a wound opens that maybe we can't solve right now. Because Jared and I both know what is likely to be inside the pages of this letter. As my mother always said, young men don't write letters to ladies they don't admire.

3

Alastair of no particular last name found me in an alley one morning. I'd run away from Storm and his True Born keep in search of Margot. My plan had not gone as expected. Instead of being helped by the kid gang I'd come across, I'd been five seconds from being pummeled to death and robbed. Ali had done a fairly good impression of being a handy merc and secured us passage across the waters, to where my sister was being held.

Though we traveled together from Dominion all the way through the heart of Russia, I learned very little about my new friend. I know he's smart. I know that when he looks at you with his soulful eyes, he sees far more than he'll ever let on. Sometimes when he thinks no one is paying attention, he lets the smart aleck fall away and he's more like a smart little boy with a lot of tricks up his sleeves. I like him best then, when there's nothing between us but the real Ali, the mischievous young man who doesn't want anyone to know he's kind.

Still, there is a lot more I'd need to learn about him before I could call him a true friend. Ali's secrets are nearly as vast and deep as our own. It was his friends who helped us in Russia—friends with mysterious mantelpieces praying to unknown gods. Friends who knew things they shouldn't. And then there is Ali himself. I've learned not to ask too many questions, but I'd like to know how it is that sometimes I've seen him throw his little pet rock in ways that counter nature. I'd like to know how it hovers there, just above the skin of his palm.

What kind of True Born gift would that be?

All these questions just mount as I stare at the True Born before me.

"He *helped* us, Jared. Saved our skins."

Jared grabs hold of one end of the letter again, though this time he makes no move to tear it from my grasp. "To what end, Lu? What does he want for his help, eh? What kind of bargain will he collect for all of his 'help'?"

My voice shakes with anger. "You have no right to imply—"

Jared's mouth flattens into a tight, angry line. "No. I don't. I'm doing it anyway. You can't let him take advantage of you. Not again."

"Who says I am?" I let go an explosive, incredulous laugh. I know he's just being protective. I know how much it grates on him, the thought that I'll be used. But I'm nobody's fool. I can look after myself, and I deserve to be treated like I can. "All that has happened is that I've gotten a letter, Jared. A letter I haven't even opened yet."

"You're vulnerable, Lu." Jared's eyes are mesmerizing fires. I could be drawn in if I'm not careful. Then burn for an eternity afterward. "You don't know who this guy is, who he's connected to. You don't know what he wants."

I pull my head back to regard the True Born coolly. He's coiled tight as a snake and twice as deadly. One of my eyebrows ticks up as I stare at him with disdain, channeling my mother's best frost.

"Vulnerable? I reckon you've momentarily lost your wits and forgotten who I am." My lips begin to quiver, so I speak more quickly. "Don't you remember all those things that make you hate the Upper Circle? The liars, the cheats, the power brokers? Those are the people who made me, Jared True Born. I reckon"—and my words dip low so I won't cry—"I reckon I'm far safer with Ali than I am with you."

I don't wait for Jared to reply, though I see by his eyes the punch hits home. I turn on my heel and rush for my bedroom, where I slam the door and lock it. But for a long time after, I still feel it on my skin, the heat of Jared's body stamped against my own.

And the burning pain that tells me we can never be.

The paper feels slippery, silky in my hands as I unwrap the fragile, creased envelope. When I pull out the letter from its sheath I'm swept by a subtle fragrance, something flowery and loamy. Wherever did Ali even get paper? It's one of the most expensive commodities, something the uppermost of the Upper Circle use to prove their vast and superior wealth.

And when I open the page and begin to read the scrawling loops, I'm taken in by a nostalgia I hadn't expected. This man was more than a friend to me—he was an ally.

Lucy,

You once asked me who I am. I don't think I gave you a straight answer, and I don't think I will here, either. There are things about me, about where I'm from, that I think could help you now, though. So I'm ready to spill some of those deep dark secrets you've been scratching at.

Some of my more interesting friends tell me that there is some stuff about to go down, stuff your guy Storm should know about. Feel free to bring him along, if you've got to, but really, we need to talk, you and Margot and me.

I'm making it sound all business, but it isn't. Sure, I want to get to know your sister a little better. I also want to visit you just for the hell of it, but that's a story for a different letter.

I'll be seeing you soon.

Yours in darkness and light,
Alastair

The words swim before my eyes as I read them over again and again, but Ali is as skillful as an Upper Circle matron at obscuring the view. The paper crumples between my fingers as I ponder the various strands of meaning. Something is happening, something Storm and Margot and I need to know about.

It had always struck me as odd that Ali had been so quick to help me when he'd encountered me in that alleyway. Most Lasters would have sold me on the black market. Ali, though, booked me passage on a first-class cruise ship and came along for the ride, putting himself in peril the whole way. It wasn't just a lark for him.

And Alastair isn't just a Laster. Is he?

I know I need to get up and tell Storm, but I just sit there, my legs weak and shaky, my breath coming in hot bursts, and listen to the clock *tick, tick, tick* on the nearby nightstand.

And not for the first time I wonder: Could Ali have a piece of what Margot and I are looking for—the truth of what we are? It's this thought that finally has me rise, like an unsteady toddler, from the corner of the bed. I shake, then shake harder, and have to sit down again to get my balance as the room spins.

It happens again. My legs wobble and I feel sick in the pit of my stomach.

A convulsive boom shakes the furniture seconds before light blooms outside my window. Jared rushes into the room, a feral nightmare ready to rip the world in two. It's only then I realize—it wasn't just me.

Someone has gone and detonated bombs right outside Storm's keep.

4

"Get down," Jared mutters through stretched lips. He takes a moment to peer out at the pink and orange tendrils licking the sky.

Another explosion rocks the building. The glass in the window rattles and shakes. Jared pulls the bedspread off the bed and throws it around his body like a sail. Then he envelops me, pulling me down beneath him, until we're suffocating.

"Is this strictly necessary?" I ask through ragged breaths.

Jared isn't listening to me. The way he tilts his head, I can tell intel is being wired into his implant. "Uh-huh," he now says softly, "she's fine." A scant breath from me, his gaze rakes my face and, though he's heavy, I can't help but tingle from head to toe.

"Sorry," he says to me.

He doesn't sound sorry. Wicked hands capped with the three-inch nails of a panther sweep gently through my hair, looking for anything amiss. "You all right?"

I nod, gulping past the twin knots of fear and longing that have mushroomed in my throat. We stay that way for a long time, so close I can study the tiny scar near Jared's lips, the high hollows of his cheekbones. His nose quivers in that familiar way. The hunter in him is scenting the air, reading the situation in ways I can't even fathom. One of my hands catches at his neck. I pluck at the collar of his T-shirt. The other is trapped against the hard planes of his stomach. When I try to break it free, his body jolts.

"Lu." He whispers my name, so low if I'd been breathing I would have missed it.

"I've got to get to Margot," I whisper, and begin the futile attempt to push him off me.

"She's fine. Sorry." The apology is so unexpected I stop squirming. "I-I should have thought to mention right off. Storm is with her."

I'd known this, of course. I've fallen out of the habit of checking the bond between us, of feeling my sister like a phantom limb. But I still receive it unconsciously: her pain, her joy. Her…dread?

"What's going on, Jared?"

The moment stretches out before he answers. "What do you mean?"

"Come on. Tell me. I deserve to know." My hand, I suddenly realize, has curled around his shirt collar. I release the thin fabric, only to watch in horror as my hands spread themselves across Jared's sharp collarbone.

If he's noticed my brazen hands, he doesn't show it. He licks his lips, elongated with half-change. His words come out slow and thick, his tongue catching on the teeth that have sharpened into killing tools. "Watchers are on the move. Some sort of armed revolt."

"Why didn't you say so?" I slide out from under him, but he clamps me down with an arm that might as well be steel.

"Where are you going, Princess?"

I roll my eyes. "Where do you think? Come on, it's been a whole five minutes without a bomb being lobbed at us. I think it's safe."

Once I'm freed of his heavy limbs, accompanied by a hollow sense of loss that I can't quite let go of, I stall at the bedroom door to wait for him. Jared crawls out from the bedspread like a languid jungle cat, sinewy and deceptively slow.

"Well then, let's go," he prompts, his eyes glittering with a promise I don't understand.

I look down and realize why. My hand has found his arm again. "I-I just wanted to say thank you. For taking care of me after…" I trail off.

"Don't mention it, Princess," he whistles as he breezes by me. "Just doing my job."

Outside my room, the scene is eerily normal. I don't know what I'd expected. People scurrying through the hallways, maybe, or acting sentry along the windows. Not this. I pass an open door and spy Torch, calm as you please, staring at a few screens rolling feeds.

"Why are they acting like this attack is no big deal?" I murmur.

Jared replies with a careless shrug. "People who panic don't live long."

I barely knock on the door of my sister's room before letting myself in. She sits on the bed, fully dressed. She is composed but I can feel her restlessness, her worry. Storm paces beside her, speaking into his mysterious earpiece, I reckon. Above his head, his crown of thorny bone crackles with icy fire.

I lock eyes on Margot. I tap my wrist, one, two times. She subtly brushes her cheek, flipping a strand of auburn hair back. Her eyes roll over to Storm, then back again to me before she lays her index finger on her thigh. I nod, small enough to not be noticed.

We need to talk.

Margot stretches and stands. "Come, Lu." She takes my hand and leads me into the *en suite* bathroom, locking the door behind her.

When we are alone, still quiet as only we can be, I let it out. "What now?"

Margot pulls at the ends of her hair. "He thinks they're after the tree." *He* is Storm, of course, and the tree is the giant tree growing in Heaven Square. *They* are still a bit of a mystery at this point, but I reckon Margot must be talking about the Watchers, led by the mad preacher man, Father Wes.

Evolve or die, as the saying goes. Spray-painted everywhere, the enigmatic catchphrase is almost always accompanied by a drawing of two red circles, overlapping in the middle. The fervent Watchers believe in a prophecy that says some sort of blood-borne, DNA-based cure can end the Plague. Father Wes thinks the prophecy is about us, twin girls born into a world without hope. *Two girls, two circles.*

But the Prayer Tree, inexplicably sprung from whatever nanotechnology was crammed into what we've nicknamed magic bombs, is another story. "Why the tree?"

Margot shrugs. "Why do the Watchers do anything?" She rolls her eyes again, communicating her belief that the Watchers are crazy.

They may just be, at that. But Margot and I have been learning the hard way not to discount the absurd. The Lasters have been hanging plague prayers on the tree in Heaven Square. More and more appear every day: the Lasters steal up under cover of night and tie ribbons to the branches, their prayers for survival, along with bells and forks and spoons, lanterns and scarves.

I was never much one for prayers. Then again, Margot and I were raised in a big house with plenty of food and taken to the Splicer Clinic for protocols more often than either of us would have liked. We had no need for prayers. We had science—and the money to pay for it.

The Lasters, on the other hand, have next to nothing. They have a tree. *And what would happen if that tree is obliterated?*

Heavy steps sound outside the door. A knock. Storm's gruff voice carries in. "Margot? Lucy?" I crack open the door. A grim Storm leans his forearm against the doorframe. "I'm fairly certain that was an isolated incident but I'm going to do a little digging. Torch will stay here with you while we're gone."

"Storm, wait." I pop my head out the door. "We're coming with you. Please?"

Storm contemplates the stubborn tilt to our chins and sighs. "Fine. It should be safe enough, judging from the number of people I see on the streets. But you follow my instructions to the letter at all times. Is that clear?"

The skyline over Dominion is a wash of orange and pink, rising to gray before fading to black. How many bombs had the Watchers lobbed? Margot's hand crushes my own, her heart beating like a panicked bird's inside me. I take a long haul of dirty Dominion air, washing out my sister's anxiety as well as my own as we skirt our way through the rubble of downtown.

Here and there the corners of buildings have come tumbling down like a set of children's blocks. We pass a boarded-up store whose brightly striped awning has caved in, along with the glass doors that have been reduced to tiny shards littering the ground like a bed of pebbles. On the sidewalk outside sits one lonely head of lettuce. Such a waste when so many Laster families, living in their car hotels, go hungry. A body drapes across a sidewalk as though the person has stretched out and gone to sleep. *Was it the bombing or the Plague?* I wonder, though I'm not brave enough to look.

Fanned out on all sides of us, Storm's team combs the street while Storm strides alongside Margot and me like a god of yore. His footsteps thump the ground as he strides purposefully in the direction of downtown, toward Heaven Square.

I tap Margot's wrist, catch her eye. She quivers all over, then hugs her body with her other arm, not letting go of my hand. But it isn't until we turn the corner and arrive at the massive tree that I understand why he's pointed us there.

A person occupies every square inch of space not taken up by the giant trunk and tree limbs. People around us make way, but everyone's attention is locked on a tall, skinny figure, elevated by some sort of stage set up at the base of the tree. His thin arms are bare where the gaping sleeves of his robe pull away. His face is gaunt, made more so by the closely shaved head. Black cosmetics band his eyes, causing the already piercing brown to stand out like coals against the lantern-lit square.

But it's the tattoo on his face that I can't look away from.

Two circles in red, conjoined in the middle.

Evolve or die.

It's the same mark we see everywhere on the walls and buildings of Dominion, only now the Watchers are wearing it. I squeeze the life from Margot's arm, and she stops and stares, gape-mouthed, at the man. He gesticulates wildly, whipping the crowd into a frenzy.

"They're not your friends, people. The Upper Circle line their pockets with your suffering. They sleep on the bed of your bones. *They'll burn your tree down.* And then they'll grow fat and rich off your suffering while they survive the Great Plague." My cheeks heat as he talks, the crowds murmuring, sometimes shouting, their agreement.

It's not strictly true, of course. Nobody is immune to the Plague save the True Borns. Sure, some of the Splicers are lucky enough to survive with the help of a little technology. Others aren't so lucky. It was only a few months ago that I watched one of the richest men in the world pass away in front of me. He'd been headed to Russia, too, looking for some secret miracle cure.

He hadn't made it to shore. And Leo Resnikov's factory, which we think likely manufactured this miracle cure, went up in flames.

In a fire that we set.

Fist pumping the air, the preacher man continues. "We can take it from them, you and I. They *have* the cure. We *know* they have the cure. And once we've taken it, we can take back the city for ourselves."

I look around, my attention landing here and there on faces in the crowd. This isn't the first preacher man to incite the rabble with a tall tale. A few years back, the police would have hauled this seditious preacher man away. Times have grown bleaker, though. There aren't enough rovers to collect the dead from the streets, let alone police to keep order.

But was the preacher man telling the truth?

"What do you think would happen if the preachers and the rabble were to rule the city, eh, girls?" he'd quizzed us. "Ask any economist; ask any of those teachers at that fancy school of yours. The rabble doesn't have the wherewithal to rule. And the preachers? Ha!" he'd scoffed. "This would be an easy power grab for them. They could make the world over with their brand of zealous chaos. Wouldn't that be a picture?"

Our father was right. I turn as a red-faced Laster beside me yells out, "That'll teach 'em, preacher man! Death to the Upper Circle!"

Storm stomps his feet, his spectral bones tossing in the night sky like a nightmare come to life. His eyes have gone liquid metal, all humanity leeched from them. "You." Storm points to the preacher man. His voice echoes like a cannon across the square. The crowd around us shrinks and drops dead silent, until all you can hear is the tinkling of the prayer bells tied to the branches of the tree and the hammering of frightened hearts.

"You," he says again, low and determined, as he picks his way through the crowd to the preacher man's stage. "You did this to my city. You and your puppet master. Where is he?"

"I don't listen to True Borns," the preacher man snarls dismissively. He backs up only to find himself trapped against the massive, hulking trunk of the tree. "I don't have no beef with you or the other True Borns."

"Oh yeah?" Storm's smile flashes like a sharp knife. The crowds part to let him pass with a wide berth. The preacher man pales but doesn't dare turn his back. "You'd set yourself up as wardens of this city but with no mention of True Borns?

What did you think you were going to do with us? I'll ask just one more time. *Where. Is. Father. Wes?*"

Wild-eyed, the preacher man turns his head to the side and nods briefly. In the shadows and off to the side stands another one in robes, who then slinks away. The preacher man pulls in his cheeks, as though sucking hard on something. Seconds later his jaw begins to tremble. His bony frame shakes and dances, as though electricity has jolted him. Then he falls, white foam coating his mouth as his eyes roll up into his head.

Storm bounds over to the man and shoves his fingers down the preacher man's mouth. He fishes out a tiny scrap of something, covered in foam. But it's already too late.

The preacher man is dead.

5

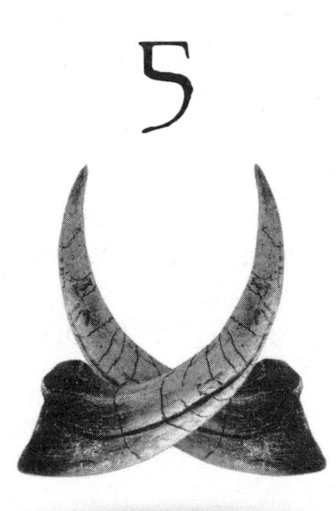

Storm beckons to Mohawk, who stands out against the Laster crowd like a flashing sign. She's the strangest mixture of clashing colors and patterns: black-and-bright-blue-streaked hair sticking up, wispy braids of her Mohawk coming down like a mane around her lovely face. Thick gold bands circle her neck, bright against her dusky skin. Today she wears a cropped jersey, faded red with the number twenty-three emblazoned across her chest in white, paired with zebra-striped leggings. She crouches next to Storm and opens a small plastic pouch fished from her carrier bag. Storm gently drops the white foaming item from the preacher man's mouth into the pouch. He wipes his fingers carefully on the dead man's shirt, avoiding the foamy parts. The dead man has gone a pearly pink color, as has Storm's fingers.

Storm speaks into his hidden earpiece. "Jared, take the twins home. The situation is no longer safe."

Of course we're safe, though. Who in their right mind would cross Nolan Storm? Most of the mob has pressed back; at least half have run away. Torch and Kira have disappeared. "Dammit. One little question," Storm says now as he gently lowers the dead man's eyelids. "Call the rovers." He turns to Mohawk. "Let them know there's a pickup."

"What did he do?" I find myself asking.

"Poison," Storm tells me, rubbing his hands together as though they've gone cold. "It's what agents have done throughout time to avoid telling their secrets when they've been captured."

Suicide? My mind reels. "But you hadn't captured him. You were just talking to him."

Storm's look turns me cold. I reckon it's the most direct reply I'll get tonight. The sky is striated with pink light, at odds with the strange discomfort of death. "When you're through making the call," he tells Mohawk bitingly, "get the girls home with Jared and take the sample to the lab. We'll be here a while yet."

The events of the night before get rolled into our school bags in the morning: just more homework to be unpacked and dealt with at a later date. Margot straightens her blue skirt and hikes her stockings up. "How do I look?" she asks, hooking a strand of auburn hair behind her ear.

"Perfect," I tell her with a smile. She returns it, a mirror image of my own, as she sits down beside me at the breakfast nook and starts spreading the toast that Alma brings in by the plateful, along with eggs and sausage and long strips of bacon.

I pop a final strip into my mouth and look over our timetables for the umpteenth time. "We don't have the genomics exam until next Wednesday," I tell Margot.

"Good," she says with a shudder.

I give my sister a hard look. "You're not skipping the tutorials."

"I know," she replies under her breath. But of course, there will be no more ditching class. No more lighthearted days for either of us. We are headed back to our familiar stomping grounds, Grayguard Academy. But we are not the same girls we were.

Over the past few months our world has tipped sideways and become unrecognizable. This is someone else's life. Some other set of girls who are reentering their school, just four credits shy of graduation. Other girls who work and live with True Borns—not the diplomat's daughters, heiresses to the Upper Circle.

Other girls, girls who have secrets cached in their blood.

I remember once overhearing a friend of my mother's telling a story about a young man from the Upper Circle who'd "gone off the rails." It was during one of their boozy afternoon sessions, the kind that ended in tears while the ladies collectively faced their fears of being Spliced. *What happened to him?* my mother had asked, her face a mask of disdain. *Did he fall into the Lasters?*

No, the woman shook her head and went on. He fell off the face of Dominion. No one knows what happened to him. *It's like he was never born.*

I think about that nameless, faceless boy as I study the thin, drawn shoulders of my sister. We are lucky, I reckon. Storm took us in. He's doing everything he can to keep us in the world we were born to. Even if that means Margot and I face the depressing and humiliating experience of returning to Grayguard. We've only to endure a few make-up lectures and tutorials, we've been told, and then we'll be allowed to sit our final exams. I shudder to think of the pull Storm has exerted on our behalf. Though sometimes I wonder at the price that will be exacted for this small slice of kindness.

Margot turns to look at me, a question in her beautiful gray-green eyes. "You realize we won't know a single person there any longer."

I nod. All our friends have finished school. We were the only two in our year—still alive—not to. And we didn't mind, not really. But our True Born guardian sure did. *You can't be part of your set without graduating*, he'd told us.

True. There is no such thing as a high school dropout in the Upper Circle. And our father isn't here to buy us our diplomas. So instead we are left with the compromise Storm has brokered for us.

My thoughts stray to the boy who'd disappeared. Every comfort we have ever known has come from the Upper Circle. Though Storm's keep is as nice as they come—in fact, nicer than many of the highest families—it is incomprehensible to me that someone would leave the Circle on purpose. I wonder now why the boy did it. Was he True Born? Was he like us, different in some fundamental way, something that would, sure as the grave, expose him?

. . .

Grayguard has changed in the last six months, though I wonder if it's just my perception of it, as though in the interim it is me who's grown. The gray bricks and iron gates of the school, manned by gun-toting security forces, seem more austere, less like a place I've been to nearly every day of my life. And, though many of the uniformed faces being ushered through the gates by their Personals are familiar, they are not friends.

Jared sweeps the yard and the buildings behind us before escorting us from the car. As he helps me out, I think I feel the slightest squeeze of my hand, though I may be imagining it. I squint against the white glare of the sky and try to ignore the rising feeling of panic gripping me.

It's more than the increased presence of security. It's Margot. She stands stock-still on the sidewalk, her head cocked like she's listening to something. I feel her heartbeat: a brittle tattoo. The curling dread in her stomach. A headache flashes through her mind. She rubs her temple as I rub mine.

Then I hear it, too.

Soft, so soft. Like the mewling of a kitten. Or a baby.

Margot turns white as a winding sheet.

"Okay?" I whisper, quiet-quiet.

She nods but doesn't speak otherwise, her hand gripping mine until my knuckles turn white and I think my bones are crushed.

Jared opens the gate, a question in his eyes. I give him the tiniest shake of my head. This is something only we can deal with, more vicious scars earned from the past few months. She can't stand it. Every time we walk past a child, let alone a baby, Margot sucks in her breath and looks like she wants to weep. It wasn't her fault. The test-tuber babies that Resnikov created from Margot's flesh had nothing to do with her, not really. But she'll not forget the sight of them, their lifeless floating limbs encased in glass. Her only choice in the matter was to destroy them, something Jared and I helped her with. And that was not much of a choice at all.

"Breathe," I remind my sister through a fake smile. "Breathe, Margot, just breathe."

It's easier once we walk up the stairs and enter the building. We suddenly become swamped by the familiar scents and sounds: lemon wax and floor polish and old, musty wood. High voices like choruses of birds piercing us from left and right. And then the bell, making us jump a little, ringing the students into homeroom. We can't hear our steps on the polished marble floors through the din. We can no longer hear our panicked heartbeats.

We sit by ourselves at lunch, an island of two, when a girl with a brash walk saunters up to us. She has the long, straight blond hair that so many of the Upper Circle girls aspire to. She stops before us, one saucy hand on hip as the other crosses over her midsection. Flipping her hair back over her shoulder with an impressive head toss, she gazes at us as though we're bugs she's come across in her living room.

I stare at the ridge of freckles spanning over her nose, the round brown eyes that would be pretty if her expression were a little kinder.

"Yes?" My tone is filled with the cultivated boredom of the Upper Circle.

Her brashness slips a knot as she continues to stare. "Are

you sure you're in the right school?" She smirks, her voice loud so that others can hear her bravado. Behind her, the volume dips as the lunchers try to overhear. "Because you look at little past your due date."

"And?" I prompt her.

"What did you say?"

"And?" I prod her along with a roll of my hands. "Surely you've heard the word before. 'And:' a conjunction that connects two parts of a phrase. It's what us old fogeys are good at, good grammar and good breeding." I throw her with a dazzling, cold smile. "*And*, meaning, have you really not got anything else?"

The smirk slips from her perfect Upper Circle face. "True Born scum lovers," she spits at us.

"Ah, there it is!" I turn to Margot, who stares at me as though I've gone mad. "Margot. Did you hear that? We're True Born scum lovers. I knew there was something special about us."

I turn back to our would-be antagonizer. Her face has turned blotchy. The cafeteria has gone silent as the grave. "I guess you know who we are, then. As well you should. I can't say we have the pleasure of knowing who you are, but then, there are so many of you. There are just two Fox sisters. But seriously, whoever you are"—I indicate with a regal flip of my wrist—"*thank you* for reminding us who we are."

I lean forward a little. The girl takes an unconscious step back. I lower my voice, but it still carries over the still, silent tables. "We are very fortunate in our choice of guardians," I tell the girl in a confidential tone, while under the table, Margot frantically pinches her leg. In answer, bright pain lances up my thigh. "Have you had the pleasure of meeting Mr. Nolan Storm? I assure you, it's not a meeting you'd soon forget. And I reckon it's always so nice to know that your friends won't be dying of the Plague anytime soon. Unlike some."

I flip my eye to her friend at the adjoining table, smirk dropping from her lips. She'll be next, I know. Turning back to the freckled blonde, I give her a sympathetic shrug before dismissing her. I can feel her behind me, burning with hate, for a long moment after I turn my back. Titters start to rise from the surrounding tables and soon the cafeteria is louder than before, loud as rabble. She storms back to her troupe of girls, storing up ammunition she'll no doubt lob at us later.

Margot rolls her eyes at me. "Did you have to go there?"

"Yes." My voice is curt. I can't wipe the steel from my eyes.

She'll try to break us, this girl and her pack of girl clones. But Margot and I, we have gone so far beyond this world of petty attacks that she is nothing more than a mosquito to be slapped.

Margot gets my attention by scraping her nail along the table. She moves the finger to the side of her face, just under her eye.

"What?" I ask.

My twin nods at the room. "Look."

The cafeteria has a large, vaulted ceiling, like that of an old cathedral. Thick wooden beams, heavy from centuries of fires, hang over the long tables in the room. The windows are high, letting in a steady trickle of gray-white light. Everything in the room is exactly as I remember it: the same pocked wooden tables, the same rickety metal and wood chairs.

The faces are different. Younger. Here and there are tables of kids I reckon are several grades below us. A young girl with pale skin draws her hair back behind her ear, nervous as a cat. *They're all nervous.* Then I notice there are far fewer kids than I'm used to seeing. And the room: The walls are studded with

Personal mercs, glowering with silent attention like watchful sentinels.

I pivot my attention back to my sister. "When did they start letting Personals in at lunch?"

She shakes her head with a tiny shrug. Her eyes are dark pools, heavy with sadness. In our absence, it seems, our school has become a town filled with ghosts and guns.

By the time Jared fetches us at the end of the day, Margot is more flushed and animated than I've seen her in ages. She practically bounces into the back seat of Storm's car, humming some little song under her breath. Jared lifts an eyebrow at me, a question in his eyes, as he holds the door open. I shrug and slide in.

Torch gets in on the front passenger side. Margot taps him on the shoulder. "Rematch when we get back?"

Torch's youthful grin fills the rearview mirror. "Yeah, sure, if Storm doesn't need me."

"Oh come on, surely even True Borns get time off?" Margot flips her hair behind her back. "I'm putting money on this match."

"What money?" I launch in, just as Jared murmurs under his breath, "This I've gotta see."

We pile into the games room when we return to Storm's keep. Jared fetches us some drinks while Margot and Torch trade good-natured barbs. With the first *thwack!* of balls across the table, I sit back and listen to the banter with my eyes closed. My sister and I had never been permitted this kind of playfulness. It's lovely, filling me with a sort of decadence that has nothing to do with fancy parties or fine clothes. I open my eyes and watch my sister blossom as she pulls her cue straight and strikes the balls, one after the other. She's good—*really* good, I realize.

Torch watches her with a face flushed with puppy love. Jared shakes his head and whistles. "You've been playing us, Margot," he says with admiration.

My twin shrugs in answer. "Been out of practice."

This was it, the thought suddenly strikes me. *This* was Margot's secret life. All those days she skipped school, before our world fell apart, all those days she'd disappear, leaving me to make excuses for her, Margot was off playing games. *This game.* The thought raises an unexpected lump in my throat. I blink back a hot flash of tears. She was *playing.*

And she never once invited me.

With a final clamor and thud of balls into pockets, Margot wins. She gives Torch a graceful victory smile while Jared lines up the table for the next game.

"My turn, shark," he teases. Margot's laugh peals like a bell across the room, spelling out something I should have learned about my sister long ago.

"Cat."

Margot sits on the corner of my perfectly made bed, watching me prepare for the evening ahead. I'm to go on yet another "strategic" outing, according to Storm, though I'm given to understand this one will be more political than the others. I pull at the sash across the midsection of the pale yellow dress that floats like gauze around me.

Margot gives up waiting for me to respond to our little game. "Here," she says, coming over to me and tightening the sash expertly. Her fingers brush the back of my hair. It's been growing since I've been at Storm's. It hangs halfway down my back now in long auburn waves. I look more like Margot than ever before.

"You're lovely," says my twin.

"Thank you." Our eyes cross paths in the mirror. I look away first.

"What is it?" she finally blurts out, her hands outstretching in exasperation. "What's bothering you?"

I'm trembling. I bite the skin inside my mouth. "You never once took me," I say, staring at the floor.

"What? What are you talking about?"

I whirl on my sister in a cloud of delicate yellow and expensive perfume. "You left me there all those times. Left me at school, left me holding the bag while you went off to play billiards. You never once thought of taking me along?"

Margot stares at me, thunderstruck. Then she laughs. My face boils.

"Don't you dare laugh at me," I warn.

"Lucy." She grabs my hand. "Come on. We both know you never would have left with me. You've always been the perfect Fox daughter."

"Perfect?" I snort. "So *not* perfect. You were the one they preferred. And how would you know? You never asked."

A slight frown puckers Margot's perfect forehead. "I reckon I needed to be sure you wouldn't stop me. You have to admit, you've always been a stickler for Father and Mother's rules." She looks at me slyly. "And now you're the model agent for the mysterious Nolan Storm."

"What's that supposed to mean?"

"Just look at you! All you've done is trade one set of Fox parents for another."

I reel back as though I've been slapped. "Margot."

She cuts me off. "You have a crush on this True Born. On all of them. It's clouding your ability to see what's happening. You're being manipulated. Just like Father manipulated us." Margot's mouth turns sour. She crosses her hands over her chest as though she's caught a sudden chill.

"It's not a crush," I try to tell her in reasonable tones, "it's gratitude. They saved our lives, Margot. Don't you want to help them in return?"

"No."

Shocked, confused, I sit down on the edge of the bed and ponder the hard lines of my sister's mouth. "Why? I thought you liked them? What about Torch?"

"I *do* like them." Margot's head tilts sideways, a sure sign she's struggling to find the words. She paces across the shiny wooden floor, her socked feet making not a whisper. "It's ironic, really, that you've become more like me than me, if you know what I mean."

I shake my head. "Not a clue, Mar."

"Usually it's me who'll fling everything away—our family, our breeding—because I have a crush on some hot guy. But this is *you*." She sinks to her knees before me, placing her hands in mine. "This is *you*, Lu. You're the sister who lives up to it all and makes it look so easy. It's not like you to throw everything away for some—"

"Hang on a moment." I hiccup a short laugh. "Are you actually telling me I'm throwing away my life for a boy? What boy?"

"Lu." Margot stares back at me reproachfully. "Storm is—"

I gape at my sister. "Margot." I lean over. "I'm not abandoning our family. Or our breeding. Not for Storm. Not for any True Born. But what choice do we have but to play along?" My throat closes over hot, bitter tears. How could Margot not understand that everything I do is for her, for the family?

"Ask yourself, Lu," Margot says with a reproachful shake of her head, "why? Why are the True Borns helping us? What are they getting in return?"

My head swims. A knot of nausea forces its way up my throat. It's not as though my thoughts haven't traveled a similar vein.

"It's not like I trust them," I choke out. "I know we're being used."

I hate the pity that slices across my twin's face. "You know it, but you don't *know* it. I like them, too, you know." Margot reaches up and touches the light curls of my hair. But the smile she gives me freezes me to the core. "But you need to see it for what it is. I learned the hard way. I don't want that for you."

6

Two men stand beside the long mahogany table in dark pinstripe suits. They could be anyone, these dull-as-wallpaper mercs. It's the men beside them who are interesting. Lasters, and not all that well off. One Laster wears a rumpled brown suit that looks like it was made for someone else, too big at the collar and too short in the arms. With his graying hair swept up in long waves over his temples, he looks like a professor from another era. His companion is younger, though the lines around his eyes and the weathered, chapped pink skin of his face makes him look years older. He wears the uniform of many a Laster: the long jean overalls with a thick sweater underneath. Glancing around the room with obvious mistrust, he cracks his thick knuckles uncomfortably every few seconds.

I reckon I don't blame him. The Lasters are completely outflanked. Besides the two in pinstripe suits, against the glass of the tall windows stand a row of faceless dark-clad mercs. Four behind, two more at the door, and another two stand sentry at the entrance. The heavy *cluck cluck cluck* of a grandfather clock marks time through the drafty room. The men in suits don't speak to us, don't acknowledge us. The Lasters seem ill at ease. I notice that the younger one's eyes, especially, dart back and forth from the fixtures to the large oil paintings of heavy-jowled Upper Circle men.

I've been in this room before, of course, visiting our father. It's one of the government buildings, the oldest, and, in my opinion, the prettiest of the three buildings where the senators rule Dominion and beyond. It could be a mansion of the Upper Circle: wood-paneled walls and vaulted ceilings give the place an air of elegance. The soft leather chairs are leftovers of a bygone age, and its glass and brass lamps lend my thoughts to cozy libraries and teas.

A moment later, Colonel Deakins limps into the room in scarlet military dress. Face shiny and red from exertion, he stops to wink at me before sitting down opposite Storm and me. I lean over, but my elbow slips on the over-waxed wood of the table and I accidentally smash my nose into my companion's large, unmoving shoulder. It smells like him, a rich symphony of musk and a hint of cloves. He glances down at me, his expression softening with amusement.

"Sorry," I say, hitching myself straight and rubbing at my nose. "Wh-What are we doing here, exactly?"

The corners of his mouth turn down. "We're getting to the bottom of a few things." He taps the tip of my nose. His touch jolts me awake.

And just in time, too. In walks Senator Theodore Nash, glowing with good health, and behind him, Senator Josiah Gillis. My breath hitches in my throat and I cough slightly. A huge hand slaps me on the back. I'm sure Storm intends it to be a light tap, but it echoes through my bones.

"Good," Nash says as he seats himself across from the Lasters. "Everyone is here. Shall we begin?" He pours himself a glass of water from the pitcher in front of him and drinks with relish. The glass is emptied in seconds. He refills it again and shares an unholy smile with us.

Storm gathers himself, and it's as though he pulls the oxygen from the room.

"It's time we talk about the future," he tells the men solemnly. "I'm sure our friends here"—he indicates the Lasters with a sweep of his hand—"agree with me. It's time we have equal and proportionate government before the chaos sets in. I've called you all here to discuss setting up a transitional council with representatives from each group that will help us solve some of our worst current challenges and maybe head off some of our future ones."

I stifle a gasp. It's unthinkable.

"Now really, Mr. Storm," the colonel blusters. He taps a meaty fist on the table in front of us. The others are just as shocked, it seems. Senator Gillis looks turned to stone.

Beside him, though, Theo Nash smirks. "Dominion already has a legal government, Storm," he drawls.

"For now," Storm concedes with a nod.

"Is that a threat?" spits Nash.

"Now, now." The colonel waves his hands.

Storm ignores the colonel. "No. It's an acknowledgment of reality, Nash. Splicers aren't surviving the Plague much better than the Lasters. And I don't think I need to remind you"—his eyes move briefly to the Lasters in the room—"the Lasters are dying."

"We'll see about that," Nash mugs.

Senator Gillis coughs loudly and clears his throat. "Gentlemen." He nods sternly. As the barbs are thrown the Lasters grow agitated, as though they aren't sure whether there will be bloodshed. "If we could refrain from insults, please." Nash sits back with a look I'd as soon call unrepentant. "Now," Gillis continues. His hands meet in a circle on the table. "Mr. Storm, Senator Nash is correct. The Senate is the elected ruling body of Dominion City. Why would we even contemplate undermining the structure that has been working well for more than a century?"

Storm pierces the senator with a look. "Because the Plague is decimating Dominion. And those bombs that rocked the city? That's just the beginning."

Nash jumps in. "The Watchers are our problem, Storm."

"No," Storm continues gracefully, "they're *our* problem. They are a problem for the Lasters and the True Borns as well as the Upper Circle. And what are you doing about it? Burying your heads in the sand."

Red-faced, the colonel half stands. "You go too far, Storm. We'll rout every last one of those little bugs."

Storm acknowledges the old war hero with a sweep of liquid-metal eyes. "Really? And how are you going to find them, Colonel?" The True Born ices out the colonel and turns back to Gillis with a quiet, "I'll not keep pumping resources into this city just to watch it burn."

Ah. So there it is. Storm has been floating the city. And there is his choke hold.

"Let's face it, gentlemen, you're not equipped to deal with this threat. The Watchers are recruiting more Lasters every day. And you simply don't have the resources to fight them."

"We have an army," the colonel protests.

Storm doesn't even glance at him. "Whose corps consists of Lasters, who are being recruited by the Watchers in droves, and the remainder of which are dwindling thanks to the Plague."

This was one of the pieces of information I'd been able to glean from Colonel Deakins a few months back. Robbie's father hadn't hesitated to tell me about the death counts. "Up to four a day now." He'd shaken his head at the losses. "They're thinking of starting conscription again," he'd told me. The last time the senators had voted in conscription, which forced Lasters only into army service, there had been open revolt in the streets.

The colonel goes silent now, his mouth a tight line of disapproval. For all his love of strategy, he likely never thought his words would come back to bite him in this way. The conscription plan must be further along than we'd thought, I reckon, as Senator Nash grins cockily at the red-faced Lasters. "I don't think that's going to be a problem."

"There's going to be hell to pay." Storm's words are quiet, but they echo around the room like a bullet. "You think the Watchers are a problem now, wait until you have half-empty barracks filled with sleeper agents."

"An idle threat."

A hand cracks down on the table like a clap of thunder. "Stop." It's the older Laster. He takes his time assessing the men at the table. I watch his Adam's apple bob up and down with the effort of swallowing whatever emotion has taken hold and turned his cheeks red. "Truth time." The Laster's voice crackles with sincerity. "Us Lasters have come upon hard times, sure. Some of our grandfathers and grandmothers remember conscription. We've learned harder lessons since then, in the olden times. But I tell you true, Senator, you bring back conscription and you lose this city."

"How dare you, Laster?" Nash yells, red-faced.

The Laster man holds up one red-chapped palm, silencing the senator with a withering glance. "We ain't the animals you take us for. Dominion puts in power its Upper Circle and says we elect them. But we don't get names on the ballot." He jerks his head toward Storm. "But this man, a True Born, would give us voice. The Lasters are in favor of a council."

"You're guilty of sedition," seethes Nash. He motions subtly with his hand. The mercs behind the Lasters take a step forward. But it's Senator Gillis who, with a frown and a shake of his head, stops the arrests.

"These men have been brought here to speak their mind, Theo. They are our guests."

"You can't be serious."

Gillis rises and adjusts the fall of his jacket. "I think it's time we call this meeting to adjournment. We'll meet again once we've had a chance to discuss your proposal."

Gillis walks over to the Lasters and shakes their hands, ushering them out. By the time Nash has left with his wall of mercs, Gillis comes back around to us. At my back, Storm's hand radiates heat and inhuman strength. He gazes down at me, lips curling up on one side. The planes of his face are dressed in shadows, but I shiver at the power in his eyes, circling his head in thick, tangled skeins. How can all these men not know what they are dealing with?

Josiah Gillis shakes Storm's hand, murmurs a word of thanks. But it is Storm who takes the meeting back. "We should meet again before the month is out. We have much to discuss. And Gillis? The Lasters need to be at the table."

"Yes, I suppose they do." He rubs his jaw like he's been socked. "Lucy." He nods at me, the afterthought, before exiting the big, empty room with his one remaining merc.

"So." Storm turns and perches on the table. I shiver again, this time from the loss of heat from his hand. The smile he gives me is light and free. "You've just been witness to history, Miss Fox. What did you think of the circus?"

How can he be like that? I wonder. One arm hooks casually across the neighboring chair. I work my throat, swallowing past alarm and panic.

Sedition, my brain says, over and over again. They'd hang a Laster for saying what Storm has said. *What will they do to the True Borns?*

"Aren't you worried?" I finally spit out.

Storm cocks his head, studying me. "About what?"

"They'll find a way to get back at you. They'll punish you, the Lasters. All of us."

He chuffs. "They can try."

"But why? Why would you put yourself and all the others at such risk?"

Storm leans over. His melted silver eyes hypnotize me. "It's the right thing to do."

"How is that, exactly? The Upper Circle—"

"Ignores four-fifths of the population. I wasn't kidding around here today. There is a reason the Watchers are gaining in popularity."

"But how will putting Lasters in front of the senators fix that?"

"It won't—not right away. But you have to start somewhere." He reaches out, his fingers running gently over a lock of my hair. I suck in a breath at the unexpected shock of it. He smiles, small and sweet, but his eyes keep watch on me. Steady and penetrating. *It's like he's changing all the rules*, I think to myself. The moment stretches out, leaving me uncomfortable, itchy in my skin. Nolan Storm isn't an old man by any means — younger than Resnikov, at any rate, whom our parents wanted either Margot or I to marry. But I've never really thought of Storm in that way before. *Maybe I'm misinterpreting the signals.*

I clear my throat. "Doesn't matter anyhow," I surprise myself by saying. "It's still not representational."

Storm grins. "How is that?"

"Where are the women, Storm? How do you have a representational council with no women?"

I expect my guardian to scoff, to tell me women can't sit on a government council. It's what my father would have said. After all, there are no female senators in Dominion.

Instead, his face lightens and his eyes gleam with what I'd call mischief. He stands, his hand returning to my back. I'm overly aware of him, the sheer size and strength and crazy power of him. Directed at me. I want to hide under the table and whimper. Instead, I stand straight and walk out of the room with my head held high, and I wonder if I hear Nolan Storm correctly as he murmurs, "I do believe you're right, Miss Fox. That's a situation we'll have to rectify."

His words are drowned out, at any rate, by a commotion at the door. Nash and Gillis are pushed back behind a wall of mercs as we near. Before the senators stands a tall, wraithlike figure dressed in the black shirt and white collar of an OldenTime preacher man. A straw boater hat perches on his head, the ends fraying and unraveling on one side. The mercs have drawn guns on him, but the preacher man just smiles a rotten-toothed smile.

I know him. I mentally sift though the dozen and one preacher men whom Margot and I have seen camped in front of audiences. *Where have I seen this one before?* But my mind has gone blank, and even duller when I spy the preacher man's knife. It's long and curved, silver steel flashing in the dim light of the hallway. The mercs yell something at the man. But instead of dropping his weapon like a sensible man, he raises it above his head with a slashing motion.

Storm pushes me behind him, holding me tight against his back as something powerful emanates from him. The blue filaments of light above Storm's head crackle and grow. He bellows one word, one word that the mercs ignore. "Stop."

Shots ring out. Three, four. I get my head around Storm's arm in time to watch the preacher man fall, the knife tumbling through the air with a wrinkle of light. A trickle of blood runs down one corner of his still smiling mouth.

All the air in my body leaves me in a great rushing *whoomph*.

"They killed him. Why did they have to kill him" I whisper into his back. The fabric of Storm's suit bunches in my hands. Storm pulls an arm around his back and holds me tight as I breathe shallowly. The air stinks of blood.

"Check his mouth," Storm orders the mercs at the door, who remain frozen above the body as though it will rise from the dead. They look at Storm dully. "Check. His. Mouth," he says again, each word a cut. This time one of the mercs lowers his gun and squats down in front of the body. He opens the preacher man's bloody, smiling mouth and pulls out a square of paper. The merc glances up at Storm as though waiting for an answer. "Bring it here," Storm tells the man.

I don't see it, but I can tell from the smell it's covered in blood. They don't ever tell you about the smell of violent death, how it fills a room with its cloying, terrible perfume. Storm pulls his arm free to open the paper. When he finishes reading it, he pulls out the square linen from his suit pocket and wraps it up before placing it in his jacket.

• • •

Outside we are surrounded by Mohawk, Kira, Jared taking point. We climb into the back of Storm's vehicle, where he keeps himself pressed close to me, the heat of his leg burning the bare flesh of my thigh, warming my cold, cold body. He grabs my hands, which have become like ice, and rubs them between his own. They are hot, rougher than I would have imagined. It's a shock. I've been living under Storm's roof for months now, but he has always been very cautious about personal boundaries.

"You all right?"

I nod, looking around with mounting anxiety. I don't want Jared to see Storm so close to me. I don't want him to get the wrong idea. But there are other things on my mind as well.

"What did it say?"

"Nothing." Storm shakes his head.

"I have a right to know," I tell him with dignity.

His hands still. Folded around my own, our hands look joined in prayer. My skin prickles with awareness. He's too big, too powerful. I feel as though I will drown in the wake of his gunmetal gaze. "There were no words," he says carefully.

"What, then?"

He sighs and pulls the slip of paper from his pocket. It unfolds in sections, and I am relieved that, despite a blotch of blood that stains one corner, it's relatively clean. But it's the symbol in the middle, drawn in a childish red scrawl, that has my heart hammering away in my throat.

Two circles, joining across the center, like a pair of crossed eyes.

Evolve or die.

7

I push my hair back with a shaky hand. "What do they want?"
Beside me, Storm is silent. He glances out the window into the deepening night. The typically gray skies over Dominion are subtly tinted with purple, a sure sign that within a few days' time we'll be experiencing one of the devastating Flux storms that can lay ruin to whole sections of the city.

"Jared," Storm calls softly. The hairs on the back of my neck rise. A moment later the van door opens, and Jared slides into the driver's seat. He turns, and I feel his eyes on me, burning coals, as he takes in Storm's closeness.

"Boss," he drawls.

"Get Lucy home. Check in with me when the twins are secure."

Jared nods as Storm removes his arm from me and moves toward the door. Even knowing Jared will misinterpret it—*and what do I care if he does?* I think rebelliously—I reach out and touch Storm's arm. "Where are you going?" It's out of line. I know it is. He's my guardian, and I'm not his keeper. I shouldn't be asking questions like this. But tumbling through the world of strange is the knowledge that he knows something. Much more than he's letting on.

Storm turns back, his lips arranged in that generous smile I know so well. He caresses my cheek. "Don't worry, Lucinda. It will all be well."

"What does that even mean?" I call into the empty space he leaves behind.

The door locks. Jared continues to stare at me stonily. I take in his attire. For Jared, he's dressed formally. In his collared button-up shirt and a formal pair of slacks I'd seen earlier, topped with a leather jacket, he could almost pass for someone who cares about his appearance. I want to smile at the thought. "Okay, Princess, Boss Man has spoken," he drawls. His expression grows pensive as he adds under his breath, "And then some," before turning around as though we're perfect strangers and gunning the gas.

Still, it takes me longer than it should to realize that Jared is not driving me back to Storm's.

"Where are you going?" I ask Jared from the back seat where I have been huddling, frozen to the core. He doesn't answer, just keeps driving with a stubborn look stamped on his face. Whatever he is planning, it can't be good. "Jared." I stretch my hand out to the driver's seat to force him to answer me. "Jared! I don't appreciate being kidnapped."

"Just sit back and relax, Princess. Everything's okay."

Sullenly I cross my arms and slide back in my seat, where I am left to study the slight upturn to his full lips, the strange glint in his eyes. I snort in reply and turn my head to look out the window as we wind our way into the northern fringes of Dominion.

Here the city is hills and winding streets, crumbling mansions falling to pieces over their high-necked fences. Most windows are dark now. Dominion has been losing its rich and mighty, those who have been building their empires in this section of town for hundreds of years. I shiver as we pass the ruins of Senator Kain's palatial home and run my fingers across the cool glass of the car window. It's still a mess from the attack all those months ago, when we first learned about the "magic" nanotech bombs.

The van swerves onto a street I don't know. Jared steps on the gas and the car shakes up a steep, winding incline. The headlights fall across a rusting white barricade. Jared stops the van, gets out, and removes it, then shuffles the van across before getting out again to close it behind us. I prick with unease. This is Jared, I remind myself. He's told me again and again he'd never harm me. Still, it's not like him to disobey Storm's requests.

I shift in my seat, overcome by a sense of panic that I'm not sure I even understand as Jared drives us through a winding copse of trees. The headlights bounce off the bark, turning the barren, stunted trees into the skeletal Lasters bit by Plague.

With a final heave, the van shudders to a stop in what appears to be midair. I freeze, my fingers death-gripped around the door handle. Outside the air is a murky brown with splotches of hazy gray that I assume are city lights.

Jared sits there for a long moment, hands resting loosely on the steering wheel. He stares out into the abyss with a thoughtfulness he usually hides behind a cocky smile before meeting my eyes in the rearview.

"Okay, Princess, we're here."

"Here, where?"

He rests his hands on the steering wheel and sighs. "Just here."

I don't move as Jared gets out and comes around the side of the van. He opens the door and bows with a mocking flourish. I pull myself out of the vehicle carefully, trying to see my booted feet in the inky darkness.

"Where is this place?" I ask, worrying at my lips. I don't understand what's going on between us, but I am somehow not sure of this version of Jared. He stares down at me impassively, his shadowy features like craggy, cut granite.

"Come here, Lu. I've got something I want to show you." The way he says this—softly, gently—melts my resistance. I place my hand in his and am instantly engulfed in the electric warmth emanating from his body. He tugs me toward the front of the van, where within a few steps the earth drops away into nothingness.

The van's headlights illuminate the few steps between the edge of the cliff and us. A thin railing separates us from the drop. It seems to go on forever, miles and miles of blackness. Here and there red or gold lights twinkle in the distance, like fireflies lighting up a summer's night. From here the city looks like bare bones, bleached of color and freed from flesh. I've never been here before, though I've often seen this place from down below.

"The Bluffs?"

Jared nods, lacing his fingers further into mine. We stand there for a long moment, admiring the view.

He's first to break the silence. "My parents used to come up here when they were teenagers." He tilts his head at me, one eyebrow cocked to suggest that maybe he can't quite believe his parents were ever teenagers.

"My dad would bring me here before…before." He doesn't have to say more. I know what he means: before his family fell sick. Before he turned out to be True Born. Before he was disowned. Jared points to a small copse of trees to the right. "He said they used to line up, all the cars, and the couples would make out like bandits." He laughs. I'm glad the night hides the hot flush of my cheeks, but Jared doesn't seem the least bit embarrassed. He turns to me, a youthful look filling his features until suddenly I can imagine a younger Jared, a happy-boy version of this young man who has become a killer. My heart breaks for that boy.

Jared's dimples flash as he shoots me a wicked grin. "My dad once told me I was conceived in this very spot."

"What, right here on the ground?" I tease.

"Dad had a muscle car. He was pretty cool." His voice becomes trailing, wistful.

I squeeze his hand. "You must miss him a lot."

"Yeah." He rakes a hand through his hair until it stands up, a riot of loose blond curls that I want to tamp down with my fingers. "My brother, Andrew, was pretty cool, too. I think you would have liked him. Both of them."

The world unexpectedly tilts beneath me until I'm no longer sure I haven't fallen headlong into space. Jared cares what I'd think about his family? He's thought about me meeting his lost family? I shake my head, certain I've misunderstood. Because surely Jared can't have meant…

I'm distracted enough that I don't move away when he turns to me, a slight, happy smile on his lips. His free hand snakes out and caresses my cheeks, sending sparks skittering down my neck and back as he pushes my hair aside. I inhale, then forget to breathe as the pad of his thumb traces my bottom lip. Sparks shoot through me.

His eyes are obsidian fires. "Lu," he says, softly, so softly.

"What?" I croak.

It's another long moment before he answers. "I can't stand it when we fight."

I sputter a laugh. His hands still on my face. "I'm sorry," I manage to say, trying to control a nervous need to giggle like a hyena. "Are we fighting? Maybe I didn't notice because it's all we ever seem to do."

A wicked grin lights his features. "That's not all we seem to do," he whispers, seconds before he replaces his thumb with his lips.

It's a soft kiss at first, tentative. Like someone asking your name. But it lights me up, sending fire shooting through my body, heat curling through my belly. I must sigh because Jared pulls back for just a moment, a question in his eyes and hunger written all over him. Then he claims my lips again, holding my face in his hands as the earth spins away from me.

I'm lost. I wind my fingers through his riot of curls, wanting, needing to get closer. Nip at his ear, his lips, the way I have imagined doing time and again. He utters a catlike purr against my lips. I splay my hands across his powerful chest, run them down his stomach. One hand slips through the space between the buttons of his dress shirt, glowing an eerie white against the headlights. Jared's breath hitches as though I've burned him, and something warm and sweet floods through me. *Can I really affect him like this?*

As my brain hazes over, I realize that I want him to not just *want* me but to want me so badly it overcomes his reason. I want him to forget himself. I want him to push me into forgetting *myself.*

He turns his head to nibble at my lower lip, tracing a hail of kisses down the side of my neck. Dizzy, I hold on to him for dear life. His fingers snake against my back, pull me closer. One moment he's kissing me and the next he's pulling back to regard me through hooded cat eyes. "Lu," he says, his voice gone ragged and deep. He lifts me up, our bodies pressing against each other, but it's still not close enough. We devour each other's mouths. I revel in the taste of him, the feel of his tongue, hot and heady in my mouth. He pulls up the skirt of my formal calf-length dress, wrapping my legs around him. Jared sways, whispers kisses into the flesh of my neck. I arch like a cat against him, digging my fingers into his arms, wanting to touch every inch of his shoulders, his chest.

He rears back. The planes of his face have narrowed, his cheeks flushed. I'm drawn to his lips, slightly swollen and infinitely kissable. His fingers tickle beneath the hem of my dress, sliding up my thighs, around, until they tease at the line where body meets thigh. I inhale sharply, shock and surprise and liquid heat stealing my thoughts. He stares at me with an expression I can't read, and then kisses me again like a dying man searching for oxygen. Jared walks me backward, pulling me up against the side of Storm's van. He pulls me tight against his hard, lean body, the still air around us filling with the ragged and labored sounds of our breathing, as sharp electric pulses course through my veins. I want. *I want.* Shudders run through him as his mouth holds me and stills, and we both pant as though we've been running full out.

Jared presses his forehead tightly against mine. Looks at me with eyes still clouded over. I can't figure out what has just happened. We don't say anything, though Jared slowly pulls his hands from my flesh, holds me tighter against his body. I revel at the thought that I can feel him throbbing, his pulse pounding through me as though we two have become one.

I lick my own swollen lips. Close my eyes against Jared's heated stare, which follows my actions like a hunting cat. When I can finally speak, I don't recognize my voice, which spills out like gravelly pebbles. "I thought you said you didn't want to do this sort of thing with me."

His harsh laugh disquiets me. "I didn't say I didn't want to, Lu." Jared shakes his head, pressing his forehead against mine. "I said it wasn't a good idea. It still isn't," he confesses quietly, his words nearly swallowed by the stillness all around us. "I'm so close to just…claiming you for my own."

That particular feminine pride I had been feeling evaporates in an instant. "Why did you, then?"

Another laugh, this one not at all pleasant. "God, Lu, do you think I'm actually in control here? You," he says, his lips coming so close to mine I can almost feel them on my flesh. He brushes them lightly, and the already swollen flesh lights up again. "You," he says again, his voice dropping into a purr as with one hand, he strokes my hair, "you're like a drug. I can't get enough of you, can't break away no matter how hard I try."

I push at his chest and force him to let me down. "You make it sound terrible," I grumble.

His voice and eyes are ragged, wild, as he tells me with conviction, "It is terrible."

"Jared," I warn.

Blond curls fall over his handsome face as he takes my cheeks lightly in his hands. I reach up and curl my own fingers over his, remembering what those hands can do. How could such brilliant, clever hands be capable of such violence? Like his hands, this man has the ability to make me feel as though I'm flying through the air one minute, bruised and sinking the next.

I try to look away, sick of the hurt, but he won't let me. Staring intently into my eyes, he whispers my name like a prayer. "Don't you get it? It's ripping my guts out because I have never felt this way before. I need to be near you like I need oxygen. And I know full well I can't have you."

The look on his face says it all. Haunted, broken. As though I really have ripped the heart right out of him, exactly as I've seen him do to others. I can't help myself. Tears begin to fall, getting caught in my lashes as I blink again and again, to hold them back.

"You're here with me now," I whisper. "Jared, I'm right here. Why does this have to hurt so much?"

For just a second, a look of pure desperation floats over Jared's features. When he finally speaks it's in a voice I've never heard before. Flat, harsh, terrible. "Because, Lu, you're destined for bigger and better things than a lowly True Born merc."

I suck in a breath. "How can you say that? How can you even think that about yourself? What does any of that matter?"

Jared's answer is to thread gentle fingers through my hair. "God, you're beautiful. Do you know that?" he murmurs, taking a deep breath.

"Don't distract me, Jared True Born," I scold. "This is the bloody end of the world," I choke out with a laugh. "I have nothing any longer. I'm no one. I rely on your boss's goodwill for my survival. And whatever is left of Dominion is being torn apart by Westfall and the Watchers. There isn't going to *be* an Upper Circle left for me to return to, even if I were so inclined. So tell me. *Tell me why.* The real reason."

But cold fingers of dread slide down my neck and back as Jared continues to stare at me, saying nothing. His throat works as he swallows something down. Then, with a look in his eyes I'd as soon call regret, Jared brushes my lips with a light kiss that leaves me hungry, wanting, and says, "You really don't know, do you? I suppose that's one of the things I love about you even though it drives me crazy. Always putting yourself last in line when you should be first."

My heart stutters to a stop. *What he loves about me?*

I think I'm going to have to break in again when he silences me with a finger across my lips. "You are important, Lucy Fox. You and your sister are sitting at the center of something so vast it doesn't yet have a name. And whatever's circling in that blood of yours... Everyone wants a piece of you."

He's right, of course. Everyone does want a piece of us Fox sisters. Scraps of our blood to do God knows what. Pieces of our social connections. No one has ever wanted me for just *me*. Until now. Until Jared.

"There's Margot," I protest, but even as I say the words, I feel a traitorous stab and know that whatever I'm thinking isn't possible anyhow.

"Yes, there's Margot. You're the two most important people in Dominion. Maybe all of Nor-Am. Hell, maybe on the planet."

"Why—because of whatever it is that's in our blood? Resnikov's cure is a fake, I'm sure of it," I say.

"There's a reason why Resnikov was doing what he was doing," he says darkly. "That bastard Nash is up to something. And all those rumors, Lu..." I recall only too well what was whispered among the elite traveling to Russia.

They say there's a cure there. And we know Resnikov was pedaling it—the snake oil he built on the back of Margot's DNA.

"It's too much of a coincidence," Jared continues.

"And the Watchers," I throw in, feeling my entire life fragment into pieces before my eyes.

He's right. I'd known this was true, but it doesn't make it any easier to bear. For a few brief, beautiful moments I'd actually let myself fantasize about a different life. One that wasn't all about duty. One where I was able to craft my own destiny. Maybe one with this True Born.

But as I stare into Jared's eyes, reading the naked truth there, I realize how delusional I have been. It's just that thought that bursts the dam, sends me over the edge. "I'll never be free, will I?"

A sob escapes me, and I bury my head into the comforting warmth of Jared's chest. He soothes my hair, whispering sweet words against my head as he covers me in kisses. "Lu, hey, Lucy, please don't," he whispers against the soft skin of my face. Then he kisses me again, a deep, powerful kiss that coils in my belly and spreads like a magic bomb's tendrils. It's a kiss mingled with tears and white-hot lust and something else, something unexpected. Something has changed between Jared and me, probably forever. It's this thought that has me pulling back enough to look at him. Shadows veil half his face. He looks troubled, restless.

Hungry.

A red light flashes across Jared, turning one side of his blond locks strawberry. It fills my eyes, making me blink.

"Uh, Jared?" I point. He turns, keeping me firmly behind his back as he searches the vista.

"Some sort of beacon, I think." He frowns.

I peer out from behind his torso. The red light fades, the afterglow still burning for a moment before it flares out again, filling a small swath of night with a blood-tinged halo.

"That's Old Town," I say, pointing down into the gully that separates the bulk of the Upper Circle from the rest of Dominion.

Jared turns and sends me a chilling look as he walks out farther, crouching down at the ledge. Dominion City is a dim and dismal wasteland lit here and there by barrel fires. I catch sight of the tree in Heaven Square, its branches sprouting up like arms reaching for salvation, dwarfing the buildings around it.

If I look to my left I'll see the vast strip of darkness of the park that stretches across the heart of the city. Nolan Storm's tower is on the other side of the cliff, not visible from this vantage point.

And this one red light. Just one.

I frown again. "Where'd they get the juice? I thought the northern power plant had been blown up," I muse out loud. The loud *pop* of exploding transformers has been indelibly imprinted upon me.

"Great question," Jared says, turning to give me a piercing look. "You'd make a fine merc."

"Such compliments, Mr. Price," I tease. But despite the lightness of my words, I reckon that things have just taken on a whole new level of sinister. I shiver and wrap my arms around myself. Not because I'm cold but because if there's a beacon, someone—or something—is being called.

As though he's lifted the thought from my mind, Jared stands abruptly and strides toward me like the hunter he is. "We've got to get you back to the apartment. And then I've got to talk to Storm."

8

I find Margot deep in the heart of Doc Raines's labyrinth laboratory. She's already dressed in her school uniform, her hair trailing down her back in sleek, shiny waves. She turns as I approach, eyes filled with shadows. I feel her teeth bite down on her lip, see it happening. Not hard enough to draw blood but close enough that I instinctively raise my hand to cup my own lip.

"What's going on?" I ask, instantly alarmed.

"Nothing," Margot says, crossing her arms over her chest.

"Cat," I caution.

"Canary," my twin chirps back, head tilting slightly to the right.

We are not alone.

"Doc," Margot calls out, "Lucy's arrived."

"Oh, good," a voice calls from several rows back. Frizzy locks bounce toward us, and soon I'm peering into the piercing blue eyes of Doctor Dorian Raines. "Good morning, Lucy," she says in her no-nonsense voice. This morning the doctor's slim frame is engulfed in a shiny white lab coat, her corkscrew curls pulled back into a tight ponytail, though the odd wispy curl pops around her narrow face.

"Good morning," I call back, looking down at the many well plates holding cells and samples, the spinning trays of our coagulating blood. "I hear there's something you wanted to show us."

Margot trails a hand over the dust-free counter. She looks up at me quizzically, as though trying to pin down what's different about me this morning. Her curiosity pushes at me like pins. My cheeks bloom with heat and I duck my head. And for once, for the first time in our lives, I am glad beyond measure that our sensory bond goes only one way.

Doc Raines interrupts us. "Okay, girls, this is going to be our little secret for now." Her thin white hands hold a long vial, bloodred, before us.

Margot and I exchange a glance. Doc Raines works for Nolan Storm. Whatever secrets are kept in that vial, they are surely dangerous.

Doc Raines clears her throat. "I made you a promise," she says softly. "I told you I would come to you first with anything I learned. I want you to know that I meant it. And I think this is the kind of information that might change a lot of people's lives. I want to give you both the chance to think about it very carefully."

"You're scaring us, Doc," Margot says lightly. But she grabs my hand under the counter, squeezing it tight.

"This, Margot, is your blood. Yours and Lucy's."

"You put our blood together?" my sister says.

My heart trips in my chest. Suddenly the room seems close and airless. I want to run away, because somehow I know this will be a moment after which there will be no turning back. *It's in the blood.*

The doc nods slowly. "I was very confused at first. Two different blood phenotypes from conjoined twins. How would you have survived? That's when I realized I had been looking at the puzzle the wrong way."

My legs tremble. I want to sink down on the cold laboratory floor. "Wh-What is the right way?" I force out from my frozen lips. Margot shoots me another sharp glance, wondering what is wrong with me.

But I don't have the words to tell her, the words that would describe endless dreams of rain, blood dripping from the sky. And somehow, some part of me knows that this is where it starts. *This is the moment.*

"Conjoined twins help each other survive. It's their very interdependency that makes them unique." Her eyebrow flips up as she takes in our clasped hands, our perfectly stoic posture. She joins her hands together on her hip. "Part of the fascination we have for twins, conjoined twins in particular, is that they shouldn't survive. And yet, here are these two symbiotic creatures. Do you know, throughout history there have been innumerable stories of one conjoined twin not living past his or her twin."

Margot and I nod. We had heard, of course. We'd made our plans should Plague take one of us. But of course, the good doctor isn't telling us what we need to hear. What we need to know.

"Can you—can you get to the point, please, Doc Raines?" I say, surprised at my own bluntness. "I don't think I can bear the suspense any longer."

Doc Raines eyes me sharply, then nods. "Girls," she starts, then hesitates again. "I don't quite know how to say this," she says, more to the air than us.

"Doc Raines," Margot implores, "*please*."

"I'm sorry." Dr. Raines lets out a huff of air, lifting a curl off her face. "Right. I'd better just show you." She turns back to the lab bench. Picking up a vial of sample blood, she uncorks the stopper and pours some onto a well plate. Dr. Raines flicks on a microscope and projects the images onto the screen as it auto-adjusts to her specs.

The blood swims and swirls, large blobs floating on the screen. "This is your blood, Margot," she says. "As I've said before, it has certain markers that tell me I'm not dealing with normal any longer."

Reaching into a small cooling unit on the lab counter, Doc Raines pulls forth another vial of blood. She removes the sample from the imaging tray, then pipettes a few drops of this new sample into the mix. "Okay," she murmurs. "Hold on to your hats. Watch this, girls." The sample is shoved onto the imaging tray and blinks back onto the view screen.

I'm surprised the doc hasn't mixed the two samples. Instead, she has placed the second sample at the other end of the viewing tray. For a moment we look at two pools of blood, each writhing like little embryos. But a few seconds later, something extraordinary happens.

As though alive and sentient, sensing the presence of family members, the sample on the left inches, caterpillar-like, over to the pool on the right.

Margot squeezes my hand so hard it goes numb. I look over. Her eyebrow lifts so high it looks painful. I forget: She hasn't seen this before. Hasn't seen my blood devour everything in its path like the Plague itself.

"What is this?" Margot hisses.

I stare at my twin. "I reckon that's my blood," I tell her sadly, "calling to yours."

"That's right." Doc Raines nods. Her eyes are winter ice, freezing us to the spot, but her words are gentle. She flicks a switch and pulls a drawer open, handing us each a pair of loops. Margot shoots me a bewildered look as she slowly draws down the special glasses.

"Of course, this part isn't new for Lucy. But *this*. This is where it gets interesting." Doc Raines touches a console on the lab bench, and the room dims. She presses another button, and the screen bursts into prismatic lines, like a gorgeous abstract painting. The doc's voice breaks through my reverie. "I've added blue fluorescent marker to this third sample," she tells us as the two squiggling pools finally join.

Within seconds, it seems, the old structures we were looking at are gone and in their place is a new structure. From this perspective it could be a house, something modern with winding staircases. "After bonding, the first two samples then go on to attract and—I simply don't know how to say this any other way—*remake* the DNA around them," Doc Raines says in a faraway voice.

The light blinks as the doc drops a third sample onto the side of the plate. Almost immediately it begins to slide toward the new DNA structure, which swallows the sample. The new DNA structure forms again, obliterating the blue fluorescent stain that marked the presence of a third substance.

"What we're left with is a recombinant DNA structure. I'll have to run a few more tests to know what this particular combination is, and then I'll run it against our DNA database."

A shiver of fear works its way up my spine. "Doc Raines." I pull the loops up. "What was the third sample, the one with the blue stain?"

The doc gives me an odd look. Part of her smile droops, as though she's told a wry joke to herself.

Her words are so simple, but they drop with the power of the bomb.

"I'd stained for Plague, Lucy."

My knees buckle and I grab at the lab bench for support. So it was true, then. *We are the cure.*

Through the gnarled thorns of the prick bushes, I can just make out the sky, the color of a dirty bandage, as though the clouds have been smeared with soot and grime. This is one of just a handful of places in Dominion that hasn't been completely gutted for firewood. The Lasters call this wooded park "sacred space." Here and there the flash of a blue tarp signals where people reside. The Lasters who've claimed this park for their own need the trees for shelter.

Beside me, Jared is restless. He bounces back and forth on his toes, sweeping his eyes sharply across the wooded area to the tips of the crumbling buildings to the east and west. Looking for something. Some*one*.

"I don't like this," Jared grumbles. He plucks at the T-shirt image sitting across his belly. It's a cartoonish jaguar in mid-scream, fangs exposed, outlined in silver glitter. A particularly twisted joke, given what Jared can turn into — a nightmarish panther man.

"What, that we're standing out here in the open? Or that

he's coming at all?"

Jared's pained expression answers that question for me. He'd as soon take me back to Storm's. That's not an option, though, and the sooner he accepts that, the better.

Two days have passed since our night on the cliff. I can't tell whether I'm avoiding him or he's avoiding me, but the outcome is the same. It's not even that he avoids eye contact—he's literally not been in the keep, and when I asked Storm about it I was told Jared had gone on assignment.

That's one of the things I love about you, he'd said.

I want to be happy about it. I want to dance with joy, preferably with Jared. But I don't know where the True Born and I stand. Except here, on the path that leads through the park, that stretches up through the belly of the city, slicing east from west, north from south. Parted by crumbling, pocked asphalt and the weight of my secrets.

Margot and I don't intend to keep Doc Raines's revelation to ourselves. At least, not forever. But we had asked for a little time, time to figure out what it all means. If we could cure Plague… It seems impossible, like something out of a dream. But Doc Raines had insisted it could happen.

"Think of this like a nanotech system," Doc Raines had said as she turned her back to us.

A second screen flicked on, illuminating the new helix structure. Numbers and letters filtered onto the screen as Doc Raines punched a series of codes into the console.

Margot sucked her lower lip into her mouth, staring quizzically at the screen. "But it's blood. How can it be nanotech?"

"I'm not saying it is. I'm saying it *acts* like nanotech. As though it has been programmed to do something very specific."

"What does mine do?" my sister asked, shooting me an incomprehensible look. But she can't hide from me. Margot's horror crashes through me with the weight of a tidal wave.

"Great question, Margot," Doc Raines replied, "but I think it's easier if we start with what your sister's blood does." I shut my eyes against a sudden bout of dizziness, half Margot's, half my own. "My hypothesis is that Lucy's blood carries the accelerator. Hers is the part that acts like the magic bombs. It draws in organic matter. That's when your blood kicks in. Once activated by something specific to Lucy's blood, some sort of DNA exchange seems to take place."

Lit with a sudden clarity, I opened my eyes. *"It Splices,"* I mused aloud.

Doc Raines turned her cool blue eyes on me. "Yes," she said, excitement lacing her voice. "I hadn't thought of it that way before, but that's exactly what it does. It Splices. Do you know what this means?"

"It means people will try to take us." Margot's voice turned bitter. "They will try to control us, or use us, or destroy us."

"Margot." Doc Raines shook her head sadly. But what more could she say? It was true and we all knew it. I drew a circle on my sister's wrist with my index finger. Margot's heart slowed, accepting my signal to let me ask a difficult question.

It was the old scientist in Resnikov's labs who led us to believe that we were genetically engineered, seeded for a very specific purpose. *He can only complete one part of his project with you, Margot,* the scientist had laid out Resnikov's nefarious plans to me. *For the other, he needs your sister, does he not? Lock. And key.*

"Doc Raines, when Margot was in Russia they were trying

to create some sort of Plague Cure with her blood alone. But the old scientist I talked to said it wouldn't work."

Doc Raines's frizzy mass springs about her face as she shakes her head. "Wouldn't have been possible. At least, it wouldn't have been stable."

"That's what he said, too. But I didn't understand what he meant."

"See here?" Doc Raines traced the bright patterns with her fingers. "This is why. The full DNA expression isn't switched on unless in the presence of whatever compound is in your blood, Lucy. There is a lot more to learn here, but essentially, I've noticed it seems to act like an anchor as well as a switch. They could have gotten some sort of short-term effect if they had amplified the sequences of Margot's DNA with some sort of growth accelerant, but it would be weak at best, unstable at worst. It breaks down without the other's input."

Margot and I stared at each other. It all started to make sense, the pieces clicking together in one gigantic mess of a puzzle. The rumors of the mystery cure in Russia, the stolen eggs. The babies—no, *things*—we'd seen floating in the jars. Things that haunted both our dreams. It was Margot they'd wanted. Not me.

They didn't need me as much then because they hadn't been searching for a real cure, had they? They'd been looking to make snake oil. And that's exactly what they made.

"What direction do you suppose they'll come from?" I ask now. I need to shake away the restless memories of the morning and concentrate on what's before me.

Jared narrows his eyes against the bright emptiness of the

sky. "Don't know. Don't care," he bites out.

"You are going to have to put your bad attitude someplace else, Jared True Born. They're coming. Get past it."

Jared's look is blank as he turns to me. For days, I've been hoping and waiting for an opportunity to clear the air, but now that it's here, a shiver of dread works its way up my spine. His shoes make no noise on the asphalt as he saunters over to me. I can't help but remember what those lips felt like on mine. How those fingers that could kill and maim a man touched me. And maybe something of my thoughts drifts across my face, because his eyes narrow even further as he steps behind me. His breath rifles through my hair, teases the back of my neck.

"Well, now, Your Highness," he says as his fingertips skate up the sides of my arms, causing my skin to break out in a riot of gooseflesh. "Are you excited about your old pal coming to visit?"

Two can play this game. "As if I'm going to answer that." I toss my hair back imperiously.

"Oh, really?" Jared turns to face me. Everywhere his body comes into contact lights up my flesh.

"Really." I close my eyes and hope the shakiness of my voice doesn't betray me.

A deep chuckle is enough to tell me, though, that Jared has heard it, too.

"Do you think your little pal is going to mind that you're not available?"

My eyes fly open. "Not available?" I cock an eyebrow at him.

Jared's hands circle my waist as he purrs. "Don't actually think he's coming here without a purpose, Lu. He's not coming to do business with Storm. He has a certain twin on his mind." As he speaks, his fingers glide up my torso, skate my rib cage. My breath hitches, and lights dance behind my eyes as those cruel, talented fingers tangle in my hair. He touches my lips with the slightest pressure. His lips hover at mine, causing a riot of sensations throughout my body. "But you're not available."

I push at his chest, hard. He staggers back a step, two, blank-faced.

"One minute you're telling me we can never be, and the next you're kissing me senseless and telling me I'm not available. Make up your mind, Jared."

He doesn't answer. He stalks toward me, cupping my cheeks in his hands. "You're mine, Lu." Jared claims my lips in a searing kiss. His lips scrape against my teeth as his tongue invades me. My stomach lurches and I'm close to being swept away until I hear the hiss of his indrawn breath, the quick stutter of his heart against my hand. But this is madness.

I don't recognize my voice as I pull away and step back, breathing so hard I might have run for my life. "I-I know what you said before. But we really can't go on like this, Jared. You don't get to be possessive of me but never let me get close. Or when we do get close… *Closer*." My fingers brush the swollen, tender flesh of my lips. My legs tremble violently. I'm not sure how I'm still standing. "You push me away. It's exhausting."

Jared stares at me in horror. "Lucy, I'm sorry." He takes a step toward me.

I hold up a hand. "Don't. You don't get to decide who I'm friends with, Jared. You don't own me. And as you keep reminding me, you never will."

"Lu—"

"Alastair has proven his friendship. God, Jared, he's put his life on the line for me. For both of us."

A scant couple of feet separate us, though it could be a mile. As we stare at each other, his eyes flicker from emerald to indigo, and I know that for now, at least, the beast has been leashed.

"I'm so sorry," he says again, so simply and quietly it all but disappears on the wind. "It will never happen again."

I squeeze my eyes shut and turn away from Jared so he won't see the tears. *It will never happen again.* He'll what—never kiss me again? Never be with me? Dread and pain lash me as I remember what life was like when Jared stayed away from me before. It was like no life at all.

In silence, we watch the path that threads through the park. A moment later, cheeks still hot and flushed, my attention turns to a small mob of people moving slowly through the skinny trees. A raven-haired man walks just ahead of the people around him. Something in my chest squeezes as Jared mutters under his breath, "Show-off."

"Jealous much?" I toss back breezily and throw Jared a huge Miss Dominion smile. He smiles back, only his grin is filled with death. "Be nice, Jared," I warn.

"As long as they behave themselves, Princess," he says cheerfully. "And that means Ali keeps his bloody hands off you or I'll feed them to him."

I roll my eyes at the True Born but have to suppress the small smile that works its way across my lips. *He is jealous*, says a little voice inside me. I tamp the thought down to better deal with the situation before me. I reckon it won't be as straightforward as Storm had thought this meeting would be.

Alastair is far from alone.

I count a solemn-faced band of seven. They are all dressed the same, in muted colors that help them blend in with the trees. Tan leathers and tall boots rise to the knees of their breeches. They aren't all men, either, I note. Two women are there, with fierce expressions stamped across fine, high cheekbones. Elaborately braided hair cascades over their shoulders. I catch gray eyes, brown eyes. Two of the men wear guns. One has a spear. And the remaining people carry bows strung across their shoulders.

But it's Ali I have my eye on. He saunters up, a glint of mischief in his midnight eyes. I'm distracted as he throws up his little pet pebble that has come out from nowhere, then catches it.

"Hey there, Miss Lucy. Miss me?" And out comes the grin.

"Yes, a little." I grin back and launch myself into his arms. He smells familiar now, the heavy scent of leather enfolding me. I close my eyes and squeeze him in a quick, tight hug.

"I'm so happy to see you, Ali," I tell him. And I mean it.

Alastair has earned a place in my heart. He's as mysterious as they come, but he risked his life for me again and again and has asked nothing from me in return. There are few in my life, I muse, I can say that of. We pull apart and inspect each other. "Didn't I warn you that you wouldn't be able to help but fall for me?" he jokes. But there is something serious to his eyes as he says this. "How's Margot?"

I nod, unsure how to answer. "Fine. She's looking forward to seeing you."

"Good." A lightning-fast smile crawls across his features, casting a fine web of laugh lines around his eyes. "But we have some formalities to get out of the way first, I'm afraid."

As one, Ali's people crouch to kneel. Shocked, I step back as Ali himself sinks down, one arm folding across his upright knee. He stares up at me with a sober look.

"I bring you greetings, Mistress Fox. I hope you will accept the friendship and hospitality of the Red Wing Clan, who are devoted to the great Horned One, Cernunnos." Ali stands, and

I step back again as he unsheathes a short sword from his hip. I've never seen its like: a curved dagger embroidered with silver thorns and knots, a set of stylized antlers resting on the cross guard. Jared takes hold of my arm. I feel his rigid warmth against my back, but he doesn't shuffle me off as I half suspect he wishes. Alastair's eyes stay tight on mine as he holds out his palm. He hoists the dagger up and slashes at the skin of his palm. Blood wells and he turns his hand over, letting drops run to the ground.

"I offer you the friendship of blood, Mistress Fox. We offer you and your friends the protection of Clan Red Wing."

Crimson pools join in small red circles. My voice trembles with shock. "Wh-why—why would I need your protection, Ali?"

"Because a war is brewing, sweet Lucy." Alastair's obsidian, thick-lashed eyes look back at me, solemn and sad. "And you'd best gather all the friends you can. Because this war is headed right for you."

9

The air is heavy with moisture as we slowly thread our way through the park. It had been the plan to bring Alastair directly to Storm's, but given the size of his contingent—and the bombshells Ali keeps dropping—Jared thought it wiser to parlay with Storm at the edge of the woods.

A murder of crows loudly communes in the barren trees. Their voices, angry and sharp, pull gooseflesh to my arms. Sinister at the best of times, these particular woods carry their own saying in Dominion. *Want to get into trouble? Take a hike through the park.* Of course, there are worst places than these woods, I think, remembering the unsavory side street where I first met Ali. Far worse places.

The Upper Circle used to come here to this park. They'd bring their children and ride horses, once upon a time, my mother said. Now it's a place where Lasters sleep on pillows of the dead, I muse, as Ali suddenly picks me up and swings me over a heap of bones half-covered in decaying leaves and rotting cloth.

"Careful."

"Thank you." I cast a look at him through my hair. It seems as though he's grown in the few months since we parted. His shoulders seem broader, his frame more solid. He glances back at me, his chestnut brown eyes throwing me questions I'm not sure I'm able or ready to answer.

"How have you been?" he says now, quiet, almost shyly. His hand floats like a ghost at my back and directs me through the woods as though he lives here. But it occurs to me now I don't know where Ali lives when he doesn't appear like magic through the trees.

"Oh, fine, I reckon. You've cleaned up some." A smile tips onto my lips. It's only as I say the words that I realize how true they are. He's in a smart leather jacket, his hair neat, though long now, past his ears and down to his chin. The longer hair makes him look less like a charming rogue and more like a capable, solid fighter, not least because it looks as though he's eaten more regularly. Unlike when we first met, there's not a single hole or stain in his trousers, and his face is cleanly shaven.

If I didn't know better, I'd say Alastair has fancied himself up.

"How are things between you and Lover Boy?" He flips a thumb toward the scowling menace of Jared, who keeps ten paces behind.

"He's not my lover," I say defensively as a blush works itself across my face.

Alastair surprises me with a laugh. "That good, huh?"

My limbs lock. I can't answer this line of questioning. Things are far too complicated for me to go there, even if I were willing to talk. "And you?" I inquire, ever the polite diplomat's daughter. I think I can continue with the niceties, but then, as though a switch has been thrown, I realize I can't. Not without some answers. I halt in my tracks. "What was that back there, Ali? What are you doing here — and who are all these people?"

Ali tugs my arm and moves me what he thinks is a safe distance from Jared's prying ears, though he'd be wrong. "I'm going to answer all your questions, I promise. Some will have to wait for a few minutes, though. Listen, you got my letter, right? I wasn't, you know, messing with you." A splotch of red works itself up Alastair's neck as he speaks. He pulls me into the shadow of a tree, his hand on my shoulder like a weight. "Lucy, I—"

"Hands off. Now." Jared stands not five feet away, arms crossed and murderous intent chiseled onto his handsome features.

"We're having a private conversation, Price." Alastair turns his back on Jared.

"Alastair," I murmur, "that's not a wise idea."

"I said hands off." Jared is closer now. Two feet. One. He throws such simmering menace I'm surprised Ali doesn't put his hand up to ward it away.

I relax an inch when Alastair seems to size up the situation correctly. "Okay, listen. We were just talking, right." He throws his hands in mock surrender. "You know, you've got some aggression issues, True Born." Ali shoots Jared a huge, knowing grin.

Jared returns the look, though it's filled with barbed wire. "Touch her again and I'll enjoy feeding your bones to the crows."

"Noted." Alastair slowly removes his hand and steps away from me one pace. Jared visibly relaxes. "But do you mind if your girlfriend and I have a conversation in private?"

Jared's jaw works furiously. To his credit, he looks at me for confirmation. I nod. I need answers, and I need to not be worried about bloodshed while I try to get them.

When Jared is far enough removed, Alastair turns back to me. "Sorry about that," he says, not at all sheepishly.

I narrow my eyes at him. "You did that on purpose," I accuse.

With a smile in his eyes, Ali shrugs. "So what if I did? Nothing like finding out the lay of the land."

"All right." I sigh. "What are you really doing here?"

An uncombed sea of leaves rattles like snakes beneath our feet as Ali shrugs and moves a few feet farther from Jared, pulling me with him. "Maybe I missed you." He smirks.

I cross my arms. "Right." I am not in the mood to play games. Not with Ali, not with anyone. Beneath a flip of hair, I sneak a look at Jared. His eyes bore into me relentlessly, hot and wild. *Girlfriend.* Ali called me Jared's girlfriend. My mind spinning and my face flushing hot, I try to play the ice princess as I prop my hand against the trunk of a tree. "If you're not going to talk to me, then we should just get going," I tell him. "Storm will be waiting for us."

Alastair grabs my elbow as I push off and begin to walk away. "No, wait." For the first time since I've met him, Ali seems unsure of himself. I turn. I'm close enough to see the light spray of freckles across his nose. His eyes are huge. "What if—what if I told you I really was here for you, Lucy Fox?"

My mouth opens but no words tumble out. I bark a laugh. It disappears into an uncomfortable silence. Alastair runs a hand down the back of his neck, ruffling the tips of his longer hair. He grins at me, the lines around his eyes deepening.

"I've shocked the unflappable Miss Fox."

My jaw gapes in the breeze. "No. I mean, yes. I suppose." Was Ali's letter a declaration? Frankly, I hadn't read it that way, and even now I'm not entirely sure I know what he's after. I try to mask my confusion by taking a few steps away. But then I catch Jared's cynical, knowing expression. The True Born watches me under his thick lashes. Hot, heavy guilt settles in my chest. Breaking Jared's gaze, I bend down and pick up a stray leaf. The small gesture gives me a precious few moments to collect myself. The last thing I want is to somehow give Alastair the impression that our friendship could become something more. Should that be what he's looking for…

"I think you'd better come and meet with Storm," I end lamely.

A drop of cold, heavy rain falls from the sky. It lands on my cheek and rests there, sliding off like a tear.

Jared's growl drowns out whatever Alastair was about to say. "It's raining," he says. "Get a move on."

Alastair holds my look. "Another time, all right?" he says, winking at me. The rock he carries around everywhere flies high up into the air and falls back into his palm as he whistles a little tune I've never heard before. I follow him onto the path, Jared's eyes devouring my back, and I can't help but think that in the space of the afternoon the world has tipped on its axis and sent me flying.

Three quarters of an hour later, we are ensconced in a boardroom I've hardly ever ventured into. Despite the large, colorful oil paintings adorning the walls, the room is cold and has the formal, barely used feeling of an Upper Circle receiving room. Alastair sits in a chair across from me, while at the head of the table, Storm occupies a massive chair that creaks as he shifts in his seat. Jared hangs back behind me, but I can feel his burning attention. No one else was admitted to our little meeting, yet another surprise.

Storm levels wintry eyes at Alastair. "Why don't you tell me about the followers of Cernunnos, Alastair."

Ali places his stone on the table before him, setting it spinning before he grins up at me. "You're True Born," he says knowingly. "So you've heard the going theory that the True Borns are a step backward in human DNA. We who follow the Horned One know better."

My mouth gapes open. I'm about to answer when Storm shoots me a look that would stop bullets. I snap my jaw shut, wincing as I bite the tip of my tongue.

"Go on," Storm says in low tones. "I'd like to hear more about this theory."

"Oh, it's not a theory," Ali says, sounding slightly smug as he lowers his hand to about two inches from the spinning stone. As though obeying some command, the stone halts its rotation. "It's a fact."

Storm folds his hands before him on the table, leaning slightly forward. As he does so, his rack of spun light shifts into sharper definition. "Enlighten me."

"We're his people."

"Who's people?"

Ali's hand comes down and slaps over his stone. "Cernunnos's. Look," he continues when Storm just stares at Ali with harsh, wintry eyes. "I know you're not as obvious a True Born as some of the others around here." Ali's eyes shift to behind me, where Jared's body heats the space at my back. "I don't know what the heck you share your gen code with, and it's really none of my business." Ali raises his hands in a gesture of surrender. "But what I do know is that Cernunnos was the first. The True Borns? They're all Cernunnos's children. Which makes us family. It also means" — Ali smiles sweetly — "that Cernunnos is almost ready to return."

"You follow Cernunnos." Storm says it again, slowly, skepticism dripping from every syllable.

Storm doesn't believe him. Not for a moment. And with Ali's next words I understand why.

"We were his servants. The Order of the Horned One. They used to call us druids. We've been serving the Horned One for millennia. But we've always been smart, see. Stayed hidden, away from trouble."

But if that's true, then why don't they know of his living ancestor? Can't they see Storm's lineage, the tangled crown shimmering above his head? I open my mouth again, ready to ask the question, but snap it closed just as quickly when Storm throws me another warning glance.

Ali continues. "We're his representatives. We are both friends and allies of the True Borns. We can assist you in the coming war."

Storm actually laughs. "You are, are you? Tell me, Alastair Red Wing, how do you suppose you and your friends can help us with this so-called 'war'?"

Ali nods as though he expected this response. "We aren't without our resources," he says. I barely catch it, but out of the corner of my eye I see Ali lift his hand a fraction of an inch. The stone on the table flies at an incredible speed and hits the window. The glass shatters, sending shards everywhere. I duck my head in my arms as Jared encircles the top half of my body.

Held within the safety of his arms, I can feel my breath

mingling with Jared's. Anger radiates from him like the heat of a sun. My heart pounds in my ears until I wonder if I've gone deaf. A long moment later, Jared clears his throat and uncurls me from his embrace. He stares at me, his eyes spitting sparks. The bones in his nose stand clear, a sure sign he's about to turn beast. But if he does, he'll spoil whatever pact Storm and Alastair are about to set up. I've not played the diplomat's daughter all these years for nothing.

"Jared." I murmur the word, trailing two fingers down his face. "Thank you. I'm okay."

Jared blinks as though he's been struck. But his eyes are a shade more human, and the persistent growl in his breathing dims. He moves only an inch away, choosing instead to linger right at my back. Not that I can blame him.

The window is a mess. Thick cracks have spun the window into a spiderweb, with one gaping hole in the middle. But it's Storm I turn my attention to. Shards of glass sit in his hair, are scattered across his shoulders and arms. He stares hard at Alastair, something in his eyes I'd not want to call up.

"Apologies." Alastair doesn't sound all that apologetic. "Sometimes I don't have a clear sense of my own power."

I don't see Storm move, not really. More like his arms tighten, holding the wood of the desk as he bores holes in Alastair. The hair on my arms stands up as the atmosphere in the room changes in the blink of an eye. It thickens, shimmers with what I think of as Storm's power. I can't breathe. I put a hand to my neck. The heavy air feels like a blade at my throat, choking the oxygen out of the room. Alastair must feel it, too, I reckon. He blanches, white as daylight, though he won't give Storm the satisfaction of an apology. The fool.

It's Jared who finally cuts in. "That's enough, Storm." And

then, when Storm doesn't seem to listen, Jared leans down and seethes, "You're hurting Lucy."

The air splits, as though the atoms have slipped a harness I can't see. Spectral bones rise from Storm's head, clear as day. I look over at Ali, watchful. *Can he not see them now?*

"You come in here with the guise of friendship and yet you wreck my house." Storm drops each word, heavy as stone, with the cold deliberation of a judge. "You took my ward to Russia under false pretenses. You *lied* to her" — his eyes narrow in disgust — "and by doing so, you placed Lucy and Margot and Jared in extreme jeopardy."

I try to sort through what Storm is saying. Did Ali betray me? I spent so many months being nothing but grateful to the brown-eyed stranger that it never occurred to me to second-guess his motives.

Storm's grip on the table, three inches of hard wood, tightens. A crack rips through the room, louder than a bullet. Storm pulls his fingers back and with them come a splintered section of the table. He hasn't even so much as stood yet. He tosses the end of the table at the wall where it whacks with a massive *thud* and punches a hole the size of a small child. Instantly, there's banging on the locked door of the boardroom. A buzzer sounds, again and again, like an insistent pest.

If I thought Alastair was pale before, it's nothing like this. Though I admit I'm curious at the way he sits there, breathing heavily but otherwise not giving away his fear. Not that I can tell, at any rate.

Storm tosses his antlers and stands, pawing the floor slightly with one leather shoe. The gunmetal of his gaze stays on Ali, and even I shiver as he dismisses the young man before him with a cold, "You let me know, Alastair Red Wing, when you and your followers of Cernunnos have something of value to offer the True Borns."

The door bursts open. True Borns and Ali's people spill awkwardly into the room. Storm steps forward and they scatter, pressing themselves against doorways to keep out of his way.

And we three are left surveying the wreckage of the board-room and one another.

"Well," Alastair says shakily. "That went well."

Jared crosses his arms. "What did you think was going to happen?"

Alastair holds out his palm. Seconds later the stone he let loose flies up through the hole in the window with unerring accuracy and lands softly in his palm. He curls his fingers around it and hazards a glance at me.

"I'm sorry, Lucy," he says quietly. And though I hear the sincerity in his voice, I don't know what he's apologizing for, exactly. And something else tells me that were I to know, I would not be very happy.

10

The stone benches in the courtyard have just finished drying off from the last rain, while I have just finished flunking my first-ever exam.

Margot slides down beside me as I hold my head in my hands and moan. "It's not that bad," she soothes. Her long hair floats into my field of vision.

"How can you say that? I didn't even remember the exam was today," I whine. I am not the twin who forgets tests, who does badly in school. But Margot was in her room studying for the past two days while I was picking shards of glass out of my hair.

These are not ordinary times.

"You should have called me. I'd have liked to have seen Ali again," Margot muses, pulling at a strand of her long hair.

"Margot." I eye her. "Which part of 'disaster' did you not understand?"

I'm out of line. I know this. But rather than call me out, Margot just snorts. "I like this new and irresponsible side you're showing, Lu," she tells me snottily. I make a face. "But really, what do you think he wants?"

"I-I don't know. Not exactly."

Ali said he was offering friendship. But the Fox twins know better than to take friendship at face value. *Everyone wants something*, as our father would say.

A long silence falls between us. Neither of us is keen to talk about it, but I know we both feel unmoored. Dependent on a virtual stranger's kindness, parentless and directionless now that our family is out of touch, Margot and I aren't sure what to think about this so-called "future" promised by our graduation from Grayguard.

Should I ever graduate, that is.

"Nash. Storm. The Watchers. Father Westfall...Alastair," Margot muses out loud. "Do you reckon there could be a connection among them?"

I blink. Sometimes my twin surprises me with how similarly our minds work. The threads are there but hidden. And I have no idea how to tease them into existence. "What are you thinking?"

"Doesn't it seem just a little convenient that Alastair should show up now, claiming to be a long-long relative of Storm's— but not *knowing* Storm—to tell us there's a war brewing? Does the Watcher insurrection count as a war?" Margot curls her pretty, pearly lip in disdain.

"You sound like one of them." I toss my head back at the rooms filled with overprivileged children. I've surprised myself with my words, but I won't take them back. We can't afford their kind of attitude. It's complacent. And complacency could get one of us killed. If nothing else, living with Jared and the other True Borns has taught me that. With a pang, my mind flashes to Jared as I'd seen him that morning. A shuttered expression to his face, as though he'd shut off everything he felt like a tap.

Was it so easy for him?

"I am one of them," Margot replies evenly. "So are you."

"I don't get it, Mar." I shake my head at my sister. I open my mouth to say more but stop when I spy Alastair walk up to us, bold as daylight. *How did he get in the school?* Visitors aren't allowed at Grayguard, though Jared has broken in at least once.

He's not alone, either. Ali has with him a companion. I take in the white-blond shaggy hair, as though leeched of all color. The pale skin with a dusting of freckles over the nose, eyes a light-light blue. He's in a leather jacket, protection against the chill of the spring air, plus a pair of brown functional trousers that seem to be common to Alastair's people.

Alastair, on the other hand, has dressed to the hilt. His leather jacket fills out across his shoulders. The shoulders are crisscrossed with stripes of red and black, so that in the brightness of the day it glints like the wing of a bird. *Red Wing*, I reckon. Under the leather is a good linen shirt, paired with smart gray dress pants. And for the first time in as long as I've known him, Alastair is sporting polished, proper leather shoes.

He saunters up to us, an easy smile on his lips for both Margot and me. He bows down before us like a story-time prince, taking first Margot's and then my own hand and raising it to his lips for a kiss. Behind the pair, a gaggle of girls swoons over the handsome boys who have just broken all the rules and crashed Grayguard to see us.

"Mistresses Fox." Ali's dimples wink at us. His hair, usually an untidy mop of black-brown, has been swept aside with something shiny that scents the air with pomade. "This is Tomas."

"Hi, Ali," Margot chirps.

Speechless, I nod at the other boy, who acknowledges us with a somber nod in return. I shade my eyes against the brightness of the white-white sky. "What are you doing here?"

He winks. "What, can't I visit my favorite twins?"

"No, you can't," I say sternly, tamping down on my panic. If we're caught, our lives will become even more complicated, something Margot and I can't afford right now. "You're not allowed to be here."

"Well, I needed to talk to you both."

Margot rolls her eyes. "So talk. But then you need to scoot. Lucy's right."

"You Upper Circle girls are so rude," he teases.

But I haven't forgotten yesterday's mess. "Rude? What is this, Ali? You couldn't tell me all the time we knew each other, on the cruise ship, or even before, that you're part of some weird druidic cult?"

"No." A stubborn look comes into Ali's eyes. "And I'm not part of a cult, Lucy. I'm *head* of the cult. *And* it's not a cult."

Margot pinches the inside of her wrist. Her sign for trying not to laugh. But I'm in the mood to argue. "Why not? Why couldn't you say something?"

"Because it wasn't time."

"And now it is?" I huff in disbelief.

Ali stares up at the blank sky as though looking for an answer. "Remember what I was saying about Cernunnos yesterday?" He shoos Margot and me over on the bench and sits down beside me.

I roll my eyes. "How could I forget?"

"Well, there's more to it than what I said."

Margot feigns a yawn and sounds bored when she replies, "You don't say. Why don't you tell us about it?"

Alastair's facade of happy calm cracks. "Well, for starters, there's the prophecy."

That catches our attention. "Go on."

"Here's the thing. I told you that Cernunnos is the father of all the True Borns, right? But when he was making the True Borns, he also chose special traits in his servants, traits that we've cultivated for the millennia since he's been gone."

"What do you mean, 'chose'? You make this ancient god sound like a Splicer doc."

"That's exactly it. He *was* some sort of Splicer. We just don't know how. And the things he's given us?" Alastair pulls out his pet rock once more. "Some call it witchery. Sorcery. We call it keeping to the old ways. Like dream casting, commanding the arcane elements." A lock of Ali's hair falls over his face. He holds the rock in his palm and, almost before we can see it, it hovers an inch above his skin before it falls back down. "One of our kind had a gift for Sight. She saw the coming of two girls who would be born special. Twins. Do you see where I'm going with this?"

Margot has gone pale beside me. Our fingers reach for and fold over one another. I squeeze hers reassuringly. "We've heard this one," I say, my voice as bland as I can make it. "It's nonsense. Father Wes told us this story. That it's us who're going to swoop in and save everyone from the Plague." Even as I say the words, I think back to what we'd witnessed in Doc Raines's lab. Maybe it is a possibility, but I'd just as soon not let Ali in on our little secret.

It's in the blood. Evolve or die.

"What if it were true? See, we're meant to be your guardians."

He says it with such sincerity that I can tell he believes what he's saying. I burst into nervous laughter.

"We have a guardian, thanks very much. And a family, I might add."

"Regardless of what you think, it's our job to protect you. I'm not asking your permission."

My chest seizes as I realize that maybe Storm was right. Maybe I'd been too trusting. "So that's what you were doing with me in Russia? Protecting me? Why couldn't you tell me?" I rub my chin, which is going cold in the spring air.

"Why do you need to protect us, Alastair?" Margot says. But her eyes are fastened onto the silent, pale blond boy with a gleam of speculation.

"For Him. For Cernunnos." Alastair's face positively gleams with the light of the fervent. I've seen this look before—most often on the faces of the preacher men and their followers. *But those men are desperate*, I think to myself. *Dying*. Is Alastair desperate, too?

"But why, exactly? What does your Cernunnos want? Why wouldn't your God want the Lasters to perish? Then all that will be left are your True Borns."

"See…" Ali scoots closer to us, his voice dropping so we won't be overheard. "Truth is, there was another part of the prophecy that wasn't stolen from our Seer. She said that the gifts from these girls would rain down on the people, showering them with unimaginable wealth. And from this rain, Cernunnos's people will be able to claim back the world as their own."

An all-over body shiver rocks me. I don't want this to be true.

Margot scowls. "Rain doesn't sound all that special. In fact, it sounds a lot like what already happens here every day."

Ali tosses his stone up, catches it. "Think of it as an allegory.

What's most important here is that when Cernunnos returns, my people will be restored to their proper place."

I think back to the pictures Storm showed Margot and me. It seems like so long ago now. And yet I can still remember vividly: the hair standing up on my arms as I studied the image of a figure at a throne, half-human, half-animal. The leopard men crouching at his feet. The trees, the same leafy variety that grew from the magic bombs stretching up behind them.

And then, with a jolt, I recall the servants in the image. Standing beside the animal men in their tabards and headdresses, the servants holding out trays of food and pitchers filled with some ancient beverage fit for a race of demigods.

Could this possibly be real?

A drop of rain splats on my cheeks as the wind picks up, turning from a caress to a biting claw. My mind buzzes and whirls so fast that I barely register the great roiling bruise-colored clouds rolling in.

"Flux storm's here," Margot murmurs beside me, gathering her things. The admiring girls in the quad pack up their books and screens, sending Ali and Tomas reluctant farewell gazes.

"But couldn't your allegory have another meaning?" I blurt out.

"What?" Ali's voice rises over the now-whipping wind.

"Your allegory," I call back. "Why would one part of this so-called prophecy be allegory but the other not? It doesn't make sense."

"What are you saying?" Ali frowns.

"I'm saying, maybe your Cernunnos isn't going to return the way you think he is, no matter what happens."

Hands fisting at his sides, Tomas looks as though he'd like to strike me. But Alastair just tips back his head and laughs.

Margot rises in an elegant sweep and turns to plant a kiss on my cheek. "Great to see you, Ali, Tomas." She grabs up her book bag with one hand, and with the other, she cradles the lit screen of her phone. "See you back at Storm's."

"Wait. Margot, where are you going?"

"I-I just— I'll see you a bit later. There's something I need to do."

Margot races to the doors of the school, bending against the wind. Ali looks over to Tomas, who has been silent this entire time. The ash-blond boy jerks his head. Ali nods, and Tomas disappears after Margot.

Then there is just howling wind and drops of rain as large as cats. And Alastair. And me. Alone.

"Lucy," Ali starts.

I busy myself with packing up my things. Regardless of what I said to Jared, being alone with Ali like this still feels like a betrayal.

"Lu," he says again. It's the tone of his voice that stops me in my tracks.

"What?"

"I want to give you something."

I don't say anything as he fishes a long, thin box out of his coat pocket. "Here," he says, opening the lid. The wind whips my hair up. It curls around my face as though dancing with it. My skirt gets tangled in my legs. But I can't help the burning curiosity I feel as Ali shows me what's inside.

It's simple. Just a small gold chain. Hung in the middle is a golden coin, so ancient it doesn't seem real. I'm fascinated by the design, so like the old coins I saw in Russia, dangling from the ceiling of the old witch's room.

"This has been in my family for as long as time. A millennia at least," he tells me. "Alongside the Great Goddess, Cernunnos was keeper of life and death, the keeper of souls. He bartered for those souls between here and the afterlife with a bag of golden coins, which he left to his servants when he disappeared. The legend is that anyone who possesses one of these coins is safe from death."

I ponder the gift. My fingers reach out to touch its raised, grainy surface. Knot work stamps the middle of the coin, which rises out into a set of twisted horns. Ali's Horned One, I presume.

"Will you accept this token?" he asks. His eyes burn into mine.

"Ali." I bite my lip. "I couldn't possibly take such a treasure. This has been in your family forever, as you say. Why would you want to give it to me?"

"Please. Please, Lucy," he pleads. He's serious. My stomach feels like lead.

"No. Really." I curl Ali's fingers around the box. "I can't take this."

"Lucy, I need you to. It really is my job to protect you. Look, I know it's just a coin on a chain, but I'm superstitious. My people are superstitious." The winds toss Ali's hair across his face. He shoves aside the strands, showing me a crooked grin. "If you take this, you'll be making me look good to them. And Lucy, I really, really need to look good right about now."

Thinking of Storm smashing his table against the wall, I give Ali a wry smile. "Not just to them, although a necklace isn't going to fix things."

"Right." Ali scratches at the insides of the box and pulls out the chain. "I also know Mr. Growls won't like this, not one bit. But think about it, Lucy. Wouldn't that be a good thing?"

I can't help but entertain the thought. Ali's people had

watched as he mangled a meeting with the most important True Born in Dominion and beyond. What would that do to a young leader who is supposed to be in league with the True Borns? *Nothing good.* If I can help with such a small gesture, I should. And then another thought scratches at the back of my mind. If I accept Ali's token, would it make Jared jealous? Would he finally admit that he wants to—no, *needs* to be with me, hang the consequences?

I'm trembling inside when I say gravely, "All right, Ali. Fine. I can't let you look bad in front of your people."

I pull up my hair and bow my head as Ali places the chain around my neck and fastens it. I touch the coin. Its burnished gold surface is already warm from my skin, throbbing with a kind of life.

"You won't regret this," he says. But I'm already having second thoughts, and third. Jared won't like it at all. If Ali notices, though, he doesn't let on as he holds out his arm, gentlemanlike, and escorts me out of the rain, face lit with some emotion I couldn't begin to name.

"Cat," Margot says, preening at me through the mirror. Her hair is long and loose over her shoulders, a wave of burnished auburn. Around her brow sits a beautiful wreath of white flowers, tightly woven together. I'm surprised that, even after a full day of wear, the petals haven't wilted. My sister smiles at me. I feel that familiar tug inside me. She's happy again, safe. It's more than I could have expected. I find myself at once delighted and oddly humbled by Margot's mood, and I can only put it down to Ali's influence.

Alastair and Tomas have called on us at school for several days now as we finish our last few sessions. They arrive each day at the same time, during our midafternoon break when the sun struggles to break through the clouds. Always outside in the quad, though I never do manage to ask how they break in. We've attracted quite the following of girls who sigh and talk behind their hands as the boys stride across the long yard, angling for us.

With each visit, they come bearing something new and interesting: a book of poetry, small enough to fit in my hands and so ancient it nearly falls apart at the touch. A bunch of white daisies that push Margot and me into raptures, especially when Tomas shows Margot how to weave them into a crown. And still, though it's all harmless enough fun, each time I see them, my heart sinks. I find myself searching behind them for a shag of sunny blond hair and a ridiculous T-shirt.

Awful pangs of conscience haunt my days and nights. Jared has been kept busy for the past few days. He doesn't yet know about Ali's illicit visits to Grayguard. Ali appears in the courtyard like magic, while Jared, acting as my merc, obeys the rules and stays at the front doors. He also doesn't know about Ali's gift. Like the coin that hangs hidden under my blouse, Margot and I have kept these little secrets to ourselves.

The necklace turns into a noose. I feel guilty. And then I get mad at myself that I feel guilty. And then I can't wait for him to see the coin hanging from my neck, to ask about it. I rehearse the scene in my head, over and over again. *Why, just a little token from Ali*, I'll tell Jared. *A friendship necklace.* Next I imagine the indigo flashing with green. The low, purring voice before his lips would come down on mine. *As long as he knows you're mine, Princess.*

My scheme is so clumsy, I scold myself. Margot would do it much better. And I'm not Margot.

"Canary." I peek out at Margot with one eye, finally answering her call to the game. I stretch out even further on her bed, wishing I could curl up and nap. Storm has had a number of political meetings of late, which means I get my exam review finished before and after the late-night talks. I'm not a complete failure yet, although with such an uncertain future, I'm not sure it matters. Still, I want to take a night off and be just Lucy again.

"You're really going to make me drag it out of you?" Margot turns abruptly, and her skirt billows out around her. Hands on hips, she gives me her best fake glare.

"What?"

"This!" she squeals, touching her finger to the bright golden coin. For just a second it's as though the coin joins us with electricity. Margot pulls back and sucks on the end of her finger with a hasty, "Ouch!"

"Ali gave it to me. It was in his family for eons."

Margot rolls her eyes. "Of course Ali gave it to you."

I don't appreciate her tone. "What do you mean by that?"

She pauses, my beautiful twin, and regards me with wise, sad eyes. Adjusting her crown of flowers, she sits carefully beside me on the bed. "You really don't get it, do you?" she says with a soft sigh.

"Get what?"

"Lu." Margot stretches her fingers across my hand. "He's courting you."

My head whips back as though I've been struck. "He is not! He said it was just a friendship present."

"And you believed that crock?" A grin bursts across Margot's face. "He is, too! And how!" She cocks her head. "Just what exactly do you think all these presents and visits at school are for?"

"Ali is my *friend*," I fire back defensively. "We've been through a lot together."

She continues as though I haven't even spoken. "And he visits you at school, away from the prying eyes of a certain green-eyed monster merc."

I can't even pretend I don't know who she's talking about. "So what? Ali knows how I feel about Jared. And I told Jared that I'm not going to stop being friends with Ali just because he gets all primitive hunting cat."

"Lu!" Margot snaps her fingers before my nose. Her hands come up and cradle my face as she pins me in place with a fake glare. "Get real. Ali has presented himself to you—to your guardian—as your protector. And he's given you a family heirloom." For a brief second a crooked smile ghosts across her lips before fading. "He's going to declare himself to you, if he hasn't already." My face blushes with heat. Did my discussion with Ali about the necklace count as a declaration? Had I been leading him on? "And I—I reckon you'd be safer if you left with him, but...I don't know if I could go with you."

It's as though I've been sucker punched. All the air in my body leaks out. "What are you talking about?"

"Come on, Lu." Her words are coated with unshed tears. "Ali will want this to be fast. Lightning-quick courtship followed by the bells and banns. Then he'll sweep you away so you don't have second thoughts."

Is Margot right? Would Ali want to marry me? Would I want to marry Ali? *No*, a voice inside me all but shouts. *Not Ali.* "You make it sound like a murder."

Margot touches the complicated antlers on the golden coin once again, and once again, a little zap pokes us both.

"It keeps biting me," she jokes, sucking on the tip of her finger. "Come on, little sister." She tugs at my arm, lifting me off the bed. I roll my eyes, knowing that this can't end in anything good, whatever is in her mind. She trolls through my closet, finding a dress with a plunging V neckline that shimmies across the knees. "Put this on," she says imperiously. "Tonight we're going to have some fun."

11

It takes all my willpower to keep my eyes off the merc in the driver's seat. I cross my ankles for the fourteenth time, smooth my dress over my legs, and stare out at the ruinous streets of Dominion.

Overnight, it seems, the streets have transformed into a war zone. Red paint zigzags across the tops of buildings, the strange pair of crossed eyes staring down at the city like demented parliaments of owls. "What do you reckon they're really after?" I muse aloud. The words sting the silence of the car, where Margot and Storm and I have been stiffly sharing company. So much for my sister's idea of a fun evening.

Storm's deep bass voice rumbles the hair on the back of my neck. "The Watchers, you mean?"

"Yes. I mean, why the soapboxing? Why the circles?"

Storm's chuckle is awful. I feel him, as much as I see him, lean forward on the seat. His spectral crown tips forward, its many points spreading out like spears. "I think only the Watchers know for certain. But if I had to guess, I'd say they are looking to convert the good citizens of Dominion. And propaganda works."

"To what end?"

The outline of Storm's broad shoulders lifts in a shrug. "They think the cure is out there. They think in terms of punishment and death and redemption. Those are powerful concepts."

"Concepts," Margot breaks in. She's been staring out the windows this whole time, withdrawn and silent, though I've felt in her a rising bubble of anxiety before it popped and became something sweet and calm. "What about what's real? What if they're right? What if—what if somehow our blood could create an honest-to-god Plague cure?"

Storm's eyes are preternaturally bright. He clasps his hands before him as he studies my twin. "Do you think it's possible?"

"I don't know," she admits. We've not told Storm about what Doc Raines revealed to us, about our blood eating the blue-stained Plague. She taps the insides of her wrist. *Pay attention.* "Doc Raines isn't sure."

"But it's worth investigating?"

"Sure."

Storm nods. One of his broad arms stretches across his body to point out at the wreck of Dominion, lit by corner fires and bordered by car apartments lining the sidewalks. "I agree. But more to the point, everyone out there thinks it's possible. If nothing else, I would ask that you please don't forget that, girls." He addresses us both, but it's Margot he pins with molten silver eyes.

Something beeps just then. In the driver's seat, Jared grabs at his ear and speaks in a voice too low for me to follow. Storm leans forward, eyes blazing.

"Tell them I'll meet them at the Junction."

Jared spins in his seat and tilts his head at us.

Margot sighs heavily beside me. "We're going back?"

Storm considers us for a long moment. "Tell them I will meet them at the Junction in half an hour," he repeats. "Serena and Carl believe they have some important information that can't wait until morning. But just because I'm being called away doesn't mean that you should go home. The restaurant is safe enough, and I want you to still enjoy your evening. If Jared doesn't mind stepping in as your dinner companion?"

My mouth gapes open. "I don't—"

"Storm," Margot breaks in. "Do you think you could take me home first? I'm not feeling well."

I frown. Margot is not ill. I would feel that. She rakes her fingernail down the back of my hand. *Let me go.*

"Of course." Storm gives us a regal nod. "I'm sorry about our evening."

A vein jumps in Jared's jaw as he turns back around and repeats Storm's orders. My eyes catch on his in the rearview mirror, causing my heart to stutter.

"So we'll just head home, then?" My voice sounds strangled.

"No. Please go, Lu." Margot squeezes my hand. "Go with Jared. Is that okay, Storm?" I look over. Her oval face is so pale in the shadows, ghostlike.

"Yes. Of course. We can't have Lucy missing out on her night of freedom."

Margot lifts an eyebrow at me, as though for once she can tell what I'm feeling. I squeeze back, pasting a fake smile on my lips. I doubt I'll fool Margot. But I'd like to at least fool Jared and Storm.

...

The car slips to the curb and Jared turns off the ignition. "I'm not exactly dressed for the occasion." He's not. Rather than a suit, Jared is dressed in a red plaid shirt, open down the front. Underneath he's wearing a faded blue T-shirt, the neck stretched a little, as though he's been tugging on the collar. A crude stick figure with scraggly strands of hair scratches his head across the front, question marks floating around him like butterflies. Jared's pants have a hole in the knee, too, I recall, though at least he's wearing shoes. He looks completely inappropriate for the swank four-star restaurant that we've rolled up to.

"Yes, I can see that might be a problem," Storm says quietly. Then he strips off his suit jacket and yanks on his tie. Soon he starts popping open his buttons, one after the other.

"What are you doing?"

He grins but doesn't slow down. Seconds later our guardian is naked to the waist. Like he's been carved from fine ivory, every single one of Storm's muscles is detailed and lean. His chest is broad, leading to the washboard of his stomach that bunches and curls with every tick of movement. But he's too close. And I can't forget the strange feeling I've been getting lately, that Storm's agenda for me is not all custodial. I send a panicked glance out the window.

"Relax, Lucy." He chuckles and raps on the glass. "Tinted windows."

Margot's appreciation for Storm's chest unspools through me like hot threads that I try desperately to ignore. I shoot her a dark look as Storm tosses his shirt, tie, and suit jacket onto the front seat.

Without a word, Jared pulls his shirts over his head and

plucks through Storm's clothing. "They'll be a little big," he says wryly, holding up Storm's shirt.

"I'll owe you a new shirt," Storm replies as he pulls on Jared's faded tee. On Jared it was loose, comfortable looking. On Storm it becomes a second skin, showing off his obscenely cut torso and chest. Beside me, Margot squeaks, possibly in embarrassment or even outrage, as would be proper for a young lady of our Circle. But I know what she's feeling…and it's highly inappropriate.

"I'll drive Margot home and rendezvous with Serena and Carl." Storm nods at Jared as Jared pulls the tie over his head. "We'll meet you at the front door or you'll hear from us." And then, quite unexpectedly, I hear a low, warm chuckle rumble from Storm's throat. He pats my chin. "Your eyes are as big as plates, Lucy. Have you never seen a man's chest before?"

I reckon everyone in the car can feel the heat of my blush right then. But I don't bother to answer. I've seen a naked chest before—Jared's, in fact, is one I'm quite familiar with. But no. What has me lightning struck is not Storm's nakedness, nor his pure, ridiculous beauty.

Shirtless, Storm is like a figure out of a book: the ancient pagan god he claims as his heritage. Part forest, part beast, part man, he blazes wilderness from his eyes and savage kindness from his smile. I've always thought he seemed godlike, but now I know it's true. *Nolan Storm isn't human at all.*

And what I really can't forget are the strange, shiny silver tattoos running up Storm's back, curving hieroglyphics from one of his ancient books. It's another elusive thing about him, ghostly markings kissing his skin, telling hidden stories I'd as soon not ask about.

• • •

Across the small, intimate table at Jacardo's, Jared looks at me moodily below his ridiculously beautiful eyelashes and plays with the stem of his half-full wineglass. In a voice so quiet I wonder if I've imagined it, he says, "You've been avoiding me."

"No." I chew carefully through a bite of delicate greens. Then, before answering, I swallow a gulp of the excellent wine, one of the things this establishment is known for. "You've been avoiding me."

Jared blinks and looks around the opulent, candlelit space. I can't recall when candelabras became the rage for Upper Circle restaurants. It has become chic to pretend both poverty and class in the same breath—though having the candles certainly helps when the power goes out, as it does frequently. And candlelight does add a certain charm to the dining experience. It might even thaw some of the frost between Jared and me. I resist the urge to finger the golden chain hidden beneath my blouse. I'm not ready to answer questions about it, and I'd as soon have a happy night with Jared, or at the very least, conflict free. And it seems to be happening. Left alone in this setting with only soft, natural light flickering on our arms and faces, we seem to be slowly, carefully crawling out from our shells.

Following Jared's lead, I look around me. Here and there scattered among the long room, tastefully dressed patrons dine in pearl earrings, suits, and dress jackets. The women are all carefully made up. Not a single Plague-ravaged limb to be seen. The waiters wear suits and carry themselves like royalty. Everything is understated, elegant, screaming quiet wealth.

It's the world I grew up in. And I am ever more conscious of it as I feel the curious, stabbing eyes of the other diners, the quiet whispers behind starched linen napkins. *That's one of the Fox sisters. Who is that she's with? Is she with a True Born?*

As though he's read my mind, Jared tips his head to the side and sends me a curious look. "Does it bother you?"

"What?"

His beautiful lips contort with disapproval. "What they're saying about you."

My hands curl around the napkin before me. I take a deep breath, let slip my napkin as I try to unbend my back.

I compose my answer carefully. "I can't afford to let it."

Jared surprises me by not replying. He stares hard at the room, chasing eyes away, and sighs. It's a full minute before he speaks again.

"I'm not avoiding you. I mean—I am, but…"

"Why?" I hide my trembling fingers under the table.

"Because, Lu, if I spend any time around you both, I'll be tempted to rip him apart with my bare hands." *Does he already know about Ali's visits to us?* Then my mind veers in another direction as under the table, something brushes the flesh of my hand, like the kiss of a tiny fish. Then Jared's hands fold over mine, the heat searing. I close my eyes tight against the sudden, unexpected gesture. It leaves me feeling as though I'm about to crack open. "And—and I want you to be able to spend time with your friend. Without worrying that I'll kill him."

My heart hammers in my chest as I feign ignorance. "Who?"

"You know who. That little weasel."

"Jared."

"What?" When I look up, he's staring at me in frank fascination as I bite my lip. "How is it that you don't have a clue how you affect the people around you, Lu? God, when I think back to how I used to think you were the most spoiled, rich brat in Dominion."

Despite myself, I smile. Jared grins back, his dimples

popping out as a lock of his hair hides his eyes, turning the hard merc boyish again. His fingers brush mine in the close of my lap before brushing my knee, my thigh. I gasp, my back straightening even more as my heart leaps. Jared's grin deepens. His eyes grow sharp and start their telltale shift.

"Jared," I say again, only it comes out breathless, uncertain. "We need to be serious for a minute."

His hand pauses its investigations for a moment before continuing up my thigh. "Uh-oh. Serious doesn't sound like much fun."

I stop his hand with mine and shake my head slowly. "It's too confusing."

"Hey," Jared soothes in a tender voice as his hand squeezes my knee. He means it to be reassuring, but it shoots flames straight through my body. I want nothing more than to kiss the panther man until we're both weak with desire.

But what would that solve?

"Hey, now, don't look at me like that," he warns, leaning back so that his hand slips from my flesh, leaving me bare and cold. "Gods, Lu, you'd tempt a saint. Which I am not."

I clear my throat. "You look nice in Storm's suit."

He's silent and watchful for a long moment, brushing the creamy linen tablecloth with his fingers. "I think that's too much weight for one person to try to hold, Princess. I think you need to let go of all that stuff you can't control for one night."

"I don't understand."

"You think I don't see it? When was the last time you let yourself be a young woman without a million and a half responsibilities?" Time slows to a halt as he stares at me. "Let's just pretend, for one night, that we're in a normal world. And I'm just a boy taking his pretty gal on a date. A real, honest-to-god date."

"That's…that's mad." But even as I say the words, a bright flare of hope pulses through me at the thought. *His girl. A* date. Jared busies his fingers along the sensitive skin of my inner thigh under the cover of the table.

"Why?" His lips curve into the smallest hint of a smile.

"Why…what?"

"Why is it crazy?"

It takes me a moment to pull myself from the fog of skittering senses and another long moment to see that he's serious.

But we've been down this road before, Jared and I. Every time I give in to what I feel for him, what I want, something steps in to remind me that we can't be. I have some sort of future to consider, they say. I have a responsibility to live up to my breeding, my class. Because I'm a Fox.

And each time I give in to what I feel for Jared, I only want him more. And it *hurts*.

I'm not certain how much more I can take: the exquisite torture of being close to him only to be set aside and held at arm's length. Jared has been telling me in a thousand different ways that there will only be these stolen moments. But maybe, just maybe, I want forever.

I consider the elegant linen tablecloth in my lap, my hand folded over it like the wing of a bird. It looks like a freedom I'll never have.

I recite the lesson I've come to think of as our family's motto. "One's duty never sleeps."

Jared chuckles, but the warmth doesn't enter his eyes, which instead fix on me with the wariness of a caged beast. "Right."

My chest sinks. Right then, I would rather do anything, be anything, than the right and proper Miss Fox. I want to be my sister. I want to be some Laster girl or True Born or anyone but me. Someone Jared could want forever.

What would I do if I were someone else? If I were free?

I can imagine us being together in a thousand other lives: Splicer, Laster, True Born. There's not a single outcome I can picture where we're together and I am who I am.

I'm not someone else. I am Lucy Fox.

"Jared." His name sounds like rust on my tongue. I'm terrified that I will lose him, just by virtue of being who and what I am. "Jared," I say again.

My hand slips under the table, hooks around his fingers. They throb with heat and warmth against the cold marble of my thigh. *I want that other life, the one where we're together until we're old and gray.* And I still don't know what I can say to this man, this True Born merc, except that I'm not ready to give him up even if we can't be. And I'm praying to all the gods in Dominion that he won't give me up, either.

The words are thick in my mouth, as though my tongue has swollen. "Jared. Don't give up on me. Don't ever give up on me."

Jared blinks. Some deep emotion washes over his eyes, like the passing of a cloud. I don't know what it means until his lips and one eyebrow quirk up, somehow making him look like a happy cat. "Do you honestly think I could, Lucinda Fox?"

We sit, transfixed in the luminous candlelight, as the waiter comes and goes. Something like a fist hammers through my heart. Jared's pupils slit to a cat's as he watches me with half-lidded eyes and listens to its violent tattoo. His fingers stay stretched across my knee. And suddenly there is no restaurant. No Plague, no political machinations to be wary of. There is just Jared. Jared Price and me, alive and together. And it feels perfect.

. . .

Without warning, Jared's head jerks back, as though he's been struck. He listens for a moment, head cocked, then turns glittering eyes on me.

Our little world of two is about to come crashing down around us.

"Dig in, Princess. Serena and Carl will be here in twenty minutes." His hands squeeze mine for a moment before releasing them, leaving me feeling instantly lost and cold. It takes a moment for me to gather my composure again.

I frown. "Didn't they meet up with Storm?" Rather than answer, Jared fiddles with a knife. In his hands the simple dinner knife looks sinister.

"Are you worried about something?" I ask.

"No. Well, I mean, yes. Everything."

"What?" I look around the room, half expecting glass to fly or people to drop dead. But no one here even shakes with palsy. Here are Splicers. People don't get sick at Jacardo's.

"Nothing to worry about, really," Jared tells me. But there's a shadow to his eye.

"Jared Price, tell me what is going on right this minute."

"Nothing, Princess, I swear." He half grins at me as his hands come up in mock surrender. The smile dies in his eyes before it falls off his lips. "It's just — I was really enjoying having dinner with you." My heart thumps painfully in my chest just as Jared's stomach lets loose a loud protest. "And so was my stomach, apparently," he jokes.

It hurts to laugh. But it hurts more not to.

Serena and Carl wait for us on the crumbling sidewalk as we exit the restaurant. An Upper Circle spot like Jacardo's would never let in a True Born like Carl. Carl is a cat, all bristling marmalade fur, tightly packed muscles, and a mean streak strewn with bullets. The trio immediately launch into a form of shorthand, a kind of merc language that would require more training than my scant few months living at Storm's.

Bored, I loose the thread until Ali's name is spoken. That catches my attention.

Carl picks his jagged teeth with a toothpick. "The kid has been staying on the other side of the park. They've got some friends there."

I break in. "What kind of friends?"

"The special kind," Serena says, pushing her long ash-white hair from her face.

"The special kind… You mean the druids really might be like True Borns?" It's not polite of me to butt in, nor is "True Born" considered a nice word to bandy about on a public street. But I'd as soon not wait for any more answers. If Ali and his ilk really are what he says they are, some sort of servants of Cernunnos, I want to know what they're about.

Serena and Carl stare at me as though noticing me for the first time. It's Serena who answers, licking her lips before forming a careful reply. "Possibly."

"None of 'em are cats, anyways," cracks Carl. He has all the sense of humor of his animal gen code, too. Which is to say, none at all.

"Oh." Disappointed, I start to turn. Serena surprises me by whipping out an arm and halting me. A plop of rain falls. Then another. I look up, waiting for the sky to ruin the evening even more.

"What?"

"Wait a minute." Her eyes are eerie blank disks. "Wait just

a second." She stares hard at me, and for a fleeting moment I feel as though the tall, lithe woman is seeing me inside out. Serena is a Salvager, that special kind of True Born, the lowest of the low according to the whispers.

Serena can see through the skin of things, trace their essence. They call her type Salvagers because they can find other True Borns. And she can see Margot and me.

I've often wondered how such a gift would have arisen, if it were a form of magic as old as the Gods themselves. Because surely, it's an unnatural talent.

But now I'm watchful as Serena reaches out one long finger and traces the horns on the golden coin that sits across my breastbone, hidden beneath my blouse. I force myself not to cover Alastair's gift with my hands as Serena's eyes narrow to slits. She makes a restless motion with her hands until, alarmed, I bring out the chain. The coin catches the light as it falls across my neck. Serena studies the coin carefully with her milky white eyes. And then, startling us all, her head tips back as she lets out a loud, braying laugh.

"What?" I stomp my foot, annoyed.

"What?" Jared parrots, pressing himself to my side. His eyebrows knit together as he takes in the necklace that, by his expression, he hasn't noticed until now.

But Serena can't speak for tears as the sky unleashes dozens of tiny hammers of rain. "Nothing," she says when she's recovered enough. She wipes her eyes with the back of her fist. "It's just—I didn't realize things were quite so tight with the kid and you." Carl and Jared and I share a perplexed look.

I scowl at the beautiful woman. "What are you talking about?"

"Your necklace," Serena says, breaking out into another

paroxysm of laughter. Rain quickly soaks the top of my sweater. I pull it tighter around me, my back straightening as I transform into the regal diplomat's daughter.

"What about my necklace? It was a gift from Alastair." Regret swamps me as I feel Jared's eyes rake over me.

"Yes, I'm well aware." Serena hiccups and tilts her head to study me. Maybe she can hear my confusion. "Don't you know?"

"Know what, Serena?" Jared jumps in. His hand tightens across my forearm, as though he's ready to bolt with me.

"This necklace. It's a promise token. Old as the hills. It means—" The laughter starts again. As her words hit, I feel a blinding faintness take hold of me.

"You've become engaged."

12

The burning in my chest refuses to go away. But the rage I feel is nothing compared to the bloody, deadly heat Jared throws off.

Jared snarls, showing teeth. "I'll kill that little weasel. I'm going to enjoy ripping his limbs from his body." He paces the sidewalk before us in long, violent strides, his legs and back gaining that telltale thickness as the bones in his face lengthen.

"No, I'll do it." I pinch at the bones of my nose in an effort to shake loose from the violent headache that suddenly come upon me.

"Yesss," Jared mouths, his tongue thick and uneasy in his mouth, "but I can break him into tiny pieces for you first."

I lean over, wanting to vomit. Ali lied to me. And I bought it—all because I thought it would help Ali. Because I had the delusional thought that it might, somehow, bring Jared and me closer. *More fool I.* The gold of the necklace jangles against my chin. And suddenly I can't stand it another second. I want it off. I stand up straight and motion to Serena. "Help me get it off."

The Salvager shakes her head slowly. "I'm not sure that's such a good idea. I think we should speak with Storm first."

"What? Why?" I paw at the back of the necklace, but I can't seem to find the clasp. In a panic, I pull on it, hard enough to bite into the skin of my neck. The chain holds fast.

"You don't recognize it?" Serena lets out an unhappy puff of breath. "Here," she says, tracing the stamped horns with her finger. Serena's voice drops to a whisper. "Can't you feel it? This coin is not just a piece of gold, Lucy Lu. It's as old as people. This tiny little coin *sparkles*. Sparkles and zaps like the Prayer Tree in Heaven Square."

"So? It will be just as sparkly off my neck."

But Serena shakes her head again. "No, leave it be, Lucy. You don't know what this necklace is."

"I can't! I won't. Carl, please, get it off me!" I plead. The marmalade cat man looks back and forth at us in alarm before stepping forward and grasping the chain of the necklace with both hands.

"Carl." Serena drops just one quiet syllable. Carl steps back, a look of regret stamped on his fur-lined face.

I gasp in outrage. "Jared," I say, lifting my chin proudly. "Take it off. Do it!" I command. But even though his eyes spit poison, as though he'd gladly tear the world in two, he shakes his head with a wry, thoughtful look.

"Maybe Serena's right," he says slowly.

My face burns. How can they leave me to suffer such humiliation? "Please take me back to Storm's," I command, dismissing them all as I look away.

Jared murmurs something, presumably speaking through his

earpiece. He's shaking with barely contained rage as he comes to stand in front of me and open the door of Storm's vehicle that has just pulled up.

"I'll take you back. And then I'm going hunting," he promises.

Storm's is quiet by the time we return. I immediately stomp in the direction of his office, Jared still heaving with anger two steps behind me. Kira pops out from nowhere, the ivory oval of her face bathed in shadows.

"Hey, Lucy, hold up there."

"I need to see Storm."

"Not right now." Kira calmly throws up a hand to halt us.

"Kira? If you don't get out of the way right now, I swear to God—"

Kira rolls her eyes at Jared. "Whatever, Prince Pain in the Ass. Hold your horses. Storm's in a meeting and can't be disturbed right now."

Jared narrows his eyes but steps back, the air of menace hanging around him notching down. "This can't wait."

"Oh, but it can. And it will." Kira twirls a strand of auburn hair between her fingers.

Jared's a narrow hair's length from turning. As the bones of his face lengthen, he snarls in the low, angry tones of a jungle cat.

If he shifts, blood will spill. And it will be my fault.

I press myself against Jared's chest, ignoring Kira and her dropping jaw. Jared blinks in surprise, too, the inhuman sheen brightening at my nearness. I trace my fingers across his cheek. Somehow the skin gets harder when he's this close to turning. But I feel him relax. A tense few moments later, Jared rests his forehead against mine as though exhausted from fighting something.

The world falls away from us. I don't know how much time passes before prickles of awareness creep in. Emotions drift through me like clouds. Joy, a sharp feeling of homesickness, and in there with the rest is a thick, awful blanket of misery. I pull back from Jared, unsure of how to put into words that something has happened. Then I feel it again: a sharp tug on that other sense, the one that marks me one of two.

Something *is* happening. And that something involves Margot.

Kira loudly clears her throat, stretching it out so there's no mistaking the fact that she's probably done it a number of times with no effect. One of her eyebrows is hitched so high it's crawled under her hair.

"You'd best keep that just between the two of you," she says, crossing her arms. "Stand down. I hear them."

Three seconds later, the door swings open. Storm's magnificent silhouette blocks the rest of the room, but he beckons us forward.

My eyes light on Margot, who sits on the cream-colored couch like a timid cat. She's pale but happy enough, so I'm able to focus on the man sitting across from her in beaten, dirt-caked leathers. I rub my eyes, happy disbelief burning a hole in me.

"Shane!" I yell.

Then I throw myself on our father's man.

The big man squeezes his fists. The gesture is so familiar it washes me with homesickness. A host of memories float through me: Shane taking Margot and me to school. Shane picking us up when we fell off our bikes. Kisses on the top of our heads. A hearty laugh when we behaved like monkeys. He'd been our father's man for nearly as long as we girls have drawn breath and was as much a part of our family landscape—in some cases more so—than our parents. Having him return is like getting back a piece of our missing life. Still, it's clear he's not the same Shane we've known for years. The creases on his face ring his eyes more deeply. His hair has grown in, a long shag rather than the tightly cropped military cut he's sported for years.

The last time we saw Shane was the night of our Reveal party. Margot and I were to learn our fate: Splicer, Laster, or True Born. Instead we learned that our future was trickier still than these. That was the night our parents disappeared and Margot along with them. We've spent months putting out quiet inquirics to learn the fate of our parents. Now, after all this time, our father's head merc may be able to finally put the missing pieces together.

The tiny cup Shane holds rattles in his large hand as though he's developed a palsy. He nods in Margot's direction. "I lost sight of Margot and your folks in the scrum that night."

Storm leans casually against his desk, arms crossed as he coolly assesses the man before him. Jared, on the other hand, greeted Shane with a warm handshake and a clasp on the back, though now he stands against the wall, one foot propped on the plaster, looking strange in Storm's finery.

"Heard through my contacts the next day they'd gotten on a private ship with that Russian count or whatever he is. And by the time I heard back from my old buddies in the Wasteland, it was too late to do 'en'thin' but look for another post." Shane blinks and stares at us.

The Wasteland. It's the mercs' word for the Siberian plains. The mercs train there because it's a hard land, we've heard Shane explain often enough.

It doesn't make sense to me. Why would our parents leave Shane behind without so much as a word? Why didn't they take their head merc? But there will be time for questions like that much later. For now it is enough to know that he is alive.

"What have you been doing to make a living?"

Shane scratches his whiskered face. "Oh, this and that. Picked up a few security gigs, nothing too stable. Kept hoping the Foxes would return to the den, reckon."

A pang goes through me, but it's Margot's rather than my own. "Do you think they're still in Russia?" she asks.

Shane nods. "I do. I have people keeping radar out. I'm makin' sure that smarmy Russian bastard doesn't do something he'll regret." The heat in Shane's words is not as surprising as the realization that he's right. All this time, I had supposed that our parents had been, at the very least, misguided participants in whatever crimes Leo Resnikov had dreamed up.

Horror washes through me, both Margot's and my own. Until this moment, we'd both barely considered the alternative. Our parents could be in trouble. They could be dead. *And then who will we be?* a little voice inside me mocks. I tamp it down, disgusted with myself, as Margot reaches for my fingers.

"You're welcome to stay here tonight," Storm tells Shane. But it's not a voice I'm accustomed to hearing from our guardian. He casts a long, tangled shadow across the room. It stretches over Shane like a shroud, ending in extravagant antlers. His eyes burn mercury. "But while I extend my hospitality, there are certain rules you'll need to abide by. No weapons. Lucy and Margot are under my protection now. And should anyone try to harm them or interfere with my guardianship, I will respond with swift and certain justice."

Shane accepts the unsubtle threat with a crooked grin, his one gold tooth glimmering in his mouth. "Grateful to you, Mr. Storm. A bed and a wash would come in handy. I just want to find some steady work and to do right by these two here." He nods at us.

"Good. We'll talk further in the morning. But now" — Storm turns his attention to Margot and me — "ladies, I think it's time you were off to bed. You have a tutorial tomorrow, don't you?"

"But—" I start to argue, only to be met with the shade of winter thrown off by Storm's eyes. I snap my mouth closed. There will be no dealing with Alastair's betrayal. Not tonight, at any rate.

The clock ticks. Eight. Nine. I turn over onto my side. The sheets tangle in my legs, boiling my too-sensitive skin. I can still feel the trace of Jared's hands on my knees from earlier in the evening. My mind hums like a swarm of bees and ticks through the relentless pieces of a maddening puzzle.

Shane. The Watchers. Father Wes. Theodore Nash. Resnikov. Our parents. Alastair. Storm. Doc Raines.

Jared.

Ten. I start counting all over again. There are so many tangles I can't possibly sort through them all. And the biggest of all: our own blood, Margot's and mine, and what it might be capable of.

It's thoughts of my sister that finally set me to my feet. I pull on a robe and tie it hastily, then shove my feet into slippers. It's not like it was at our home, when Margot and I would dash into each other's rooms as though they were our own. Here we are separated by yards of hallway, walls, doors that don't join our rooms. And most troubling of all: Margot's secrets.

I rap softly on her door. "Mar?" The door isn't locked, so

I let myself in, feeling the strange distance between us, like a skin we no longer share. The room is quiet, still. The curtain flaps gently at its ends where the window is cracked open. The form on the bed doesn't move. But she is not sleeping.

Her wakefulness calls me. "Margot," I call out in our quiet-quiet way. Threading my way through clothes strewn about the floor like land mines, I sit on the bed beside her. My hand rests on her ribs. "Mar."

She turns and stares at me through glittery eyes. For a moment I have the vertiginous sense of looking back at myself through her eyes. An illusion. Must be. Margot flips to her back and moves over. I flop onto the warm spot left by her body. Our fingers reach out automatically to touch.

"What's wrong?" The silence of the room almost swallows my sister's hushed voice.

"Don't you mean, what's wrong *now*?" I try to joke, but it comes out flat. This is no laughing matter.

"Sure. That." My sister lets go of my fingers and eases a hand over my hair. Her touch is soft, gentle. It soothes me in ways I can't describe. It almost breaks my heart.

I swallow past the lump in my throat. "Turns out I might be in a bit of trouble."

"You?" There's laughter in her voice. When did the tables tip so completely? When did I become the trouble-magnet sister? "Well, might as well tell me, then. Maybe I can help."

"It's Shane. Well, it's sort of Shane."

Margot plays with a skein of my hair. "It's wonderful to see him, isn't it?"

"Yes," I admit.

"So why are you upset? What has this got to do with your troubles, Lu?" She props herself up to see me better.

"Makes you realize, I reckon. They had such high expectations for us. How can we ever live up to them while we're here, living this life?" And high up on their list, along with top grades and making the right connections, was achieving the right marriage. In our world, marriage is a political alliance that furthers the family's interests.

Margot's hands still, her expression grim. "Why do you think we'd have to? It's enough that Storm has us finishing our degrees."

"We're still the Fox sisters. They're still our parents. They may come back."

"Lucy." Margot lets out a huffy breath. "I think you need to face facts. It's really doubtful they'll come back."

"Why? What do you know?" Because she does know something. She's holding back. I feel the wall between us, so thick it might as well be a prison.

"I know they've likely washed their hands of us."

"But why? What did we do?" The tears start, the ones I'd been refusing since the moment our house was demolished and Margot was ripped away from me.

"Nothing. We did nothing, Lu. Listen to me." And I can't help but respond to the note of authority in her voice. "We. Did. Nothing. This is their fault."

I ponder this thread for a moment before speaking again. "Would you have married him?" She doesn't need me to say the name. It hangs there between us. *Resnikov*.

"Yes," she coughs out.

"Really?"

She doesn't answer. But inside her unfurls a hard, bright emotion I don't have a name for. *She's hiding this from me*, comes the treacherous thought. And then, *What did that lunatic do to her?* For a lunatic Leo Resnikov surely was. And our parents—God only knows what kind of deal they had worked out between them, but I reckon it was a bad one.

"Mar." I still her hand on my hair and touch her cheek. "You know you can tell me anything."

She nods, her eyes bright with unshed tears. But there it is, a still seed within her, a secret she won't share. I hate it. It makes me feel sick that she'd keep things from me. And yet, I have to admit I have been keeping my own secrets, too.

As if she's read my mind, Margot asks in a bright, curious voice, "Will you marry Ali?" I choke and sit up to cough it out. Mar pounds me on the back. "You okay?"

I nod through the tears, feeling foolish and about ten years old. Because I don't think I can admit to my sister the truth of my folly, the mess I'm in.

"No," I finally say, but in answer to which question, I'm not sure.

"No, you're right," Margot muses with a peal of laughter. "You'll likely marry Storm."

"What?" I screech. My stomach curls into knots and I find I want to dive under the covers rather than reply. Has Margot seen the shift in Storm's attitude towards me? "Why would you say that? He's our guardian."

Margot shrugs. "It's the smart move. Storm is the most powerful man in Dominion right now."

"You reckon Father might have matched us?"

Margot sighs, and a husk of her hair floats away from her face. "I don't know, Lu. I don't think I know what our parents would or wouldn't do any longer. And I'm not even sure it matters." There it is again: a secret. "All I know is, Nolan Storm is quickly becoming one of the most important men in Nor-Am.

And on top of that, he's our guardian. And on top of *that*…" Her smile is lopsided and strange, accompanied by something sharp and bright in her words, her heart, that I don't understand. "I reckon he's grooming you for the position."

My mouth flaps open and closed as I sit there in stunned silence. And yet, Margot's not wrong. I can try to ignore it or deny it all I want, but maybe it would be smarter to start thinking about what Nolan Storm might want from me, and me alone. "You're joking."

"I'm a Fox," Margot says in tones so black I'd as soon call them shadows. "I'd never joke about marriage."

You can smell despair on every street corner as the preacher men set up their soap boxes and talk of the coming of peace, of Plague Cure. Yet safe in Storm's keep, we're treated to the crumbs of our old life of privilege, safety. Certainty.

Blinking, I drag myself out of bed and try to ignore the sinking feeling in my gut as I stare at the empty chair across from me, its lacy, girlish pillows intact. But this morning is different, I remind myself. Everything is different today.

Margot's brightness zings through me. I rush into the kitchen and throw myself into Shane's arms for a massive hug. His biceps are huge, covered in the intricate Celtic knot work he says is his religion—if a merc like him could be said to have a religion other than death dealing.

"Mornin'." He snuffles into my hair, then pulls back to put a heavy hand on my head. "Holy Plague Fire, you girls are growing up to be fine ladies." He grins that familiar grin. But the lines of his face are tight, and the smile doesn't quite stretch to his eyes. I sit down beside Margot. We watch our father's man happily for a moment as he quietly sips his coffee and studies us from under half-lowered lids.

"You got a reason for staring, you sassy Foxes?" His voice booms across the room.

Beside me, Margot giggles. I delight in how she feels, lighter than she's been in months, as though suddenly the hands of the clock have tumbled us back to a simpler time. I grab a piece of toast from the pile Alma has left, though she's nowhere to be seen.

"Shane." She giggles some more, half covering her mouth. "Will you take us to the school this morning? For old time's sake?"

Shane sets down his coffee mug and shoots us a curious look. "Now why on earth would you girls be heading back to Grayguard? Didn't you finish that place off last year?"

Margot and I share a startled glance. She taps a finger on the table. *You tell him.*

"Well…" I pause to diplomatically compose our downfall— though to save Shane's feelings or our own, I'm not certain. "Margot was in Russia and didn't get to finish the year. And I was… Well, I was too busy to finish…" I blush. "So when Margot returned, Storm made a deal with the school that will see us finish up our credits."

Margot's mouth turns down into a pout. "Essentially he's making us do this. He says the piece of paper is important. We're almost there, though. Just two more exams."

Shane's face crumbles. "Oh, girls." He hangs his head. His long hair tangles down so I can see dirty blond streaks mixed with white and black. When Shane finally looks at us again, his eyes are suspiciously bright. He runs a hand over his stubbled cheeks. "I don't even know what to say. You don't have a clue how many nights I lay awake just praying you were both alive." Alarm skitters through me, though it's not my own. "I owe you both a debt of honor, and I hope you'll forgive me for letting this happen to you. I'll do whatever it takes to make it up to you."

Shane's eyes travel back to his hands, where he grips his coffee mug like it's a pistol. I fold my fingers over his callused flesh. "This isn't your doing, Shane. Mother and Father..." I start. But I am at a loss as to how to finish that thought. I offer him a brittle smile. "We're fine. The True Borns took us in like we were their own."

"They shouldn't have had to save you. It should have been *me*." He thumps his chest with a meaty hand. But what is the sense in wading back into the past? I wonder. It's littered only with the bones of what might have been.

We enter the cavernous foyer of Grayguard. I feel sick as I rehearse what I'm going to say should Ali be foolish enough to show his face today. At the same time, I try to ignore the feeling of déjà vu that pricked me with unease, like a squeeze to the neck, as Shane dropped us at the huge wooden doors of the school this morning. Margot gently reaches across my back and tugs a lock of my hair. It feels soft and sweet, a reminder of times past.

"What is it?"

I heave my bag higher on my shoulder. "Doesn't it feel strange to you?" I whisper back.

Eyes on us. Eyes everywhere as the other students fill the

hall, rambunctious with laughter and chatter. I lower my gaze and concentrate on my feet as we walk toward our lockers. If I can't see them, maybe they can't see me. Margot clears her throat. I know she's feeling the same way I am. *Exposed.* "What? This?"

I shake my head. "Shane. Here he is, returned and picking up right where we all left off. But how can he? Our old life is gone. I don't know how to make the two fit."

Margot takes a second to consider before she nods. "I reckon you're right." Her chin dips she answers me. "I sometimes wish we could go back, believe it or not. Things were so much…simpler. There is no way, I know that. But I'm not sure I can imagine a way forward, either. And…what if we're just stuck, right here, forever?"

"Do you trust him?"

I don't realize how much I want my sister to say yes, she trusts Shane without reservation, until she nods. "As much as anybody, outside of you. I mean, I trust him more than Mother and Father. Don't you?"

"We have only a handful of allies, and he's one of them. We don't really have the luxury of mistrusting him. Do we?"

We stop in the midst of the crowded hall, our troubled eyes locked on each other. Murmurs and grunts of disapproval fill the air as all around us the student body flows like water flowing past two rocks.

There's an old proverb in Dominion, bandied about the Upper Circle, but it flies like a poison arrow to our hearts.

An Upper Circler won't survive without family.

13

The air is a sullen gray mass as Margot and I push open the doors of the school and blink against the brightness. We scan the schoolyard, teeming with surly-looking men in uniform. Across the street, an entire squadron of blue hazmat suits enters a building. I shiver, feeling that familiar cold seep inside my bones, and pull my jacket tighter around me. It's never a good sign to see more than two rovers at a time—it's likely to mean a nest of Plague victims has been found. It happens that way sometimes. Sometimes whole families will drop dead near to the same time. Our genomics teacher explained that this is because there are similarities in genetics inherited from generation to generation, blueprints that give us our hair coloring, our eyes…even the likelihood of our deaths.

I feel a nudge from Margot. "Someone's here to see you," she trills in a singsong voice.

I follow her gaze to the stone obelisk of the front gate.

Alastair stands there, a bright posy of flowers held close to his chest. Under a flop of his long brown hair, Ali wears a "guilty as charged" look. At least, I think to myself, he wasn't stupid enough to break in to the courtyard today.

He's lucky he's still wearing his head, I reckon. Serena had gleefully told Storm about Ali's little necklace trick. And I doubt Storm wasted any time in voicing his opinion of the situation. I simply chose to ignore Ali's calls that had lit up my phone ever since.

"Oh, brother."

Beside me, Margot giggles, her eyes flashing mischievously. "I think it's sweet you've got so many beaus, little sister."

I grit my teeth in a rigor mortis smile. "Don't you dare abandon me, Margot."

"Oh, I wouldn't miss this for the world, Lucinda, don't worry," she teases.

Ali takes a few tentative steps forward, a hopeful look taking the place of the guilt, as Margot and I descend the long marble staircase of the school. As we draw near, Ali all but throws the bouquet at me.

"For you," he mumbles.

I gaze down my nose at Ali, giving him my best ice-princess glare. Margot titters into her hand, her laughter coursing through my veins. The silence lengthens. I notice Ali's ash-blond friend, Tomas, lurking behind him with a bland expression. Ali swallows loudly.

When I say nothing, Alastair dives in. "Lucy, look. I know I probably should have said something about the whole betrothal thing." I didn't know my eyebrow could hitch higher, but it does. "It's just that it's a tradition in my clan, and I didn't want to scare you... I mean—"

I cut him off with an imperious swipe of my hand.

"Get it off me. Now."

I pull my hair back, fully expecting him to move around me and obey. But he doesn't move.

"Ali," I say through clenched teeth. "Get. This. Off. Me."

But instead of acting, Alastair puts a hand to his chest, as though in pain. "I want to do as you're asking, Lucy. I want to. You have no idea how badly I want to. But see, the thing is, I can't."

My eyes pop wide. Panic claws at me. Margot places a hand on my shoulder, as though she expects me to lunge at the young man in front of me. "What did you say?"

He looks sheepishly at the ground. "I'm saying I can't."

"Why?"

"Because. Once the promise is made, it can't easily be broken."

"So? I didn't make any promise."

"Also, it requires a special person from our clan to do it, and that person currently lives…in Russia?" His inflection rises. "Remember him? Tom? Cilia's husband."

I don't have words. I am speechless. But I do have an anger that has mounted out of control, zipping through my veins like electricity. I don't even notice myself doing it. And so it's likely with as much shock as I read on Alastair's face that I haul back and punch him square in the face.

I pull my aching fist away, wondering if I'm going to do it again. But his friend has stepped in and shields Ali from me just as Margot yanks my arm and marches me away. Alastair leans over his feet, grabbing at his cheek with both hands.

Good, I've hurt him, I think to myself, consumed by a burning rage. And I'm ready to do more.

He straightens and pushes his friend away, still holding his face. "I deserve that." He spits a tiny round of blood onto the ground in front of me and raises a placating hand. "But you need to listen, Lucy. The coin is not just a marriage promise, and that wasn't my primary motive for giving it to you. It's a very powerful talisman of protection. For my people there is nothing so sacred as a coin of Cernunnos."

"What do I care? I'm not one of your people."

"But you are. Both you and Margot." He takes us both in. "You know you're different."

I blink, trying to understand what he's saying. "We aren't True Born."

"You're not like the other True Borns, true," he says.

"We're *not*," I insist. "We've been through this. Through rounds and rounds of Protocols. We don't have the Talismans."

"But you wear this Talisman around your neck." The way he says it, with reverence in his voice, makes me wary. He reaches out, tapping the coin before I can pull back and swipe his fingers away.

"Don't touch me."

Alastair is undeterred. "They've seen it. The Red Wing Clan. They've seen how it comes alive around your neck."

A shiver snakes up my spine, raising the hair on my arms and neck. "What are you talking about?"

"The coin. It's part of what was seen. Cernunnos's coins would come to life when worn next to the skin by the twins meant to usher His time back into the world. The Seer said it will be something in their blood. Something that will sing to the coin, activate its magic."

It's in the blood.

"It's not magic, Ali," Margot says patiently. "It's just an old coin."

At this, Alastair graces Margot with an apologetic look. "I'm just sorry I had but one coin, Margot. Most leaders only have one in their safekeeping."

Margot's voice is raspy. "That's just fine, Ali. I'm too young to get married."

I shoot my sister a dirty look and make an effort to unclench my fists before continuing. "Stuff and nonsense," I chide. "There's a perfectly reasonable explanation for whatever it is you think is happening—*if* it's even happening at all. I can't see or feel anything." But then I'm full of doubt as I recall Serena's blank eyes, drawn to whatever strange material lies buried in the coin.

"You can't hide from the truth forever, Lucy. It's in your blood. Yours and Margot's."

"Forever?" I scoff. Still, his words are enough to send a bolt of dread into my belly as I recall the vivid dreams I've had since wearing the coin—even more vivid than my usual dreams where I see what's to come.

In this dream I float high above Dominion, filled with a grief so terrible it doesn't have a name or shape. And as my tears fall down over the city, it becomes rain. Rain, washing the streets clean.

Blood drains from my face. Panic gallops through my veins. I take deep, even breaths to calm myself. Is Alastair just like all the rest—after the secrets of our blood?

"What are you going to do, Ali? Are you going to try to take us, like all the others?"

"No, I would never." He steps forward, hands outstretched beseechingly.

I slap his hands down as they come to wrap around my upper arms. "I said don't touch me!" He keeps coming forward.

I back into Margot, stepping on her toes as I close my eyes and flail my arms. I'm fighting Ali's grasp but also the ghosts who would steal our lives away: Resnikov, our parents. Father Wes and his Watchers.

Must I also fight some ancient band of druidic loons?

I scratch and claw and push and shove while Ali tries to grab my arms. Someone approaches me from the side—I assume it's Ali's friend, who tries to hug me around the torso. I lunge forward and snap back, kicking one of them as hard as I can. Margot's screeching drowns out a groan and muffled curse.

"Stop it! Don't touch her! Someone help!"

And just as sudden as a Flux storm, it's over. Alastair and his friend are both on the ground. Shane stands before Margot and me, barely even breaking a sweat.

"S'a good thing Mr. Storm let me come and pick you up today."

His knotted tattoos shine like black snakes under the white light of the sky as he swipes at a lock of his greasy hair and snarls at the boys. "So much as look at these young ladies again," he says, anger transforming us to "leddies," "I'll skin yas alive. How does that sound, lads? Fun? Or maybe we won't wait. Maybe I can do it here and now in the schoolyard, save us all a lot of years of misery." Shane's smile is ugly, tight. As if to punctuate his words, he pulls out a knife, serrated on one side. At least five inches from scabbard to tip. He juggles the thing expertly between his hands. Judging from the feral gleam in his eye, I'd assume he's not fooling.

It takes me a moment to process the prone form of Ali on the ground. Flowers, blue and gold and white, are strewn around his body like lost buttons. He's up on one elbow, the stuffing apparently knocked out of him, I notice with some small glee.

"No," I tell Shane, putting my hand carefully on his arm. It takes a moment to steer his attention away from spilling blood. "Take us home, Shane. Just take us home."

I barely spare a glance for Ali and Tomas as Shane leads us away from the curious glances of some of the mercs and their young charges. Some of these Personals, House mercs, greet Shane by name, slapping him on the back as we pass and uttering the phrases common among the mercs for a save on the job.

The council chamber smells of mildew and wax, dust and the sweat of nervous men. Dominion is gloomier than usual today; the sky remains wrapped in a shawl of gray shadows. Power was cut from the main generator station, Storm tells us. Watchers, he suspects, judging by the red eyes and writing left behind, dripping from every surface.

I study the gaunt faces of the Lasters at the table in the flickering, candled half gloom. The old man isn't here today. But the younger one is, flushed in his overalls, almost handsome as he roves a nervous eye around the room. Beside him sits a skeletal man in a long-sleeve shirt rolled up from the wrists, exposing white-white arms that jut from his body as though they've lost their skin. This man wears a cynical smile like a mask.

And he's bold for a Laster.

"Well?" The Laster arches up a thick black eyebrow and burns a look at Storm and me. "Are we going to sit here and die of boredom?" His anger chops the air.

Storm inclines his head politely, a slim finger of an antler catching the light. "If you don't mind, we'll wait a few more minutes for the representatives from the Upper Circle."

"Don't we have a representative of the Upper Circle sitting right here?" The man motions to me with the back of his hand.

"Tonight Miss Fox is a representative of the True Borns." Storm smiles, but I'd as soon not be on the receiving end of a smile like that.

"Isn't that convenient?" throws back the man. "A rich True Born and a rich brat from the Upper Circle teaming up? Sounds as stacked as the deck they'd offer us." The Laster nods toward the door to indicate the absent senators. My breath catches. It's not the worst insult I've ever been thrown. Still, it hurts, knowing as I do just how untrue his impressions really are.

"If you really thought that," says a sober Storm, his skin crackling with power so strong I want to push away from the table, "why are you here?"

The man laughs, bitter and ugly. "And miss all this? This is better entertainment than the dross they put on the Feed, expecting us to eat it all up like hungry babies." The word stretches and rolls. *Bae-baes.*

Storm's body shimmers with unearthly power, the air suddenly evaporating from the room. The young Laster pulls back in his seat like he's been shot. Even the skeletal man blanches, though he's too arrogant to show much else.

"You'll be civil to this young woman."

"Or you'll what?" the skeletal man crows.

I suck in a breath and bite my lip. *What will he do?* But apparently Storm doesn't feel the need to make threats. He simply stares at the Laster man, his eyes glowing hot metal in a face absurdly beautiful, utterly alien. It seems to finally make an impression, though. The man sits back with a thoughtful expression.

And then the real problem sails through the door.

"Don't bother to get up; we won't be here long," chirps Theodore Nash. None of us was making to stand anyhow, so it's just as well.

Nash wears an ascot today, the official red of his office, and the kind of well-cut gray suit that only the finest tailors could produce. Healthy color stains his cheeks. I take in the white linen handkerchief folded neatly in his breast pocket.

Perfectly folded. Senator Theodore Nash doesn't mop away sweat any longer. Either the man's Splice took hold, or he's a lucky man.

No one survives. That's what they say. When it finally sinks its teeth into you, there is no coming back. So what happened to Nash? I look over Nash's shoulder as he takes a seat at the table and folds his hands together, but no Gillis appears. Nash pulls his lips into a thin, bloodless line. "Well, how nice that we're all here."

Storm tilts his head as though he's hearing something from a whole other frequency. "Where's Gillis?"

"He won't be coming back to these meetings. For that matter, neither will I. The Upper Circle is officially denying your request to start a council. There's a curfew on, eh? Better scurry back to your hidey-holes." He smiles then, a hate-filled, arrogant smile. Even I want to punch him. But as the two Laster men turn to give each other knowing looks and start to stand, I can't help myself.

I've seen my father do it often enough, I reckon. I clear my throat loudly, my own hands coming together on the tabletop. "Excuse me, Senator Nash. I guess I'm a little confused as to how you have the authority to speak for the rest of Dominion. I thought Senator Gillis outranked you?" I say it in as polite of tones as I can muster, which isn't much, I'll grant. It's enough to mottle Nash's face as he stands and walks over to me.

"That's right, Lucy, that's right. Gillis outranks me," he all but spits in my face. "But he's not here, is he?"

"What happened to him?" I ask. Innocent enough question. But something has happened; something is wrong. Because Nash lunges for me, his hands heading for my neck as though to pick a nasty weed.

Just as suddenly, Storm grabs Nash. The senator's red ascot dangles as his feet leave the floor. The lines of Storm's face could be carved of marble as he stands there, the words slow and careful.

"Come near Miss Fox again and I'll feed you your own hands and light you on fire," he says in a conversational tone. But I believe every word. And apparently, so does Nash. "Apologize."

Nash is lowered to the floor, face beet red. "Suh-suh-sorry," he gasps, but he can't bear to look at me. I've been frozen to my seat, not just through the threat of violence that lingers in the air like fine perfume but something else that niggles at me, like a dream where I see things.

Nash. Something is very *wrong* with Nash.

D oc Raines calls out to us from somewhere in the bowels of Storm's lab. "I'm back here, girls." The room's cold metal, as familiar as a nursery rhyme to Margot and me, glares at us under the harsh lights.

Margot grasps my pinkie with her own. "Whatever happens," she says. Our oldest bargain. Me and her, no matter what.

"Whatever happens." I nod.

Doc Raines appears in a puff of frizzy hair. "I've discovered something significant. I thought you should know right away."

We've heard this before. It's always something new, something we don't fully understand. And no matter how hard I try, the answers to the real questions seem to elude us.

What are we? That's the most insistent question, the one that drives all the others. *Why are people after us? Why did our parents disappear?*

Margot tenses, pulling my pinkie. I focus on Doc Raines, whose sharp blue eyes blink, huge and owlish, behind her lab loops. She pulls them up so they sit on top of her hair. Only this time, rather than jumping in and bombarding us with information, this time she just stands there, hands on hips, and takes us in.

She wipes at something on her forehead. "I don't know how to prepare you for this."

14

Alarm courses through my body. "What?"

Doc Raines rakes her eyes over us. "You do realize, don't you, that your DNA is breaking all the rules of science as we know it? Remember I told you I was going to try to match whatever DNA expression your twinned blood created with our central database? Well, I got a hit almost immediately."

"What is it, Doc Raines?" Margot gives my hand a death grip.

"You're not going to believe this. Once combined, your blood starts creating True Born Talismans. I didn't recognize it at first, because it's an expression of the Talismans I'd never seen before."

My mind whirls noisily while Doc Raines continues. But I can't hear her anymore. The True Born Talismans are what make the True Borns unique, separate from their human counterparts. When the Talismans are present in a person, all sorts of physical anomalies appear, like Carl's cat fur or Jared's shifter abilities. The Talismans are why True Borns don't catch sick with the Plague.

Lock and key. Splicer and True Born. But how can we be both?

It's Margot who speaks first. Clearing her throat, she asks, "Not Plague Cure?"

Doc Raines shakes her head. "Very astute of you, Margot. Not exactly. It's not that simple. But it is more elegant. The structure that we looked at *did* get rid of the Plague sample, as I showed you. But it did so by first transforming the host DNA into the True Born Talismans. As you know, True Borns don't fall ill because the Talismans protect against the Plague. But no one has really had the opportunity to study why. Granted, we don't know whether your blood acts exactly the same as the natural expressions. It essentially looks like an archaic variant of the Talismans, but really we're just guessing."

Doc Raines is so ecstatic you might think she's won the Dominion lottery. Beside me, Margot frowns.

But an idea is forming in my head. "Doc Raines, what would happen if a Plague-struck was given our combined blood? Would it cure them?"

Margot cuts sharp eyes at me. I can feel her heart thumping. She needs to know. We both do.

"I'm honestly not sure about that, girls. We'd need to run more tests. It's more likely to proliferate True Born Talismans throughout the genetic matrix. Clearing the body of the Plague's rogue DNA would simply be an added benefit."

"So you think it would turn people into True Borns? What about just Margot's blood?"

"Margot's alone would give a boost to natural immunity. That's all."

"They wouldn't *evolve*." I try out the word self-consciously. "No, I doubt it."

I look at Margot from the corner of my eye. "But it would help someone survive the Plague."

Now it's Doc Raines's turn to frown as she puzzles it out. "Yes. Temporarily…it would need the anchor for stability, but like I said, when it's combined…" Doc Raines cuts off and abruptly shoves to her feet. "You there," she calls, rounding the corner. Following close behind, Margot and I are just in time to see Shane hold his hands up in mock surrender. "What are you doing here?" Doc Raines orders.

"No need to get upset, missus," Shane says dismissively. "I'm just here for the girls."

"That's *Doctor* to you, thank you very much. And I'll ask you again. What are you doing here?"

"Sorry." A small smile frames Shane's mouth as he stares down at the thing in Doc Raines's hand. It takes me another moment to grasp that she's pulled a gun on Shane.

"Doc Raines, this is our father's man, Shane." I step in front of the gun, forcing the doctor to lower her hand. "He's been with us since we were babies. We'd trust him with our lives."

"No one is supposed to enter here without my express consent," the doctor continues as though I hadn't spoken.

"Sorry, I just didn't know how else to get their attention," Shane says with an air of abashment. "It's time for the twins to get off to school. Wouldn't you know it? Mr. Storm has given me a vote of confidence." He winks at Doc Raines. "Girls, for the next little while I'll be your school merc, Just like old times. I'm earning my stripes with your friend."

She doesn't put the gun away. "We'll take this up again later, ladies," she tells us while Shane holds open the laboratory door.

Then we sail off into an ordinary day, Margot and I, knowing that nothing will ever be ordinary again.

"Ali didn't come to see you today," Margot observes.

We lie on her bed, hands threaded together as they were when we were born, fingers twining like DNA.

"Do you think Doc Raines is telling the truth?" I whisper. It's not just that I'm avoiding the subject of Ali. It's that the bomb Doc Raines dropped on us earlier in the day feels like a much bigger deal than a boy. It's a life-and-death secret. And we girls, the Fox twins, are its keeper. *Lock and key.*

Margot taps at her cheek and lets go a chuff of air. "I reckon she believes it."

"What do you believe?"

My twin is silent. I can feel the storm clouds gathering in her, stretching out over everything she is. When she finally breaks her silence, I can feel the wetness rushing out over her cheeks. I don't move to comfort her, though I want to. She'd not want me to reach out right now.

"They thought to sell my DNA as Plague Cure is what I think." Her voice is bitter, twisted. This version of Margot hurts me somewhere I don't have a name for.

I think back to how I found my sister again. Hundreds of people on luxury cruise liners, on trains, seeking a cure. *Was this what they were after?*

"We destroyed the lab, so it doesn't matter," I soothe.

"No, Lu. We destroyed one factory. That doesn't mean they don't have tiny pieces of me they're growing someplace else."

Horrified, I squeeze her hand. But there's nothing I can say to ease this. She's right. We don't know how much they stole from her or how far it's traveled. A man like Resnikov would have backup plans. He'd have business partners. Friends.

Margot shifts and buries her face in the pillow, her hair falling around her in a tangled mess. I can feel her heart beating, wild like a trapped bird's. I catch myself wondering if we'll ever be uncaged from this mess.

"But what if we could make a cure? A real cure? With both our blood? Then no one would want their snake oil."

It's then that I feel it, like a door closing inside of myself.

"I-I want to be alone for a while," she murmurs. I touch her hair, my heart breaking for both of us. But she doesn't want my comfort. "Please."

I nod. Pain lances me, sharp needles of it stabbing me in the heart. That's one thing she's never done before, neither of us has. We've never made each other be alone until now.

I don't realize I'm crying until I walk into my bedroom. A candle is lit, though I barely register it before Jared is there, grasping my arms.

"What's wrong?" If I didn't know better, I would say he was angry.

I swipe at my eyes. "Nothing."

But he'll not be swayed. "Why won't you tell me?" He leads me over to the chair, which is still warm from the imprint of his body. He's been here a while, I reckon. And as I take a moment to register those facts, he pulls me down into the chair, me across his lap, as he soothes his hand down my hair. "What's wrong?" he says again. Only this time it's just above a whisper and filled with something I'd as soon call desperate.

But Jared doesn't get desperate. Jared is a merc, a soldier. My mind is too busy to work out what's happening as he runs fingertips light as rain across my cheek, erasing a track of tears.

"Lu." His lips are so close to mine, so hot and warm. I can smell the faint waft of cinnamon on his breath even if I can't make out much more than a black T-shirt that bunches under my fingertips. Jared's eyes are hooded from the light of the candle, fathomless orbs that hold me still. Then, with his eyes still holding me, his lips come down.

He looks as surprised as I feel as the spark dances between us, an instant inferno. His absurdly long lashes flutter over his eyes once, twice, covering the spark of his eyes. His lips part as I press into him again, curling my fingers in the wavy softness of his hair as I bring myself back for more.

At first I can feel him holding back, as though he's afraid to break me. But I've already broken once this evening. I can't break any further. I bite his bottom lip, sucking it into my mouth. Jared moans, and my stomach curls and clenches. He pulls his fingers through my hair on either side of my face, tilting it to the right before bringing his lips back down onto mine.

He kisses me like a man starved of oxygen. Heat fills my veins, and I moan into his mouth. His tongue snakes into my mouth, hot and demanding. I want more, need more. I grab at his shoulders, willing him to press more deeply, take more.

One of Jared's hands skirts up under my shirt. His fingers trill against the soft flesh of my side, and my back arches. He pulls his lips from mine and runs hot kisses up and down my neck, nipping at the spot behind my ear. I gasp. His mouth comes down again, wild as a starved animal.

He pulls back a moment after his hand touches the soft bud of my breast. His eyes are mesmerizing, stormy emeralds. I've never seen a man as beautiful as Jared Price. His lips are slightly swollen as his glazed eyes try to focus. "What are you doing to me, Lu?" He runs a light finger across my bottom lip, then my top. I nip my tongue out, surprised by my own brashness. As is he, I realize, when his eyes widen then narrow, as though he's just figured out we're not yet certain who's the hunter and who's the prey.

"You keep doing that, Princess, and I won't be responsible for my actions."

I keep my eyes on him until I'm close to his ear and then indulge myself, running my lips up the hot, tangy flesh of his neck. I take his earlobe into my mouth, enjoying beyond measure the strangled sounds he makes. His fingers tighten on my body. *Good*, I think. *This is definitely not one-sided.* And best of all, it drowns out everything else: Margot's pain, my own, the weight of the world. Suddenly I feel in control and I feel out of control. And I want more.

"What if I don't want you to be responsible for your actions?" I purr, continuing to lick my way back down his neck to the tender bone of his collar. I can feel him, his desire pulsing against me in time to the rhythm of his heartbeat. I can feel my blood call to his. I have never wanted anything so much as to feel the skin of his chest against mine.

Jared slowly closes his eyes. A pained expression falls across his features, turning the shallow planes of his cheekbones to stone. Hot skeins of embarrassment roll through me as Jared holds me at bay.

"Oh. I'm doing it wrong."

"Oh, Gods, Lu. Oh, holy Plague Fire you are so not doing it wrong." Jared takes a jagged breath. Another. He swallows hard, his body tense and still. Then he holds my face in his hands with such tenderness I could cry. "How could you even think such nonsense?" I want to get angry, lash out, but there's such genuine confusion in his eyes. And something else, something I'm not sure I have a name for, that thrills me to my toes.

"What, then?"

"You know," he whispers, pressing his forehead to mine. Like we can share sensation that way.

"No," I tell him, genuinely bewildered. The tears gather another storm and are set to loose. "I don't know."

He breathes me in. I can feel him pulling in each tangle of scent, the taste of our mouths mingling, our heated skin. "I'm about to get carried away, Lu. I am about a hairsbreadth from losing control of myself."

My eyelashes tremble, skating against his skin. "I think that's what I want to happen right now," I confess. "Just right now. Just tonight." I tangle a finger in his hair. Bold as daylight, I pull his lips down to mine, exploring the contours, the ridges of his fine, fine lips. Jared lets loose a gasp and rears back.

There's a note of hysteria in his voice as he says, "What are you doing to me, Lu?"

I can't help but smile. I've never felt so powerful as right now. But when I come to kiss him again, he grabs at my wrists and holds me at bay. Jared's eyes are hot coals, burning into my flesh.

His voice is a hoarse whisper. "I want to —"

A knock sounds at the door. Jared and I stare at each other, wondering if whoever is on the other side of that door — especially in a house full of True Borns — can hear the clatter of our hearts. The knock sounds again, insistent and dense against the wood of the door.

"Just a second," I call out shakily. I climb from Jared's lap and arrange my skirt, which has hiked up considerably. I watch as Jared runs his fingers through his hair, neatly pulling the blond strands back in place. He reaches over, a small smile tugging at his lips, and corrects some locks of my own hair.

Jared nods, and I turn and open the door. Shane has propped his shoulder up against the doorframe, the knotted work of his arm tattoo bending out of shape as he leans forward. "Lucy, I wanted to ask you about—" He stops as Jared silently comes up behind me. "What are you doing here?" Shane doesn't look happy.

Jared gives Shane an unholy grin. "Hopefully same as you. Security issue," he explains with a nod toward me.

I roll my eyes as Shane bristles. "Sorry, Shane, was there something you specifically needed? Jared was just leaving, and I'm tired." I've seen that look before. Shane the hunter. Shane the merc. But he's no match for Jared Price. "Shane?" I prompt.

"It can wait." He drawls out the words slowly, as though expecting one of them to detonate. "Jared, can I have a word? When you're through, of course." No one could miss the sarcasm.

Jared's eyes burn across my skin like a fleeting kiss. "Sure." He shrugs. The careless, casual death dealer is back. "Just give me a second to catch Lu up on some orders."

Shane takes a step but doesn't exactly give us any privacy. Jared's hands tighten around my arms as he pulls me behind the door. His heat presses against me, my head swimming with his nearness. For a moment I think he's going to say something as he gazes at me with a lost look in his eye. But then his lips come down, scraping against my lips. Lightning heat ignites between us again. His chest heaves as he struggles to stay in control. Hands come up to cup my face, and when he pulls back, those eyes of his are embers again. Bright. Hot. *Wanting me.*

Jared gulps air. My stomach pitches and rolls. I find my hands on his arms, anchoring myself in place as the room spins. And a distinct cough in the hall signals that our time is up.

Lips brush mine a final time, too much like air, and then he's tickling against the tender flesh of my ear. "We'll finish this discussion later, Princess," he warns. His teeth graze my earlobe, and I shiver as his lips press the soft spot under my ear. "And it's going to be a long talk." There's a flash of mischief in his eyes, a tilt of a smile as a dimple appears.

And then the panther man is out the door. His light footsteps ring in the hallway, followed by the heavy tread of Shane's dusty black boots.

It's a frosty morning, but all the ice I feel is being thrown by my father's man. *Former man*, I remind myself as I stand by the breakfast table receiving the cold shoulder from him. He's no employee of my father's now. Yet he'll censure me just the same, keep me in the same prisonlike box that Margot and I lived in our entire lives. *You'll be friends with who we say you can be friends with, girls. We will decide which boys you date.* Shane keeps his back to me, his whole body spitting sparks. Margot furiously rubs at her knee and raises an eyebrow. *What the hell is going on?*

And that's all it takes. Between one heartbeat and the next I realize I'm not interested in that box any longer. I'll not sit idly by and be told I'm not behaving well enough for the Upper Circle or for my parents, who abandoned us. Not by Shane. Not by anyone.

"Lucy." Storm breezes in, distracting me. His body is solid and yet, like always, it's hard to look at him. This morning he's dressed in a casual suit. Blue linen. But the gray-white of his eyes tells me that something has happened. "Come and join me in my office for a few minutes?" His smile is small, not entirely welcoming. I don't like the sudden tremble that takes over my body.

At the table, Margot shoots me a look she doesn't use much on me. *What the hell have you done?*

I shrug and slide away from the kitchen, following in Storm's wake.

"Did I do something I'm not aware of?" I start the moment I step into his office.

He turns slowly to face me. "No." A genuine smile cracks across his face, warm and welcoming. "Has someone given you that impression?"

"Maybe." I bite my lip. "I don't know," I admit, "things seem strange this morning."

Storm nods and gestures to the couch. "I understand. Sit down, Lucy." He doesn't lean against his desk or stand at the window as he normally does but comes to sit beside me. His hands rest on the cream leather and idly, as my mind sifts through the number of catastrophes that could have occurred while I slept, I study his hands. They are long and solid, large but not overwhelming, strong but not overly callused. His fingernails are clean and blunt. It occurs to me that I've never thought to wonder at Storm, at whether his body changes shape the way Jared's can.

"We have a situation." I can see from the winter in his eyes that I'm not going to like it. My stomach churns as my imagination takes over. *What could it be now?* "With Nash rejecting the creation of a council, I think I'm going to have to go another route to get everybody on board and talking."

Oh. I'd been expecting this conversation, at least, for days now. Without the Upper Circle's support, Storm doesn't stand a chance of forming a council. He'll need senators on his side to obtain that goal.

Storm crosses his elegant ankles, hitching his pants legs up a little. He frowns down at his leather-clad feet for a moment before looking up and holding my gaze.

"I need you to keep an open mind on this, Lucy," he says softly. His lips pucker into a sour smile before softening, the skin around his eyes creasing into deep laugh lines. *Does Storm laugh?* The notion is an odd one.

I nod. "Okay." And I'm sure I can, until he utters the words that can never be taken back, never erased, never understood.

"Peace is not going to happen without our help. I still think it can be achieved, but we need more ammunition—we need to make a formal alliance. So I propose," he drawls, the words echoing in my ears like shots fired, "that we marry."

Marry.

"Marry. As in, the union of marriage?"

Storm's lips twitch. "Is there another kind?"

Most young women my age would not bat an eyelash at Storm's proposal. I'm nearing nineteen, the time when most Upper Circle are ushered into political matrimony. In a majority of the cases, the groom is chosen from among a father's cronies. They're often much older than the young lady. Far older than Storm is. And Storm, at least, is handsome, kind and powerful. *But do I want him as my husband?*

I look down at my hands, clasped bloodless in my lap, and rehearse the lines every girl from the Upper Circle has memorized since their tender ages. "I am very sensible of the honor you do me…"

But Storm is not a fool. Not like so many others. "No dissimulation, Lucy," he cracks out. The floating wreath rising from his head becomes a tantalizing shade of silver-blue, until I can almost reach out and touch the bony fingers. "I realize there is an age gap between us. And it's an unusual situation, given that I'm also acting as your guardian. But the proposal I seek is a political alliance. This would be a marriage of convenience if that's what you'd wish. Do you have any other objections?"

Does he really not know? I feel sick as my mind fills with Jared. That shock of blond hair that fell over his eyes just before his lips arched down, burning me. His hands tangling in my hair, running down my back until I dissolved. How would I even tell Jared?

"My parents—" I begin, but Storm cuts me off with an impatient swipe of his hand.

"Your parents. If they were here, they would want you to make the most advantageous match you could, one that would ensure the future of the Upper Circle and, by extension, Dominion. That is me. In part I'm doing this to help ensure that you and Margot have the brightest future possible."

"How do you know my parents would approve?" I ask, genuinely curious. "They've made it clear in the past what they think of True Borns."

Storm leans in slowly. I fight the urge to draw back at the swirling intensity that gathers around him. "I don't know they would approve. But I am well aware of what's happening out there, Lucy. As are you. The balance of power is shifting."

Nervous, I wet my lips before continuing. "That's just it. How do you know an alliance with me will make things better? The longer our father stays away, the more the Fox twins are likely to become Upper Circle pariahs."

"Right again." Storm nods. "It's not a certainty that your social connections will hold up." If there's one thing I admire about Storm, it's that he cuts to the chase.

"But then—"

"Lucy," he cuts in, not impatiently but with the confidence of a man destined to win. "I've been fairly clear all the way. The Lasters' time is almost over. The Splicers will not be able to keep things going. They are going to need us working together. You think things are bad now? Just wait until their numbers dwindle even more," Storm promises. "Picture what the Lasters will do when the preachers and their followers figure out we're all facing an 'end of days' scenario. You think some gunmen at Grayguard or the Watchers we've seen are all you'll get? *Picture* it, Lucy."

And I can picture it. I see in my mind the Lasters sitting at the council table, their eyes sharp and hollowed with wild grief. I think about the bodies that have been not picked up lately, the rubble on the streets. The squadron of hazmat suits. We've always prided ourselves, Margot and I, on the fact that we've not turned a blind eye to what's happening in Dominion and across the world. But I wonder now if somewhere along the way I've shut down—if we both have?

Still puzzled, I ask, "What could you gain, then, by marrying me?"

Storm remains still as the sky, but I can feel the power coiling and gathering around him like an electrical storm. Then he smiles, and it's as though the sun has blinked out. "I think you and your sister are very special."

I mull this over. "Why not Margot?"

"Margot has been through a lot, and she's not as strong as you. She needs time to recover."

I'm shocked to hear him say this, even though secretly I've thought the same thing. "Are you in a rush?"

Storm folds his hands on his lap. "The sooner we create an alliance, the sooner we build a power base that stands a chance of ousting idiots like Nash from power."

Still, it's not a reason to marry the man sitting before me. The man I'd grown quite comfortable thinking of as my guardian.

"I need time to think," I tell him honesty, biting my lip. *There's Jared to consider.* The thought rolls through my mind like thunder.

But I've been raised to understand marriage as a business transaction, a political gambit. Girls from the Upper Circle do not marry for love.

Love. Once the word seeps into my brain, I know it can't be taken back, can't be hidden.

I stare at the threshold of my future. It's become something unrecognizable, something I could never have imagined just a few short months ago. Love or political marriage to a True Born?

Do I love Jared Price?

Yes, a voice whispers, soft as mist.

"Thank you for your offer." The flat formality customary of the Upper Circle comes out again. "I will think over what you've proposed very carefully."

Storm's lips quirk again. "I appreciate that." I pop off the couch quickly and am almost to the door when Storm's voice calls me back. "One more thing, Lucy. Shane will drive you and Margot to your last exams. Jared has been reassigned. Shane will be your new main school security."

I swivel on my heels. "Why?" The word explodes from me, more revealing than I'd intended.

The ice and metal of Storm's eyes lend me no clues as he

shrugs. "He's got an impressive background and skillset, as well as seeming to care a great deal about you and Margot, I want to give him room to earn my trust."

"Oh," I choke out, and turn back to the door so that Storm can't see the flaming heat of my face. My mind leaps into sorting the various possibilities, but they're like scattered pieces of a puzzle I can't solve.

Did Shane report Jared and me to Storm? Does Storm know that Jared and I... My thoughts veer off. What would he even know? I don't know what we are, and though it was a big enough deal to me, what does fooling around mean to Jared?

Another thought drops through my brain like an unwelcome guest. Did Jared want to be reassigned? And if he did, why?

Love, I think in despair.

15

I stare out the windows of Storm's car. The streets of Dominion are strange and blank. Blank like me. The hurt in my chest keeps blossoming, unfurling with every block. Absently I rub at the spot in my chest where it feels like my heart has been ripped out. I feel a pinch on my arm, though no hands touch me.

Margot.

I gaze over at my sister. She looks bright as sunshine on the other side of the back seat. Her hair is pulled into a severe ponytail, exposing the high, long line of her neck and the fragile bones of her cheeks. The mirror image of myself. I don't know what to say. I can't share without giving away all my secrets. So when my lip starts to quiver, my eyes blinking back rain, I pretend to look terribly interested in the drab morning scene.

It looks like every other day in this dying city.

From the corner of my eye, I spy a Laster on the street.

The man puts out a hand to brace himself against a wall. Not long for this world, I reckon. I watch him shake just before he doubles over, an arm slashing over his bloated, empty stomach. I am about to turn away, not able to take a second more of the misery to be found in the streets, when a figure steps out from the shadow.

I would have known what he was even without the long robe flowing down over his long torso. On his face is a stamp: red circles, conjoined in the middle. Not an ordinary preacher man, then. A Watcher. He steps behind the Laster, a hand outstretched, perhaps to comfort the dying man.

"Margot," I murmur, sitting up straighter. But by then we've cruised past the scene, and I will never know what it was the Watcher was going to do. Margot's eyes are curious as I look over. *Watcher.* I mouth the word, not sure I want to say it out loud.

Margot's eyes go wide as she realizes what I've said. They've been in hiding, or so we thought. So we've been told. So what does it mean that the Watchers are on the streets again?

What does it mean that we haven't been told?

The hair on the back of my neck stands at attention. I receive the double prick of Margot's, a gnawing knot of anxiety that grips my gut. Within the flicker of an eyelash, Margot and I have made a pact of silence. We'll wait until we're alone to discuss this. The car pulls to a stop, and Shane glances at us through the rearview.

"Everything all right, girls?"

"Fine," we singsong. The door locks open and we pile out, blinking against a gray-white sky.

Shane frowns at us as he steps around. "You know you should wait until I'm door side."

We know the drill. It's protocol to let the mercs escort you from the car to the doors of the school. But something is going on today. Not the least, I reckon as I look around, is how far away from the Academy we've stopped.

We can see the school through the gaps in the buildings, but it's still a good three blocks away. Barricades stretch across the necks of streets, fencing us in, each topped with barbed wire.

"What's going on, Shane?" Margot asks. I can't swallow past the lump of fear in my throat.

Shane shrugs and sweeps an expert eye at the rooftops. "Bomb threat, I reckon." He flicks an impatient finger at us, but his face tightens into a scary mask. "Let's get moving, girls. I don't like you being out in the open like this."

Margot bends down and pulls up her right sock. "Coming," she says. Slowly she stands tall, her eyes casting a hooded look at me.

Something is wrong. We both sense it.

Just one other car has pulled up ahead of ours. It's too soon to know who will spill out. But we don't like the eerie quiet of the streets. The blue uniforms of the school's security blaze behind the barricades. Our heels make funny *clackity-clack* sounds on the pavement as we scurry toward them, Shane's heavy tread carrying behind us. Maybe that's why we don't hear anything. A long foot emerges from the shadows. Then a leg, a torso. Then a head.

And a gun.

The man stands there as though he's not got a care in the world. And maybe he doesn't. His cheeks are heavily pockmarked. That hasn't stopped him from coloring his face with the insignia of the Watchers, though on this man it looks like he might have drawn it in with red lipstick without a mirror.

Part of one circle is smudged, and when he smiles, it stretches back across his cheek. It's a yellow-toothed smile. One tooth is missing from his lower jaw, so that he looks lopsided and comical as much as terrifying.

"Girls," Shane barks from behind us. Margot and I pedal to a full stop. "Get behind me."

The man steps forward. One step, another. His gun butts forward like an eager nose, long and thin. Still, the man says nothing, does nothing. Shane shoves us behind him.

"We've no quarrel with you," he tells the Watcher in his gruffest tones. With one hand he holds us at his back. The other hand raises in peace.

Margot pinches my arm, and I turn. She points to the roof on the building opposite. *Sniper.*

The shots whistle down around our ears, but they aren't meant for us, I realize. They're meant for the blue-clad Academy's men who run toward us in zigzagging lines, shouting. From the side street, a dozen or so Watchers emerge, all of them as scraggly and worn as the man before us. All are anointed with what looks like fresh war paint on their cheeks.

"Shane," Margot whimpers. Her voice falls to a whisper as she and I both realize what's happening.

We've just sprung a trap.

"Mar." I hurriedly dig through my bag. "Get your phone. Call Storm." I try doing the same. My fingers fly over the buttons as more shots are fired between the roof and the school. I look up in time to watch a man crumple to the ground fifty feet ahead. Frantic now, I dial the numbers.

The phone takes an eon to connect the number. Then

Alma's voice comes on the line. "Hello, Lucy."

"Alma, we're under—"

That's all I have time for before an explosion rocks the building the sniper had been standing on and the top corner of it evaporates before our eyes. A massive shelf of mortar and cement slides down from the building with a bone-jarring, earth-trembling crash. Tidal waves of ash and debris close over our heads, and we gasp for air in the deafening roar. Margot's arms are around me, our faces pressed against each other's necks to protect each other from the dust.

A rough hand is a talon at my shoulder. It rips me from Margot's embrace. I lean forward and kick blindly, satisfied when I connect with something hard. The talon softens but doesn't let go. It aches when I twist, but twist I do, meeting a Watcher face-to-face. The hair prickles on my arms as I stare into crazed eyes, streaked with red and coated with dust. His skin is rubbled and ruined, pocked with blood and ash. I bring my elbow up and dig into the hollow chest. The man grunts and steps back in surprise. It's enough time for me to yell, "Margot, run!" Then he starts for me again.

Margot coughs. Clouds of dust erupt from her, as though she's learned to spit smoke. She shakes her head. Reaches out her hand. In a split second, I catch a glimpse of Shane wrestling with two Watchers, though they're not the kind of preachers' kin I've ever seen before. Their arms are as muscled as a merc's, their legs long and powerful under their tunics. I can't see Shane's face, but the Watchers seem almost amused as he bats at them, swinging fiercely. And there is something comical about the way Shane is holding them off, something exaggerated and strange as he flips one over his back as easily as flipping an egg—

No time. I grab Margot's hands. We go like bats toward the thickest of the dust clouds, hoping for a bit of cover. The man's long arm reaches for me again, nicking my shoulder. I thrust my arm up to break his hold. Between that and Margot's momentum, it's enough to break us free.

The ground beneath our feet is like a minefield as we skip over chunks of concrete and brick, shattered glass and twisted metal poles. No one shoots at us as we make our way to the mess in the square, but the debris slows us down. Margot chances a look behind us, her lips pursing.

"Almost," she croaks through a mouthful of dust. They're behind us then, and closing fast. I sweep the streets for somewhere to hide.

"Black door," I tell her, pointing with my eyes rather than my finger. No need to give ourselves away. We scramble over a pile of rocks, staying low to the ground. At the top, I pause to take in a scene of chaos. A gun war still blazes between the school and the rooftop snipers, who pick off the Academy's mercs like so many flies on a wall. I spy the rocket launcher near the Grayguard gates and three men crouching behind splintering riot shields as they load another round.

From our rocky crest I have a better view of Shane, who crouches in a fighter's pose. The men surrounding him stand looser. Shane stops and glances around. Looking for us, I reckon. I'd call out, but for the moment, at least, Margot and I are invisible in the muck and din of battle. He straightens, his mouth moving. From here I can't tell what he's saying, who he's speaking to. The Watchers who have him cornered look around restlessly, scanning the area for us. My stomach balls into a knot of dread as I realize what's wrong with the scene.

They aren't punching. They aren't fighting.

Setup.

"Mar." I crouch, pulling my sister down on top of the rubble. "Back around this building instead."

Margot looks up uneasily at the building behind us. It looks for all the world as though it's about to fall down on top of us, a thousand pounds of death. My sister just blinks at me, nods.

"Careful," she says.

We pick our way over a dozen chunks of a former wall before we hear a shout. It's coming from the roof of the four-story building opposite. I look up; a rifle points down at our heads. A man yells for backup. Seconds later, the roof explodes in a shower of sparks and flames and brick. Margot and I duck and sputter, but then I grab her hand, threading her through the chaos as quickly as I can when we're both blind and deaf from the roar of the explosion.

Think, think, I order my chaotic mind as a Watcher scrambles onto a pile of rocks not twenty feet from us. *What would Jared do?*

Rip them to shreds, comes the instant answer. And here I've no iron claws.

But thinking of him calms me. Jared would tell me to use my brains. He'd tell me to run and hide and be smart, like a mouse.

And mice go to ground in holes.

"Quick, Mar," I shout. They're everywhere, the Watchers. And Shane. *Shane.* My guts twist in fury. The side of the building we're near has a huge crack down the brickwork, as though it's been torn.

Ahead of us is an alley that seems relatively quiet and clear, the rubble confined more to the corner that had been ripped apart. I open my mouth to tell Margot we're nearly there but snap my jaw shut when the shadows ripple. Out step a dozen or so Watchers, all with the messily painted cheeks of the newly initiated.

Margot and I scramble back. Her fingers are soft and wet with sweat. I hear her labored breathing, a match to my own, the hammer of her heart echoing in my chest. The wall…the wall has a six-foot drawing of their sign. Beside it, someone has taken the time to make the letters huge and straight. *Evolve or die.*

I have time enough to whip my head around when a rough hand grabs me. I bat at it, kicking and screaming. Margot yips. A Watcher's guttural warning sounds in my ears as she sinks her teeth into the hand snaking over her mouth.

My sister's fingers are pried from my grip. My hand suddenly free, I have more room to fight. I swing around, catching the terror on Margot's face as a Watcher pulls her to his chest. And from the corner of my eye I spy Shane, standing behind the ring of Watchers, hands on his hips, something grim and sinister stamped across his features.

The last coherent thought I have is how glad I am that Jared isn't with us, as surely he'd get himself killed. Then I think of my lonely, naked fingers, so opposite the weight of Margot's panic as she struggles like a little bird in their grip. All that before something heavy comes down on my head and knocks me into oblivion.

16

y head throbs. I struggle to open my eyes. All I see is
red. It takes quite a bit longer than it should to realize
why. I'm staring at a stone brick wall covered in the
Watchers' symbol.

My heart gallops as I reach through my senses for Margot.
There she is, slumbering inside me. I try to turn my head. My neck
is sore. The effort is almost too much. I try to pull my hands up to
cradle my aching skull, but they're stuck. Fastened to something.
I'm seated on a chair. Cuffed. My legs have gone numb, and I
have the violent urge to pee. A wave of pain swallows me as I try
to move. I sweat through it, although, soon enough, I'm retching,
and it splits my aching head in two.

Maybe it's this sound that wakes Margot. She stirs not far
from me. I'm comforted by the little burst of breath that always
signals to me that she has come awake, the inner spark I feel
that accompanies this.

"Mar." My voice does not sound like my own. Fragile. Lost. I turn my head carefully to the side, one inch, two.

Margot's hair falls down around her face so I can't see if she's been hurt. Streaked white from the explosions, her head bobs up once, twice. She's a scant three feet away from me. It might as well be a mile. I can't touch her, can't reach through our bond to get to her.

"Mar." I say it quiet-quiet. The way sneaky girls do.

My sister's head snaps up. She stares, wide-eyed, as though she's seen straight through to hell.

We don't speak another word. Margot pulls slightly at her wrists. The heavy ache of iron tugs through me, my arms leaden and tired from the weight of two sets of cuffs. They *are* cuffs — the kind of iron bands they throw on the worst violators in Dominion.

My sister eyes the sparse room. Her eyebrows flare as she takes in the bright red dripping symbol on the brick wall, set up before us like a static NewsFeed.

My sister turns her head back to me. I read the question in her eyes.

Watchers?

I wince and gasp as I try to move my head around. Margot winces in sympathy, shakes her head slightly. They've done something else to her. Maybe drugged her. She looks behind us, then back at me, eyes sharpening.

Door, she mouths.

Trapped on the chair, sweating with pain, I try to unclench my aching jaw and shove my panicked thoughts away. *What would Jared do?* I think again. He'd tell me to recover, breathe, think. The ball of rage in my belly — not just against the Watchers and their ilk but the beast who gave us up to them — expands. I feel light-headed all over again.

How could Shane have done this to us?

After watching us grow up, shepherding us to and from our events, sheltering us day and night… How long had our father's man been working for Father Wes? The thought makes me sick to my stomach and I retch again, wishing the poison in my soul was easier to get rid of. For I feel as though, at this moment, I'll never be able to wash myself clean of his betrayal.

It feels like an eternity before we hear the metallic snick of a lock behind us. The heavy shove of a door. It slams, making us jump, and the lock jigs again. We hear the tread of feet on the gritty stone floor. Those steps materialize before us as a tall, gangly Watcher.

Margot and I regard our captor uneasily. He graces us with a bizarrely tender, utterly insane smile. Thick lines of flesh run down either side of his face like he's been melting, crisscrossed by the sloppy red circles. His eyes are set far back in his face, framed by heavy eyebrows and a large, crooked nose.

He doesn't seem to be in a hurry to speak to us, though, so I decide to move the conversation along. But when I open my mouth, I'm surprised at how my words come out, slurred and strange. "What do you want with us?"

The Watcher's smile deepens, widens, until he looks almost serene. His hand opens at his side, large and callused, his fingers thick as sausages. I'm still watching the hand as it comes up and whips my face, bringing back the darkness like an endless river.

・・・

Jared's breath tickles my neck. *Don't you dare give up, Princess. You give up I'll personally kick your ass. No, worse, I'll hand you over to Kira and have her kick your ass for real.* The threat makes me shiver. I open my eyes a crack and peer at my blond avenging angel. His skin pulls tight, the lines of his flesh drawing down the way it does when he's ten paces from changing. *Do you hear me, Lucy? I will* not *let you die here. Do* not *let me down.*

I nod weakly. Eyes cold and bright and filled with a thousand emerald suns watch me. He doesn't touch me. I lean into him. I want so badly to feel his hands. The True Born doesn't smile exactly, but the corners of his lips curl up. In a blink it seems like some weight has been lifted from him. *Good. Good.* He presses his lips to the space under my ear. If I could move, I'd squirm as the hairs on my neck stand up. How does he manage to do that when I'm tied to a chair in a Watchers' dungeon? *Lu*, he whispers, the words hot on my neck, *Lu, Lu, Lu, I love*—

And just like that, the switch is flipped. Dream Jared disappears in a painful cloud of disappointment. In his place comes a singsong voice I know as well as my own.

"Lu. Lu Lu Lu Lu Lu." *Margot.*

I struggle through a knot of cold, helpless emptiness. Pain has become fastened onto the back of my eyelids, cementing them down. The coin tied around my neck jingles slightly as I struggle, but the moment I start to move, my head throbs violently.

I hold still for a moment before experimenting with my lips. They are swollen and tender, my mouth filled with the coppery taste of blood. "Mar-got." I mouth the word in our quiet-quiet way, unwilling to take another blow. I'm not sure I'd survive, at any rate.

And if there is one thought I take with me through the shadows into the light, it's this: I want to survive. *Need* to survive. Not just for Margot. *For Jared.*

The thought becomes a loud roar in my mind, thick through all the cells of my body. *I need Jared Price.* I need to see him again, touch him again, with a desperation I don't understand.

"Lu, Lu," Margot's voice insists. She tugs on one arm, the tight band on her flesh clawing at her wrist. I would have missed it in the inventory of our bodies had she not called attention to it.

There. That small scrap of fragile flesh where the forearm meets the elbow. It has been months since I've felt that same tender bruising, exactly like it feels after we've been pushed through a round of Protocols.

Our captors have been stealing our blood.

I lift my head. The Watcher is gone. My sister's face is wan with concern, still streaked from plaster and building dust. But I see in them something else, something I'd give days and nights of my life to erase. *Fear.*

My lips barely move as we enter our private patter, but they still split and hurt. "What're they after?"

Margot gives a tight shrug of her head. "Dunno. No words. Just Protocols."

I spit a small circle of blood on the ground. It barely makes an impression on the rough and filthy stone flags. "How much?"

"Four." Four draws. That's quite a lot of blood to work with for whatever test they had in mind.

"How long?"

Margot's lips compress into a tight line. She knows what I'm asking. "An hour maybe. Losing track already." Her eyes glitter with words she hasn't said, the panic that I can feel jutting into my bones at sharp angles. This isn't her first time playing captive. She'd never spoken of it, but I knew that was one of the things that bothered her most, both after Clive and the attendants at the Protocols clinic took her and then, especially, once she'd come home from Russia.

Time doesn't work the same when people keep it from you, she'd told me. *I've lost what feels like years of my life, though it's only been months.*

Margot clears her throat. "What now?"

I think this through. *What would Jared do?* What would he tell me to do, since it's unlikely I'll be able to rip apart our captors with my bare hands and snarl at them until they wet themselves. What would Jared *want* me to do?

"We get smart," I tell Margot, barely recognizing the sound of my voice as the kernel of my plan takes shape in my mind. "Picture," I say, plastering a bright smile on my face.

I feel brighter the moment she gets it. Margot blinks once, twice. "Tell," she says. And like we have a million times in the past, like we're children with nothing to gain but our mastery over the world, I lay out my plan for our survival—*our victorious escape*, I tell myself fiercely—through the hushed, staccato rhythms of one of our oldest word games.

I almost smile as I start us off. *"Door."*

We'd gone silent a long time before a new Watcher comes in, though it takes us a few moments to realize that there are others, too, hidden behind us. The shuffle of their bodies and the scrape of their shoes on the flag floor the only signs. A small, whiffling cough.

The Watcher stands before the symbol on the wall, eerily

haloed by a light I've only just discovered. He's shorter and bulkier than the other, biceps straining under a tight, dirty white shirt that looks as though the neck has been ripped off it. I take in the straining breeches, the beginnings of a tear starting in the knee.

He looks like any other Laster you'd pass on the streets, though perhaps a shade better fed. His face is shiny under the glow of the lights. A greasy lock of his hair pulls over his forehead. No symbol on this one's face.

The thought burns through me, stomach dropping to my numb toes, as a crackling sound, like the scratching of metallic claws, fills the tiny chamber. Margot and I hazard a glance at each other. Her rising panic fills my veins with adrenaline. I shake my head slightly, the pain helping me to break Margot's hold on me. She taps her chair with one bent finger. *Picture.*

Listen.

A tinny voice booms through the air. "Misses Fox." I wince as the voice curls up into a high-pitched whine. Even the man before us hunches his shoulders. But worse — I know that voice. It haunts my dreams. Margot taps insistently at her thigh, trying to get my attention. She knows, too, I reckon.

Father Wes has finally claimed his quarry.

17

"Now, girls." The voice booms and crackles through an inept speaker system. "You must be asking yourselves why you're here. No?" He continues as though we were supposed to answer. "Perhaps we'll leave that tale for another time, then."

Margot and I share a look. Should we have spoken up? Yelled? Acknowledged him in some way? The last time we came across Father Wes, when, with an army of Lasters, he attacked and destroyed our home, he struck me as a man who needed an audience. The preacher man will tell us eventually—he won't be able to help himself. I give Margot the slightest shake of my head. *Stay silent*, I warn her with my eyes.

"Here's how this is going to go. Brother Noah there in front of you is going to unlock you one at a time and escort you to the bathroom. You'll be given food. Then it will be the other's turn. Should you give Brother Noah here any trouble, we'll start chopping off your fingers and toes. Any questions?"

I can hear it in his voice, clear as day. He's longing for a chance to hurt us. I nod at Brother Noah. Whatever happens, we want him to believe we're cooperating.

But I reckon I have a perverse streak, because I can't help but croak, "What happens when you run out of fingers and toes?"

Margot swivels her head over to me, the look on her face showing me what she thinks of my dumb heroics.

Father Wes's metallic chuckle fills the air. "Why, we'll start killing your darling True Borns."

Not our parents, I notice. Not our friends from the Upper Circle. If he's not threatening our parents then he likely doesn't have them. *What intel has Shane been feeding them?* Because if there's one thing I'm certain of now, it's that Shane is working with these monsters. I choke down a sob. The man I once trusted with our lives was just another betrayer. He doesn't deserve my tears.

"Thank you for the clarification."

The chuckle dies to a dull rasp. "One false move, little Fox, and I'll be cutting off your tail."

I ignore him and turn my attention to the man before me. "Her first," I tell Brother Noah bravely. His eyes are mean little pebbles set back in his face. Bluish lips twitch from side to side. He just stands there, looking at me as if I'm a bug he'd like to squash beneath his heel. The loud voice of Father Wes breaks through the air again.

"Brother Noah, please see to the girls. Mouthy one first."

As Brother Noah's shadow falls over me, I try not to recoil. He reeks of boiled cabbage and urine and the peculiar stench of the unwashed. I lean back in my chair as far as I can as the

Watcher takes his time, no doubt enjoying this.

My hands come free. I rub the skin of my wrists, a raw tattoo. My jailer's face is lost in shadows as he grunts and indicates with a nod of shaggy hair to follow him through the narrow door.

I take a last look at Margot. Her eyes flicker to catch the subtle tap, *one two three*, of my finger on my wrist. Her eyes widen slightly, then flutter closed briefly. Satisfied that Margot has understood, I rise on unsteady legs. I'm clumsy as I follow the dirty, stinking Watcher past his robed brothers guarding the room and out the small metal door. My muscles ache from sitting, accompanied by the needlelike sting of blood flowing again.

We pass through a narrow, garishly lit passageway, all but three feet across. The walls look like earth but harder. In a few paces we come to a small room with moldy tile walls covered in the filthy red insignia of the Watchers. There is a bathroom stall, a sink, a mirror caked with red circles. Brother Noah motions me in.

I stand there, eyeing him with obvious reluctance.

"Are you just going to stand there?" I ask, looking down at my feet. "I don't think I can if you..."

Brother Noah snorts. He finds my feminine shyness amusing, no doubt. Crossing his bulky arms, he moves to stand around the corner but no farther. He'll not be worried about my escape in here. And as I examine the space, I can see why.

The lock has been torn from the stall door. The walls are barren, without images or windows save the Watchers' signs. *Evolve or die* cuts across my mind like an endless litany. Needing a distraction, I picture Jared. He springs vividly to mind. I can see his serious face, drawn and pinched over the nose, can almost smell that peculiar cinnamon scent of his skin. *First things first*, Dream Jared tells me sternly. *Pay attention. What do you see?*

A few embarrassing moments later I shuffle out of the stall and stare at myself in the mirror. In the reflection, my face is crisscrossed with red circles, one line coming up under my cheek like a violent swirl of blush. My eyes are huge, the pupils blown. *Concussion*, my addled brain decides. The long waves of my hair have become helplessly tangled. I touch a tender spot on my head. It comes away red. I pull at the water taps; it takes as long, grinding moment for the water to pour. A trickle appears and it's rusty, the pipes near to bursting with air. Then it runs in spits and sparks, though foul.

"This smells like fish," I call out to my guard.

A snicker is the only reply I get. I slap the foul-smelling water on my face, keep my wrists submerged as long as I can as a memory hopscotches through my mind. How had the childhood lesson gone?

Clean and pure piped in for the Splicers, sitting in their towers.
Fetid and fishy 'round Lake Dominion's shores.
While the Lasters in the center have their plugs pulled.

It was a children's rhyme, one we Upper Circle kids had passed down from generation to generation. Just words, cruel and unkind. But they taught us who we were, where we were from.

Where we *are*.

"Hurry up."

"Coming." I twist off the tap.

We must be near the lake.

When they're being kind, they call this area the Lowlands, though I've heard it called the Graveyard, too. There's nothing around the area rimming the lake but industrial buildings, crumbling to dust from lack of use. The kids' song is meant to make us afraid. Everyone knows that the lake has been used as a mass dumping ground for years, when the Plague came on too strong and in the chaos there weren't enough hands to bury the dead.

Which is worse? Drinking the flotsam of the dead? Or having no water at all?

It's a question I'd as soon not ponder as I'm marched back down the long earthen tunnel. He doesn't touch me, but I can feel Brother Noah's eyes raking over my back. I send Margot a breezy smile as I sit back in the wooden chair like a duchess at her tea and wait for the Watchers to lock me up again. And then I fight the urge the smile when they don't seem to know what to do with this attitude.

Once they have me clamped, Margot is loosed. I keep a keen eye on her as she rises, stiff and sore, but am relieved that my sense of her is strong and sure as she slowly makes her way to the door, head held high.

Margot taps her leg. "Well?" she whispers in our quiet-quiet way. "You reckon there's any way out?"

My neck is sore as I turn my head to speak. "No."

A dull look comes into Margot's eyes. I can't afford to have her give up. But it's not my way to lie to my twin. Besides, she's seen it herself. "I think we're underground. Near the lake."

Margot's voice swells with conviction. "They'll come for us, though."

"Yes," I say at once. She's right. I know the True Borns will look for us, too. At least, they'll try. I've avoided thinking about Jared for the past several hours, but now he flares back to life in my mind.

Is he going crazy right now? After all, this is the man who tracked me onto a cruise ship, who'd gone through hell and back to be sure I was safe. But if he cares about me, why has he all but disappeared from our lives, ever since Shane came back? *But Shane is a traitor*, I remind myself. He's been working with the Watchers, which can only mean... It was all a set up. Shane somehow convinced Storm to reassign Jared.

And even if Jared does come for me... How will he track us underground?

Serena's milky white eyes and wide, generous smile float before my thinning vision. *I see you*, she's told me. Serena sees nothing, nobody, but True Borns. It's her Salvager gift. *But she can see us, too.*

"Don't worry, Margot," I croak. I'm fading and I can't hold on. "Just remembered they have a Salvager." It's my last thought before I'm rushed to painful sleep.

A tearing pain at my wrists pulls at my consciousness. Drops of heavy black rain fall on the insides of my eyelids, remnants of the dream that won't go. I stir and glance over at Margot, who saws the thin blades of her wrist back and forth beneath the thick metal cuff of her restraint. The skin is scratched to ribbons, with thin rivulets of blood rolling beneath the metal.

"What are you doing?" I whisper.

Margot turns mad eyes on me. "Got to get out of here." Her teeth chatter. She feels cold, numb. Hot. *Crazed*.

"Margot, calm down. Stop panicking and get smart."

This stops her in her tracks. "You weren't here."

I send my twin a wry smile. "I passed out. Not by choice."

"Don't *do* that," she pleads.

"I'll try not to," I promise her. "How long have I been out, do you reckon?"

Margot shakes her head. "There's no time in the grave."

It's true. There's a distinct lack of clocks, noise, anything other than the shuffling of our feet on the dirty floor or the breath in our chests. We're used to doomsday clocks. We're used to large grandfather clocks in foyers and drawing rooms that while away the hours with the Upper Circle socialites.

We're not used to tombs.

"You're hurting me." I nod my head to her wrist.

"What does it matter if you're dead?" she whispers.

"But I'm not dead."

"Will be."

"Mar," I break in patiently, "we can't afford to think like that."

My beautiful sister shakes her head. "You don't understand."

"Explain it to me, then."

For a moment I think she won't. Her face draws in on itself, shuttered and tortured, while her panic ricochets inside me. But she holds it together. "I learned some things while I was…away."

I perk up. "What kind of things?"

Margot glances around, worrying at her lips. "Do you think it's safe to talk here?"

I consider this. Though I can see no evidence of listening devices, it doesn't mean there aren't any. "Safer to assume not."

She nods. "Once they get what they want from us, they

plan on killing us."

My tone turns sharp as a knife. "How do you know this?"

"Something Leo said." She hides her face behind her hair.

"You tell me what you know. Right now," I warn.

She doesn't look at me as she nods, just sits behind the shiny curtain of her hair as though contemplating something. Then she raises her head and shrugs. "What does it matter if we're going to die anyway?" I open my mouth to protest when she tugs at her wrist cuffs. "While I was with him, I was put through so many more Protocols. But he was angry. Like Father with the rabble. Remember?" A ghost of a smile pulls at Margot's lips. "Leo said his partners had betrayed him. That's why I had to go through so much more, because he had to get it first."

"What? Get what, Mar?" I burn with anger. How could they treat her this way? And then I heat for another reason: how could Margot keep something so important from me?

But Margot shakes her head again. "Don't know. Something about our blood. Mine. They had...plans."

I nod. "The babies. I know." Sharp lightning bolts of pain crack through me. "Mar, get a hold of yourself," I tell her sternly, "I can't think through this." I take a deep breath. *Turn it off; just turn it off,* Jared's voice whispers to me. I've done it before, but never with my sister so near. The link between us doesn't disappear completely, but Margot's overwhelming emotions fade to a dull roar. "So what was it?"

"What?"

"The plan? What was being betrayed?"

"Plague serum. One for them—a real cure. And for everyone else a temporary cure they could control to make gobs of money."

The chains rattle on my wrist as I sputter. "A-And you're

only thinking of telling me this *now*?"

"You can't believe anything they say," she argues.

"I'm beginning to think I can't believe a word *you* say."

It's the meanest thing I've ever said to Margot. And as I stare at my sister, the person I know best in the world, I can't help but think she's a stranger.

"How can you—" she starts defensively.

But my anger spills over like a storm cloud, and I unleash it on her. "How dare you keep this from me, Margot? You may have information that could have prevented this. You could know things that are so important to our future well-being, to our *family*, yet you selfishly decided to keep them to yourself. You kept them from *me*, Margot." I can feel my face flush, my skin hot and bursting in time with the painful throb of my skull. I turn my head, unable to even look at my sister.

"You don't understand, Lucy. They left me there."

Something about Margot's tone has me drawing back. "Who?"

"Mother and Father. They took off. Two days after we arrived."

I roll my eyes. "Of course they did. What did you expect?"

"They didn't even say goodbye!" my sister cries. Tears track down her pretty, haunted face. I reckon the sting of knowing that Mr. and Mrs. Lukas Fox put their own ambitions above everyone else—even above their favorite daughter—has been more than Margot can bear.

"*I* didn't leave you there, Mar." And when it's clear she can't take this in, I change course. "Do you know where they went? As opposed to the 'I don't know' line you've been throwing me?" The words crack out like ice. I may understand what lies behind my sister's treachery, but that doesn't mean I'm ready to forgive her. Or let her off the hook.

"No. But…" Her words trail off. She sucks in her quivering lower lip. I feel her misery and guilt, heavy as a black cloud, and marvel at the fact that she has hidden this so well from me.

"Tell me," I press her. "*Tell me*, Margot."

"H-He never said it outright, but I couldn't shake the feeling that our parents were counted among Resnikov's betrayers. He became so angry after they left and after that…everything went off the rails."

"Do you remember anything specific?"

Margot shakes her head. With her hair bouncing around her face and her eyes wide and wild, she looks like a lost little girl. *But she's not a little girl any longer.* The traitorous words echo through me with all the power of a bullet. Because suddenly I am keenly aware that regardless of what has happened, everyone has worn kid gloves around my sister. We've been treating her like a child. Letting her get away with this. Even me.

And now she'll have to clean up her mess, I muse angrily. If we survive. "Fine. Do you have any suspicions as to who his other partners might have been?"

Margot shakes her head again. Her tears leave behind pale tracks on her cheeks. "No names or anything. But I get the sense the other partners were in Dominion, too."

"Why do you say that?"

She shrugs. "He kept having his people set up secure transcontinental calls. And some of the network security protocols seemed Upper Circle."

Our father liked to brag about the security his job came with. The encryption process for his "diplomacy" calls was tighter than the Senate's.

"You saw them?"

"No," Margot mumbles. "They'd throw me out of the room by the time the passwords were pulled up."

"Then how?"

"Same blue screen."

Right. With shore-to-shore Protocols, they'd set up a secure portal. If the partner was from Dominion's Upper Circle. *If he was a member of the government.*

"You reckon he's a senator or something?"

"Something like that." Margot shrugs. "I don't think he was talking to our father."

My mind buzzes so fiercely I almost miss Margot's next bombshell. "…just want to know what happened to him. If he survived, I mean."

She's talking about Resnikov. The man who kidnapped her, who nearly kidnapped me, as well. The man who took her stolen eggs and made monsters out of them. "Why?" I earnestly want to know. "What good can come from knowing the fate of that monster? Does it really matter?"

Margot stares at the rough, red-hewn wall before us, dry-eyed once again. And then she drops the mother of all bombs.

"I need to know if I'm a widow."

18

I'm surprised at how measured and calm my voice is. "What are you even talking about?"

Margot's face flames with embarrassment. "I-I didn't want to tell you."

I picture Leo Resnikov, his face a mask against a room on fire. His eyes haunting my sister, raking over her as though he owned her. Because he thought he did own her. The way he'd kissed me—thinking it was her. A kiss of pure possession.

"Why?" But she won't answer—can't answer as she bursts into tears. "Mar. Mar—stop it," I say, cool as ice. "We don't have time for this right now."

She looks out at me from under a dirty lock of hair, eyes red-rimmed and angry. "You're always so perfect. You always know what to do. I hate it, Lu. I can't stand feeling like I never get anything right." A bright, hot strip of her jealousy rips through me.

What is going on with you, Margot? It never occurred to me that my sister could harbor, let alone hide, such awful feelings for me. But I don't have time right now to process or deal with it. I have to get smart. And I have to get Margot back on task. There are things we need to do.

Jared has drilled it into me again and again. *If you're ever in a real bind, never just sit there. Never just let it be. You have brains, Princess. Use them.* And then he'd repeat his instructions as though I were a child. At the time, he'd wanted to warn me about the dangerous game I'd been playing, gathering information for Storm.

And now I'm in a real bind, a life-and-death situation, and I'm grateful that his words come flooding back to me.

"Listen, Mar," I whisper. "We need to focus. We don't know how long it will take for them to find us — "

"*If* they ever find us."

I shake my head. "No, they'll find us," I say. What had Serena told me? *I can see your blood through walls, Lucy-Lu.* "In the meantime, though, we need to do our part. What do we know about these people?"

"Why don't we just sit tight, then, if you're so convinced they'll find us? What if we bungle things?" Margot gazes steadily back at me, her face bathed in shadows.

"We know Father Wes is here — or was. We know they want us to cooperate. We know what they're after." *It's in the blood.* No need to voice it.

Margot hiccups. "They don't make sense because they're nuts who believe in some prophecy. And — and they've got terrible fashion sense."

My head splits with pain as I crack a slight smile. "But they haven't killed us yet."

"What are you saying? They're not going to kill us?"

"I'm saying they have a need for us. For now. We can use that as leverage."

Her voice rises. "To do what?"

"Shhh. Quiet-quiet time," I tell my wild-eyed sister. "Did Father not teach you anything?" I joke, trying to penetrate the fog Margot has wrapped around herself. "Gather your wits, Mar. Pay attention." Her eyes narrow as she blinks and focuses.

I clench and uncurl my fingers several times, trying to break free of the sharp pins and needles, and tap two fingers on my leg. Margot closes her eyes with a shiver, then nods.

Then I hatch my plan.

"My hands are numb," I explain to the broad-shouldered Brother Noah. For good measure, I send him a small, apologetic smile with a bit of teeth. I wiggle my bum on the chair. "Let me get up and walk around the room a minute first?" The tray of food he's brought me sits untouched on my lap, but not because it looks about as appealing as a room full of corpses.

He makes me wait another thirty seconds before taking up the tray and letting me get to my feet. I'm shaky, and for a moment the room spins so hard I wonder if I'll be able to move. Margot must be worried about it, too, as she spies me from under her hair.

The door to our cell room isn't closed. It's clear as day they're not worried about escape. As I walk by the metal door, I count two Watchers standing guard just outside, long hoods cutting shadows on their faces. A few more steps and I'm at the far wall. I brush my toe against the dirt and stumble, holding out my hand to catch myself. In the far corner, at the ceiling, is tucked a small black box. It sits there watching us like a spider.

"Stand up," Noah says.

"Sorry." I pull away from the wall sheepishly. "Need to get my sea legs under me."

Brother Noah looks not the least bit impressed. "Hurry up."

"Yes." I stagger down the length of the hall, my hands rough against the caked dirt walls. Here and there my fingers trace through the red, leaving faint pink flakes on my fingertips.

There's nothing else to discover on the walls, so I stagger back and fall onto our captor's burly chest. "Must be hard working down here, like a rat in a maze. I'm sorry you're stuck babysitting us." I give him a shy look. "I'm so dizzy," I tell him as he grabs the flesh of my arms, holds me there against him for a second or two longer than he should, a slight smile splitting his not-unhandsome face.

"You promise you'll come back to let me use the bathroom after?" I say it like I trust him, like he's a good man. Our jailor, though, seems fairly immune to my innocent act. He nods once before disappearing out the flat metal door.

Margot examines me as I daintily take up the tray and shove the mystery meat into my mouth.

"Get everything you wanted?" she asks drily.

All I can do is nod. I tap once, then lift my finger in the direction of the camera. "Eyes on us. Likely ears, too."

"Well, we've always been good at giving a show, haven't we, Lu?"

I swallow past the disgusting lump of food and smile at my twin. "Haven't we just?"

"Speaking of which...don't you think you were laying it on a little thick back there?"

I bat my eyes at my sister. "It worked, didn't it? He didn't have a key on him. I suspect it's bolted from the outside, which is why they have guards rather than just locking us in. Besides" — my smile splits into a grin — "I bet you a Dominion dollar that he lets me have more time than you in the bathroom."

"You and your little pantomimes." Margot wheezes and rolls her eyes. "Where did you learn to do this, sister dear?"

"Only from the best, dear sister." I smile sweetly. "From you."

It's the voices that pull us from our light doze, the sleep that fills uncertain hours. Black-red rain had been falling behind my eyelids. The sky was a black cloth, wrapping over the crumbling ruins of Dominion City as I gazed down at it. Tears. Endless tears. The empty park was a wasteland. The canopy of the giant tree, like a weeping eye, stared back at me.

I pull my head up, sure that someone is in the hallway just outside our room. But no — I turn my head. The sound comes from somewhere inside. Just the hushed-hushed murmur of someone speaking quietly. *Or with the volume turned down low*.

The ploy worked. Jared would be so proud.

I had finished bathing myself as best I could in the rust-filled sink. Noah grunted and nodded as I stretched my arms behind my head and chirruped brightly, "How is Father Westfall able to speak to us from wherever he is?"

"Didn't you ever hear curiosity killed the cat?"

"I'm okay with being a cat. Cats have nine lives," I prevaricated, stretching out the remaining tether of my freedom.

"You better hope you got nine lives." Brother Noah snorted

before nodding up at the ceiling at the camera eyeing us at the end of the hall. "The cameras are one- way. The sound sure ain't."

"Oh." I was actually startled that he'd answered. "You mean I can hear you guys talking from — from wherever you are, if only you turned on the sound?"

Noah took two steps and opened a small, discreet panel in the wall. Tucked inside was a vid screen, buttons and dials. He fiddled with one and the hallway suddenly filled with the static of dead air. Voices in the hallway. The scuffle of shoes on dirt. Quick as air, he spun the volume down and shut fast the panel.

But he must not have turned it down all the way, I realize now. It's the only explanation I can come up with for the strange, disembodied voices we hear.

"...behind schedule. We'll have to ramp up production if we're going to make the deadline." I'd know that distinctive, rolling preacher-man voice anywhere. It's the voice that haunts my nightmares.

Westfall.

"Increase the draws, then," a second voice nags.

A pause ripples through the conversation. "If we do that, they could die, which would jeopardize the supply if something were to go wrong."

"What could go wrong?" The other voice rises. "I'm living proof, aren't I? It works. It's successful. They're no longer needed."

That voice. *That voice*, my mind yells at me as Margot pulls herself from a drowse and looks at me. I shake my head, draw a short line on my thigh. Quiet-quiet time. Time to be like mice in the walls.

"That's not good business."

"Look, Westfall, how much proof do you need? The bombs worked, didn't they? Look at that damned tree. You can't even burn it down. Remember? We tested the technology and it worked. Now that we have the girls you'll see. It works in humans, too."

"It's not meant to be a full cure. The girls are insurance."

The bombs…The girls. *Us.* It makes a horrible sense. They must have used the same kind of acceleration technology in the magic bombs as they did when they engineered us. *So how do our captors know what we were made with?*

"Since when are preachers businessmen? Why don't you leave the heavy thinking to us?"

"Watch yourself. You don't get to make those decisions."

"Yes." The voice rolls out its vowels. Not quite Upper Circle but close. Not quite Laster, either. But something about the snarky, arrogant tones…

My eyes seek out Margot's as recognition finally dawns on me.

"Don't forget. The partner is on his way, Westfall. Prepare yourself," says a voice carrying the twang of the country.

The voice belongs to Senator Theodore Nash.

My mind is buzzing so hard I nearly miss their next words. "…Next Protocols… Sending in Noah now."

Margot and I immediately drop our heads, feigning sleep. The voices disappear, as though they've walked into another room. And just in time: Noah tromps his way into the room, a brother with a tray bearing the quaint instruments of Protocols torture by his side.

They don't bother to wake us. Noah simply bends down and pushes up Margot's sleeve, taking only the faintest trouble to disinfect her skin before plunging in the needle attached to the bag.

Her blood ebbs quickly, painlessly after the first sharp jab "What are you doing?" Margot asks in a sleepy voice.

"Nothing." He doesn't bother to look at her. But his eye drapes over me like a secret. Then it's my turn. He takes his time with me, running rough fingers against my arm before jabbing in the needle.

"Please don't," I start to say. Noah shakes his head and nods to the corner of the room where the camera watches us. His fingers tap a small beat on my arm as the blood trickles out. I feel light-headed more quickly than I can ever remember. A sharp pain throbs behind my eyes. "Can I have some water, please?" I must look terrible. Noah pulls out the needle as I begin to slump over, calling out at someone in the hall.

But for me, the world slips away, and behind it, a screen of black-red rain.

Margot is humming a song I've never heard before. I open my eyes. She stops her humming mid-bar. "Thank the gods," she says in a breathy voice before taking up the chorus again.

The walls are still the same: earthen and crumbly like moldy cheese overlaid with the stain of red paint. *Evolve or die.* There's a tang of blood where I must have bitten my tongue. I blink at my twin. She stares back at me like a stranger.

"Picture," she says in a bright voice.

A game, then. A game to keep us safe while we converse.

"A bed, feather duvet. Soft like a cloud. After a bath, of

course." I frown down at my wrinkled, sore body. The pain in my head is gone, but it's been replaced by something large and thick that keeps me from thinking too quickly. I feel my eyebrows knit together unhappily. "Did they give me something?"

Margot nods, another deep, fake smile on her beautiful face. "Uh-huh. Okay, my turn."

I nod grudgingly. "Okay, fine. Picture."

"Knights coming to the rescue." She sighs. "Combing through the city until they find us."

The True Borns are looking for us? How does she know? I think feverishly.

"A life of no more Protocols." She sighs again, dramatic and heavy, and pulls against her restraints.

I need to know more. I throw in a note of teasing. "Father and Mother giving us a loving embrace?"

"No." Margot shakes her head. The mask of the game slips. "You don't understand. Father and Mother. They left me there with him."

"Who—the Russian?"

Margot blushes. "God, I want to tuck my hair behind my ears so badly. Yes, the Russian. Him." The blush floats scarlet down her neck, tints the tip of her pearly ear that I can only just get a peek of.

"Picture a crush," I throw back. I only mean to tease, but my sister's face takes on a stormy look. Her emotions pulse through me like lightning. And it's only then, as her walls collapse, that I see.

"Oh my gods," I murmur, unable to stop staring at her as though she's a complete and utter stranger. "You *love* him."

There is a long beat of silence between us before she throws back defensively, "So?"

"So nothing. How did you manage to keep this from me?"

I say with a note of marvel.

Her lips come down over her teeth, turning her smile into a broken string of pearls. "You always did think I couldn't escape you, little sister. But I'll find a way."

It's a terrible thing to say. I don't even know how to respond. I fidget and struggle to get comfortable on the chair. The coin at my neck jangles against my skin.

"You think maybe hubby is the partner?" I forget all about the pretext of the game as I stare hard at Margot.

"No, I don't think so."

"Why?"

"Because. Because he'd never—"

The sound of footsteps cuts off her answer, not in the hallway outside the room but on the elusive sound system. Westfall's familiar voice carries over the air. "…I told him not to take too much. We could accidentally kill them. I told him you'd be here to assess—"

But it is the accompanying voice that has the skin on the back of my neck skittering.

"Gather more genetic samples and then we'll see," the cold, clipped voice orders. "We'll take no chances until we're certain that we can manufacture it. And we need a little more time to study our little human guinea pig."

"Of course." I can practically hear Father Wes bowing and scraping.

Margot mouths the word I cannot bear to think, the man whose life consists of people bowing and scraping to him. I picture the man: the tight line of his shoulders. The hands, strong and squeezing the life out of a pair of black leather gloves.

Father?

19

Bright spots flicker past my eyes like the lights when the power is about to go out. The room goes silent, save the sound of Margot's ragged breathing and my own shallow pull of air. I feel as though I've been sucker punched.

I reckon we both have, my sister and I.

The idea that the secret partner was Resnikov, somehow miraculously survived from the destruction of his factory, has crossed my mind a time or two. Perhaps it was someone from the Upper Circle, I'd thought. Senator Kain was a suspect on my list.

But this—this betrayal cuts so deep that for a moment I think it will kill me.

Tears track down Margot's face. I can feel her retreating, the stabbing wound too deadly.

What of our mother—does she know about this? Is she in on it as well?

But even as I ask the question, I sift back through the evidence and piece together an awful story.

Mother at our Reveal, telling us that she's sorry.

Resnikov's old scientist, with his tale of two girls born from a cocktail in a test tube.

Margot and I still don't quite know what we are, let alone who. Yet the most important question of all presses us with urgency. *What does our father intend to do to us?*

"Wh-What do we do when they come back?" My sister's words bring me to my senses. Because of course, she's right. They will be back.

Anger rattles my already shaky bones, makes me flush hot and cold. My teeth chatter in my jaw until it feels like I'm grinding glass. And still we sit there. Dead ducks.

Margot's hushed voice cuts through the red fog of anger. "They'll kill us."

I shake my head. "No, he'd never."

"Yes. Yes, Lucy. You need to face this." Margot's bottom lip quivers with upset.

But how can I? How do I accept that my own father is behind our kidnapping? Desperately, I call to mind my True Born, his eyes bright and clear, cutting through the storm of my confusion. *Think, Lu. Be smart.*

"He said 'human guinea pig.'"

"What?" Margot's voice carries low in the room.

"Not us. *A.* Singular. Human guinea pig. He wasn't talking about us."

Margot nods. "They're testing it on someone. Maybe…Leo?"

I wince at the hopeful tone of her voice. "No." I shake my

head. "Can't be. He wasn't sick."

Margot cocks her head, staring at me like a pretty bird. But I'm right—and she knows I recognize the scent of approaching death. There's been only one person who'd been sick lately, and then not.

Only one person who's evaded death's sure hand.

Theodore Nash.

The clang of the door interrupts my train of thought. In walks Brother Noah with another of the Watchers, face smeared with red, carrying a tray with drink and syringes and tubing. Noah bends down to swab my arm; I swear I can see a glint of pity in his eyes. And behind him, like a flag, the glowing red obscenity of two circles, conjoined.

It's worse this time. I wake bathed in throbbing, intense pain. Behind my eyes the black-red rain falls, mixing with my tears. And the world beneath me turns first crimson, then a luscious green, as though each inch of Dominion has been seeded with the magic bombs that transform into prayer trees.

But something is missing. Something is vanished. And when I turn and understand who it is that's missing, a howling grief takes hold of me, more desperate and terrible than anything I've ever felt in my life—

The coin around my neck jangles as my head snaps up. We're not alone.

Sitting in front of us is Westfall, his arms draped around the back of a wooden chair. *Wood*. I thought only Upper Circlers could afford wooden chairs.

The stubble on his cheeks has grown into a short, curly

beard patched with white and gray. Lines divide the flesh on his cheeks. He looks old and sick and tired. His trousers are thin blue cotton, of the cheaper variety. The pattern of his shirt, over his heart, is a colorful explosion, making it look as though he's been shot and is bleeding a rainbow. He looks us over. First one, then the other, a mad sheen to his eyes. Behind him, Brother Noah stands with his arms crossed. He gazes down at us inscrutably. A scuffling noise in the hall behind us alerts us to the fact that they are not alone.

Three feet from me, too far away to touch, Margot sits straight-backed, legs crossed at the ankle. Like she's at an Upper Circle social.

"Did you know there are ten pints of blood in a human?" He doesn't seem to expect a reply as he continues. "Girls, there are a few things we should talk about before we get down to business." Father Wes turns his attention back to me, eyes hovering at my neck. His gaze makes my skin crawl. "Where did you get that coin?" he asks with genuine curiosity.

When I don't answer, he tells me, "I could beat it out of you. Beat your sister until you tell me."

I smile a mouthful of knives. "How about we play a game? You tell me something, then I tell you something?"

Father Wes tips his head back and laughs, a deep belly laugh. "You think you're in a position to bargain, little girl?"

"I think you're not going to harm us until you get what you want."

"And what do you think we want, Little Fox?"

I stay silent as Father Wes rubs his knuckles on the back of the chair. They're raw, chapped and covered with scabs. Hands that look as though they've seen several hard winters. Now I notice them: spots on his face. Tiny scabs near his ear, one sitting above his right eye, blemishes that the beard can't hide. Recognition washes over me. A familiar feeling curls like a rotten flower in my belly.

Father Wes has the Plague, that little voice inside me insists.

"I reckon you're looking for Plague Cure." I eye him meaningfully. "And you think it's inside us somehow."

Margot shoots me a death dagger, but she doesn't know. She doesn't know what I know. Father Wes considers me anew.

"And how do you figure that?" He draws the words out slowly as he reaches around and fiddles with something at his back.

I shrug. "I'm a clever little Fox."

His grin freezes me. "And so you are." The preacher man lifts his eyes to the ceiling. "Noah, collect the blood."

Noah steps forward, his face a blank. He bends low, does his best not to prick too hard as he shoves the needle in, draws the blood. It's when he pulls a breath that I realize he's genuinely not happy with what he's been asked to do.

"It's okay," I whisper to him.

His head snaps back, and he stares at me, his face an unreadable mask. I nod slightly, letting him know I understand, though why I should be so kind to him is beyond me.

Father Wes hasn't noticed. He's still talking, and I catch only his last words. "…girls, there's something you ought to know. We intend to make the world anew, and you're going to help us. Do you know how important that makes you?"

But I've had enough of the preacher men and their grand schemes. All I want right now is answers. "Did you arrange to have Margot kidnapped at the clinic?"

That stops him cold. "What did you say?"

"Last year, before you appeared at our school. The clinic?"

For once the preacher man is without words. He stares at me, jaw and eyes hardening into a stubborn set. "What are you talking about?" he grumbles.

"Surely you had your eyes on us. Surely your young boy knew Margot had been taken. He came with another big man to get me."

It's then that I notice it. He tries to hide it, but I see it in the throbbing vein in his jaw, the twitch of his little finger. "Yes. Of course," he says. But his words are wooden, automatic. Then I know for sure.

Someone betrayed him. Someone very good at politics. Someone like—

I've only begun to process the thought when Noah finishes draining me of a pint of my blood. He makes a production of it as he turns to Margot. I wince as a new needle goes into her arm, the pain crawling through my own.

And then we all freeze as a voice ghosts over the intercom.

"Get all your men to the entrance. I don't think they'll storm us, but I'd rather not take the chance. And for pity's sake be sure to get rid of that damned preacher when you exit," says the man with the cold, clipped syllables of our father's voice.

Nash's dry tones float close before softening out of range. "He could still be helpful. His people control the city."

"But you'll be controlling all the food out there in nowhere land. All that magically abundant food. And Plague Cure. He's a complication we won't need."

We sit a frozen tableau in the tiny dungeon. Noah's hand on the needle, just pressing into Margot's arm. His increasingly uneven breathing. The mad look to Father Wes, standing now behind a halo of red circles.

In the end, it's he who breaks the silence with a grin that

turns my remaining blood cold. "Noah, leave off the needle," he drawls.

"Father." Noah obediently drops the needle on the small collections tray. As he steps back, the acolyte bows his head. But I can see the way he watches us under his lashes.

"Seems I have some housekeeping to do," Wes says after an eternity of silence. "Seems some people don't believe in my quest. But you know what?" He bends low over me. I can see each and every pore on his face, the gray-streaked stubble around his chin. Up close, the scabs are bitter and seeping. On my face, his breath is fetid, the smell of a sick man. "You know what, Miss Fox? I think all our suffering is at an end." The words, so soft and utterly menacing, spike up and down my spine.

A sudden crash sounds through the building. The ceiling booms, the walls shake. Dust trickles down from a seam in the low ceiling. Father Wes raises his eyes upward. "Looks like the cavalry has arrived," he says to no one in particular. "Noah, time for you to leave."

Noah steps forward. "But Father—"

Wes turns his head as he lumbers over to my sister. "I told you to leave. If you manage to stay alive, find me. The True Borns are here."

It's too dangerous, I think, even as my heart leaps at the news. What if they're hurt—what if Jared is hurt? Margot and I share a frantic look as Father Wes berates his man and orders him out of the room.

Margot whispers, "Love you true, Lu." Time only for those four words to be uttered, barely a sentence, before Wes's body drops a shadow across her beautiful, pale, tear-stained face.

Time stands still as something leaps, bright and shiny, in Father Wes's hand. Excruciating pain lances me through and through and keeps going. Crimson sprays everywhere, draping me in the fine spray of my sister's blood. I can't catch my breath. My heart hammers horror in my chest as I try to take gulps of air and find nothing. Nothing.

And then I feel it letting go, that thing inside me. The shimmering line between my sister and me as her eyes dull.

I am dying, I suddenly realize. No.

I feel my sister dying.

Father Wes leaves Margot slumped and bleeding in her prison chair and turns to me. "Your father thought to double-cross me? There's nothing so pure as the light of the almighty," he cries, triumphant. There's a knife in his hands. A hunting knife. A knife for hunting little girls, still sopping with my sister's blood.

He presses the knife to my neck and slices before it catches on something. He can't get it through, so he lifts the blade from my neck and tries to chew into me anew. But the grooves of his knife have stuck fast.

Warm trickles of blood flash hot. A shout. Then a flash and a bang and smoke. Father Wes abandons his knife and steps back and away.

Jared, I think as I sink into an endless black. *Jared, please save Margot*, I think desperately as I hear a rattling gurgle and know in my bones that behind me now lay two more corpses for Dominion's coffins. Father Wes and Noah have been killed.

"Jared." My voice is nothing but a gurgle as I choke on my own blood. "Margot."

I catch sight of a living nightmare, primal rage twisting an inhuman face into a death mask. He's got something in his hands, and it isn't until I blink once, twice, freeing my eyes from blood, that I realize it's a head.

It's Father Wes's head, the eyes dull and open in terror.

Jared screams, and the room stops. Jared's beast nose twitches and the awful scream tears at me again. I reckon he can smell our fear, the galloping arrival of our deaths. Because in that instant I know, I know, that I, too, am hurtling into death.

He screams in that panther voice. I think he's calling my name. It rattles me back to my senses, long enough to mouth the words, *Save her*, before the sparking brilliance of Nolan Storm's thorny crown swarms into view, and Jared's blood-soaked hands.

The world tilts on its axis.

And me? I slump into nothingness, hand in hand with my sister.

20

Screaming. There's screaming in my head, the sound of a siren's wail that I can't make my throat do. And the dull certainty, the silent, empty room inside me.

Margot.

So this is what it's like to be one instead of two.

The loneliness is more than I can bear. I expect to burst into flames, to be swallowed by the nothingness of death. *How can I still be alive?* I must be alive, I reckon, because there is an endless ocean of pain. A wail bubbles up, but the pain in my throat is excruciating. It comes out more like a mewl.

Someone squeezes my hand. My head is frozen in place, but I know by the subtle weight and feel, even before turning my eyes, that it's Jared. For the longest time he doesn't say anything, just stares at me with a look so deadly I'm surprised I don't die again. I must have died, if only for a time.

I watch the bobble of his Adam's apple as he swallows. He

licks those perfect lips, lips that up until a few days ago I would have watched with keen interest. But now…

"Don't try to talk." He peels back a slick of hair from my face. A frown puckers his forehead. His eyes are hollow sockets tinged the color of a bruise. I notice he looks thinner, less of himself somehow. His cheekbones have grown sharper for some reason other than his own shifting.

It's as though I'm seeing him through a distance of a thousand years. He's so close, but he might as well be on the moon, for all I can touch him, all I can absorb. I am frozen and lifeless, a dead thing. A Laster's corpse on the side of the road. I pull my hand from his. I just want him to leave me to die, but I can't get any words out.

Raising a hand to my throat, I realize why. The bandages are thick. A burning pain accompanies my own swallowed tears. Cautiously, slowly, each inch a bout of torture, I turn onto my side on the bed, away from him and his prying eyes.

"Lu." Jared's voice is tortured, but then he says nothing. He keeps his vigil by my bedside for a long time, silent as a statue, until I hear him slip out the door like a whisper.

But I don't look. I don't say a word.

No one should have to see a grief like this.

Time has lost all meaning. Someone has pulled the blinds back. In the glass, I spy a spitting electric blue, shimmering and dancing like flames. I don't want to turn over, but something in Storm's voice commands me.

"Lucy, I know you're awake. Look at me."

He says it gently enough, but his tone makes it clear there

is no room for debate. I turn far enough to see him where he stands before I float my eyes away. Storm has his hands in the pockets of exquisitely tailored trousers. He pulls them out and places them on the bed, lowering himself into a chair. He says nothing for a long time. It gives me the chance to study him closer.

This is Nolan Storm in mourning clothes. Black shirt, stiff and buttoned. Black suit, perfectly tailored to his muscled body. But it's his face I study. There is more stubble across the hollows of his cheeks than I've ever seen before. Smudged purple circles rim his eyes, which are haunted and filled with something I'd as soon call war. And then there is his spectral crown. The ends have grown longer, thicker, their jutting protrusions tangling more intricately than before.

"We need to talk." He doesn't move his hands from the bed, where they lay like an open book. He doesn't try to touch me, for which I'm grateful. I stare at the ceiling, my throat still a raw, throbbing mess, and listen while his words rumble over me. "The Watchers are gone. You're safe now."

He doesn't understand. Did he see? *Does he know?*

His voice gentles even more. "Nothing can fix what was broken…what happened to Margot." He blinks and closes his eyes momentarily as his crown of bone flares hot white. When he opens his eyes again, it's as though an alien god has replaced him, as his gunmetal gray eyes roil like the clouds of a Flux storm. "By tomorrow morning the preachers and the Upper Circle will receive identical letters." And when his lip flips up on one side in a grimace of a smile, I want nothing more than to cower under the covers. "That letter will tell them in no uncertain terms what I will do to Dominion City should anyone rise against me or my people again."

What will you do? I want to ask. But I reckon I know enough.

Nolan Storm is going to tear down Dominion, brick by brick. He'll kill them all, as impersonal as a hurricane. He'll wipe them off the face of the earth.

I feel my own lips stretching into the suggestion of a feral smile.

Good.

W hen I next see the sky, it is wearing its familiar white robe. Kira holds my arm like I'm an invalid, much to my horror, though I'll admit I'm weaker than I'd like, and escorts me down the elevator.

"Don't worry, Lucy." Kira says with a wry smile, pulling me closer. "You're not my type." She's clearly trying to coax a smile from me, but my face remains a frozen mask.

They tell me fresh air is good. I would argue with them that Dominion has no fresh air, but I've no desire to speak. Despite the bandages having been removed from my ripped-up throat, I don't even know if I can.

I haven't seen Jared since the night of my return to Storm's keep. Haven't seen him, heard from him. He's probably forgotten all about me. I tell myself it's for the best.

As bleak as I feel, Kira puts on fake cheer like she does four-inch stilettos. "Hey, wouldn't it be nice to take a load off and watch the world go by?"

I let her lead me to the bench near the building's entrance. We sit awkwardly as I watch the occasional city bird swoop down on the hunt for food. They've gotten fat and bloated from the corpses, those birds, practically becoming another species. Over the tops of buildings farther downtown, a canopy of lush greenery explodes and spills. The Prayer Tree. The air is clammy, as it is before a day of rain. I can smell it in the air. Iron and dirt.

Like blood.

Kira is far gentler to me than I knew she could be, though she's still about as tactful as a machine gun. She glances at the scar cutting across my throat. "Looks good, Lucy. Almost like it didn't happen. I've never seen a wound heal like that before."

I wouldn't know. There had been no point in me looking at the wound on my throat. Mirrors are for the living.

Tentatively I run a finger lightly over the track where the knife's blade had kissed me. I feel a line, nothing more. Below that, Ali's necklace. I pick up the coin, feeling its ancient weight, its strange heat, in my hand.

"You know," Kira muses, "I think that necklace might just have saved your life. The cut should have severed everything," she tells me with professional interest. "The necklace was wedged so deep in there it had clotted right into the wound. By the time we got you to Doc Raines, she had to cut into you to get it out. They had to work around it, though. Couldn't get it off you."

I stare hard at the lethal assassin beside me. I gulp past the painful knot in my throat. When I finally speak, the sound of my damaged voice, a low, guttural thing, shocks us both. "Where is Ali?"

Kira blows out a deep, whistling breath that pushes the bangs off her face and looks away. "They didn't tell you."

I shake my head. Something terrible knots in my belly.

"Ali...went in with us. He was pretty good, too. But the

Watchers had guns, Lucy. He—Ali...Gods, Lucy, it shouldn't be me telling you this." The assassin's mask slips, and I see genuine regret in her eyes. "He didn't make it."

It's the dream that shakes me awake. The same dark red rain. My tears mix with it, turning the hills and fields around Dominion a blooming crimson. Only this time, I understand its cryptic message. *Margot.*

And this time, when I open my eyes and blink away the tears, feeling the hot wetness on my pillow, I also know I'm not alone.

He can tell the moment I shift from sleep to wakefulness. One long, lean leg comes uncrossed in the chair across the room. Beside his rumpled form, on the ground, is a litter of pillows he has undoubtedly stomped on. The lamp beside the chair switches on, throwing off enough light to see him by. Enough light for him to see me. He runs a hand across his forehead, as though it pains him, his eyebrows drawing in. I can just make out the white pattern of one of his favorite shirts. Across the front dances a skeleton, which somehow matches the frayed holes of his jeans. He looks...tired. Lost. Defeated. The silence between us lengthens.

"You're alive. I don't know how to tell you what it was like when I thought... You were sitting in that chair all covered in blood, and I thought for sure you were dead." After a few moments, he calls out again from his perch across the room. "Can I...can I come sit with you, Lu? Please?"

It's not Jared's way to be tentative or unsure of himself. Jared does what he pleases. And I hate that I've taken this away from him, too, like another little death. Still, the moment draws out before I decide to say yes. A moment longer than he likes, I reckon, as I hear a rumble, low and deep, in his throat. "Lu."

When I finally nod, Jared all but flies out of his chair, faster than my eyes can track. His weight sinks the mattress. There's a look to him more wild than wild. His eyes marble: green, indigo, green, indigo, like exotic traffic lights. He's not been sleeping, I can tell. The smudges beneath his eyes make him look as though he's been punched.

"You look terrible," I rasp.

His laugh comes out in short, chippy bursts. "Thanks. I know." He eyes me. "You don't look so hot yourself." I don't have any reply to this, and he doesn't seem to expect one. "Sorry. I didn't mean…" He combs anxious fingers through his hair, the blond skeins standing straight up. "I'm just…I'm just so damned glad you're alive." I stare at him in wonder as his chest heaves. "I've been going through hell, sitting by your bedside whenever you're asleep. Knowing what you must think of me. Finally I couldn't take it anymore. I decided I had to be here anyway."

I shake my head in confusion. "I don't know what you're talking about. What are you talking about…what I think of you?"

"I'm sorry I wasn't there for you. I'm so sorry I was too late." Jared takes my hand in his two. He raises my hand to his lips, savoring the scent of me before flipping my hand over and gently pressing a kiss to my palm, another to the soft skin at my wrist. The kiss ignites me.

My body leaps to fire. My mind slams that door firmly shut. But not before Jared murmurs, "You even smell different now."

A flare of annoyance ignites inside me. "That's because I'm dead."

He blinks owlishly, as though I've spoken in a foreign tongue. "What?"

"Don't you get it?" I wrench my hand from his. "Don't you understand? I'm. Dead." I don't bother to glare; I simply turn my face to the wall. I can practically hear his horror as he continues to sit there. Slowly, creaking off the bed, Jared walks out of the room. Maybe for the last time. Maybe I've finally pushed him away for good this time.

It's all right, I remind myself. Because the dead don't have regrets. The dead don't love.

21

From here, high above the city, safe in Storm's office, the heavy twirl of smoke among the buildings doesn't seem that sinister. I know this is a distortion, like seeing the world through glass. If I were standing on the ground, I'd know that houses were on fire or that there was a battle on the streets. Or that the Rovers are clearing the dead.

"Rovers," a deep, masculine voice behind me says, confirming my suspicions. My reflection in the glass, one hand laid across the faint track of scar on my neck, disappears in the glow of the magnificent, forked lightning around Storm's head. As he comes to stand behind me, I feel his heat, power emanating from him with a heavy throb. And where I once would have described his scent as the loamy smell of a forest, now all around him is the smell of ozone.

The scent of a gathering storm.

I nod, turning my back on the chaos of Dominion, and stare

up into the handsome, chiseled face of my guardian. With a tilt
of his heavy head he says, "The Watchers tried to burn down
the Prayer Tree again last night." That explains the smoke, then.
"My ears on the ground inform me that, now that Wes is dead,
his people don't quite know which way to turn."

"Nash? The council?"

Storm nods and leans his hulking frame against the glass.
From here, so close, it looks as though he's about to fall out over
the world. *But he wouldn't break*, I think to myself. *Unlike me.*

"Nash hasn't been seen or heard from since we stormed
the house."

My still-ravaged voice comes out broken. "My father?"

Storm tosses his head again, the gray of his eyes molten
lava. "No."

I stare down at my hands. The skin around my wrists
remains a delicate pink as it heals. I whisper, "You believe me.
Don't you?"

I told Storm, of course, as soon as I'd been able to hold a pen.
Wrote down for him what Margot and I had heard, what we'd
seen—how complete our betrayal has been. Until this moment,
though, I don't think I realized I expect he won't believe me.
And I wouldn't blame him; I hardly believe it myself. It grows
quiet in the room. I hear the heavy hand of the clock fall over
Storm's desk and marvel at how meaningless time has become
to me. I hiccup on a sob, holding it in. I have no desire to cry
in front of Nolan Storm.

But he takes my chin in gentle fingers. I feel power throbbing
through his skin as he forces me to look at him. With his other
hand he gently brushes my hair from my eyes. A stray tear
breaks free and courses down my cheek, but he brushes it away.
All gentleness, though his eyes still burn winter.

"Lucy." His voice is so soft I almost don't hear him. In a bizarre parody of what Jared had done, Storm takes one of my raw-boned wrists into his hand and presses a slight kiss to the thin skin. "I know you feel lost, but you're not alone. You have us. You have me. And I'm not going anywhere."

I nod my thanks, unable to speak for the tears that would threaten like rain and feeling more than a little uneasy at sea. Standing on weak and trembling legs, I face the man god who has, perhaps against reason, taken me in.

I croak over the giant lump in my throat. "What would make me feel better is if we destroy them. I want to destroy them."

The planes of Storm's cheeks stand out under the shadowy glow of his thorny crown. Slowly, so slowly, he nods.

"Yes." I almost think I've imagined his answer until he says it again. "Yes, Lucy. We will destroy them." His voice is deceptively calm as he sits down casually on the couch, as though we're discussing the weather at an Upper Circle tea.

But his eyes tell me everything I need to know. Nolan Storm will help me avenge Margot.

It's a bleak day, the color of ash, when Mohawk and Jared drive me up to the gates of Grayguard. The security guards have been replaced, I notice. A line of shiny new faces mans the fence, the blue of their uniforms crisp against the old stone of the school.

Jared turns around to look at me from the driver's seat, his face inscrutable. "Are you sure you're ready for this?" he asks in a neutral voice.

"No," I tell him truthfully. "But I'm doing it anyway."

Beside me, Mohawk smiles a terrible smile. "Good for you,

Dolly. And anyway, you won't be alone." Mohawk opens the door, her sharp gaze sweeping over the terrain before holding out a hand to indicate I can exit.

They'll take no more chances, Storm told me.

Mohawk's strange print skin sticks out under her white cutoff shirt and long shorts. I'm certain Grayguard has never seen the likes of one such as her, I think, recalling the True Born merc with blue-tinged skin who I used to see a lifetime ago. I sigh and let Jared pull open the doors and usher me through. His fingers burn at my back, and for a moment I long to press into them, to ease the suffering. But I can't let myself unwind.

We've arrived in the middle of the day, hoping to avoid the crush. But it seems we've come between classes. The halls are packed with uniformed bodies pressed into polished leather boots. The air is thick with their chatter and laughing, overlaid with the smell of wax polish. And it's through this crowd that I walk, two True Borns at my side.

The bodies part almost magically. The din falls mute. Our footsteps echo on the hard marble as I steer toward the bank of lockers at the far end of the hall. I don't look at anyone as I pass.

The bell rings and, save for us, the hallway remains a frozen tableau. Then a rumbling of feet and the bodies disappear into heavy-doored rooms coated in bulletproof glass.

Mohawk holds open a large canvas bag into which I stuff Margot's books and a Grayguard jacket. She's closed the bag and makes to leave as I twirl open the lock on the adjacent compartment.

"What are you doing?" she asks. Jared, for his part, wisely says nothing.

"Cleaning out both our lockers."

"You don't need to do that."

"Yes, I do."

"You're coming back—"

"No. I'm not."

"C'mon, Lu." Mohawk steps toward me.

I raise my palm. I need the distance as bitter pain wriggles through my bones like the ravages of Plague. "No. And we're not talking about this." I slam shut the locker door but stop short, staring down the long, deserted hallway. The whole point of coming back to Grayguard was to move forward with our lives. With our degrees in hand, we'd be stepping into our pedigree, claiming back an inch or so of the life we'd left behind. But now, with Margot gone, I can't seem to see the point. *And anyway*, I think cynically, *Storm will make them give the degree to me now, finished or not.*

Leaning against the lockers, looking utterly relaxed, Jared tilts his head. A blond curl bounces across his cheek. "Let's take a walk."

I shake my head and pull my few remaining things to my chest. Doesn't he know I'm barely keeping it in check? Doesn't he understand? I can't be here. "No."

"Come on," he says again, this time taking my arm. I watch his eyes go to Mohawk—telling her to stay put, no doubt—as Jared hands her my things and half drags me toward the inner courtyard door. "Let's go to our secret spot."

The benches are the same as when I'd last been here, the stone mossy with polluted rain, the scattered tables bare. Jared came to speak to me in this very spot what seems like a thousand years ago. I'd last sat with Margot, I realize, back when Ali was sneaking in here every day. I fight back another wave of grief for the both of them, and pull a breath in through my nose, almost as if I could scent her again.

But it's Jared I smell, no one else. Jared, with his cinnamon and male scent, and whose body moves lithely and gracefully beside me.

"Let go of me," I tell him woodenly, which he ignores. He leads me to a seam where the walls meet in the octagonal yard, pressing my back against the warm stone and brick. Still he doesn't let loose my arms. My skin sends traitorous signals up and down my body as he continues to gaze at me as though I'm some meal he's contemplating. "I *said*, let go of me." I try to shake him off but know I'm nothing next to True Born strength.

"Cut it out, Princess. You're not impressing anyone out here." This catches me off guard.

"What did you say?"

"You heard me." The words are deceptively mild. He reaches out and oh so gently strokes hair off my face, leaving in its wake an electric frisson of pleasure.

I swat at his hand. "Don't."

His body is so close to mine. Barely an inch stands between us. Jared looks at my hair, his fingers tangling with the strands so that I can barely think, barely breathe. "Remember when I told you to shut off all those impressions Margot was sending you? Remember that?" he murmurs. His face bends closer so I can see the scar near his lips.

But my heart is so heavy. So heavy. Doesn't he understand? We were betrayed by those who supposedly loved us best. And Margot…she was all I had left. Without my sister, I don't even know who I am. "What, are you telling me to just shut down? To cut Margot out of my heart? Well, I can't do that. And I don't need your stupid advice, Jared." I weakly try to push him away, but he moves closer. My hands become trapped against his solid flesh. He reaches up and frames my face with his hands, cradling me there against the wall. My body throbs with his nearness.

Jared just smiles a funny half smile, as though he can tell what effect he has on me. "No. I was going to say, before you so rudely interrupted me, that right now you need to do the opposite."

Annoyance flickers through me as I stare at him. "I don't understand you. And leave me alone."

"No." He smiles tenderly, his lips wide and generous. I can't stop looking at them.

"What did you say?"

"I said no, Princess. You're not going to shut me out. I won't let you. So what I need you to do is this. I need you to let it all in. All of it. Every last single ounce of it. Let it in, Lu. I'll be here. I'll be right here. I'll catch you, will hold it with you."

I stare at him, the wildness of my heart just inches from the surface. "No!"

"Yes," he insists. "Yes, Lucy. You need to feel her."

"I *am* feeling her!" I stomp my feet.

"No, you're not. You're letting her kill you."

I pull back, aghast. "H-How can you say that?" The angry sparks within me fan into an inferno. "How can you say that?" It's as though I'm watching outside of myself when I first strike him. A punch to the shoulder. He doesn't move, not even an inch, which makes me even angrier. I haul back and slap at his chest, watch him barely twitch. "How dare you?" I scream, punching him in the arm and chest for all I'm worth. But he simply stands there, a look in his eyes as wild with sorrow as I am, like a lost thing. A cruel and useless thing.

And then I'm done. One of my hands goes to his chest. There's a red mark on his cheek that I don't even remember leaving. I half sob, half hiccup, "I'm sorry. I'm so sorry." Then my other arm curls up around his neck as Jared gathers me close, shushing me. His heat warms over my shame as the first fat tears fall.

He pulls me so tightly against his body, sinew and strength, running his hands down the back of my head and cradling my skull. "It's all right. It's going to be all right. Just let her in."

Then I really start to sob. His lips murmur across the soft flesh of my ear, and he drops tiny kisses on my face, tilts my head back to kiss my forehead, my eyelids, my soaked cheek. Then he pulls me back against his body, cradling me in his arms as the storm inside me takes over and rages.

As Margot's final spark of life ebbed out of her, I'd done what I needed to survive. I'd switched it off, whatever that thin, fragile string was that had bound us our whole lives. But I needed it. I had always needed it to feel whole. And now, when I miss my sister so much it feels like I'll die, I need it all the more.

It's just this thought that has me searching the seams for that other sense until I feel it flicker back to life. Then the cord opens fully, and the sensation floods me, as though a dam has broken. She's not there—there's nothing, no one, on the other end.

But strangely, I'm not alone, either. *Something is happening*.

It's as if all at once a switch has been flipped and a machine hums suddenly to life inside of me. The sensation is so odd that my tears abruptly halt. I pull back to look at Jared.

My face is soaked with tears. His shirt is soaked, too. We both look like a storm has rocked us. But it's what's going on inside of me that worries me the most. "What's happening to me?"

22

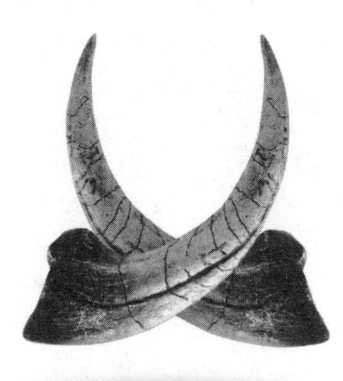

J ared holds the door open, his hand resting on the small of my back as we make our way into the lab. I can hear the hum of machines, the small swooshing sound of particle separators.

Doc Raines looks like she's gained some years back since the last time I'd seen her, after she'd sewn me up. With her tight curls bouncing in a high ponytail, her body clad in a long white lab coat, she resembles a child playing dress up. She looks up at us as we come together, her eyes owlish with the high-powered ocular device that allows her to see things less than ordinary.

And as usual, she gets straight to the point. "What are you doing here, Lucy?"

"I need you to put me through Protocols."

A deep V appears on the doc's forehead as she frowns. "I was just packing up, as a matter of fact. There's no more need for Protocols, is there?"

"Doc Raines." My voice is short with rising panic. "I need

you to run the Protocols again."

"Why?"

"You said our blood creates True Born Talismans."

"Yes, I said that. When properly combined," she emphasizes.

"So our blood can trigger True Born mutations. Which means we can keep people from catching sick."

"Yes, but Lucy, Margot is gone. That dream is over."

"How does it work?"

"Lucy, really." Doc Raines clucks and turns away, ready to dismiss me.

My best ice-princess voice roars from my mouth. "Tell me!"

I'd had time to think as Jared and Mohawk escorted me back to the van. Time to contemplate those seconds when Father Wes had brought his knife down on first Margot, then me.

Lock and key.

That's what has been rolling around in my mind. An accelerant and an anchor, the doctor had told us — that's what our genetic codes were. Yet linked, tagged to each other. And when the two puzzles merge, True Born mutations are triggered.

I pull my cold hand out from under Jared's warm one. My fingertips trace lightly over the thin smile of a scar.

"Kira said it healed too quickly," I say.

Doc Raines stares at me as though I'm a stranger. She glances at Jared, apparently satisfied by his continued silence and stony face that I'm not to be dismissed as a crazy person. She turns and places her hands demurely in her lap. Staring at my neck thoughtfully, she motions to us.

"All right then, pull up a stool and get cozy."

• • •

The sky is turning when I wake. From a purple-black bruise it lightens, almost imperceptibly, to a medium gray. Soon it will be as white as a winding sheet. I don't have to turn to know Jared is there, asleep in the chair across the room. I've come to learn that he's attuned to my every movement. When I open my eyes, so does he.

"You're awake." Still half asleep, he raises his arms in a satisfied feline stretch. His red T-shirt with crude white lips below Kiss Me, I'm Available!, lifts with his movements, revealing the rippling muscles of his belly.

"You're still here." I'm grumbling, but it's half-hearted at best.

Jared Price hasn't left my side since we visited Grayguard.

"Yep." He gives me a sleepy smile. I snort and pull myself from the warmth of my bed to go over to the window. From here, so high above the streets and roofs of Dominion, everything below is the size of crawling ants. Everything, that is, except the Prayer Tree.

The smoldering fire blazed for a day and a night before the Lasters finally put it out. If there was any permanent damage done to the tree, I can't see it from here. I run a finger across the almost nonexistent line at my neck, just above where Ali's coin necklace sits. I pull on the coin, feeling the familiar spark nip my fingertips. To, think, not so long ago I would have done anything to have the necklace removed. Now that Ali's gone, I wouldn't part with it even if I did know how to get it off. It's all I have to remember my friend. *And he was right after all*, I think with bitterness. It did save me.

What else had he told me about the necklace? The thought of forgetting something so important depresses me. Two hands, brawny and strong, appear on either side of my body at the window frame. I slowly turn, coming face-to-face with a pair of inhuman cat eyes peering out from under a shag of sunlight hair.

"What do you think you're doing?" I say imperiously. I want to cross my arms, but he hasn't left enough room between our bodies to let that happen. I become keenly aware of the heat rising from his flesh.

As though he's read my mind, he gives me a slow, sensual smile. "What does it look like I'm doing, Princess?"

"Getting in my way," I grind out.

"Oh?" Jared cocks his head mockingly. "Am I in your way, Your Highness?"

"You know you are."

"Good," he says. His tongue licks his bottom lip sensually before he kisses me with desperate intensity. His hands tense on the window frame. He places one, then the other broad hand on my back, pulling me closer. I can't think as my fingers automatically come to rest on his shoulders, fists curling in his T-shirt.

Jared nibbles at my bottom lip, causing me to shiver from head to toes with desire. I open my eyes to look at him. He regards me through half-lidded eyes with frank hunger. It's this, this intimacy that is so great, and far too important to me, that has me wanting to run scared.

"Lucy." He sighs.

"Jared," I warn. His lips find my ear, trace down the sensitive skin of my neck until they hit my collarbone. He nips at the tender tendon in the space beside my shoulder, and I nearly jump out of my skin. Frissons of heat and ice dance through my body. I am suddenly, electrically alive.

For a moment my traitorous body wants to give in. I feel the surrender washing over me, an automatic reaction. My body hugs closer to his, my hips fitting tightly against his powerful thighs.

But then I think of Margot. My other half, who is dead instead of me. I push myself away, panting and shaking. Jared looks as bewildered as I feel.

"Are you okay? What's going on?"

He doesn't know, doesn't understand. I feel dead, like I'm trapped in the ground with Margot, drowning in betrayals. And I don't want Jared there with me. Jared is sunshine and heat. Cinnamon and forest. Green and gold and indigo. He's more alive than anyone I've ever known. And I can't sully him with the way I feel. *I won't.*

It's his tone, a hair shy of imperious, that gives me the fuel I need. "What's going on? What's going on is that you're hot and cold with me. One minute you're telling me we can't get close and the next you're holding my hand in the lab and kissing me. Make up your mind, Jared."

"I *have* made up my mind." His eyes are smoky, a hue I've never seen before. The seriousness of his words, the quiet magic of them, bespells me. "You're right, Lu. I can't say I blame you for saying that. I know I've been an idiot, that I've been making about as much sense as a postage stamp. I've only ever wanted to protect you, and then I go and bungle it up because I want you so badly. I know I've hurt you. And I'm sorry. I need to explain…When you were captured everything became clear. Nothing else matters but you. You and me. Everything else— Storm, duty. None of that matters anymore. Not to me."

But I can't listen. If I listen, my resolve might crack. *He needs to be away from me.* With that, my mind whirls, machinelike, until it fastens on the most hurtful thing I can think of.

"St-Storm…" I stumble on the words, knowing what a

betrayal they are. "Storm asked me to marry him."

Jared hisses. He cups his ear and leans over with a savage look. "What did you say? I can't have heard that right."

For a moment, before I lower my gaze to the floor with cheeks hot to the touch, I catch sight of Jared's face. He's ashen, with a look I'd more associate with someone who's been kicked in the gut. All the light and sparkle drains from his eyes. I put a fist to my stomach, feeling sick.

"I haven't given him my answer. Yet." I back down from saying the worst: that I'll likely have to say yes. Marrying Storm is really not a choice—Jared and I both know it's the sensible thing for me to do. And it's the perfect excuse to get Jared to walk away. But I can't. "I-I need to think about it."

I refuse to meet Jared's eyes as the remainder of my heart cracks in two. I don't look back as I walk away, shaking. Leaving him behind.

Because if I do, he'll see I don't want to.

23

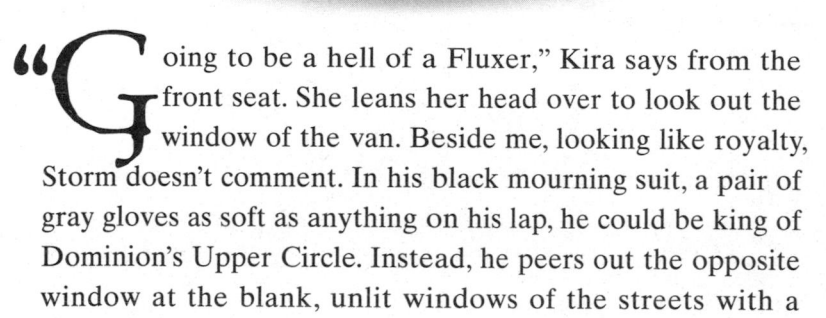

"Going to be a hell of a Fluxer," Kira says from the front seat. She leans her head over to look out the window of the van. Beside me, looking like royalty, Storm doesn't comment. In his black mourning suit, a pair of gray gloves as soft as anything on his lap, he could be king of Dominion's Upper Circle. Instead, he peers out the opposite window at the blank, unlit windows of the streets with a thoughtful expression.

The sky is as surreal as the day. It's lit gold and lime, a combination I've never seen before and too much like Jared's eyes. It's far too gorgeous to be the day I bury my sister.

Our caravan tracks over the rubble of a dying city. We pass a barricade where a small, tidy pile of bodies is stacked, likely waiting for the Rovers. On the top is a corpse so small and thin I can't bear to look.

...

"What do you think it will be like?" Margot had once whispered to me, snuggled up in one of our childhood canopy beds.

"What?"

"You know. When the Plague... What comes after."

"You take my hand and we wander in a vast blue city together," I'd told my twin with a smile.

I'd earned a crack of a laugh for that. "Why blue?"

"Picture," I say, invoking one of our oldest games. "The color of the sky the way it's supposed to be, a moment before the sun sets. That's where we'll be, Margot. Together."

I reckon I lied to my sister about death. But now I wonder: what *is* she experiencing? Is she in there somehow, a part of her tucked away inside me?

It's a crazy thought. Still, the flat awareness of *something* changing inside me has jumped to life since Jared and Mohawk and I visited the school. If anything, it's been intensifying as the days trudge on, gathering like its own storm cloud. At times I've been too warm, as though I'm coming down with a fever. At other times I've felt occupied, yet there's not that pulsing, unique awareness that was Margot.

I'd tried to describe it to Doc Raines as she'd plucked and scraped at me with her instruments the day before.

"Imagine growing a person inside you, only he or she doesn't have a mind."

Doc Raines stared hard at me, her lips turning down in a frown. "That's unnerving."

"N-No," I quickly cut in. "No, it's like...knowing you're not alone. I don't feel so lonely now."

Doc Raines finished drawing a final pint of blood. She sighed and wiped a stray wisp of curl away from her forehead. Her gloved hand rested on my shoulder and pressed hard on the pinpricks from the needle before giving me a tight smile that didn't reach her eyes.

"That's all that matters, then."

Like a butterfly, that secret life, the one I associate with Margot, flutters awake inside me as we pass Heaven Square. A bunch of Lasters ring the Tree, some on their knees. I watch as a girl, maybe a year or two younger than me, painfully thin in her cotton gown, hangs a picture of someone she's lost.

I hadn't been aware that I was leaning over Storm's lap until he throws an arm around me. I tense but try to relax into his solid, electric warmth. *He wants to comfort me*, I tell myself. But I'm very glad that Jared is in the other car. No matter what I've told him, my heart feels the traitor.

"What is it, Lucy?" his deep voice rumbles.

"Nothing." I shake my head. "Just thinking about the Prayer Tree. It grew back after the fire?"

Storm strokes a hand down his chin as he considers his answer. "Almost overnight. Whoever engineered those nanotech bombs knew what they were doing."

"You think it was the same people who engineered our DNA. Margot's and mine." It's not a question; it's a statement.

Storm's hand tightens around my shoulder, squeezing slightly for comfort. But his palm tingles with power barely leashed.

"That is a likely scenario at this point, yes."

The burial site is in the old graveyard, exclusively kept for the Upper Circle. This is what the Old World must have been like, I've always thought. Whenever Margot and I have been here in the past, it was for the funerals of important people or their children. Here the Lasters haven't been able to tear down the trees. They rise up like comforting guardians, bending and weeping over their dead. There are too many fresh graves in this part. But as kids, Margot and I wandered through the older sections, wondering over the marble angels and kingly mausoleums. The graves blend in against the white-white air like unburied corpses. The wind whistles in my ears. It's the only sound I hear, making me feel as though I've gone deaf.

Storm leads me to a quiet, shady spot. A tree arching over the plot reminds me of our old canopy beds, the way they nestled us in from overhead. *Margot would like that*, I think. It's the kind of decadent touch she'd approve of, though it's not our family plot. The Fox family plot is on the other side of the graveyard, tucked away in the giant, vaulting mausoleums. We'll not give our father another victory.

It's dead quiet. No other mourners have shown up yet. As we round the top of the hill, I spy Jared. His hunter's eyes train on me, hooking me with raw power. He's in a black suit that fits his body to perfection. His hair falls in loose curls around his face, but somehow I can still see the sharp slant of his cheekbones. My heart is drowning, but I can't tear my attention away from him. His hands cross in front of him, feet slightly apart like a proper merc. The line of his back is rigid. I can tell he's scenting the air for danger. But his lips, drawn into a severe line, soften as I near.

How can that even be? I pull my back straight and my chin up. *Too late*, I remind myself, even as the ghost of a smile that drifts past his lips distracts me.

I don't even feel the crackling pulse of Storm's touch as he leads me to the side of the grave. I'm so distracted by the pummeling grief and the presence of Jared, just behind me, that I barely register the mourners winding their way through the cement- and marble-strewn paths to where I lay my sister.

"Lucy?" a familiar voice calls me. I look up, eyes burning. It takes a full moment to recognize a man staring out from what I last knew as a boy's face.

"Robbie?"

"I grieve your loss." He rattles off the familiar, expected line. All the same, I can see he means it.

"Look at you. All grown up." My lips twist in a grimace of a smile as I take him in. My sister's former beau and son of Colonel Henry Deakins, Robbie is the epitome of the Upper Circle young man: dashing, handsome, rich, and carefree. But he's not. None of us is.

"You look so much like her today, Lucy." His eyes well with tears as he touches one of the curls Kira insisted on putting in my hair before we left. A shot sounds from somewhere in the city, but Robbie doesn't blink. Instead, he looks down at the toes of his expensive, shiny shoes. "I'm sorry we fell out of touch."

The Fox sisters have been getting the cold shoulder from the Upper Circle for so long now that I'd not even noticed Robbie's absence. We were at his Reveal party, when he turned eighteen and was declared a Splicer. He was one of the few boys we knew who was at ours. We used to see Robbie every day. At lunch he'd tease Margot just to make her blush. And I suspect he was her partner in crime for skipping class.

But as I stare at the handsome young man who will inherit our Circle, it strikes me that I don't miss our old set. I don't miss being one of the crown princesses of the group at all. Somehow it makes the heavy burden of my loss an inch easier to bear.

"Never mind. It's nice to see you. Thank you for coming. Are your parents here?"

Robbie's eyes shift uncomfortably as he coughs into his fist. "Ah…no. They couldn't make it." A faint stain of embarrassment lights his cheeks.

"Oh. Well. Give them my best," I tell Robbie woodenly and turn to face the small stream of black-clad bodies.

For every mourner, it seems, there are fifty missing.

The line of mourners left to greet me trickles down to a small end. Then only a handful of bodies is left to ring the grave like a necklace: Kira, Mohawk, Jared, and me. Storm has gone a little ways down a path with a business associate. Torch leans his slender body against a tree. Clothed in a gray suit, his thick black hair slicked back, he appears to be wiping away a tear before he turns. The air is thick with unshed rain.

"Lucinda." A voice breaks through the fog of misery that engulfs me at the thought of having to leave my sister behind in the dirt.

The hair on my arms stands to attention. Not least because someone has called me by my full name. It's the voice, deep and lilting, with that peculiar accent, that has my head whipping up. *Lyoo-cinda.*

I hadn't even seen him approach, though clearly Jared did. He elbows me out of the way, a sinister snarl on his face.

"Wh-Wh—" I stutter, trying to push my guardian out of the

way, and when that doesn't work, I simply peer over his shoulder. And stare into the long-dead face of Leo Resnikov.

Resnikov. The man who stole my sister. *The man my sister says she loved*, a voice reminds me. Loved and *married*, even.

"You're alive." I say the words but I still don't believe my eyes. I blink as I look over his ghost, though surely the tall, dashing figure is not a specter. Dressed in an impeccable suit in that foreign style of his, with the straight, raised collar and long coattail, his hair long and unkempt, brushing his collar, he looks like the Resnikov we knew before. But there's something different about him, too. He's lost weight, I see. The hollows of his cheeks have become even more pronounced. He stares at me with a weight of grief I didn't think possible.

He opens his palms to me and shrugs, as though he, too, is surprised to see me. "I couldn't stay away. But it is not smart for me to have come."

"I thought you were dead. What are you doing here?"

He tips his head and glances at me strangely. "Surely you know."

"I'm going to be so happy to kill you." Jared walks up and smiles through a mouth of deadly teeth. But I can't have Jared kill the man before us—not yet, at any rate.

My words are impatient. I squeeze Jared's arm, hard as I can, hoping I make a dent. This might be important. "Know what, Leo?"

"Your sister and me," he begins. But then he bows his head, hands going to rest on his hips.

Utterly forgetting himself, Jared snarls, razor-sharp teeth drawing down in his mouth. "Your sister and me *what*."

But then Resnikov and I lock eyes. And in that moment I think I know all I need to know. "Tell him," I say softly.

"I loved her. She loved me. We were married. We've been meeting secretly these past few months."

Jared roars. "Liar!" With just seconds to spare, I throw myself on Jared's body to keep him from lunging at Resnikov's throat. I push him back with all the strength in me as the other True Borns stand at attention.

"Look at me." I say it with all the imperiousness a Fox sister can muster. Jared's gaze darts back and forth between Resnikov and me. "*Look*. He's telling the truth."

Jared pales. "You didn't tell me."

And that's when I feel the tears finally well, threatening to spill and never stop. My chest aches with the barometric pressure of an impending storm. "She didn't confide in me. Just about the marriage, near the end. When we thought we were going to die." I stop. I put a hand to my chest and wonder idly how it is that my heart continues to beat. "I didn't know they had been seeing each other."

"Lu." In the moments since Resnikov's appearance, Jared's eyes have gone wild. His fingers have turned to claws, but he gentles them on the skin of my arms. "Lu, you should have told me."

"What does it matter? She's dead."

"And that is why I'm here," Resnikov breaks in. "I needed—I need to say goodbye to my wife." His voice breaks, and for one tiny moment, I glimpse what it is that Margot saw in this man. *Watch him—he's treachery*, a small voice inside me warns. I'd be wise to heed this little whisper that reminds me of what Resnikov was willing to do to get what he wanted from us.

My voice grows hard and firm. "Where is my father?"

"I don't know."

"Tell me the truth or I'll let Jared rip you to pieces."

But Resnikov just sighs and rubs the bridge of his nose as though it hurts. "Don't you see? Our alliance was at an end when I let Margot escape."

I laugh, the sound as bitter and hollow as I feel. "You *let* her escape?"

Resnikov pins me with a wry look. "You think it would have been that easy for you and this True Born to take her, had I not wanted you to get her out of there?" For a moment the world is hushed, holding its breath, while I consider Resnikov's words.

"We blew up your factory." I can hear the smile in Jared's voice.

"Yes. Another ultimately empty gesture. You did me a favor." The Russian shrugs.

My fists clench at my sides. I have never wanted to hit someone more. "How do you reckon?"

But now he laughs. The lines at his eyes spread with dull mirth. "We knew pretty quickly that the therapy was not complete without your blood, Lucinda. Margot's DNA could almost be used on its own, but not entirely."

I might never have this chance again. The questions are worth the risk, especially if Resnikov really can't tell us where our parents are. "Who made us? Was it that scientist in your lab?"

There's genuine amusement on the tall man's face as he hooks his hands together at his back. Jared grows ever more apprehensive. I can feel his heart thudding in his chest. I try to calm my own beating heart in the hopes it will help him stay under control.

"It was a team. But you girls were always a surprise. I was

very young then. It was my father who struck the devil's bargain with your own. He did not live to see the results, sadly."

"What was the purpose?"

Resnikov tilts his head. "How can you ask such a silly question?" Jared's warning growl fills the air as Resnikov motions with his arms, his body signaling boredom. "Stand down, kitty. I'm not here to hurt her."

"What was the purpose?" I ask again.

"To control the Plague. To control who is healed by it."

We already knew this. I want to know the mechanics. I want to know how they planned to profit from our genes.

"What does my father want?"

Resnikov turns his face to the ground. His hands fold inside the pockets of his pants as he shoots me a murderous look. "Your father? Your father is a man I'm going to kill."

It doesn't matter that I know he's the devil in flesh. My blood runs cold in my veins as I take in the sincerity of Resnikov's pledge. He means to kill Lukas Fox.

I feel sick as I ask it. "Because of Margot?"

"Because of Margot. Because he betrayed me." He gestures at the funeral guests, the faces of the mourners as they anxiously watch the scene between us. "Look around you. You think this is all an accident? Any of it? It's not. That man has machinated all this. All of it."

"Margot and me."

Though Jared is a solid buffer, Resnikov leans over and spits. "You were little pawns in a very large game, Lucinda. And the game isn't yet done."

"Can I kill him now?" Jared seethes.

I pause to carefully consider Jared's request. I reckon Resnikov sees I'm serious, because he takes a step back, then another. "No," I say thoughtfully. "Any enemy of my father's is someone we'd do better to keep alive. And Storm might need information from him later. Can't get intel from a corpse."

From where I stand, I can almost see Resnikov's hackles rise. He looks at me as though he's never seen me before. I can't blame him. I don't know when I crossed the line and became a bloodthirsty girl. I don't recognize myself. Then again, I don't recognize anything now that Margot is gone.

Resnikov takes another step back. "I knew it was you, you know," he says. Behind him, the row of mourners is like a solid black canvas. "I knew all along."

The kiss. He's talking about the kiss.

When Jared and Ali and I crossed the world to free Margot from Resnikov's base, I ran into him. To save my cover, I played my twin sister. But Resnikov surprised me by kissing me. I'd thought it strange at the time. Now, with his confession, I find it even stranger.

"Why did you do it, then?"

He rubs a hand across his chest as though it hurts. "To make Margot jealous. I wanted her to escape. But not without telling her that I loved her."

It's such an unexpected answer; it catches me off guard. I tip over, hiccupping a sob. Jared's nails have grown to daggers, so it's harder for him to catch me as my knees begin to buckle. He retracts his claws with a ferocious, ear-splitting yelp, loud enough to wake the dead. I barely notice the small mob of mourners drawing back in alarm.

I have wits enough still to understand what the madman before me is saying. *He knew Margot was watching*. Knew that it was me, not her, who he kissed those many months ago. He really did want my sister to escape. And as the realization sinks in, I feel like another burden has been lifted from me.

Margot was loved.

I don't know why it's important. She's dead now, and the dead feel no pain. But it hurt me somewhere I didn't even know to think that my twin could have lived and died without feeling loved, deeply loved, by someone other than me. I wanted Margot to fall in love, to get married, to have a family. I reckon I wanted her happiness even more than my own. That she was loved, even by this madman…it's not enough, but it's something to ease the pain.

Two of Jared's claws have hooked into the tender flesh of my arm. The skin isn't broken yet, but I read the panic in his eyes as he realizes he's hurting me. "I'm all right. I'm okay, Jared," I tell him, even as I hold on to his broad shoulders for strength. His nose quivers as though trying to smell a lie. I reckon he finds none, because the tips of the claws slowly retract, human fingers regaining their form.

When I look back over my shoulder, Resnikov is still there, facing Margot's grave with a wild look. I watch his lips move, though no sound comes out. *I'm sorry, krasavitsa.* He calls her his beautiful girl. And then his lean, tall body melts back into the crowd like a ghost.

"Jared." The word is hardly more than a whisper. But I know he hears me. "Take me away from here."

Jared cocks his head. The bones along his nose have flattened, so that he looks both younger and deadlier. He pulls me close, his voice scraping against the soft flesh of my ear. "You'd regret it, Lu. Think about it."

I blink back another river of tears. "I don't know if I can do this."

"You can." He presses his face into my hair. "You need to

say goodbye to her."

I breathe against Jared's solid chest for a good solid minute, just listening to the tick of his heart, steady and sure with the rise and fall of his chest. There are birds singing somewhere amid the branches of the tree. And there's the sound of the wind, the ever-present wind, whipping around the gravestones and singeing the air with cold.

My eyes have nearly cleared when I see Storm's spectral bones rising over a crest. He hurries toward us with a powerful stride, and I catch that glimmer once more, that strange illusion, as though all the air around Nolan Storm has turned into something liquid, malleable, splitting the world in two. A thunderous look is stamped across his bluntly handsome features, his long fingers curled into fists. Storm's head swivels slightly, and the heavy rack of bone around his head tilts left before straightening. Nolan Storm looks as though he's ready to rampage.

Something is wrong.

Mourners scatter out of his way as he strides past the open grave toward us. "Lucy, Jared," he calls, and the air shakes. "Don't move."

My attention snags on a little red dot that inches up Jared's chest, little by little, until it rests over his heart. Looking behind me, I see a similar pattern splayed on my back. Then I spy the black-clad body on the top of a marble mausoleum about two hundred feet away, lying before a long gun. I glance back up at Jared. From the expression on his face and his sudden stillness, I reckon he's seen it, too.

Sniper.

• • •

Past Jared's shoulder, behind Storm, more bodies in black gather. But these aren't mourners. The insignia of Dominion appears on batter shields, splays across each bulletproof vest and helmet. Heavy guns hold steady to squinted eyes.

And before them all, standing at the front of the small army dressed in full military gear, is Theodore Nash.

We're under siege.

24

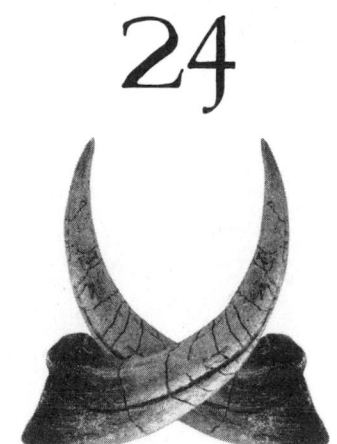

"Do *not* move." Storm raises an arm and points at us. I dare not breathe. The muscles in my belly pull taut as I stare helplessly at the glaringly red bull's-eye painted on Jared's white shirt.

They'll likely shoot if I move. And if I throw myself on Jared to protect him, it's more as like the bullets will pass through us both. If there's one thing I've learned to appreciate through my childhood in the Upper Circle, it's the strength of Dominion's elite firepower.

My jaw clenches like a trap. "J-Jared."

"Don't worry, Lu. Everything's going to be all right. We've got this." His tone is soothing, but I can see the wild take over his eyes.

"Liar." I crack a laugh. And watch in wonder as one half of his lips curls up in a smile, exposing a perfect dimple.

"Have I ever let you down before, Princess?"

"Repeatedly."

Jared frowns. "How so?"

But then the bulk of Storm's body coming into our orbit with the strength of a hurricane interrupts us. In seconds, he's inserted himself between the sniper's assault rifle and us. I turn, not wanting to keep my back to the gunman. The red bull's-eye travels north to rest between Storm's eyes.

"What's happening?" Jared murmurs to Storm.

"Our buddy Nash seems to be staging a coup of some sort. And here I didn't think he was smart enough."

"That will teach you to underestimate the cockroaches of this world."

I shake my head, throwing my gaze between them. "He'll not last long. He's dying."

Jared tosses his hair. "Again?"

"I want you to take Lucy and head to safe house one. If one is compromised, go straight to three."

"Got it."

"What? No!" I cry.

But the men ignore me. "Wait until my signal," Storm tells Jared.

"Wait, Storm—what are you going to do?"

He smiles at me then, and the blood curdles in my veins. "I'm going to negotiate."

Storm turns his back on the sniper, as if the threat is no more than a mosquito, so he faces the rapidly advancing Nash and his men head-on. I lose count at thirty in full riot squad gear, but there is at least a handful more.

Storm lazily stuffs his hands in his trouser pockets. "Here to pay your respects, Nash?"

Nash is close enough now that I can see the sweat beading

on his forehead. Though he must be hot in his flak vest, I can tell he's not well. His face is flushed with fever. I reckon it won't be long before the full symptoms make their appearance once more.

"True Borns are now illegal in Dominion. I'm here to arrest you."

I didn't think Storm's smile could get more terrifying. I was wrong. "Since when have True Borns become illegal? Illegal in what sense?"

"You're not human. The government of Dominion believes that the True Borns pose a significant threat to the safety and well-being of the human population."

"How so?" Storm crosses his arms, clearly amused. "Just because I'm going to kill you?"

If Nash is scared, as well he should be, he blusters through convincingly. "We have good reason to suspect that the True Borns caused the Plague. Therefore we must eradicate the threat to public safety."

Storm tips back his head and laughs. "That's a remarkable stretch even for you, Nash," he drawls in a dangerously low voice.

"We have scientific evidence to back us up."

"Do you? And just what kind of evidence is that?" The air vibrates with the power of Storm's words.

"An informant has stepped forward. Someone who has shared with the government the true origins of the True Born Talisman mutations. We know what you are."

"And what are we, Nash?"

"Abominations," he spits.

"And just who is this mythical informant? Why should anyone believe you?"

Nash nods to one of the soldiers. "Bring the prisoner," he commands. The lines part, offering a startling glimpse of platinum hair and milky eyes. Two soldiers stand on either side of her cuffed hands. One stands behind, gun trained to her back. Although a line of thick red tape covers her mouth, her eyes remain uncovered.

They don't know, I realize. They haven't covered her eyes because they don't think she can see anything. They don't know that she can see whatever is in our veins. She'll not see the gun behind or beside her, but Serena could track us through walls.

Storm doesn't so much as blink. "Yes," he drawls, as though we're having a casual conversation. "I can see you've been well informed. What interesting tales Serena must have for you with her mouth all glued up."

Nash rolls his eyes and motions to one of the flanking soldiers. He rips off the tape covering Serena's mouth. "Son of a bitch," she swears as the tape rips from her skin. Red welts instantly appear on her face. But other than that, Serena seems intact.

"Tell them." Nash points at us, his focus trained on the Salvager.

Serena shrugs, her cuffed hands jangling. One corner of her shirt slips down over her shoulder, exposing a pale, slender shoulder blade. "It was my duty to tell them. I have a responsibility to the citizens of Dominion." Jared and I lock eyes. *What is she talking about?* He shakes his head, almost unnoticeably, and we turn back to stare at the icy figure before us. "More important, I have a duty toward my people, the Horned One's followers."

My head buzzes, and I feel faint. She's one of Ali's people? But didn't Ali say they'd do whatever it took to keep us safe?

I can't work through the terrible and twisted logic. And in any case, there's no time.

Nash pushes Serena back behind a wall of thick-bodied soldiers. "There, you see?"

"What does Gillis have to say about any of this?"

"Gillis doesn't have anything to say about this. He's not the one in charge here."

The earth shakes as Storm paws the ground. Even Nash has the brains to look ashen for a moment. "I'm about through speaking with you, Nash."

Margot's mourners had been staring slack-jawed at the volleys between the men. But now, as Storm's power gathers, his eyes roiling like a mad beast, they begin to back away. One soldier with a trembling gun shouts something as Storm tosses his antlers. A gun explodes, the shot cracking through the air like lightning.

Storm places himself between the bullet and us. It pierces his shoulder. Blood spurts in a crazy torrent. He lets out a bellow, loud enough to rattle the dead, and for one long moment everyone freezes.

Then the mourners scatter like hens, squawking and scrabbling as they flee through the headstones. Nash's men shout among themselves. Guns explode in the air. And, though white-faced and trembling, Nash holds his ground. An angry, defiant frown pulls at his features, making him look like a stubborn child. Telltale sweat drips down his face. He mops at it as he starts shouting commands.

"Storm," calls Jared, "what do you want me to do?"

The leader of the True Borns turns blazing eyes on us. "Get her out of here," he snarls. "Take her to number three directly. Don't go to one."

Jared gives a curt nod. "Understood." He carefully pries my fingers off his shoulders and jokes, "Careful, Princess. I'm precious cargo, you know."

It's only then that I realize that I've been digging into Jared's shoulders. A red stain covers his arm. Storm's blood, I realize, feeling faint. And then the jeweled red of the sniper's laser gun sight travels up to Jared's forehead and locks between his eyes.

"Jared, look out!" I screech and throw myself against him as the air splits and thunder rolls from the arc of the bullet. We fall to the ground and roll slightly to the left over the uneven dirt and grass. Though I'm on top, the air still whooshes from my lungs. I stop moving for a moment, wondering, through the haze of pain, whether we're alive.

Beyond us, a soldier sways, his face a ruined thing, then topples. The bullet found a home, then—just not in us.

Jared looks at me, primeval rage etched across his fine cheekbones. Can't be dead if he looks like he wants to tear something into pieces and eat it. My heart slows, relaxing with the knowledge that he's still alive.

Storm, though, might not be as lucky.

Another bullet rips through Storm's other shoulder as he advances on the line of knock-kneed soldiers. Storm lifts his head. The sky splits with the sound he issues, the very air shaking with his power.

The lines of Storm's body begin to blur, and he seems to loom larger than himself as he reaches out and grasps the gun that wounded him. He rips the metal with his hands. One half he throws at the line of soldiers. It takes out one man, the head bending with a sickening crunch, and he falls. The other he hurls into the graveyard, amid the scattering mourners and gravestones. The line of soldiers backs up a few paces. Storm stands still and paws the earth, his antlers glowing like an unearthly beacon. Then he charges the line of men like a mad minotaur, while above the sounds of a rising wind and fray, Nash screams, "Stop it, we need them alive!"

I'm too caught up in what's happening, the terrifying force of Nolan Storm, to move. Jared says something I don't hear as Storm grabs the nearest man in two hands, picking him up like he's nothing more than kindling. He hurls the soldier at his comrades, many of whom scatter while others fall, pinned beneath the man's weight.

Suddenly the earth moves, and I'm no longer splayed across Jared's body but beneath it. "Shhh." His warm breath tickles my ear as I struggle. My fists pound his flesh uselessly. "Seriously, cut it out, Princess. I can't save you if you're wriggling like that." He pulls back and traps my fists on either side of my head. Something about his voice, the strangeness of his eyes, stops me.

"How dare you," I murmur. "I saved you just then."

Jared chuckles, a warm, rich sound that jogs me all the way to my toes. "That you did. So why don't you let me return the favor? We can go halfsies on this one, all right?" He flashes a dimple at me, the lines of his cheekbones so arresting I can barely think. *He's trying to distract me so I don't panic*, I reckon. But the din around us is maddening. And we're in mortal peril. I nod, hoping he'll let me up.

Jared, though, is no fool. "Promise me you're not going to fight."

I let out an angry whistle of a breath. But a second later, I nod again. Jared flashes his teeth. "That's my girl."

He pulls me up to a half crouch, one hand on my arm and another on the small of my back. I make a point of landing on his foot as hard as I can as I right myself.

Jared leans down and rubs at his toes. "Ow! What was that for?"

"Miserable, arrogant cat," I mutter to myself. Then, for his benefit, I toss out, "That's for calling me a 'girl.'"

Another burst of dimples as his nose quivers and he starts to lead me through the winding row of headstones. "Duly noted, Lu."

But just as Jared pulls me to relative safety, something—someone—catches my eye. A blur of slick hair, a square, strong jaw covered in its low beard. And the reflective glare of black leather gloves.

"Jared, wait!" I work to free my hands from his. I'm no match for him, though, and end up struggling uselessly. "Please!" I screech.

"What the hell is wrong with you?"

"I thought I saw—" Though when I turn back around to look, the face has disappeared.

Just like a Fox, I think to myself. *A Fox going to hole.*

What is my father doing at Margot's funeral?

25

"Did you see him?" I feel sick at the thought. My father. The man who betrayed us.

Jared doesn't answer, just winds me through narrow, dirty alleys. We're in a part of town I've never set foot in before. His attention flickers over me briefly before it goes back to scanning the street with the fine and professional intent of a merc. I can tell he's cataloging the environment with more than the tools of a professional gun, though. Jared Price was born to kill.

He could have been killed, that small voice reminds me. No matter how deadly, Jared could have died tonight. It doesn't matter if I don't think we can be together. If something happens to Jared... Bile rises in my throat, burning and itchy. I stop to fight back my racing brain.

"See who?" Jared murmurs.

"Lukas Fox. My father."

The True Born stops mid-stride. "What did you say?"

Here the buildings are shorter than in other parts of town, built more of brick than stone. I lay my hand on the brick, faded with age and moss. It's rough under my hand, like a cat's tongue, and covered with graffitied eyes. Two joined as one.

Only just one now, my mind corrects. The ache in my chest intensifies. I rub at it, though I know it will never really go away.

Jared's fingers steal across the flesh of my hand. "Lu," he says patiently. He looks around one more time before he backs me up against that brick wall. His fingers tangle in my hair, frame my face. But he won't let me go, holding me with the intensity of his blazing gaze. "Tell me."

"Saw him as we were leaving." My voice rattles out in unrecognizable, raspy gasps.

Jared tilts his head. His body is so close, so close, the heat rolling from him in waves. And until I feel that basking warmth I have no idea how cold I am. Just being near him makes my body break into shivers. I wrap my arms tighter against my belly, the thin cloth of my mourning coat stretching meanly over my shoulders and elbows.

Gently he takes my face in his hands. One finger traces the soft skin of my bottom lip. He looks…*hungry*. "You'll have to fill me in on the details when we get to our destination."

I swallow, fighting against the sensations stirring in my gut. "Which is where exactly?"

"Can't tell you. Top secret."

"Why?"

Jared's lips quirk up. "Just in case. Besides, you'll have to see it to believe it."

"Fine." I study the street. The rubble of a broken-down city is strewn everywhere. Across from where we stand, the husk of a car sits at a curb, one door rusted open, as though waiting for someone. Unease creeps up my spine. "Let's just get there."

It's quiet. Too quiet. And if there's one thing I've learned in my brief association with the True Borns, it's that quiet is dangerous.

Jared soothes a strip of hair from my face, studying me as though looking for bruises. But my cuts are under the skin, so deep they can't be fathomed. I turn my face away, just in time to see a dog-size rat poke its quivering nose out from behind a beat-up box. I make a face. Jared pivots, then lunges at the beast with a hiss.

The rat makes a high-pitched squeal and runs away.

"They've been known to take down small children," Jared says, matter-of-fact.

He didn't need to remind me. Gorged on Plague victims, Dominion's rats are the stuff of every Upper Circle kids' nightmares. I shiver and wrap my arms tighter around me. "Can we get out of here now? Please?"

"Yes, Your Highness." Jared smiles, his lips settling over his back-to-human teeth.

I trace the red circle drawing one last time. Its coarse texture feels chalky under my fingers. Jared tips his head out of the alley to conduct a final sweep. I expect him to signal to me and tug me out into the street.

Instead, he flattens himself against the wall, pinning me back with an arm.

And then I hear what he must have: the heavy tread of feet on cement. Coming directly for us.

· · ·

I try not to whine as Jared pulls me deeper into the rat-infested alleyway. He shoves me behind a Dumpster where he discovers a hole in the side of the building. Wedging the Dumpster far enough away, he leans down and takes a good look at what's in there.

"Time to discover your new castle, Princess," he teases under his breath.

"I am *not* going down there first," I argue. "There are *rats*."

Jared gets that stubborn tilt to his chin I've learned to hate and admire. A dimple flashes, but I'd as soon say he's not amused.

"You know what's on that street, Princess? I hear at least forty soldiers. A squadron. Do you know what squadrons do? They fan out and search nooks and crannies like this godforsaken alley."

"You think they're looking for us?"

He stares at me, hard, as though wondering where I've left my brain. "When's the last time you heard of the army being called up to do anything?"

My awareness of the situation suddenly shifts. Questions buzz through me like a blanket of flies, but there is one certainty here that I can see from Jared's face.

These soldiers are hunting for us.

Jared takes my face in his hands and kisses me. It's brief, just the softest touch of his lips zinging against mine, striking me with an electric spark. A second later, he's pushed my head into the hole, and I'm falling, arms akimbo into the void...

And landing on a hard dirt floor.

I roll over onto my side, a slight twinge in my wrist, moments before Jared lands beside me, on two feet, like a cat.

Jared takes in the basement with the alien eyes of a predator.

Even in the dim light I can see his nose twitch before he sneezes. All I smell is dirt and decay overlaid with the scent of mold. But at least there are no rats. Jared takes a step closer. Instantly I'm engulfed in his smell, cinnamon and sweet and a hint of the woods.

Just stop, my mind shouts before I shake the thought away. This is not the time to turn moony over Jared Price — especially since I have made up my mind to let him go.

"What do you see?" I think I feel something crawl up my finger, and I shake it off.

"Ghosts and rats." He snorts. "C'mon, there's a set of stairs two feet to your left."

I shiver involuntarily and swivel my head to see, but there's nothing except a wall of deep, dark black. He takes my hand in his, rubbing my fingers between his flesh as slow heat curdles in my stomach. I straighten my back.

"I can walk."

Jared snorts again, though this time in amusement. "I know you can walk, Lu," he tells me suddenly. "I bet you could walk through fire. You're the bravest woman I've ever known." I blink against a sudden rush of tears. No one has ever said anything so kind to me before. "And you're the strongest woman I've ever met." He gentles a finger through a strand of my hair. I imagine an insect he's flicking away. "I know today has been more than hard on you." There's an uncomfortable silence while Jared's eyes glitter on mine, and I think I can see the line of his jaw tighten. "I need you to stay strong, though. We can't let them win, Lu."

The words are so simple, so softly spoken, but they hit me with the force of a punch. He's right. Whatever unfinished business lies between the True Born and me, whatever I'm afraid of, rats or soldiers, needs to be put aside for now. It's more than a matter of survival. It's a question of doing what's right. For Storm. For Jared and me.

For Margot.

I nod and twine my fingers through his, liking the steady hum of his blood through his flesh. His fingers feel at home holding mine, as though despite all our differences, our flesh recognizes each other's. Jared's breath hitches. Outside, we hear boots strike the ground like hammers. He straightens, and I think I catch the slight curve of a smile lighting his face.

We pass the day in a round, tin-roofed hut in a poor section of Dominion, listening to the rain drum down with light staccato fingers. No more than six feet across, the hut has thick gray concrete block walls scribbled over with colorful graffiti. The streets smell of dead things and weeds and the iron-tinged rain that falls from the sky in light sheets. Occasionally we see a haggard, soaking Laster with bushy white hair and beard push a cart past the entrance of the hut. I'm surprised he never attempts to seek his shelter beneath the tiny roof, and I say so.

Motioning me away from the entrance, Jared pats the hard-pressed dirt of the ground beside him. He snorts. "That guy? He wouldn't be able to fit his cart in here." Then he sobers. "Lots of the Lasters don't like being in enclosed spaces."

"Enclosed," I repeat woodenly. The sensations pooling through my body distract me as Jared takes my hand and rubs his fingers over my knuckles. He flips over my hand and traces a light melody on the sensitive skin of my wrist. "Why?"

The corners of Jared's mouth flip into a grimace. "Some

think that the Plague is like one of those ancient sicknesses you'll have studied in school. Spread through the air. They believe that the close quarters of being inside spread the disease and bring on death."

My heart stutters in shock. I lick my dry lips, feeling unsure of myself. I'd heard that theory, of course. But not its consequences. "Do you believe that?"

Jared shrugs. A shock of his golden hair falls over one eye as he takes up tracing something on my arm. "Doesn't matter what I believe."

"It matters to me."

The creases next to Jared's eyes crinkle delightfully as he looks up and smiles. It's as though the sun has come out. "I knew you'd see things my way eventually, Princess," Jared teases. "But to answer your question: I know the Plague doesn't spread that way. Still, if a man believes that a life spent outdoors and away from others will keep him alive, who am I to argue?"

I mull this over. "So you're saying that you think faith keeps him healthy?"

"No." Jared rolls out the word, stretching it as he holds up his fingers and trails them lightly down my face. "I'm saying he likely thinks so. And who am I to interfere with how he lives and dies?"

Something fierce grips my belly and holds me. My eyes burn with unshed tears as I think about our broken world, the devastation of the Plague, and how many lives it has ruined. "What if it could be fixed?"

"What?" he says softly, just seconds before his lips come down, soft and sweet, like a question mark. He tilts my head and brings his lips down again, this time the hunger licking at us both. I moan into his mouth, and his hands freeze on my face. "Gods, Lu, you're going to be the death of me."

I grab at the hand that holds me still. "Don't say that," I whisper fiercely. "Don't ever say that."

Jared's smile twinkles. "Careful, Princess. You might give the impression that you care about me."

I know it's not right. I know I need to push Jared away, for his sake. But suddenly I can't hold myself back any longer. "Shut up, True Born," I tell him imperiously. And then I chase his lips with my own through the end of daylight and rain.

The "safe house" is squat and brick, with a rickety, falling-down fence and weeds growing up through the cracks in the pavement. All along the street are rusted tin cans, broken boxes flattened by rain, the rubble of broken asphalt and glass. We arrive just before dawn. The streets are quiet, still slightly damp, and smell a bit like motor oil. There are no cars on this street. Most of the windows and doors have been boarded over.

"What happened here?" I whisper as Jared punches a code into the Identi-pad. The door opens with a snick, and a thick miasma of dust assaults us. I cough and cover my face.

Jared tugs me over the threshold and secures the door behind me before saying a word. "This was one of the early neighborhoods."

"Oh," I say, looking around me.

When the Plague first started, it flamed through whole sections of the city. Originally, no one knew what it was. But those who survived the purges to their families, gaps appearing in generations like punched-out teeth, took their gear and relocated, leaving whole neighborhoods deserted. Some, they say, moved out to the country where the fresh air was thought to be more wholesome.

Not that it saved them.

"So where are we?"

Jared doesn't answer, just holds a finger to his lips and peers around a corner. I watch his reflection through a dusty mirror hanging on the hallway wall opposite the door, a large gilt-framed affair that reminds me of my old home. Who were they, the family who once lived here? Were they like us?

But as I peer around, I reckon they were a regular family living a happy, regular life until the Plague hit. A tidy wooden piano perches in one corner, hooded with dust. A red-striped rug covers the floor, inviting bare feet, and next to it, a sofa that looks warm and inviting. The curtains are drawn, keeping out most of the light, but here and there a finger pokes through, casting the living room in a nostalgic air, as though all its inhabitants are just a hairsbreadth away.

By the time Jared has scouted the small house, I've gotten acquainted with the photos on the wall — a smiling gray-haired couple and three adorable bronze-skinned children missing teeth — and rifled through a menagerie of animal knickknacks. There are pouncing leopards; a long-legged ostrich, its neck comically bent; a lion with a huge mane; a doe-eyed deer; a seagull; a huge, ugly frog.

One in particular catches my attention: sitting high up on a glass-and-metal shelf gone white with dust is a hand-size golden elephant. I pick it up and nearly drop it. It's much heavier than I'd imagined. But its golden skin shines in the light, its body sleek and cool in my hands. The elephant has a trunk raised in perpetual greeting, its tiny tail swishing. It has weight and substance and magic. *Like Storm. Like the True Borns*, I think to myself as a smiling Jared Prince saunters up to me.

"You find some treasure, Lu?" Jared teases. His nose crinkles delightfully.

I give the True Born a measured look, wanting him to see my double meaning. "Yes."

It isn't until the word is out and I wish I could take it back that I realize it is also true. What would I have done without them? Without Storm's support? Without Jared's warmth — and for a second it's as though the room spins as I contemplate how close I have been to shutting down my heart entirely.

And how much I owe Storm, a small voice reminds me. It niggles at me, the thought that I am beholden to my guardian. I need to take his suit seriously, and not just for that reason. If Storm and I make an alliance, we have a shot at building a council, with True Borns and Lasters at the table. At the very least, the Splicers would have to listen politely. It's worth contemplating. It's the kind of match our parents might have made for me as the axis of power shifts.

But there's the blond-haired True Born before me to think about, too.

"Jared, I—"

But Jared covers my lips with his fingers. "You know what, Princess? Let's not do that right now. Let's just enjoy the relative peace for a few hours, okay?" He doesn't seem angry or even tense. Just watchful. My heart clenches like a fist.

Hands in the pockets of his dress pants, the man I'd once thought of as careless studies me from beneath a flip of hair. Then, quick as lightning, he brings his lips down for a short, hard kiss. His hand grabs my shoulder in a light, impersonal squeeze before he releases it.

"Why don't we forage for something to eat? I hate cranky princesses."

"Okay," I toss back breezily, though inwardly I'm shaky and bruised.

As Jared leads the way to the small kitchen, tossing over his shoulder a measured grin, my sinking gut makes it clear that somehow something has shifted between us. And that maybe, just maybe, I've messed things up beyond comprehension.

We've whiled away more than a dozen hours when a fist raps on the front door. It's a driving, staccato rhythm that pulls me out of a doze where I've curled up on the couch.

Jared gets to the living room in seconds. He swears lightly under his breath.

"What is it?" I hate the shakiness in my voice as I call out. Worse is the liquid weakness filling my limbs as I lift a hand to my hot forehead and watch the room briefly spin.

Jared just closes his eyes and pinches the bridge of his nose, which is thickening with an unexpected change. *Can it be that bad?*

But then the knocking comes again, more insistent. Then two sets of hands: one lighter, the other heavier, muffled, accompanied by the low, full sound of a woman's voice. "I know you're in there," it calls in a singsong voice.

Then a heavy voice, raspy with smoke, sounds. "You gonna make us wait outside here all day?"

How did they find us? I mouth at Jared, who frowns as though he'd like to eat the people at the door.

I reckon I don't blame him.

"I see you." The high-pitched woman's voice comes through the door. "C'mon, Lu, Jared. We have a lot to talk about. I promise we're alone and we weren't followed."

Jared rushes to the back windows, obvious relief etched on his face. Then they're telling the truth. Soldiers don't surround us. Yet.

But we'd be fools to trust the people at the door. Because these visitors aren't just anyone—they're traitors. It's Serena and Carl.

26

"Well? We're going to attract attention standing out here."

"Let us in, True Born." Carl's deep voice vibrates the heavy wood of the door.

Jared freezes, turning to look at me. A hundred expressions float across his face. Anger, a burning desire to rip them to shreds, a ghost of regret, and an expression I'd as soon call helpless. He doesn't know whether to let them in, I realize.

But if there's one thing I've learned being the daughter of Lukas and Antonia Fox, it's how to receive visitors. I slip my feet onto the floor, toes together, straighten, and pull back my shoulders. The rat's nest of my hair I smooth down with my fingers, rub at my eyes, and pinch my cheeks and lips to give me color—a trick Margot and I learned from the girls at school. I straighten the skirt of my mourning dress, wrinkled beyond recognition at this point. *Never mind*, I tell myself, looking up in time to catch Jared, with a shock of blond falling artlessly over one eye, staring at me in amusement.

I grace him with my blandest, most ice-princess expression. "Please let them in."

Silence stretches out between us for a moment as he considers whether I've lost my mind. Then, finally, Jared reaches over to kiss the top of my hair.

"Your wish is my command, your imperious pain in the ass."

Outside, Carl's low, ticking chuckle fills the air. The hair on the back of my neck stands up as Jared saunters over to slowly, carefully, open the door.

"Finally," Serena says as she wipes her perfect pale forehead and steps into the small house. "I thought we were going to have to resort to show tunes."

"And you're tone deaf," Carl tosses out, chucking the butt of a cigar onto the weedy sidewalk outside. "That would be painful for everyone."

"Says the cat who thinks yowling is an art form." Serena halts just inside the small foyer. Carl comes up behind her and discreetly arranges her hand above his elbow, then guides her to the large black chair beside the couch. She sinks gratefully into its deep pocket, sighing, and gets comfortable. Carl leans on his elbow to stretch across its back.

"Nice place you've got here," Serena says breezily.

Jared looks fit to explode, so I cut in with a noisy clearing of my throat. "To what do we owe this…*unexpected* visit, Serena?"

I'm not certain how I think she'll reply , but it isn't to throw her head back and laugh, long and loud. Even Carl can't help but be moved by its infectiousness. He makes a ticking purr of a sound deep in the back of his throat.

"I beg your pardon." My words are ice. "I'm afraid I don't

understand your amusement."

"Oh, I'm sorry. I just— It's amazing," she tells me, wiping tears from her eyes.

I bite out my words. "What is amazing?"

She meets my gaze with her unearthly one, all hint of humor evaporated. "How utterly ignorant you are."

I'm stunned to silence, while Jared, who'd been leaning against the door as though he hadn't a care in the world, bares his teeth and steps forward.

"Jared." I say his name under my breath, certain he can hear the panic in its tone. I don't want a bloodbath in such close quarters.

Serena wears the same black leather pants as earlier, in the scrum, but she's dressed now in a black halter top. A bruise slides along one shoulder. Her right cheek is decorated with a red welt. I decide to change tacks.

"They hurt you?"

Serena makes a dismissive noise. Her hair falls along her back like a white curtain. Carl's claws flex almost by instinct on the upholstery. "They wish."

"But you're bruised."

She puts a light hand to her face. "Oh, this? They got lucky. It won't happen again," she says as Carl touches his bullet belt.

"If I'm so ignorant, perhaps you would be so kind as to enlighten me."

Serena focuses on a spot at my neck. I don't like her concentrated attention on the flow of my blood.

"It's happened," she whispers. Reaching out for Carl's paw excitedly, Serena sits forward to examine me more closely.

"What's happened? What are you talking about?"

"The miracle we've been waiting for."

"Serena," Jared breaks in, "you've got about ten seconds to explain before I lose my patience and toss you both out of here."

Carl snorts and scratches at his neck. "You wish."

Jared's eyes flash. The air grows heavy with the scent of bloodlust. I jump up and wedge my body between them as Carl paces a step forward.

"Not here. There's been enough bloodshed today. We're calling this neutral territory. Okay?" I turn around to face Jared, then Carl. "Okay?"

Carl hisses but steps back. Serena drawls, "Sit down, Carl, would you? You're blocking my view." She raises her arms in a feline stretch as she yawns, a bored expression on her face. "Listen, it's been a long, long couple of days and we have a lot of material to get through and not much time to do so. So why don't you get your pretty-boy butt into the kitchen, Jared, and make us all some coffee, and we can get to it. Hmm?"

An hour later, coffee mugs litter the small glass-topped side tables. An empty pot leaves brown lunar rings across its surface. Carl licks at his paw and scowls as I pull up my feet and hug my knees to my chest. Jared leans back and puts his arm around me. His warmth seeps in, taking the chill from my bones, just as we hear a copter's roar rip over the house. It's close enough to make me flinch.

Sweat pools on my lower back and under my arms from all the coffee. My heart has gone jittery, my mouth dry. And a raging tide of panic threatens to drown me. I fist my hands in my lap and stare at them, wishing I could undo what I've heard.

Because, in the space of an hour, my worldview has been shattered.

All this time. All this time, and I never suspected that the Salvagers were different for a reason. They used to talk about people like Serena, the Salvagers whose special gift it is to sniff out other True Borns. A senator friend of our father's had once famously suggested putting a Salvager or two on payroll. *Keep a bird in hand so we know how many are in the bushes*, as one laughingly said.

But I've never heard of one, not on payroll, not anywhere, who would work for the Upper Circle. Now I know why. Because the Salvagers are followers of Cernunnos, the Horned One. They're the Order's holy people.

And their one occupation?

To find me. To find Margot and me.

And to read what is written in our mingled blood. *If Serena's right.*

"There's a name for you." Serena had traced the scar across my neck. "Salvagers call you *aingeal*. It's our story, the tale of our people, told through centuries and passed down from generation to generation. The one," she told me happily, "we have been waiting for. *Aingeal*: the memory of the gods.

"You know what DNA really is, Lucy? It's a memory chip of eons past, switching things on and off like a computer program."

"What about our DNA? Doc Raines says it doesn't act human. More like nanotech."

"That's because it's not fully human. What I read in you… What I see in you…" Serena looked over my limbs as though they were word-filled pages. She lifted a long, slim hand to trace down my cheek. "It's the most awful thing, losing your sister. But she lives on in you. That day…" I almost don't hear Serena's next words through the pounding of blood in my ears. I can't even think about that moment, when the knife came down. "Her blood mixed with yours. And the truth was revealed."

"What truth is that, Serena?"

"You are Cernunnos's child."

Jared jumped in. "Now hold on. Lucy doesn't need more of your tall tales."

But the sightless woman just shook her head. "It's true. I know it sounds fantastic—" Jared snorts. Ignoring him, Serena continues. "I know it sounds crazy."

Wanting nothing more than to hide, I pulled myself as far back onto the couch as I could. "How do you know I am…what you think I am?" I rasped.

She looked me over, her eyes flitting across my neck. "How do I know? Because I see it. It's there in your veins. Like sap in a tree. It's rising. It's changing."

"You think somehow my father and his partners got ahold of your god's DNA and Spliced us with it." It's not a question. And Serena doesn't seem to take it as one.

The pretty young Salvager turned and faced the window. "The DNA was separated. And a strand was put in each of you girls. You reassembled the strands. The DNA was made right again. It brings back what we lost so long ago."

Two circles, conjoined. Margot and me. Sisters of two bloods.

My head reeled as I considered the implications. "How could something like that even happen? It sounds like a fairy tale."

Serena shrugged. She reached out a hand again and traced the scar across my neck. Her touch burned like cold fire. "Was her blood on the blade that bit your neck?"

. . .

"I don't know if I can believe any of this," I tell her now as I turn my attention to the Salvager and her sidekick. Carl picks at a matted clump of fur on his belly. Serena taps her long, thin fingers on the armrest of her chair.

"Can't blame you. But there it is." Her fingers turn over, empty, as though proof of her honesty.

"But what for? What's it good for?"

"Don't you see?" White-blond hair floats around Serena's face, making her seem like a young girl. "If Cernunnos's people come back, then we'll all be free."

"But aren't Cernunnos's people the True Borns? They *are* back. So why does everybody need my blood?"

"You still don't understand."

Our conversation is cut short as the air becomes charged. Jared and Carl jump up. Jared rushes to the back of the house where the kitchen windows look out onto a weedy backyard. Carl pounces over to the front, his tail twitching furiously.

"What is it?" I croak.

They say nothing. Serena strains as she glances blindly around the room.

"They hear something." She shakes her blond mane. "We thought we weren't followed, but it's probably best if we go now."

I grab her thin wrist just as she's rising. "No! There's more I need to know."

"You're right." Serena squeezes my hand and looks to Jared and Carl. "Lucy needs to know what she's capable of."

"And yet I'm wondering why I should trust anything you've said. You were with *them*." I nod my head to the door, in the direction of where I expect soldiers and Senator Nash to appear at any second.

Serena takes up both my hands in hers. "Listen closely, Lucy. You and your sister were sown with Cernunnos's seed. Do you understand what that means? You were both made perfect but incomplete. But when the two lines, born together, rejoin... My mother said a new race would be born. The strong children of Cernunnos, children from the ancient times. And then we'd all be free." Her white eyes gleam with the light of the fervent. *Just like the preacher men*, I think cynically. I try to ignore the twinge of my conscience reminding me that, until today, I thought of Serena as a friend.

"But you betrayed us," I admit, confused. "And you betrayed the True Borns."

"No." Serena shakes her beautiful head just as Carl does a little jump. "It was necessary to make them believe we were helping them."

The orange cat man leans his head back to regard us. "We got some people at the gate. Time to skedaddle."

"You were with them," I hiss, ignoring Carl's warning. "You helped them. They've outlawed the True Borns."

Serena turns her unerring eyes on me, a tendril of a smile blooming on her beautiful face. She holds a soft hand to my cheek. "You'll see. There really are no sides to choose. This is just one piece moving across a vast game board. And everything, everything, sweet Lucy, is accomplishing the will of Cernunnos."

"What are you taking about? How could any of this—"

Before I can get my answers, Serena is up and moving toward the front door. Carl is already there, throat rumbling, as something hard taps on the front door. *A gun*, my mind supplies.

Then Jared is there, hauling me to my feet with burning

eyes. He nods slightly to Carl, who nods back. Jared leads me to the back door and we're out, pushing our bodies through head-high weeds that tug and grab at us. Out front are raised voices, shouting. A burst of gunfire sounds like the staccato beat of a drum. And then, above the fray, Carl's high-pitched yowl.

"*RUN!*"

27

We run like our hair is on fire through the wreckage of Dominion's tin-can neighborhoods. Block after block blurs by before Jared lets us slow to a fast walk. It's early enough still that there aren't many Lasters on the streets, save a few pushing carts or those handful of humped bodies, wrapped in blankets. Finally we get off the sidewalks and streets. Threading me through a small apartment complex as he surveys dilapidated balconies piled high with junk, Jared just stops and tucks me against a wall so I'm not exposed.

"Stay here. Don't move. *Please*." He needn't waste his breath. I'm so tired from our flight I have to fight the desire to sink down to the ground. But from the glittering fire of his eyes and the stubborn set to his jaw, I know he'll haul me to my feet again. So instead I push my head back against the concrete frame, hands on hips as I try to bring my heartbeat back to normal. Jared disappears into the shadows to emerge once again on the far side of the courtyard. He leaps, his body lengthening as he grabs on to the balcony above him and pulls himself up, hand over hand, one floor, then another, until he stands on a fourth-floor balcony blocked by clothes drying in the breeze.

He rifles through some of the laundry, then tosses down a few items, pale, bodiless arms and legs, before he climbs down a story or two and jumps bonelessly to the ground. He joins with the shadows again after gathering his bundle, reemerging before me.

I pluck from his arms a shirt hardened from drying in the air. "How do you reckon they found us?"

He pushes me back into an alcove. "Probably put a tracker on one of them. They likely didn't know they were putting us in danger, if that's what you were wondering. Here, change your clothes." He tosses a few more pieces at me. I must look crazy because his lips quirk up and he *tut*s at me. "Don't be difficult, Princess. I don't want to have to strip you myself. A lot of people got a good look at us. We need to change our clothes. I promise not to peek." He winks.

He's right, I realize with a sigh. Despite the lack of privacy, it's our best option for getting around the city. Seconds tick by as I look around for Peeping Toms. The yard appears empty at the present, but that doesn't mean there's nobody watching.

"Before midday, please, Princess?" Jared's face has gone stiff, his neck frozen as he holds up a towel to guard my privacy. "What's the matter?" He gives me a wicked smile as he drawls the word out. "Scared?"

I snort. "Not likely. Just… make sure no one can see, all right?" As I push the fabric of my soiled gown down over my shoulders, though, something changes. I'm no longer worried about anyone in the yard watching. Just Jared. A muscle twitches in his jaw, leaving in its wake deep dimples. His eyes rove from my shoulders to my mouth, where I realize I've been biting my lip. A low sound rumbles through the air. It takes a moment for me to connect the sound with Jared, who stares at me with the intensity of a true predator.

After a long, wavering beat I slowly bend to pull on a pair of trousers under my long slip. I pull the silky fabric of my slip up and over my head. Jared's knuckles grasp the towel so tightly they turn white. His face is a mask of quiet intensity. But it's his eyes that grip me, so alive and filled with fire they could burn a house down. I take a quavering sip of air into my lungs. Another. The world stands still as we take each other's measure.

"Jared." The words are still on my lips as his mouth comes down on mine, hard and solid and hot. His lips part mine, his tongue scraping against the tender flesh and teeth as he drinks me in. The world spins in vertigo color as he backs me up against the concrete wall. His hands cover me in the towel but then traverse down my length, fingers dipping below the waistband of the too-large trousers.

Jared's teeth abandon my mouth. I'm bereft until I feel them scrape along the tender skin of my belly under the towel, inching up to my collarbone, inciting a riot of flesh each step of the way. I shiver and press a hot kiss against his shoulder. Power rips through me as I feel his huge, solid body shudder and draw me closer. Closer.

Just as suddenly as a storm, he stops and rests his forehead against my own.

"Lu." He presses the word against my flesh with a tender kiss. His voice sounds ragged, as though he's been fighting. "Lu, this isn't right. We can't. We've got to keep moving."

He's right. Still, I can't help but feel a tiny part of myself grow smaller as I pull on the long-sleeve shirt Jared has found for me. *And I've done it again.* I've given in to my hunger for the True Born knowing full well I should be backing away. I have been proposed to. It's not the same as being promised, not really. But I do feel like I inhabit a strange limbo state almost as strange as death since Storm's request. That twilight state is constant for me now. I'm but a ghost of my former self. The mere thought of my twin leaves me feeling itchy dread, tingling with cold.

I should be in the ground with her. *We promised.*

But Jared — Jared pulls me back to the living. His fingers restlessly hike up the fabric over my shoulder, his gaze hungry on my flesh. "Don't take this the wrong way, Lu." He flashes a grin and strips off his own shirt. My mouth waters as I take in the carved muscles of his torso. "But I think we need to keep your clothes on. You are way too distracting."

The knot forming in my throat dissolves. Jared locks on my mouth. I swallow. The True Born tracks the movement with the concentrated attention of a hunter. The air between us grows heavy, weighted.

Kkkk-rrr—ooo! The long, shrill croon of a rooster in the yard pulls us to our senses. Jared pounces as I turn, only to watch the small, uninterested bird strut across the courtyard.

"They keep chickens?" The rooster sounds his alarm again, wrecking the silence of the early morning.

Jared shoots me a puzzled look. "How else do you think the Lasters survive?" And then, finally in a new gray pullover that settles too tightly across his shoulders and abs, he tugs me into action.

Still, I continue to hear that rooster's cry long after Jared winds me through the labyrinth of streets.

· · ·

It is somewhere near sundown when Jared's phone pulses, rousing me from sleep. At first I can't tell where I am: the air has become a wash of fog, with objects disappearing in the white mist. Jared's arm, tucked close around me, jerks as he reaches behind him for the gadget.

"Yes." He says it quietly enough, turning his head away to help me stay asleep. But the restless heat of our bodies pulls me further into wakefulness. *Too hot, too hot.* Every inch of his body had been pressed against mine, and where he pries away now, coolness seeps. I shiver feverishly. He's been gone just for a brief second, but already I miss his arm. Most of all, I miss his light, tickling breath against my neck.

And it's wrong, all wrong, I remind myself. I reach out, feeling the still, empty cord that marks Margot's absence as the familiar litany takes root. *She's gone, she's gone, she's gone.*

I stuff back tears, deciding to focus instead on the taut lines of Jared's back and our makeshift campsite. We're bedded down underneath an eroded iron bridge, black with age and covered in thick trails of rust. In front of us flops a boulder-size concrete block. Part of it has crumbled away, giving it the appearance of a chipped tooth. Another, with a rusted broken pipe sticking out from it, guards us on the other side, offering us a convincing illusion of privacy.

The bridge skips across the water but sags so low in the middle it looks like it's sticking a toe in the water. The air is still and quiet, the water's trickle a lullaby, and something about the emptiness of the place had rocked me into the first deep, healthy sleep I've had since before Margot and I were captured.

"Uh-huh, okay," Jared murmurs beside me while sweeping the area like a proper merc. When he feels me watching him, he fastens his gaze to mine. "Uh-huh, okay," he says again. I watch his lips, the perfect full arc of them, and lose myself in a daydream about them rifling over my neck.

If I thought a life with this True Born was impossible before, it's nothing to how impossible things seem now—now that Margot is gone, now that my father wants to murder me. Now that the leader of the True Borns has expressed a desire to marry me.

What would we be like if we'd met in some ordinary way?

"'Kay, Doc. I said okay… An hour." Jared flips the phone shut. My stomach rumbles loudly. It feels as though a week has passed since we've eaten.

"What's happening?" The overhang makes my voice echo and sound tinny.

"We're going to take a little field trip to Doc Raines's."

I absently clutch at the front of Jared's now soiled dress shirt, feeling hot and dizzy. "Jared. Be serious for once."

Jared stares at my hand as though he's never seen its like. His fingers worry at my nail, chipped in the dash from our safe house to here, and filthy to boot. "Lu." There's something soft and open to Jared's face as he seemingly plucks my thoughts from my mind. "What if all this stuff wasn't happening? Do you think— Would we still want to know each other?"

My mouth gapes open, but I have no words. What would my life be like without him? Awful, I reckon. But…had my life continued as before, a princess of the Upper Circle? A small finger of doubt prods me.

Had my life continued as before, would we even have grown to care about each other? My parents would have made sure we never became friends no matter how often we were thrown together. And me? I likely would have been more than happy to do my duty by marrying whichever of the rich elites my father chose for me.

The silence goes on just a beat too long. But by then it's too late. Jared turns his head and pulls our bodies apart, ripping my heart in the process. He sniffs and turns away. "The doc's expecting us, and it's a long way off. We'd better get a move on."

We pluck our way through the ruins of unnaturally quiet streets. No faces appear at the windows of the car motels, where people sleep in burned-out automobiles stacked four and sometimes five high. There are no preacher men, nor their followers. No one. Yet the staccato beat of gunfire sounds somewhere to the west, not far from where we snake past buildings that could have been bombed for all I can tell.

Jared flattens me to the side of a building. I frown at him as I try to catch my breath. My chest feels crushed, not just by his arm but by the terrible sadness brewing in me. His nose twitches as he pins me, murmuring, "You need to take a shower, Princess."

My frown slides into a glare. "That's so…so…impossibly rude!"

Jared tilts his head with a charming smile, as though we're at a garden party. "And you're so easy to rile." He leans down and moves his iron bar of an arm from my chest, only to take me in his huge hands. His lips brush the soft skin of my ear, sending shock waves through my protesting body. "Keep it together, Princess," he whispers, nipping softly as my stomach tumbles. "We're almost there."

Our eyes meet then, electric and fierce. *It wouldn't matter.*

The realization hits me like a Flux storm. It wouldn't matter if, in another life, Jared and I had never crossed paths. *We've met.* We've met, and now nothing will ever be complete again without the arrogant, beautiful True Born. I don't know when my hands snake out and grab at his, holding on as for dear life.

"Jared." I want nothing more than to tell him, no matter the cost to me.

I take a deep lungful of air filled with ash and smoke and death. I cough and can't continue. There must have been a fire, I reckon, as plumes of smoke begin to fill the sky in earnest.

A shout fills the emptied streets. Gunfire erupts. Jared's eyes swing to the left, his body flattening against mine. His lips crush against my ear, the words so quiet I'm not sure I hear them. "When I say so, we're going to roll into that alley. Got it?"

His body is tight with tension as he waits for me to respond. With a gulp, I nod and try to peek over Jared's broad frame. But in the falling dusk I can see nothing, none of the dark-clad bodies of the army. Nothing but emptiness, though I hear the bullets ricocheting across the alleys. Dust spills down on our heads from a bullet that hits the wall above us. And the steady metallic hum of a large vehicle. The ground shakes as it nears, more dust raining down on us.

As much as I want to ask where it's coming from, what's heading our way, I can tell from Jared's tense, sober expression that now is not the time. Now is the time for— *"Now."* He snarls fiercely and pulls me close as he pitches me to the ground. We roll against the wall and nearly fall as we round a corner. The gunfire immediately sounds further away—

And we are faced by the stuff of nightmares.

• • •

I've never seen one on Dominion's streets, though I've heard of them. Robbie Deakins has told us often enough about Dominion's military might over the years that I'd know it by sight. The metal carapace the size of a car motel stitches its way through the streets on rotating tracks. With every inch it takes, its canon gun zooms around, looking for a fight. And it's loud, so loud I can't hear myself think.

Nash has loosed tanks on the streets of Dominion.

Jared doesn't wait for the tank to find us. He pulls me into a crouch, and in seconds we're trailing through debris-strewn streets. We weave past a Plague-bit body, and Jared tugs me toward a narrow gap between buildings.

By the time we arrive at the stately brick townhouse, deep in the section of Dominion where the rich doctors and lawyers live, clustered like bats in a cave, we're breathless and bedraggled. I've worn a hole in the knee of the Laster breeches Jared stole for me. My shirt is filthy. There is something stuck in my hair I'd as soon not ask about.

Jared fares hardly better than me. A streak of dirt smears across one cheek, making him look even more dangerous as he glowers at Doc Raines's tall oak door.

"You need to push the button," I remark drily as he continues to stare at it.

"Sass?" Jared quirks up an eyebrow at me. "At a time like this?"

He's joking, but that's all it takes, just those five little words and my knees start knocking together. I'm scared—and not for myself. What if they've taken Doc Raines?

The door flies open, and a springy set of locks bounds out toward us. Glancing around like a merc, Doc Raines wordlessly extends her skinny white arms and hauls us both inside.

I open my mouth, about to ask her what's happening. She shuts me down with a finger to her lips. She turns, still silent, and bids us to follow her up a set of floating wooden stairs. We pass a large drawing room on the second floor, the expansive white walls rising at least forty feet covered in large, bright canvases.

She continues past these, not even glancing back, and, with her thumb, opens another wooden door with an Identi-pad. The door leads to more stairs, narrower than the last, and as auto lights come on when we head up the stairs, I smell what has become familiar to me these past few months: sterilizer and chemical soup overlaid with the steady purr of fridges and cell separators. We pass through another set of doors, another Identi-pad, and enter Doc Raines's personal lab.

It's the longest, brightest lab I've ever seen. Six floor-to-ceiling windows, rounded at the tops, line one wall. Doc Raines touches a small pad near the door and the windows tint, masquerading the room from clear light to dim.

"What?" I begin to ask. Doc Raines shushes me quietly. Her hand goes to the panel, and she enters in a series of numbers. A light noise filters through the room, sounding a bit like the crackling of paper.

Beside me, Jared raises an eyebrow, impressed. "You've got an interceptor system, Doc?"

"I've learned that a healthy dose of paranoia is not a bad thing," Doc Raines drawls. The mechanical hum fills the room as the doc turns and strides quickly down the long bank of bench space filled with whirring machines. She opens a walk-in fridge, her frizzy halo of curls peeking out. "Well? Come on.

We don't have all day."

When Doc Raines returns a few moments later, there's a small specimen tray balanced in each hand. She closes the fridge door with her foot and a blast of chilly air puffs up like smoke. I rub my arms against the cold of the lab. Wordlessly, Jared walks over to the wall where a line of white coats hangs like bodies in the breeze. He grabs one, examines the tag briefly, and comes back to shake it out over my shoulders. "Thank you," I murmur, just as Doc Raines turns her attention to a screen and lights it up.

"Yes, get cozy," she says absently. "We have a lot to talk through and I suspect we don't have long."

"What do you mean?"

"That buffoon Nash has declared a civil war on the True Borns. It's only a matter of time before one of my colleagues turns me in for being so closely associated with the True Borns. I'm certain they've already bugged my house."

My heart begins to pound as I jump to my feet, looking for the exits. "We have to get you out of here."

Doc Raines levels me with a quiet, determined look. "There are more important things to discuss right now. Sit down, Lucy. We need to talk about the new genetic mutations your body is producing."

28

New genetic mutations. Serena hadn't had time to explain what it was she saw written in my blood.

Doc Raines picks up a test tube and shakes it, packing it in a tray before neatly stacking the rest of the tray with the others.

"You asked me to run Protocols. Remember? After Margot died."

I shake, feeling like the explosions rocking the city outside the building are happening inside me, too. Jared puts a steadying hand to my back.

"Yes. You have some results?"

Doc Raines nods and picks up one of the petri dishes. "What happens in this little dish is one thing. What happens in a live person is a whole other story."

"She got inside me, didn't she?" The words come out as whispers. The hair on the back of my neck rises as Doc Raines nods.

"I don't know how to say it any other way, Lucy. Maybe it was just a trace of her blood, but it seems to have acted like what you called magic bombs. The exact same kind of accelerated proliferation rate that's behind the Prayer Tree. Not only did Margot's blood respond to your anchor and trigger, it went nuts, like its programming was tripped. It started creating the True Born Talismans at a remarkable pace. Those expressions are growing inside you, Lucy."

Jared's hands squeeze my shoulder and neck. Black spots swim before my eyes as I'm swamped with horror. "What do you mean? Am I going to die?"

Doc Raines shakes her frizzy nest. "I don't think so. But I believe it has an important purpose. A function, if you will. Just like good nanotechnology would."

"What purpose?"

Doc Raines bends down to look me in the eye. I've never seen her so serious. "It would be so simple to harvest the strains."

"Counter-Plague," Jared murmurs. "Right."

"What? What?" I repeat woodenly. But it all makes sense now.

Lock and key, that tiny voice inside me murmurs. *Evolve or die.*

"It acts like an antidote to a snake bite, or an inoculation. See, both the Plague and True Born Talismans remake the DNA in the human body. The difference is, the True Born Talismans make the host subject stronger. The Plague, on the other hand, reprograms the cells in the human body to eat themselves. And here's where things get interesting. Jared is right. I really think that the stuff your body is producing can be given to others."

"Like a natural Splice?"

Pursing her lips, Doc Raines considers this for a moment.

"Yes, we can go with that analogy. There's nothing natural about it, mind you. You've definitely been engineered, you and your sister. Like perfect doomsday clocks in reverse."

My head reels. Jared leans in and asks in a low voice, "So how would you go about infecting people with the cure, Doc?"

"It looks like it could accommodate multi-modal transmission. I think the skin could easily absorb it, for one. If it were to enter the water supply, or were injected... Think about the way the Prayer Tree was made, using a bomb format." Lasters were rioting on the streets the day the Prayer Tree was created. Margot watched as a bomb was thrown. There'd been an explosion. And a few hours later, right where the explosion had ripped up the concrete, sprouted a tree. A tree that became giant almost overnight.

"Maybe I don't completely understand." I'm trembling from head to foot, and I'm colder now than I've ever felt in my life. I must look lousy, too, because Jared puts a hand to my forehead.

"She's burning up, Doc."

Doc Raines unfolds her crossed arms and spins into action. "Yes, that doesn't surprise me. Lucy, your body is manufacturing the specimens at a unique, exponential rate. You must have been experiencing the effects for the past few days, haven't you? You're liable to feel ill, as though you've come down with the flu."

The past little while suddenly makes sense: the impression that something was happening in my body, like an ignition switch had been thrown, accompanied by waves of heat and dizziness. I nod and pluck Jared's hand from my forehead. "You said I'm like a doomsday clock. Am I dangerous?"

"No, not in and of yourself," Doc Raines says, pulling a thermometer gun seemingly from thin air and sticking it in my ear. "One hundred and eight," she murmurs, tucking a swear in under her breath. "We've got to get your fever down, Lucy." She adopts the stern tones of a Protocols nurse.

"Will it kill me?"

Doc Raines pauses her whirlwind of activity to consider me. "Not if we're careful. I think extracting some of the Talismans your body is producing will help. Right now your body is both an incubator and a factory. It's burning a lot of fuel as it manufactures its code. But if you think about it, factories are rarely self-destructive. There comes a point when the body's natural defenses will shut down the production. Which also means that the present moment is critical."

"What do you mean?" I ask the question but am not so certain I want to hear the answer. Margot's death has swept me like a raging fire, cold and heartless as it burns out of control. But as an inkling of an idea takes shape, I can see, for the first time, the glimmering outlines of hope: that something good might come of her loss.

I might be able to wreak a measure of revenge against those who've betrayed my sister and me—and against our makers. Maybe we don't have to be pawns in everyone else's game.

Maybe we can be our own destiny, Margot and I.

Doc Raines looks sad as she stops, one lock of frizz wavering in the currents in the air. "They're not really after me or Jared, or even Storm." She doesn't bat an eyelash. "Are they, Lucy?"

And in a wash of guilt I understand: the war declared on True Borns, the tanks on the street…are all just bait to get to me.

The house rumbles and vibrates. Jared hurries to the window, turning feral before my eyes as he curses. Fine fur has sprung up along his wrists and hands and the nape of his neck.

"Tank," he says thickly. Another spatter of gunfire sounds in the distance, an echoing one closer by. "How many exits you got, Doc?" he asks, his features melting once again into a gorgeous man's.

"Three. What's going on?"

"I suspect they've come to call on us."

Doc Raines whirs into action. She throws test tubes into bags, then jumps into the walk-in and returns with trays curling with icy vapors.

Jared steps into her path. "Just what do you think you're doing, Doc? We've got to go."

Doc Raines flips a corkscrew from her eyes and stares at Jared balefully. "I'm not leaving our samples here for them to find. Lucy." She nods at me. "Grab my instruments, please. If we become separated, we need to meet up at the sugar refinery near the port."

"Sugar?"

My disbelief must show, as Doc Raines arches an eyebrow at me. "Doesn't look as though you've got a lot of choice but to trust me, Lucy. But yes, Storm put together a backup lab for me there."

She's right. I have exactly two people on my team at present. Three of us against an army of Dominion's finest, including tanks that haven't been deployed in a generation. All looking for me.

And no sister to keep you careful.

The world tilts again as I consider this heady freedom. No Margot to worry about, except the pieces of Margot locked inside me.

"A backup lab?"

Not a second later, a light blinks off and on in Doc Raines's lab coat pocket. I hear the buzz as she extracts the small phone and taps it on.

"Yes." Her tone curt and sharp as a scalpel, Doc Raines smooths a hand over her hair. I watch as her eyes harden into cold planets.

I think it's an accident that I can see her fingers trembling. Then, a moment later, she extends the phone to me. Her eyes are round as marbles. Her face has gone white as a winding sheet.

"It's for you."

Jared pounces before I take the phone. He holds my wrist close to his ear, a warning light in his eyes. I bend in and listen to the quiet hum of air and wonder if it's Storm calling. Then the world drops out from under my feet as the familiar voice that has shaped my life spills into the sterile lab.

"Lucinda." It's a harsh voice, bitter with cold.

"Father." Panic floods me. *How does he know where I am, who I'm with?* "What do you want?" I'm glad I sound harsh and full of hate, not like the quivering child I am inside.

"You foolish little girl." His voice is thick with contempt. It's a tone I'm familiar with: the scathing tenor he uses on business partners who disappoint him.

My heart pounds. Sweat gathers on my neck and back and hands. I clear my throat. "I said, what do you want?"

I'm shocked when a tinny laugh echoes through the phone. "I want you, of course, my darling daughter."

"I think at this point we can firmly establish that I'm not your daughter."

"Legally you are. And True Borns are holding you against my will."

Jared hisses as I walk myself through his logic. It's still not enough to warrant tanks on the streets, but then again, Lukas Fox has friends in the highest of places.

"What's going to happen, *Father*," I mock, "when I tell the senate and the rest of the world that you've been pedaling fake Plague Cure?"

His voice is sinuous and thick. "Which is why I need to get my darling daughter back. Think of the millions of souls who can be saved."

"You're *sick*," I spit, overcome by rage. Jared's lips rise in a snarl, but he curls a hand over my arm, holding me steady. Reminding me I'm not alone. But I'm lost in a storm that has been brewing, unbidden, inside me. And it breaks with the suddenness of a Flux storm.

"You killed my sister. You killed my sister, you murderer!"

A pause. I hitch a deep breath, readying myself for whatever bullets will next fly from my mouth.

"That was a mistake that I regret," he breaks in.

It's not lost on me that this is the first time in my life I've heard my father come anywhere near apologizing for anything. But it doesn't make a dent in the inferno whipping about inside me.

"Because you figured out you needed her. And now it's too late."

"I didn't kill her, Lucinda. A madman killed your sister."

"Wes wielded the ax, true." I grab at my neck, feeling the memory of his blade. "But he was your hand. *We heard you. I* heard you."

The line falls static and empty for a moment before my father's voice pumps in again. "The doctor's house is surrounded with tanks and an entire squadron. I'd like you to come out first.

Keep your hands on your head or they'll shoot. We'll let the True Born and the doctor come out second. If they cooperate, they'll not be killed."

"Go to hell," I snarl, and click the phone off. I haul it back to hurl it at the window when Jared plucks it from my fingers.

"We've got to go, Luuuuu," he says. I watch as his face swims into brown and black zigzagging dots. "Luuuu? Luuu, honnnn…"

Which is all I hear before the world crawls to black.

It seems like hours later that I'm dragged away through a river of tears, tears raining down on the world like red death. I feel as though my body is floating, fragmenting into a hundred pieces. Rough hands grasp me. A buzzing sound fills my ears as the world swims back, and I surface from the dream. I blink and try to anchor my eyes on Jared. A ferocious light pierces my eyeballs and wavers back and forth.

"Good." I hear the low, rumbling tones of Doc Raines. "She's responsive."

Somehow I've ended up on the floor, head cradled in Jared's lap, which explains why his face is upside down. I try to move but am racked with a sudden intense chill that puts my body into spasms.

"Dammit." Doc Raines opens her medical bag and pulls out a hypodermic. She thrusts it into my neck before I can say a word. Moments later, the chill melts away in a sea of warmth. "It's not going to last long." She cocks an eyebrow at Jared. "Let's get moving."

And the windows explode with a parade of bullets. *So much for amnesty.*

Glass shatters across the room, spilling out like confetti in thick shards. Holes the size of my palm riddle the opposite wall. Jared plucks me up into his arms as though I am no heavier than a rag doll and crouches through the row of glass-coated benches. We arrive at a door tucked beside the walk-in fridge, all but unnoticed. Doc Raines is already there ahead of us. She keeps her body low to the ground while she lifts her thumb to the Identi-pad. The door *shucks* open to reveal a passageway. "I built an escape hatch," she says, dry as toast.

I'm locked in weightless, spinning vertigo as I'm carried over an invisible threshold, down a set of dimly-lit stairs. Jared's hands are warm anchors on my flesh. I can feel each trip of his heart as he breathes, in, out. And despite everything, despite bullets and tanks and my father, I feel safe.

Doc Raines's voice floats up from below. "One more flight." A crack of light appears, and I catch the frizzy blur of Doc Raines's hair as it bobs out of sight. "This way."

I can feel the rumble of the tank, echoing up through the floor and in Jared's bones. I squeeze my arm tighter around his neck. "Whatever happens—don't let them get me." I swallow. "Kill me first."

In the darkness, Jared's face is a smear of white that lightens with each step. And then he's gazing down at me with wild, soft eyes. "No one is ever going to take you from me, Lu. Not even if they try to pry you from my cold dead hands."

A rattle of gunfire below. Jared stalls and pushes his back against the narrow stairway. He shifts some hair away from my ear. "Can you stand?"

"Think so." My feet come under me, and for a moment it's like I'm back on the large cruise liner that took us across the ocean. Everything sways. My heart stammers in my chest as I wait for the wave of dizziness to pass.

"Lu?" Jared props me up against the wall, his lips curling down in concern. "Don't move, okay?" Touching his ear, Jared begins to whisper into his implant communicator. "We've hit some trouble at Doc Raines's house. Never mind why we're here. Long story. Can you get a crew to the sugar refinery? Yeah. Be there in a few hours."

The silence of the stairwell is suddenly wrecked by a shrill yell, followed by another dash of gunfire. Jared eases himself down the stairwell and waits by the open door. He peeks his head out and returns to me a moment later, pulling at a lock of his blond hair.

"Okay, Princess. Don't fail me now."

I glare at him imperiously. "When have I ever failed you?"

Jared's dimples flash as he contemplates this. "Never, Lu. Not once." His lips come down, smooth and soft against mine. He scrapes my lower lips between his teeth and takes my face gently in his hands, tilting me slightly to better capture my mouth.

My head spins. I stare up at him. "You don't think we're going to make it, do you?"

His silent breathing is confirmation enough for me. "I should never waste a single opportunity to kiss you senseless, Lucy Fox. I shouldn't waste a single moment not telling you—"

But I don't hear the rest of his words. The high-pitched whine of incoming bombs drowns them out. Behind us, the night explodes.

Jared flattens me against the wall. "Plague Fire," he curses. As flames lick up the walls, the True Born pulls me down the rest of the stairs. He stops just shy of the door and peers out before dragging me out and around the corner. Seconds later, a belch of smoke and flame erupts from where we just had been standing. The streets fill with noise as people stream out from their houses.

"C'mon." He tugs me into the fray, and I follow, shucking the white lab coat, letting it land on the street like a lifeless body.

We turn the corner. A soldier in full riot gear blinks and rounds his rifle on us. "You're under arrest!" His gun shakes from side to side as he trains it on us.

Jared neatly plucks the rifle from the startled man's grasp. He hurls it to the ground so fast the soldier barely has time to register. I don't even catch the movement when Jared's hands rip the man's helmeted head until it makes a loud *thwack*ing sound. He sinks noiselessly to the ground. I shiver with dread as Jared steps over the corpse and grabs me under the armpits to swing me over. He takes my hand without a backward glance as a platoon of heavy feet tramps our way.

"They're coming," I whisper. I know Jared hears me, though he doesn't make a sound. He runs us over one alley, across another street where the sidewalks are lined with car hotels on either side. He drags me to the second one, stopping only briefly to look in the window before hauling me up and throwing me into the top car of the four-car-high lodging.

By the time I've scrambled to sit on a rock-hard vinyl seat, Jared has jumped in behind me. He darts his head around, looking to see whether the soldiers have spotted us. The car smells like unwashed bodies and rotting food and something that stinks a bit like old car oil. There's a huge rip in the seat that we're on, the vinyl cracked and exposing a chunk of musty yellow foam. I open my mouth to complain about our hidey-hole when two pairs of wide brown eyes and shags of brown hair peek over the front seats at us.

"I thought you checked this one out," I hiss at Jared, who stares at the children as though they're enemy soldiers.

"I can't see in four cars up, Princess."

"Shh. Don't scare the children."

Two young boys by the look of things. Raggedy kids with the gaunt, hungry look of Lasters. One boy's mouth hangs open while the other scratches his head.

"Our pap said no strangers." The head scratcher leans back to take us in.

The snarl melts from Jared's face. "Your pap is smart."

"You're a stranger."

"Yep. But how about we be friends for a moment until the bad soldiers outside go away. How about it?"

The boys seem to think about this, conferring with each other with a look. It reminds me so much of Margot and me that I'm hit with a stab of wild pain. The head scratcher clears his throat. "Yeah, okay." The gaping-mouth kid, clearly the younger of the two, leans over to his brother and whispers something behind a folded hand. It's too faint for me to catch, but a quick glance at Jared tells me he's heard. Then the head scratcher is back, an all-too-wise look on his face.

"Rupe says five bucks."

"Five—what? Robbery!" Jared crosses his arms and glares at the children, who rightly enough pull back and rethink the matter.

The young one, Rupe, pulls a sticky finger from his mouth and points out the window, toward the street. "Soldiers."

Jared and I immediately duck down. The head scratcher leans over the seat and smirks. "Five bucks," he repeats.

"Shark." Jared's eyebrows meet in annoyance, but he pulls a bill from his pocket with a hint of a smile and hands it over.

The boy takes it, turning it over and over like he's never seen its like before.

"Listen, mister, we don't got change." The boy tries to hand it back, but Jared waves him away.

"The first five is for keeping quiet now. The second is for keeping quiet after we're gone. Not a word to your folks, right?"

The boys exchange another look. Then, satisfied, the head scratcher nods. "Deal."

Rupe points. "Soldiers gone in there."

I follow his finger. The building is a small tower, with windows up ten floors. The roof would overlook the street nicely, I reckon. The perfect place to keep watch. Jared, of course, has gotten there ahead of me.

"Time for us to go, kids. Remember." Jared puts a finger to his lips. "Not a word."

The head scratcher loops two fingers together, interlocking them in the middle. "Swear." It's the symbol scrawled now on nearly every wall of Dominion. Conjoined circles. *Evolve or die.*

Jared starts to climb out of the car, but I grab the back of the front seat, startling the children. "Wait. That thing you just did. What is that?"

Rupe shrugs. The older goes back to scratching his head. "What thing?"

"The — the thing. With your hands."

"It's the swear."

"What is the swear?"

The boy scrunches up his nose as though I've said something stupid. "Where do you come from, lady?"

"Please."

"It means 'swear by eternal life' or something like that."

The younger boy pops a finger out of his mouth again. I'm

distracted by a gleaming gap in his mouth where he's lost some teeth, until he says, "You swear on Plague Cure."

"What?"

"Lu, we don't have time for this."

"Oh, right." The elder boy breaks in. "When the Plague's broken." He rolls his eyes. "Like that's ever going to happen. Anyway, when the Plague's done, if you've broken your swear, you don't get to live the long life like the rest of the saved."

"Who taught you this?"

"Comes from the preacher men, I reckon." The boy shoots me another dirty look. "Ain't you a Laster?"

"Sure I am," I say absently.

But all I can think about is the furious beat of my heart. *I get it now.* Father Wes and the Watchers had stolen the prophecy from Serena's mother, then they partnered with the one man in Dominion's Upper Circle with twin girls. Knowing what was possible, what my father and his Russian backers were planning for us, the preacher men and the Watchers taught the Lasters a sign, a byword about a miraculous cure coming to the worthy. And as it spread from building to building, hand to hand, the sign all but promised that the Lasters would do Father Wes's bidding…and make billions from their snake oil.

A knot of nausea grips me as Jared interrupts my train of thought with a furious whisper. "Get your butt down here *now*, Princess."

I shimmy out of the rolled-down window and slip into Jared's waiting arms. He squeezes me briefly, as though to assure himself that I'm safe, before we melt into the shadows and run for our lives.

29

"Gods, I can't stand it." Jared's nose quivers in disgust. We're still a good five hundred meters from the factory, but even from the shadowy bank of the river where we hide, the air is pungent and thick and cloyingly sweet.

My stomach rumbles in disagreement. "I'm starving." There's a hole in Jared's shirt just under the collarbone. He worries a finger through the hole as though judging its size. But at least he has the good grace to wear a hangdog expression.

"I'm sorry, Lu."

We'd come across an open grocer, one that even stocked food, but Jared had given most of his cash away to the Laster boys, and I had none. In the end, we'd settled on splitting a roll and a bag of nuts behind the store. It was little enough for one let alone two, but it had cut the sharp pains in my gut. The intense throbbing of my head had also begun to ease off, as had the nausea brought on by the fever.

"You think it's safe?"

"It's never safe, Lu. Not ever." He doesn't mean it as an admonishment. For Jared this is a fact of life, as true as breath or morning or the sharp edge of a sword. *I'd be wise to remember how true it is, too*, I remind myself.

This is not the Dominion I grew up in. The city is filled with an alien presence. The sky is dotted with drones. Around every corner, a tank and a line of soldiers in their black riot gear stand in sharp contrast to the bleary white of the sky. And everywhere, everywhere, there is the noise of the hunt. There's not a single Laster to be seen, save the dying or the dead. And everywhere, there are the haunting pictures resembling the children's hands. Two conjoined circles.

Plague Cure. *All the Lasters know it.*

Evolve or die.

Jared pulls a strand of my hair from my mouth, gazing at me with an intensity as sharp as my hunger. His eyes fasten on my mouth. Self-conscious, I run my tongue over my lips. Jared's hand jumps to mine.

"Don't do that."

"Why?" I whisper.

"Because if you do I'm going to kiss you senseless, Lu. I'll lose my mind and get us killed."

"No you won't."

"Oh, I will," he promises. I stare at his lips and watch his jaw tighten in response. My heart trips again and I take in a sharp, jagged breath.

"Gods, Lu, please stop. I'm afraid I won't be able to control myself."

And in that moment I realize he's speaking the truth. No matter what the circumstances, he's an inch shy of forgetting himself. It thrills me to high heaven. It scares me to my core. But I reckon it's a quality that calls to something inside me. Because when I'm with him, it feels like I lay myself aside and am reborn as someone else.

Is this what love is?

I don't get to answer this as a sharp, shrill whistle pierces the air. Jared pulls his head up like a rabbit from a hole.

"They're here." He climbs up the small bank and holds out a hand for me. I grab it and end up balancing tight against his body, electric frissons sparking wildly through my veins. "Lu," he murmurs into my hair as he holds me close. "One day we're going to finish this conversation."

"What conversation?" Instead of answering, Jared silences me with a hot, searing kiss. And then he drags me across an asphalt jungle to the bleak, graffiti-covered doors of the abandoned refinery.

The air inside the building is a chalky mixture of dust motes and moss, almost as opaque as the skies of Dominion. With its strange half-light, the wide-open floor with its pipes and machines makes me shiver. Mohawk leans over Doc Raines's shoulder with a flashlight as she tinkers on a flat black box. "There." She smiles in satisfaction and flicks a switch. Lights go on in a row all down the floor.

"Turn them off, Doc." Jared stares daggers.

"Jared, I need them to—"

"Turn them off. The army is searching every corner of the city. You don't think they're going to want to check out the building that's been abandoned for the past twenty years but that just happens to flare to life tonight?"

Doc Raines drops her shoulders in defeat. "I should have considered that." With a flip of the switch, the refinery floor dims again. Mohawk sneezes, leading the light from her flash to bounce chaotically across the floor and the pipes that line the wall like thick ribbons. Jared paces until finally Torch returns from his upstairs sweep.

"Nothing but some rats," he reports. "Though a ton of 'em."

Mohawk shows off her pointy teeth. "Good. I may get hungry later."

"Well, we'll still need a bit of juice and light running into the generators." Doc Raines shakes her bag at the True Borns.

Jared nods at the young man. "Torch, find some juice for the doc. Then stand watch on the upper deck. I want plenty of warning if we're going to have guests."

"Why does he get all the fun?" Mohawk crosses her legs. The muscles in her powerful thighs ripple, making it appear as though the strange patterns on her skin are moving.

Jared crosses his arms and glares. "You need to keep helping Doc Raines."

"Isn't 'the boy' supposed to be the one good at tinkering with machines?"

"Penny." Jared slashes in annoyance at a golden lock that has fallen into his eye. "I need you here on the floor in case we're surprised or overpowered. You need to get Lucy and the doc out of here. Or die trying," he adds grimly.

Mohawk preens, running a hand over the black crest of her hair. "In that case," she purrs, "I'd be happy to."

"What of Storm and the others?" I tug at Jared's sleeve.

Jared's jaw clenches. "We're not to get in touch for a while."

"Why?"

But I know why. Even before Jared lowers his eyes to mine

and says, in a quiet-quiet voice, "So we're not traced back."

I translate mentally. Jared must think Storm is still in custody. "Are you worried?"

"No," Jared tells me quickly enough, though a shadow falls across his eyes as he does.

Something buzzes and pops. A machine blinks on in Doc Raines's hands. "Good. We're in business," she says.

They pump me and prime me and put me through something like Splicer Protocols. Fourteen hours. Just fourteen hours is all it takes to pull from my skin and blood and bone the strange mixture of Margot and me.

As I lie on the floor, my head cradled in Jared's lap, I idly wonder about the Laster men who'd sat for Storm's council. I imagine Theodore Nash's smug, smiling face, crumbling to dust. I try not to think about Margot, or Ali, or the bloody head of Father Wes. And when the fever takes me, it's as though I'm flying, my body so light and unchained I wonder if I still have skin.

I really am dying, my feverish brain supplies. *If I die, Jared will be free.* But Jared keeps me tethered to my body. He wipes the sweat from my forehead as Doc Raines used her laparoscopic pic needles to pull the special True Born Talismans from my body. Twinned strands, one for each of the girls, wound so tightly together they become something else.

I doze. I wake. Sometimes I do both at once, unable to separate wakefulness from the weight of dreams.

And in my more lucid moments, I speak to Jared about the biggest danger we face.

"He owns the Watchers and the army. Don't you see?"

The single greatest threat to anyone, to everyone, is my ruthless father. Lukas Fox.

"Yes." Jared simply agrees, gazing down at me with an unfathomable expression.

"What can we do?" I whisper. A tear escapes to leak down my face. Jared soothes it away with the gentlest of motions. "No one can win against him."

The True Born flips out his cockiest smile. "Don't be so sure."

I snort. But Jared shakes his head. "Look, your dad is undoubtedly a master tactician." I marvel at the word "dad" used to speak of such a man. He's no one's dad. At this point I have trouble thinking of him as anyone's father.

"Yes," I mimic.

"We're ahead of him on this one, Lu." I know Jared means what he says. I know we think that. *But is it true?*

"Five minutes." Doc Raines's voice floats over from somewhere nearby.

"Good." I sigh with relief. "I can hardly wait to get up and walk around awhile."

"You'll need to take it easy." Doc Raines shakes her head in warning. "It's been a long stretch since your last break. You'll likely experience dizziness, nausea, fatigue. And then there's the fact that I have no idea what will happen to you now that we've extracted so much. I can't guarantee you'll be stable."

"Gee, Doc, don't sugarcoat it or anything," Jared mocks.

And then time stops again. I hover in a space between the minutes, where there is only rain. Crimson rain mixing with ashes and tears, falling on the land and turning the parched world new again.

Margot, I was wrong, I muse out loud. *Death is not a glimmering blue at all.*

And when I return to the world, nimble fingers pull wires and tubes from my skin, leaving behind tiny pricks of displeasure. I'm so distracted it takes me a moment to register the chalky white face and drawn expression that mars Jared's handsome features. I raise my hand to touch his cheek but find I can't control it well enough to make contact.

"What's wrong?" I'm weak as a kitten.

"We've got company, Princess. You well enough to stand?"

"Why? Can't we stay here a while longer?"

It's hard for me to read Jared's face in the dim light. At some point it must have fallen dusk again, because now only a garish white light scours the side of his face.

Something is terribly wrong.

I struggle to sit up. "Smell that?" Jared tips his chin to the doors by the far entrance. The one we've locked and double locked and then barricaded for good measure.

A deep, powerful voice trembles the air as the creep of smoke and ash and the horrible, clawing scent of paint and burning wood fills the air.

"Jared, it's now or never." As Nolan Storm swarms into view, Jared nods.

"You've been out for quite a while now, Lucy. How are you feeling?"

My eyes bounce and glide off the powerful leader of the True Borns, a trick I've almost become accustomed to. He's still in his dress shirt from the funeral, though it's become dirty, torn and frayed at one cuff. A pale splatter of red mars one side of his chest. Something like a slight yellow bruise kisses the skin beneath a red welt on his left cheek. They've beaten Nolan Storm. *Beaten him.*

"They hurt you," I say, as if that will somehow make it less true.

"No, Lucy." Storm takes my hands. Between him and Jared, I'm turned upright and set on my jelly-filled legs. I'm struck by a feeling of lightning, the strange unearthliness of the man before me, whose eyes sing of death. He gives me a hint of a smile now, the jagged, tough planes of his face revealing nothing. "They can't hurt me."

"Did you see my father?"

Storm sighs. "Yes."

Jared hooks one arm around my waist and drapes half of me over his shoulder. Storm holds my other arm, and between the two of them I'm carried over to the stairs leading to the second floor.

"I don't think I want to go up there." I give my escorts a baleful look. "I hear there are rats."

"Don't worry," Jared answers breezily. "I think Penny ate most of 'em."

I shiver. Storm lifts my arm, and before I can blink, I'm on the first stair. I glance back at him.

"Did they tell you?"

Storm nods. "Yes." And my foggy brain wonders if he knew before or whether he suspected that Margot and I were of Cernunnos's line, just like him. Was that the reason he's protected us all this time? Is that why he asked for my hand?

I become aware that I've been staring as Jared hoists me higher on his shoulder and squeezes my hand.

"I reckon we're kin, then." I toss the word out bravely, as though this is an everyday announcement. But my legs are tired and weak. My throat is on fire. And I feel as though I've been burning in the everlasting fires of hell forever.

"Something like that." His tone is reassuring, light, but then he smiles at me in a way that tells me his courtliness is a sham.

"Not quite kissing cousins, if that's what you're worried about."
Beside me, Jared grows stiff as a board.

"What happens next?"

"Oh, you and Jared are going to take a little trip."

My mind slips, becomes unpinned from my body. I feel as
though I'm floating. "Is this a dream?" I ask.

"No." Storm's voice is gentle, but it shakes with power. "No,
not a dream. I am going to take the city now, Lucy, so I need
you to go with Jared and be safe. Once I'm finished, we'll get
back to discussing our future and the future of Dominion. All
right by you?"

I don't know whether I nod or not. Storm's arching crown
twists and turns, spidery thick snakes of power rising, and I
become lost in their splendor. But I do feel Jared's hand at my
back, burning hot against my chilled bones.

My throat is parched. My words rasp from a painfully dry
throat. "Are you going to kill him, Storm?"

Storm stares down at me with relentless liquid eyes. "Yes,
Lucy. I'm going to kill your father."

And then somehow, though I'm swamped with disgust and a
strange, elated thrill I can't bear to think about, we're suddenly
pushed through a small door to find ourselves outside, staring
into the mouth of hell.

The sky on all sides of the slightly pitched and warped roof
of the refinery is a gaping, open wound. The typically gauzy sky
bleeds red and orange. Everything is obscured by thick, acrid
smoke heavy with the unmistakable scent of burned sugar.

"What's happening?" I ask, but there's no need. I reckon I
know. Lukas Fox is happening.

My father has set us on fire.

• • •

The wind whips my hair all around my face, but through strands that I bat at with weak fingers, I can make out the heavy pipes of tank guns pointed at the refinery. All around the building are soldiers in SWAT gear. Quickly I pivot my gaze, looking for the sniper who will snuff us out. But a quick glance around proves there are no buildings nearby. Storm chooses his castles well.

Storm gazes dispassionately at the scene below and plucks my thoughts from my mind. "We chose this location for its strategic value. They'll have trouble burning us out, I think. Time enough to do what we must."

My puzzlement over this is broken by the sound of a phone. Storm pulls out the slim device and stares at its screen. We both know who's calling.

A metallic-coated voice rises up from the base of the building. "It's no use, Storm. Send me down my daughter or you'll all die like the little rats you are." Storm doesn't react, except to smile. It's one of the scariest things I've ever seen. Then, a moment later, "Lucinda, listen carefully. All your little True Born friends are going to die. Their blood will be on your hands unless you do exactly as I say."

Prickles of hot shame pop out on my skin. A sudden bout of nausea grips me. I lean over and heave, but there is nothing inside me. Nothing left. Jared holds me with one arm, his hand soothing my back while the other flips my hair away from my face. "Don't worry, Lu." He holds my head as I heave again. "Doc Raines said you'd likely be ill after all that you just went through."

But I know it's more than that. It's the burden of knowing my friends are at risk because of me. *Because I exist.* Still, even had I wanted to listen to Lukas, to give in and give myself up, I reckon I know better.

There have always been whispers among the Upper Circle. Us girls were never meant to know. It was repeated often enough at parties, folded behind fans, that quiet-quiet girls like us were able to hear. *Lukas Fox is the scariest man alive.* I remember hearing this for the first time when Margot and I were maybe eight years old. *He'd serve his mother's organs for dinner if it would get him more power.*

Blinking back a rush of tears, I reckon I can't afford to cling to any illusions now: Lukas Fox will hunt us all down, one by one. He won't let anyone survive. Not the True Borns. *Not Margot,* whispers that terrible voice. Surely not me.

The heavy, whirling buzz of a copter cuts through the mayhem. Choking on the smoke, I watch as it hovers over the building and begins a slow descent as bullets ring into the air like tiny firecrackers.

Jared flattens me onto the ground, his body my shield, just as Storm yells, "Get down."

The scent of Jared suffocates me: the stale scent of Laster laundry soap, his cinnamon woodsy smell strong after such a long time on the run. But I feel safe. Utterly safe, though the world burns.

"You all right, Lu?" comes his anxious voice. He peers down at me, one eye popping green.

I elbow him in the ribs. "God, you'll have to lose some weight if you're going to keep falling on top of me like this, Jared True Born." I don't know what possesses me to joke at a time like this. But it works.

Jared grins, a lazy wicked grin. "*If* I'm going to keep falling on top of you, Lu?"

I snort. "Sometimes you're so weird."

"Yeah." Jared's gaze follows the curve of my cheek, my

mouth, restlessly darting to look me square in the eyes. "But I'm your weird, Lu. All yours."

I can hardly breathe suddenly, and it has nothing to do with his weight. "Jared," I start. The heavy thud of Storm's booted steps interrupts my train of thought.

"Come on." Storm's eyes glow mad with rage. "It's time."

The whine of the copter engine stops, and within seconds, the only sound is the crackling of fire. Storm walks to the edge of the refinery roof and gazes at the chaotic scene below. It's as though the True Born leader sheds a skin, and all this time what I've known of Nolan Storm has been an illusion.

His form ripples. His thorny crown of bone swirls, and he pulses with power. When he speaks, he keeps his voice low. But still, the sky splits and peals with the sound of his low, gravelly voice.

"Fox. This is your last chance to do the right thing."

My legs shake with exhaustion and fear. I'm not sure how long I can stand, though Jared keeps a watchful hand under my arm. The fire's rippling fingers reach for the roof of the refinery. Burned sugar, sticky and cloying, overtakes even the reek of burning wood and paint and metal. There's no way we're getting out of here unless it's by copter.

And we're surrounded by flames, and by blank-faced soldiers and tanks.

By a madman.

"Give up, Storm. You're surrounded."

"Naw." Storm gives my father a cocky grin. "You are."

Storm tosses his bony crown and brings one foot down in an elegant stomp. It crashes like thunder, the boom resonating not just here on the roof. I can hear it down below, echoing through the buildings. The True Born opens his mouth. He speaks a word, a single word. It's a language I've not heard before but it sounds ancient, primordial. The hair on my arms pricks. My gut clenches. I want to curl up in a ball and hide from the power of its call.

Which is the moment I realize it *is* a call, as suddenly, hundreds of thin, wan faces emerge, swarming like silent rats through the streets. Some carry guns and knives. Others planks of wood with nails or metal pipes. There are children mixed in with the raggedy crowd, too, thin-bodied and racked with hunger and the seeping onset of Plague. They all have hollowed eyes, blank with misery. It's an army of hundreds—*no, thousands*, I calculate through the strange floodlight of the fire. And each one of the rabble army wears as their uniform a sharp look of defiance. These people will fight to the death.

And they're Lasters. All of them, Lasters.

Occasionally one stumbles, and a neighbor helps them to their feet. I'm swamped with a horrible sense of déjà vu, but when I look over at Storm, he's carefree and smiling.

Nolan Storm has unleashed this human storm. This is civil war. And he is their captain.

30

"What have you done?"

Nolan Storm tips his head toward me to indicate he's heard but peers silently into the teeming human sea below. Lukas's army is now completely surrounded, barricaded in by a thick human wall. The armed soldiers turn masked faces to the crowd in a feeble attempt to hold back the Lasters. There are maybe a hundred guns with which to kill thousands. *Not enough, I reckon.* I lean closer to the building's edge, far enough that I can watch the roving eye of a tank's gunwale, restlessly passing over the crowd as though searching for a good target. I spy my father, dressed more casually than I've seen him in years, in black trousers and shirt. His silvered hair whips around in the breeze as he stands on top of a tank with some sort of device in his hands. As if he can sense me, our eyes meet.

My father glares at me. Disappointment and anger show

visible in the rigid lines of his body. He raises his arm and points one black-gloved finger at me.

Get down here, he mouths.

I tremble violently. I'm not stable as Storm stomps his foot again and the ground beneath my feet ripples, the shock waves hitting my knees, making me sick to my stomach. The jolt is just enough to send me pitching forward. I feel my feet leave the roof and I plunge into the night and the flames.

A primal scream wakes me from the descending darkness. Like a puppet I dangle, held by one hand over the chaotic scene below.

"Lu! Do *not* let go." Red-faced and snarling, Jared's bones grow sharp under a bank of blond bangs.

"Jared." My ribs feel caged in steel, so it's difficult to breath, let alone talk. "Jared." Tears leak from my eyes. *This is how Margot felt, this letting go.*

But Jared holds on. I stare into his terrified eyes as he hikes me up an inch, two, high enough that Storm is able to crouch down and extend his fingers. "Give me your other hand, Lucy."

Both of my hands are fastened like slippery cement on Jared. I can't bear to let go. Jared's eyes grow fierce. "Do it, Lu." He nods at me. "Please. Do it."

I flap around in the breeze as I let go and extend my other shaking arm to the rooftop. Storm takes it and between the two of them I'm winched away from the dark jaws of certain death below. Seconds later I'm sitting on the roof, gulping in air, adrenaline spiking through my brain like the hum of electricity. I feel as though I've been hit by lightning.

Below, chaos unfurls. The Lasters mob the army, tearing at the soldier with bare hands. They beat the soldiers with whatever tools they have in hand as the tanks roar to life and crush bodies beneath their ridged tracks. I scream, horrified by the violence as I watch a child sink beneath the belly of a tank.

I lose track of my father in the terrible chaos.

"What's happening?"

Storm crouches beside me. His heavy hand comes down over the back of my hair, soothing me, though I'm far from pacified. "After the last council meeting, the Laster representatives and I came to a mutually beneficial agreement. The Upper Circle will no longer rule Dominion."

I stare at him, certain I've misheard. It's unthinkable. Unimaginable.

But so is this, my feverish brain supplies.

Is there any other way? Not that I can see. Not ever again. Not after what Nash and my father have been up to. The Upper Circle can no longer be trusted to hold the reins of power.

"Who, then?"

"We'll strike a council, like before. All represented."

I lick my lips. "And you'll lead them."

"I'll lead the True Borns," Storm agrees calmly. "You'll stay on the council, too. Either as an Upper Circle representative… or something more." There's a thread there I can barely follow. I'm not certain if Storm means that he'll have me sit on the council as a True Born hybrid or whether he's talking about something else… Something like marriage.

Yet I can't think about councils or the future while the roiling storm of bodies continues beneath us. While some of the foot soldiers retreat, the tanks are immobilized but holding fast in their metal carapaces. And more Lasters are mown down. Some soldiers are torn from their uniforms as the sky lightens with the hazy glow of fire. I want to cry, but where are my tears? *Where have they gone?*

Jared's hand holds fast to mine. Squeezes. "C'mon, Princess. Don't fail me now."

I turn and give him my best, most haughty look. "I do *not* fall apart. Not ever."

Jared's grin spreads slowly as he helps me to my feet. "That's the truth, Lu. You do not."

He pulls me up into his arms and starts toward the copter. I raise one hand in salute to Storm, who nods and, with a slight smile, turns to head back down the stairs of the refinery.

"I can walk, you know," I grumble at Jared.

His grin grows wider. "I know you can, Lu, but how else can I cop a feel?"

I stare at him, utterly bewildered. "How can you joke at a time like this, Jared Price?"

This sobers him. "Because you're alive, Lu. That's good enough for me."

The copter's blades whirr to life as we reach its metal belly. Jared tosses me in, and I struggle against his hands as he buckles me into a seat. "I can do it!"

"But then I don't get to feel you up." He follows me in with a wink, pulling on a headset and making a whirling motion with his hands. The pilot nods, turns, and smiles at me. Though a hat and his earpiece obscure his face, I suddenly recognize the long, thin cheeks, the slight bluish-white cast to the man's skin.

"You're the merc from Grayguard," I yell, though the copter's hum steals my words. I'd once followed this man around the halls of Grayguard. He was one of the few True Borns hired as a Personal to guard the young masters and mistresses of the elite private school. I'd hoped to learn more about True Borns from him.

Jared throws a headset on me, and I can just make out the

man's words as he nods at me. "Miss Fox."

"Jared, do you know who this is?"

Jared busies himself before his voice tunes in to my ear. "He can hear you, Lu."

"I'm sorry. I never got to ask you your name. I always wanted to know."

"Gideon."

"Gideon. And how…?" I stop myself just in time, remembering myself. These days even a career merc can find themselves without a job when their family is bit by Plague.

The copter lifts off the roof, and as it takes to the sky, an idea digs its roots . Flowery petals of fire open all around the refinery. And an idea flowers inside me. *So simple*, staring me in the face the whole time. It's the biggest idea. The one that will change everything, forever. And it comes to me in the quiet-quiet whisper of Margot's voice.

Evolve or die.

Shaky and unsure of myself, I eye the medical chest shoved halfway beneath the seats of the copter. Grabbing at the seat belt, I lean over and watch as the multitudes combat in the streets. I can see more army coming: lines of black moving orderly through the streets from out near the city edge where they're hosteled.

"Jared, look." I tug at his sleeve and point.

Grim-faced, Jared grabs his mic. "Gideon, open a channel, please." A whining noise fills my head as Jared talks, though I catch a few words: *two hundred men. Rocket launchers. Light artillery.*

The communication ends, and Jared nods at Gideon, who

flies us back over the scene. Smoke hangs everywhere, stinking heavily of sugar and billowing around the torch-like refinery.

Gideon makes a noise in his throat. "Shall I continue to make passes?"

Jared considers this a moment and sends me a sidelong look I'd as soon call torn. "No. We need to get Lucy to the country."

"Wait," I break in, touching the back of Gideon's seat. He catches eyes with me in the rearview, that strange, startling alien quality to him causing me to pause. "Gideon," I say, scrambling to get my thoughts in order, "Gideon, I need to talk to Jared about something very important and very private. And I know you'll be able to hear it, too…"

Gideon shakes his head. "No. No need." He flicks a switch and with a crackle and a smile I realize he's cut himself out of our loop. I flash a smile and turn back to Jared as I unbuckle my seat belt.

"Just what the hell do you think you're doing, Lu?" Jared storms as he moves lightning-fast to re-buckle me.

"No. No, no, no. Jared, listen to me." I take his face in my hands, marveling at the rough-smooth quality of his skin. The stark beauty of his face, the lovely, elegant slant to his nose, the unquenchable spirit in his eyes. If anyone will support me in my crazy scheme, it will be this man. "We can't just run away from this mess."

"Yes we can, Lu. And that was a direct order from the big guy." He twirls his fingers for punctuation just as the copter lurches. It takes me a moment to realize that the tiny blurs floating upward past the open doors is a volley of bullets. Jared swears and screams at Gideon to take us higher and move away from the scene. My hair whips around my face, obscuring the dangerous view, and I hang on to the unfastened strap of my belt for dear life. Jared clamps an arm across my body, holding me fast. The copter jerks again and dips before heading toward Storm's keep, rising like an obsidian tower in the lowering dark of the city.

"Jared, stop, wait. We can stop this. I need your help. Please, please, Jared. We can end this," I plead.

This stops him. "What are you talking about, Lu?"

"We have what we need. Everything we need is right here." I sweep my hand to indicate the chest at our feet, the city below. "Please, Jared. I'm begging you. Please. Please help me."

He's still, my True Born, as he contemplates what I'm asking. And I reckon I can tell the moment he's grasped the extent of my plan: the moment his pupils dilate to tiny pinpricks and his jaw drops.

"You can't be serious." A moment later he heaves a breath and continues. "We have no idea what it will do to people. It's not been tested at all."

I nod and swallow past the massive knot in my throat. "I know. I know that. But they're going to die anyhow, Jared. Either by bullets or Plague. At least this way they're given a chance. And—and it will even the playing field."

Jared runs a hand over his face. "I can't believe you're even suggesting this."

Tugging his hand away from his chin, I force him to look at me. "You know as well as I that Storm and his Laster army are no match for the entire army of Dominion. They'll win, Jared. And what happens when they do? Think about it. The Watchers belong to my father. The preacher men. The countryside. They only way to stop his game is to take it away from him. To *change* it."

To bring things full circle. Two circles, conjoined. Lock and key.

"I can't, Lu. *We* can't."

I nod but grab his hands, pulling them to my chest where my heartbeat trips. "I can't do this on my own, Jared. I need you."

"No." He frowns, every inch of his features stamped with stubborn. "I'm getting you out of here. And you're going to the country. Storm will join you there. And you'll be safe."

My eyes widen in shock. "*Storm* will join me there?" After a beat, his meaning sinks in. "You're planning on being my babysitter until Storm shows up. And then what?"

"Then you go on to your happily ever after," he spits out miserably.

"There is no happily ever after." I bark a harsh laugh. "This is Dominion."

There is war and famine and Plague in Dominion. There are starving children being murdered by the army. There is a madman taking over the government.

"Jared." I return my hand to his cheek, bringing his forehead down to mine. Our eyes still meet, lock, and for a moment I'm lost. "Jared, there's no life in Dominion unless we do something. Not even Nolan Storm can survive this. Not without help. Not without his people."

It occurs to me that if I do this, if we do this, I'm giving in to their prophecy. Giving in to everything Serena and her Horned people — or whoever they are — want. But is there another way?

No. And in the end, I reckon Jared knows it, too.

For a long, tense moment he contemplates me from beneath his absurdly beautiful lashes before his lips come down to claim mine. It's the softest, sweetest kiss I've ever tasted from him. And it makes me tremble with its power.

"Okay." He rips the word from his lungs like it hurts. "Okay, Lu." He soothes the hair from my face, his fingers trapping satiny locks with his fingers. "I-I can't believe I'm doing this," he grumbles. But underneath I can feel him shaking.

"There's no other way, Jared. There's no other way," I reply with conviction. I leave dangling the words that don't need to be spoken. *Not without so much bloodshed and death.*

Reluctantly, Jared turns to Gideon, but he holds fast to my hand. He raps a fist on the roof and Gideon leans over, flicking a switch before meeting our gaze with a politely inquiring look.

"Change of plans, G," Jared drawls as the three-way radio flickers on with a crackle. My heart breaks open as Jared twirls his fingers in the air. Gideon zooms up and over Storm's tower, back toward the bloody fray.

31

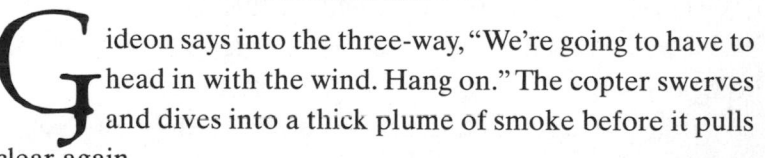

Gideon says into the three-way, "We're going to have to head in with the wind. Hang on." The copter swerves and dives into a thick plume of smoke before it pulls clear again.

And reveals a scene of mayhem.

The refinery is lit like a massive beacon, the air thick and choking. All around it, bodies litter the ground. From this vantage point they look like rag dolls in Lasters' trousers, bloodied and bent, torn by bullets. One of the pipes running up the side of the refinery gives a sudden lurch and crashes, crushing against the topside of a tank. The fire spreads to a large metal garbage bin where Laster children have been stashed for safekeeping. I scream in horror as I watch them leap like little fleas, some of the youngest of them being pulled out by hair covered in burning embers, or clothes, or whatever there is to reach.

Jared grabs my hand and holds on tight. "Lu. Lu, look at me." I turn away from the carnage below. "If we're doing this, we're doing it now. I think we've got about a three-minute window."

I nod, speechless. Yes, time enough for mourning the dead another time.

"Okay." I wipe at the senseless tears that I find streaming down my face. "Okay. Now."

Jared slides Doc Raines's medical chest out from under our feet. He pulls two keys on a ribbon from his pants pocket and unlocks the lid. Dry ice escapes in a puff of white. Gleaming dark nodes, encased in opaque squares, sit neatly on trays. Jared lifts one, two, three, each one containing at least fifty or more of the tiny cubes, and more trays beneath.

"Ice cubes?" I lift an eyebrow at Jared.

He grins and squares his shoulders. "Well, it's hot out there, isn't it? I think the people could use a little something to cool things down."

"I think you're right." I swallow down an emotion so big it threatens to drown me. I take in hand a tray Jared offers. He takes another.

"We won't be able to take this back, Lu. Once it's done—"

I stop him there. "I know." With a lift of my chin, in a voice not even shaking much, I tell him, "No regrets. This is the only way."

Our eyes lock. For one long second my True Born and I are alone in the world.

Without another word, I tip my tray out the side of the copter.

The fire is an inferno as we near, hot as a sun. In moments the ice melts, leaving behind a trail of wet black spots that streak against the smoke-choked horizon. Jared tips his over the side, hands me another tray. Within minutes the crowd below is splattered red. Crimson black streaks fall from the sky, fall on the upturned faces of the Lasters, who stop to stare at us with watchful, hungry expressions on their faces.

I think the skin could easily absorb it, Doc Raines had said. *If they were to enter the water supply or were injected...* With any luck, the crowd below will absorb the Talismans made from our blood, Margot's and mine. They'll be able to transform the DNA of this broken world. They'll help the Lasters ward off the worst ravages of the Plague.

The copter circles back around, and I can see it now, the air filling with drops of blood, as though the sky is bleeding tears. I am shaken by a deep sense of déjà vu, as one of my dreams charges into waking life. *The same dark-red rain. My tears mix with it, turning the hills and fields around Dominion a blooming crimson.*

The copter finishes its pass and the thick, billowing gray smoke curls and clears for Nolan Storm, who emerges on top of a tank. This Storm is an angry god, ancient and mysterious. Hair whipping about his face, Storm turns his face to the copter.

"Oh God." I freeze. "He's going to kill me."

"No, honey." Jared's voice is thick with sarcasm. "He'll kill us both."

The air around Storm parts. He snarls, his face a death mask. It takes a second before I see the lone soldier rising to meet him from the belly of the tank. Another blink of an eye, and Storm has thrown the man's head one way, his body the other. Storm stomps and the tank lid crushes down as though it were made of cardboard.

He stops. Jared and I watch as Storm extends his arm,

pointing one long finger at someone. *It's my father*, I realize. Lukas Fox cowers behind a bank of maybe a dozen soldiers in riot gear. It's not enough to save him.

Storm pounces. Bodies leap out of the way. Then the True Born leader stands before my father's war party. One machine gun goes off with a staccato burst. Storm flips the gun sideways, somehow missing the bullets meant for him. He throws a kick. A line of men falls, limbs cracked in two. And then, with an ugly light in his unearthly face, Nolan Storm takes my father's neck into his bare hands and wrings it.

My father's body slips to the ground, lifeless. *It's done, then.* Lukas Fox, the power behind Dominion, the true puppeteer of the Watchers, is gone. I wait for more sadness to grip me, but I feel nothing but icy numbness spreading through my heart.

The True Born leader makes a running jump onto the top of a second tank. He tips his head back, throat exposed and crown of bone substantial enough now to be splattered with the blood of his enemies, and roars. Impossibly, we hear it over the copter's purr, a bone-shattering, air-ripping horror that raises the hairs on my neck. It vibrates through the metal carapace of the copter. Shakes the ground.

Laster and soldier alike freeze. No one moves, even through the thick smoke and violent fire. Storm surveys the scene as though claiming everything with his eyes. And then he tips his head up, staring right into the copter where we sit. I can tell he sees us, sees me. His lips curve with the smallest hint of a smile.

That's when I see it. That's when I know. Nolan Storm isn't going to kill Jared and me for what we've done. Nolan Storm will be king of them all.

King of a world of True Borns.

• • •

I sink back into the vinyl of the copter seat, sucking air into me as though it's a scarce commodity.

Gideon's voice breaks in. "Where to next, folks?"

Beside me, Jared seems equally stunned. When I finally come back to awareness, I realize he has my hand in his, where he slowly shuttles a finger across my skin. Back and forth, back and forth, as though it can comfort us both. Jared raises an eyebrow at me in mute question and seems relieved when I nod. "Take us to the main water tower." His gaze never leaves mine. "Might as well do this up with style."

The water tower is the main water supply for thousands of Lasters. Once we dump the last tray in there, many more can be saved from the wasting Plague.

"Aye-aye, captain." Gideon's face brightens with humor. From the corner of my eye I watch him flip a switch. The headset flares with a crackle. Jared and I are as good as alone.

"Do you reckon he's had this planned all along?"

"What?" Jared peers down into the ragged streets.

"This." I spread my hands into the sea of chaos below.

"Naw. I think he sets up shots and lets other people knock them down as they will. Or not."

"You think we were set up?"

Jared levels me a serious look. "I think you've been set up your whole life. Don't you?"

Truth. We were designed, Margot and I, to be pawns in these men's games of power, first by our father and Resnikov, by the clever hands of the scientists. Our very DNA was imprinted with Cernunnos's will, which his faithful followers made known to the Watchers. As daughters to the Upper Circle, Margot and I were gussied and groomed to become exactly what our parents wanted of us.

But somewhere along the way I stopped being and doing what everyone else wanted of me. I'm not sorry about what we've just done, Jared and I. I reckon this night we'll have saved thousands upon thousands of Lasters from the grave.

I may not recognize who I am any longer, this young woman who's gone as rogue as Plague-bit DNA, but I know she's doing no one's bidding but her own.

"You know he's serious." Jared's softly spoken words interrupt my thoughts. "Storm's going to want to marry you."

Our knees knock together. I gulp back a string of tears. I'm not ready for this conversation. I nod as though I am. "I know."

"You should marry him, Lu. It's the right thing for you. Will you?" He sucks in his lip with a breath, and I realize he's as close to tears as I am.

"I-I know I should. I don't want to."

"Don't, Lu." Jared's lips are inches from mine as his eyes burn into me. "Don't. Don't marry him. I know you should, but don't. Marry me, Lu. Be with me. It's selfish but I can't—can't seem to help it." Jared blinks away a tear and takes another expectant breath, as though waiting for a blow. A shock of blond hair falls over his face as he looks down at his open hands. He folds my fingers into his. "You asked me a while back never to give up on you. And I never will. I can't. No matter what you choose."

My heart stops, then thunders into a gallop. He curls a lock of my hair around his finger. Fingers that can kill and maim. Yet these are the fingers and hands and arms that soothe me more completely than any but my sister's. Dominion's heiress apparent, I am becoming something else: the mother of a new world. I know where my duty lies. But there's a choice, for once. A choice for me alone to make.

Heart or duty? Heart or head?

It doesn't help. I've been raised for duty, not love.

What would Margot think?

And with that thought, everything clears.

I take a moment, feeling the rush of the cool, wet night air on my skin as the darkness falls across Dominion, blending with the bloodred rain that gently coats the dying city. One day soon it will turn everything green and new again. Tomorrow the Lasters will wake up changed. And maybe the lights will start coming on again. Maybe the cars will be driven and the houses lived in. Maybe tomorrow, mamas will kiss their babies good morning instead of goodbye.

Maybe the Plague will be vanquished, at least for many. And the rest? We'll get to them, in time. All I know right now is that I'm exhausted. *And free.* Nolan Storm has won his kingdom. I reckon he won't see the need for a political marriage after all.

Jared holds my stare, beat for beat, measure for measure. *Lock and key.*

"I could never marry someone else. Not Storm, not anyone. You are mine, Jared True Born Price. Mine forever. You're stuck with me whether you like it or not. And don't you ever, ever forget that you like it," I say with a little hiccup.

Jared stares down at me, an emotion like wonder stamped on his too-handsome face, as though something irrevocable has happened.

And it has, I reckon. We are one now, he and I. I have lost everything. But maybe I've found home.

"That's as it should be, Princess. And don't I know it."

His head comes slowly down to claim mine in a knee-weakening, heart-stopping kiss. Just a whisper from my skin, I freeze him with a faux-haughty look.

"That's queen to you, Jared Price."

"Queen Lu," he murmurs against my lips. And then I'm lost in a sudden maelstrom. "Yes."

Acknowledgments

The solitary writer at her keyboard is a cliché. It's also not true. The True Born series has indebted me to so many, but let me start by thanking my agent, Robert Lecker, who has been such a fierce guardian of my work. Liz Pelletier, thank you not just for your editing but for believing in this series. You have continually amazed me with your insightful, generous mentoring. Everyone at Entangled Teen gets big high fives from me, but especially: Heather Riccio, who always returns my emails (thank you!); the brilliant Stacy Abrams, whose razor-sharp insights helped shape a good book into (hopefully) a great one; and Melissa Montovani, who is not just an amazing publicist but a friend. These books would not be so gorgeous without the talents of the gifted designers and layout artists. Thanks also to Fernanda Viveiros and the folks at Raincoast Books for their efforts to make these books visible in Canada. Thank you, Craig Wattie, for copyediting my galleys and being the best darned assistant and cheerleader this writer could ever dream of. Finally, I want to send a huge shout out to the bloggers, reviewers and readers. Delighting any one of you for a length of time is my ultimate ambition. That you take the time to tell me I have is my greatest reward.

GRAB THE ENTANGLED TEEN RELEASES READERS ARE TALKING ABOUT!

UNRAVELED
BY KATE JARVIK BIRCH

Ella isn't anyone's pet anymore, but she's certainly not free. Turns out the government isn't planning mass rehabilitation... they're planning a mass *extermination*. With the help of a small group of rebels, Ella and Penn set out to end this for good. But when they're implicated in a string of bombings, no one is safe. If she can't untangle the web of blackmail and lies, she won't just lose her chance at freedom, she'll lose everyone she loves.

RISEN
BY COLE GIBSEN

My aunt has been kidnapped by vampires, and it's up to me to save her. Only...I had no idea vampires existed. Then there's the vampire Sebastian, who, yes, is the hottest being I've ever come across, but there's no way I can trust him. He swears he's helping me get answers, but there's more to his story. Now I'm a key pawn in a raging vampire war, and I need to pick the right ally.

ASSASSIN OF TRUTHS
BY BRENDA DRAKE

The gateways linking the great libraries of the world don't require a library card, but they do harbor incredible dangers.

And it's not your normal bump-in-the- night kind. The threats Gia Kearns faces are the kind with sharp teeth and knifelike claws. The kind that include an evil wizard hell-bent on taking her down.

Gia can end his devious plan, but only if she recovers seven keys hidden throughout the world's most beautiful libraries. And then figures out exactly what to do with them.

The last thing she needs is a distraction in the form of falling in love. But when an impossible evil is unleashed, love might be the only thing left to help Gia save the world.

ZOMBIE ABBEY
BY LAUREN BARATZ-LOGSTED

1920, England

And the three teenage Clarke sisters thought what they'd wear to dinner was their biggest problem...

Lady Kate, the entitled eldest.

Lady Grace, lost in the middle and wishing she were braver.

Lady Lizzy, so endlessly sunny, it's easy to underestimate her.

Then there's Will Harvey, the proud, to-die-for—and possibly die with!—stable boy; Daniel Murray, the resourceful second footman with a secret; Raymond Allen, the unfortunate-looking young duke; and Fanny Rogers, the unsinkable kitchen maid.

Upstairs! Downstairs! Toss in some farmers and villagers!

None of them ever expected to work together for any reason.

But none of them had ever seen anything like this.

entangled teen

an imprint of Entangled Publishing LLC